Bound Across Time

Bound

Book One

Annie R McEwen

BOUND ACROSS TIME

ISBN: 979-8-9890320-6-8

Published in the United States of America by Harbor Lane Books, LLC.

www.harborlanebooks.com

To John, a true romantic.

ONE

"Is it haunted?"

Four and a half months of Candlelight Castle Walks. Fifty-seven versions of that question. This one came from a middle-aged woman in a plaid tam o'shanter. The dog in her handbag had the same cap only much tinier, held by an elastic strap to its head at a jaunty angle. She shouldn't have let the woman bring the dog, but the group was so small tonight, only nine walkers. What was one Yorkie, more or less?

CeCe made herself smile at both the woman and dog as she answered. "Not that I'm aware of."

Why did her walkers always think there were ghosts? St. Rhydian's Castle wasn't famous for bloody battles, witch burnings, or even family arguments that ended with His Lordship bashing Lady Frippery's skull in with a candle lantern. No history of strolling spirits or dead earls on the ramparts. Yet, every Saturday night, questions about the supernatural wrenched her tour from history to histrionics. *Uh-oh, they're dawdling again.*

"Let's all stay together, folks! Don't want to lock anyone in for the night!" Faint laughter from a few walkers. Shouts of,

"Brill!" and "I belong inside, Officer!" from the pair of snarky teens at the back of the group.

CeCe picked up the pace. With luck, she could get them out the door before there were any more ghost questions. One more of those and she'd start barking like Purse Pooch.

Saturday night. Technically Sunday morning since it was just after midnight. Her group wobbled raggedly toward the exit. Of course, they wobbled. Most of them viewed the Walk as the capstone of a pub crawl. CeCe silently cursed the Anchor and Bell a couple dozen yards outside the grounds.

Dang, it was sticky tonight. Living her whole life in Savannah should have made her immune to humidity, but there was something about north coastal Wales in summer, the briny mist rolling from the Irish Sea...

Her wool eighteenth-century bodice stuck to her, and the boning of her stays poked into her underarms. The drawstring that held up her top skirt sagged, so she kept tripping over the hem. Despite its label (*Water-resistant coverage!*), her makeup was no match for sweat and was slowly sliding off her face.

She forced enthusiasm into her voice. "Almost at the exit, now! Follow the light!" Follow the light? Stupid, but better than "Follow the battery operated candles!" CeCe's scalp itched, and she worked a finger under her ruffled linen cap to scratch it. She'd already made a big concession to entertainment by wearing a costume for her tours. As of that morning, she'd been told to summon spirits. She'd had such a good career plan. How had it gone so, so wrong?

Job. *Check.* History job. *Check.* History job in a beautiful castle. *Check.* History job in a beautiful castle, leading to a full-time staff position—

No check. Not even a hyphen. The worst thing about her plan falling apart—actually, there were two worst things. The first was how fast it happened. Between nine and nine-thirty that morning, when the Programmes Director called CeCe into her office.

"Your history tours are—informative, Miss Gowdie," Eunice Tattersall had begun. "But they don't seem to be attracting visitors the way I had hoped."

"It's only been a few months," CeCe pleaded. "They'll build."

"Let's think about how we can build them now. Ghost walks are immensely popular, and I think it's time we had one here at St. Rhydian's. Besides, I know you want to secure long-term residency in the U.K. A cultural worker visa can do that, so look at this as a viable path to staying on here."

Had that been a bribe, or a threat?

She'd continued, "This assignment should not be difficult for you, Miss Gowdie. With such a long past, St. Rhydian's must have plenty of ghosts. Take a couple of weeks. Find them."

That was when CeCe choked down her irritation and walked away from the PD's perfect office (like a suite in a boutique hotel) and her perfect presence (sleek chignon, couture suit, Jimmy Choo size nines). She'd been so sure that when the Castle admins got to know her, they'd see she deserved more than a part-time tour guide position. She didn't mind starting at the bottom, and she could be a team player, but why did she have the feeling that her promotion potential was slipping downward, or at best, sideways? At least when the PD ruined CeCe's day, she'd said her surname right. Most people didn't. "It's from Scots Gaelic," she explained over and over. "Sounds like *goh dee*."

From the middle of the group, a noise like a cat hawking up a hairball distracted her. *There he goes again.* "You okay, Mr. Cranwell?" A man with a world class dust allergy and no meds was along tonight. He'd had a coughing and sneezing fit every five minutes for the past hour. CeCe dug in her skirt pocket for a small packet of tissues and gave it to the walker behind her. Walkers behind that one dutifully passed it to Mr. Cranwell, whose *thank you* was muffled in another expectoration.

Thank heavens, CeCe thought once they reached the Grand Staircase. "Home stretch, everyone. Mind your step, please."

She trudged doggedly down the stairs, followed by her little flock. Anger over her career slide returned like a tour taker who'd stepped away for a minute and was now back. The second worst thing about it? It had happened before. Savannah, two years ago. A fight to the death between her "Real History of French Savannah" tour and an upstart called "Ghostess of the South," a stupid spin on the city's nickname, Hostess of the South.

"Ghostess" dribbled phantoms across three hundred years of the city's past. Truth? Not a shred. Just made-up stories of bloody deeds and grudge-holding haints. But "Ghostess" was *hugely* popular. Six months after it launched, CeCe didn't have enough people on her tours to justify trying to find a parking space in the Historic District.

At the time, she thought there might be one good thing about it—the guide, Jasper Marcotte. Lean and long, with a wicked smile. Devilish good looks to go with the black fitted coat, the crisp Edwardian shirt, and the snug leather pants. What a package. Just in case she might have missed a chance to add insult to injury, CeCe unwrapped it.

"Still my friend, sweet cheeks?" Jasper cooed after he dumped her.

"Always," CeCe lied.

Worst Things One and Two had led her directly and dismayingly to tonight. To what she'd thought was her dream job but was starting to look like "Ghostess," only without Jasper Marcotte.

Obsessing instead of walking fast, it was her own fault one of the snarky teens and his question caught up with her.

"So, Ms. Gobee—"

"Gowdie."

"Right. Do you believe in ghosts?"

What, young sir, no questions about the fascinating sixty minutes of local history I just reeled out? "Um, I'd have to put myself in the unbeliever camp." *Because ghosts don't exist.* "Not that I have a problem with those who say, yes, there are ghosts." *However dim-witted I think those people are.* "Oh, look, here we are at the Forecourt!" *And I don't have to chat about ectoplasm anymore. At least, not tonight.*

"Goodbye, everyone! Thanks for joining my tour of St. Rhydian's. Drive safely. Please visit us again!"

She patted the Yorkie-in-a-bag and pointed the last of her walkers toward the car park with a cheeriness she didn't feel. Groaning, she tugged the heavy Forecourt door shut from the inside, then leaned back against it. She was tired all the way to her toes. If only she could follow the group to the parking lot.

But the night wasn't over. She still had to retrace her route to douse the candles, "douse" being poetic license since all she had to do was flick a switch on each one. The Castle was Grade I Listed, so fake was the only kind of candle in it. There were forty-two along her tour route.

It was a hike, but she'd start as she always did at the farthest point, the west Tower, then work her way three floors down to the Great Hall and then the exit. It took fifteen minutes if she hurried. Tormenting herself with thoughts of her soft bed in the micro-flat she rented in the town outside the Castle gates, CeCe headed for the Grand Staircase.

———

Thirteen minutes. She'd beat her usual candle-dousing time, top to bottom of the Castle. Now, she was out the Forecourt door, turning the key in the modern lock, punching in the digital alarm code. All the while, she tried to think of some excuse she could give Eunice Tattersall to wriggle out of being Casper the Friendly Ghost's new nanny. Ghost walks! Any actor in a cape could drag phantom-obsessed tourists around every Saturday night. Why stick her with the job? Her degrees were in History, not haunting.

She started across the Forecourt, threw a last look over her shoulder at the Castle, and spun around in surprise. *No, no, no.* There, high in the Castle wall, was a faint glimmer in the slit window of the Tower.

CeCe groaned. Somehow, she'd missed a candle. Not just any candle. The one farthest from the exit. Impossible. She would never forget trudging up those fifty-eight steps to the Tower Room, would she? Maybe there was something wrong with the switch, and the candle had un-doused itself. *Dagnabbit.* It had been a really long night after a really long day. She supposed she might have been so preoccupied that she only thought she switched the damn thing off.

Muttering bad things about castles and towers and candles, she went back to the Forecourt door, unlocked it, and pushed open the heavy oak. Now, she'd have to go up three floors and climb the nearly vertical stairs to the Tower, just to put a plastic candle out. *Dag-doubledog-nabbit.* It was late and her feet hurt. All she wanted was to go back to her flat and peel off her itchy, stuck-to-her-skin clothing. Instead, she was looking at aerobic exercise in the middle of the night.

She hesitated in the Great Hall. Even if the candle were real and even if some stray draft blew it over, there was nothing to catch fire in the Tower. It was an eighteenth-century folly, a faux sentry post in an era when no one expected Vikings to land on the rocky beach a mile away and storm the Castle. An empty chamber at the top, bare stone walls and floor, no furnishings. Open to skeletal rafters, since a rotted wood ceiling had been ripped out in eighteen-eighty and replaced with the era's miracle stuff, iron. Once the sun came up, no one would even notice the light. She could just let the battery run down.

CeCe, you know you're gonna climb up there.

Conscientiousness. What a bitch. Sighing like all of Wales and half of England was on her back, she dug in her skirt pocket for her cell phone. A tap on the phone's penlight, and she began following its thin beam along the route she had just walked to turn all the candles—correction, all the candles except that one—off.

Hurrying the whole way. Not paying attention. Still grumbling about ghosts. By the time she went up the fifty-eight steps and lurched into the Tower Room, CeCe was gasping for breath. Stars danced in the corners of her eyes. Wobbly and wheezing, she spotted the candle glowing opposite her. Glowing and snug and lustily fake in the wall niche where a couple hundred years of real candles and real oil lamps had left the stones permanently blackened.

She lunged for it. Grabbed it, upended it, and flicked off the switch underneath.

Well, aren't you brainy, Miss Celeste Gowdie, M.A. cum laude. She'd just put out the only light in the castle other than the one in her cell phone. At least she had that and—

Smarter and smarter, CeCe. She'd forgotten to charge her phone for—two days? Three? Just to spite her, it started beeping drearily, then faded from Low Battery to None.

The penlight was gone. In its place, there was only darkness as dense as the inside of a peanut.

Don't panic, don't panic. She still had the fake candle in her other hand. *Switch it on and light your way to the ground floor, easy peasy.* She felt for the switch with her thumb. Flick. Flick. Flick. *Why isn't it working?* Flick—

The candle lit up just as the back of her neck prickled, the short hairs rising. With the sensation came smells. Tobacco, sweet and strong, like pipe blend. Sea water, sharp, saline, fresh. Peat smoke, slightly acrid and homey.

CeCe whirled around.

Oh, God. A man stood not eight feet away. He was tall and wide-shouldered, strongly built. A loose linen shirt, thin and soft from wear and open at the neck, clung to his broad chest. The shirt was carelessly tucked on one side into brown knee breeches. *Knee breeches?*

He stood like a cocky son of a gun, solidly planted, legs apart, arms relaxed at his sides. Mustard-colored hose gripped his meaty calves and disappeared into black leather shoes with dull silver buckles. *Knee breeches and silver buckles?*

Just what was he doing in the Castle? Why was he dressed like that? Should she be screaming?

Her eyes skidded up from the buckled shoes to the man's face. *Yowza.* It was the handsomest face she'd ever seen outside of a Ralph Lauren ad. Handsome with blue-green eyes that stared bold and unblinking into hers. Handsome even with the six-inch whitened scar that lanced along his temple and through his right eyebrow, barely missing the eye on its way to his cheekbone.

The scar. A jagged bolt of fear shot up CeCe's spine. She knew this man, and he was really, really dead.

He took one step forward and reached for her. Everything went black.

Two

Holy Mary, Mother of God, please tell me I haven't killed her.

Patrick bent over her still form, saw the subtle rise and fall of her chest, and let out his own breath. *Not dead, only swooned.* Swooning was—acceptable. Swooning after shrieking like a banshee—also acceptable. Not shrieking or swooning long enough for him to converse with her—that was the pinnacle of his desire.

Instead, she'd taken one look at him and collapsed like an empty sack.

He cursed himself for doing so many wrong things in so few minutes. It was a poor excuse, but he'd lost all control when it was clear that she saw him.

Saw him. Looked straight at him with her fine, big eyes the color of amber held up to the light. Eyes filled with himself who hadn't been seen for so long by any living creature, much less a beautiful woman.

Then, she swooned. Predictable, perhaps, but confounding. He didn't have many skills with swooning women, it wasn't usually what they had done around him. Perhaps, now and then, from a surfeit of pleasure. That, he could manage. But this...

He'd given no thought at all to what he would do when —*No.* There was never a *when.* There was never so much as an *if.*

Even had he allowed himself to imagine an *if* and a *when,* there was no one to advise him on how to behave should either come to pass. There was no society in this place, this *condition,* where he'd been for so long. Not society of his own kind.

His own kind. What in the name of all the saints and martyrs was his kind? Dead, yes. Dead was the only requirement for society here, society meaning the other souls that wandered and lurked and drifted around the Castle and its grounds. The small army of cutthroats, melancholiacs, purveyors, and victims of violence and gross perversion with whom he shared a roof. He'd long ago put a stop to discourse of any sort with them.

"Damn your blood to hell, you burnt-arsed, madge-faced, buggering fuckwits. You will sodding well leave me the fuck alone." After a thoughtful moment, he added, "Or I'll tear what's left of you into so many pieces there will be fuck-all left to haunt a keyhole."

In truth, he had no idea how he could make good on the threats. But he'd put everything he had into them, and they'd done the job. The years crawled by. He was left totally, shatteringly, endlessly alone.

Until now. Until this night. All that being true, there was no way to determine in advance the social niceties, the *politesse* of whatever the holy miraculous sodding hell was happening in the Tower Room to him and this woman.

He checked her breathing again. She was still at it, a relief and an invitation to linger in contemplation of her face and form.

God in Heaven, how fine she is. He'd seen fine women. In

Paris, they fluttered in the Jardins des Tuileries, on the grounds of the Palais-Royal, like butterflies among the trees and flowers. But this woman was so far above the others, above *him*, he couldn't think how he dared to even look at her.

He'd nearly missed her altogether. He'd watched her snuff that candle as he'd watched her snuff it many times before. And during those many times, hopelessness had carried him away and back to the long gray. But for some reason, on this night he felt if he could just get a flame from the wretched thing, it would light her back to him. So, after she went down the steps, he stood there like the sapskull he was, trying to figure out how the candle worked, only to realize the wee black bit at the bottom was a sort of flint and...

He got it lighted. It drew her as he wildly hoped it might.

And then, he ruined everything.

You're an idjit, Patrick. Death was always too good for you.

He should have gone slower with her, no doubt about it. He was a lout, a brute, to startle her so thoroughly, and that was never his intent. He could have—no, he should have—whispered, or moaned, or shimmered from a distance. Instead, he was hasty.

Hasty? He was a burning brand of desire. Who could blame him after two hundred-fifty...how long had it been? He'd lost count of the years.

That was still no reason to be an imbecilic knave, popping up like codswalloping Punch on a puppet stage while wearing the same filthy linen he was tipped overboard in when the Earl didn't have the decency to give him a proper burial. At least the sea water had washed away the blood.

His honor, his common sense—perhaps they'd washed away as well. Within reach of this woman, he could remember nothing he'd learned of subtle romance and courtly manners. All he could think of was making her his, now until the end of time.

What an embarrassment he was, to his sainted mother, to his upbringing, to the gentleman he was reared to be. An embarrassment to every Irish bard who ever sang songs or wrote poems about women who were doves, and lilies, and other things he couldn't remember. He did remember that they were fragile and easily startled. Easily driven away.

Next time, I will be slow. I will slowly and gently explain things to her. Unusual things. Highly unusual, uncanny, frightening nigh incomprehensible things.

Sure, now, Patrick, me boyo, that'll be a stroll along the banks of the Shannon.

By the right hand of God, but she was beautiful. Slumbering on the stone floor, her skin smooth ivory but gilded, as though the sun had kissed her once and then fallen in love, unable to leave. She'd lost her cap, and her hair—rich, deep brown and burnished with red, like brandy—tumbled around her neck and shoulders. Her sun-brushed skin, high and perfect cheekbones, the delicate slant of her eyes, the plump swell of her breasts above the top edge of her bodice, the curves of the body he could imagine pressed to his own aching and lonely one...

Beauty itself, she was, not only of body but of mind. In the weeks before she'd seen him, he'd watched her exercise that beautiful mind among the slower thinkers of the Castle, who doubtless envied her. She was stubborn, spirited, and quick-witted—he liked that.

He crouched over her crumpled form, not touching, only taking in her scent. Rose attar and mint—he liked that, too.

The only thing he didn't care for was the name she went by, See-see. What sort of name was that? It was something you called a canary. He would never call her that, not when the French name with which she'd been christened was just like her.

Céleste, meaning *heavenly*.

She was waking now. He rose and backed away. Time for him to depart, as he must, and breathe a prayer. Not for himself, there was no point to that. If God had ever listened to him, he wouldn't be where he was, and he deserved no better. His prayer would be for her, the angel who defied or escaped God's curse to light his endless night.

Come back, Céleste Gowdie. Please come back.

THREE

CeCe's brain cleared enough to realize she was lying on her side, on the rough limestone floor of the Tower Room. She carefully pushed herself to a sitting position, and just as carefully looked around. The space was empty. There was nowhere to hide, so wherever the man was who'd been there before, he wasn't around now. His scent still was. Tobacco, sea water, and peat smoke.

She cautiously moved her arms and legs. Everything seemed to be in one piece, except for her shoulder. It hurt like hell where she'd fallen on it. No, not fallen. Had the vapors, kissed the canvas, conked out.

She'd fainted a couple of times before. Once in high school, when a girl six inches taller and forty pounds heavier had pitched a softball directly into her chest. Once when she accidentally slammed a car door on her finger. Never because of a—

Her cap had fallen off. She picked it up, thought about pinning it back on, and decided it wasn't worth the trouble. Leaning against the cold stone of the wall behind her, she turned the cap in her hands and rehearsed her choices.

Low blood sugar. Her four aunts in Savannah were always nagging her about skipping meals, but she'd been busy as hell all day and dinner had disappeared from the agenda. Physiology happened. Wouldn't be the first time she'd explained bizarre behavior with it. Hadn't she been using it once a month since she was thirteen?

Panic attack. The conversation with the Programmes Director had left her stunned, agitated, and worried about her job. Worried enough to see things? Even her thesis defense hadn't worried her that much.

Traumatic memories. Sure, she had them. But why surface tonight? Her memories were the same as they'd always been. Partly-forgotten childhood, unknown father, mother drowned in the St. Mary's River when CeCe was five. She'd never had visions, and then fainted, from her emotional baggage. Cried and fumed, yes. Hallucinated, not once.

Intruder in the Castle. Scary. Maybe even enough to pass out. Some crazy reenactor slash stalker who'd spent one too many weekends dressing up like a Jacobite rebel and thought he would slip into the Castle to make her acquaintance. A crazy who looked exactly like a not-known-to-be-crazy but well-known-to-be-dead man she recognized from his portrait in the Castle's Grand Staircase gallery.

The dead man led her, kicking and screaming, to Door Number Five.

Ghost. No. Emphatically, implacably, immovably, *no*.

Shakily, CeCe got to her feet and jammed her cap into the pocket of her skirt. She patted down her clothes. Nothing seemed to be out of place, untied, or ripped. Whatever and whomever the man was, he was gone. Tomorrow, she'd take measures to make sure he stayed gone.

Moving stiffly, like she'd been in a car crash and taken a punch from the airbag, she crossed the room and picked up her useless cell phone. The battery candle...

It was back in its niche, merry and bright, as though the little devil hadn't plunged her into darkness where any old intruder could sneak up on her. The candle acting all ship-shape and functional now was doubly odd, because she distinctly remembered trying and failing to turn it back on, then dropping it when she saw—him. She took it out of the niche and flicked the switch off and on, off and on. It worked perfectly, which wasn't the weirdest thing that had happened tonight, so she shuffled it to the bottom of the weird deck.

Holding the candle in front of her, CeCe carefully went down the fifty-eight steps, the three flights of stairs, and out the Castle door.

Her nerves jangled the whole way. She couldn't explain the weirdest thing of all. The scent that had come with the man in the Tower—it didn't go away. It was like walking into an empty room and smelling the cologne of someone who'd left it earlier. Except CeCe was the one who'd left, while the scent stayed. Stayed, as she passed under the arching yew trees bordering the long paved walkway to the car park. Stayed, as she went to her car. Stayed, as she opened the door. By the time she got into the driver's seat, she was shaking so hard she could barely fasten the seatbelt. Her key fell out of her hand three times before she got it into the ignition.

Four

CeCe slept the rest of Sunday away. She woke in the wee hours of Monday morning, asking herself questions about reality. No answers came, so she hid under the covers and slept some more.

When she opened her eyes again, sparrows were bickering in the linden tree outside, and daylight flooded through the window over the kitchenette sink. She lay in bed for a long time, thinking about what she knew. Not about reality, but about the Grand Staircase of St. Rhydian's Castle. The Portrait Gallery along the wall. The painting of a man. A man whose identical twin had reached for her in the Tower Room, right before her brain and body experienced a temporary service outage.

She had no idea who the Tower man was. She could say who he *looked* like, but she didn't think she should say that out loud to anyone, ever.

Hauling herself out of bed, she made some strong tea and dressed, but not in the business attire she wore at the Castle to impress the admins. Definitely in the way her graduate mentor, Dr. Pauline Grisham-Chu, told her to dress if she wanted to be taken seriously.

What, a faded pink UGA tee and artistically shredded jeans aren't serious? Hey, Dr. G-Chu, the price tag on these jeans was shockingly serious.

CeCe had a perfectly good reason for un-seriously dressing. Research. Not the academic laptop-on-fire kind that produced reams of notes and a published paper. This was covert research, the behind enemy lines kind. Or, rather, swallow the cyanide pill if you're caught, because you are *not* telling anyone you're researching a dead man you saw in the Tower—that kind.

Her mission started well. In summer, every day was tourist day at the Castle. CeCe showed her staff card at the door, and then merged with the crowd of people in khaki shorts and camera bags. No one noticed, a half hour later, that she hadn't budged from the bottom step of the Grand Staircase. Rooted on the step like a tree that had sprung up overnight, she fixed her eyes on the painting above her on the wall.

Sean Patrick Ó Loinsigh. She reviewed what little she knew about him from the files she'd read when she first got the tour guide job. He was born in 1730-something, the half-Irish bastard son of the Earl of Trawsgoed. Earl, that is, until his death from sepsis in 1762. The son was reputed to be a warrior and a scoundrel, though few details were known about his adult years. Even his death was a mystery. No record of the date or cause. No known grave.

Sean Patrick Ó Loinsigh. *Does he go by Sean, or Patrick? Whoa, CeCe, wrong verb.* What forename *did* he go by? Back *then*, when he *was* alive, which he *isn't* now. Why was she even stumbling over verbs for somebody who hadn't drawn a breath in more than two hundred and fifty years?

She let a noisy gaggle of sightseers get past, then went back to staring at the portrait. He might not have been breathing now, but when he was, he was—hot. That unsettled her. She couldn't remember thinking such a thing about any historical figure she'd seen in books, paintings, or online. When they were alive, she supposed any of them might have given women's hearts the pitty-pats, but all she'd ever felt was curiosity. How uncomfortable was that starched cravat? Did he have lice crawling around in that powdered wig? This historical figure, though...

"Oh, sorry, sorry!" she blurted to a couple behind her wearing Swedish flag T-shirts. CeCe scooted over, smiling at them as they passed. Their Birkenstocks scudded on the stair treads as they smiled back at her.

Context, I need context. She went up the stairs to the landing, to the top of the Gallery. She needed to look at the portraits in order. Really look, not just *oh-yes-guidebook-page-nine* look.

There were six large paintings along the wall, a parade review of the founding family that ruled the Castle and the estate from the early to late 1700s. At the top, His Lordship the Earl, Richard Thomas Alchester DeBlaes. Through the darkened lacquer of the painting, CeCe could just make out a long-nosed, square-jawed, light-eyed man in a wine-colored coat. Next to the Earl, his wife, the lawful one. Edith Aurelia Fantelle, Lady Menton, Countess of Trawsgoed, was a pale blonde woman with a vacuous expression. Her blue and silver gown must've taken a year to embroider.

CeCe moved down a few steps, to a group portrait. The Countess in later years, posing with two teenage boys—the heir and a spare—and a little girl. The elder boy was John something—John Harold? John Hadley? He died shortly after succeeding his father to the title. The spare was called James

Hugh. She couldn't remember the daughter's name. Malvina? Mary?

Two more steps down, the younger son had his own wedding portrait beneath the group, a formal one made when he was Lord James Hugh Marquand DeBlaes, eventual inheritor of the earldom. The newly minted Earl was stiffly posed with a dull-faced, unsmiling woman, also stiff in a gold-lace-on-white gown. There had been no issue from that union. The title went to a cousin when James Hugh died.

Letting more tourists crowd her against the wall, CeCe descended the last four steps. There it was, at the very bottom, the portrait that completed the family, albeit grudgingly. It was as large and well-rendered as the other paintings, but most visitors didn't get a chance to appreciate it, since it was partially obscured by the thick English oak newel post and urn-shaped finial at the base of the stairs. She'd bet her bottom dollar that wasn't an accident. In the parade of titled persons that a house gallery represented, who chose to put an ancestor in such a bad spot? *You're an also-ran*, the location said. *An afterthought, a by-blow.*

Sean Patrick Ó Loinsigh. If he was her ancestor, CeCe certainly wouldn't stick him in a dark corner. His looks alone would have made her want to claim him. *Take a look at these genes! You don't see DNA like this every day!* Her Francophile Aunt Diane, who still got around for a woman of forty-something, would examine the portrait, make a low humming noise, and then say, *"Beau, très beau."* Tante Diane reserved her French for the most delicious things in life: food, wine, and men. And if Sean Patrick Ó Loinsigh wasn't delicious, then neither was *crème brûlée*.

Unlike CeCe, the man in the portrait was wearing serious clothes. A dark blue jacket over a waistcoat of the same color. Both over a white shirt, an austerely knotted cravat. The waistcoat and jacket were probably superfine wool; they had that soft nap and nicely falling folds. The shirt was certainly linen, cotton being unusual at the time. CeCe could almost feel the crisp texture of the cloth, hear the gentle whisper it made when the man in the portrait lifted his arms, moved his shoulders. His powerful arms, his very broad shoulders.

And then, his face. The face that had stunned her off her feet the night before. Leonine cheekbones, strong jaw, long straight nose, bold, arched black eyebrows that matched the unpowdered hair pulled into a queue at his neck. Rare, aquamarine eyes, with something resolute and unyielding in them. Ó Loinsigh hadn't been a ditherer, a conciliator, or a diplomat. Every line of his face said, *I do as I will, and damn your eyes if you disagree.*

But his mouth—that was made for deep living and deeper pleasure. Full, but not fleshy. Lifted at one corner, as though a laugh wasn't far away.

There was nothing laughable about his scar. She hadn't seen it for long last night, but she'd say Tower Man got it just right, as right as a fake scar could be. Latex and stage makeup could never reproduce the scar the real Sean Patrick Ó Loinsigh bore on his face, the one the artist hadn't tried to conceal in his portrait. A sword, a dirk, or some other lethal weapon had produced that scar.

Who dealt the blow? Did you give as good as you got? "I hope you took him out," she whispered, then caught her breath and surveyed her surroundings. Had anyone noticed her crazily talking to a dead man in a painting?

Crazier still was that she yearned to touch the portrait, even as her museum training screamed, *We do not handle historical artifacts!* If she could only run her fingers along that scar, restore the cheek so it matched the other perfect side...

Imperfect or not, Ó Loinsigh was a handsome bastard, literally. She had to wonder what his mother had looked like. In the eighteenth century, wives were chosen for bloodlines and mistresses for beauty, so it wasn't surprising that this bastard made his legitimate half siblings look like range cattle standing next to a prize Angus bull. Another reason for hiding his portrait, no doubt.

The canvas had been in a worse position than it was now, according to the Guidebook. Hidden away in storage for decades, it was only hung in the Gallery in the late 1800s, when some genealogy-mad DeBlaes in Victoria's reign ordered the portrait moved to the Grand Staircase, so there wouldn't be any gaps in the painted record of the family. Even so, the legitimate DeBlaeses could hardly be asked to move over so a love child could take a seat at their haughty board. Sean Patrick Ó Loinsigh went to the tail end of the Gallery, a place setting squeezed onto the Thanksgiving table for a distant cousin who wasn't really expected to attend.

"He's my favorite, too."

CeCe's shoulders jerked in surprise. She whirled around to face the thin, gray-haired woman who had noiselessly appeared beside her. Somebody who worked at St. Rhydian's, but what was her name? Lancaster? Litman?

CeCe immediately slapped on her smile for senior colleagues, though she wasn't really sure where the woman fell in the Castle pecking order. Above an American tour guide, for sure. Before she could say anything, the woman spoke again.

"Would you like to see the charcoal sketch?"

CeCe remembered a footnote in the Guidebook. "The sketch the portrait was painted from? Yes, I would love to see it." Her memory churned frantically. *Lytton*, that was it! M. E. Lytton, D. Phil. Cambridge University. Castle Collections Manager. "Thank you, Dr. Lytton."

"Miriam, please." The woman tilted her head toward a door at the end of the ground floor hall. *No Admittance. Staff Only.*

Miriam walked toward the sign and CeCe followed, like a balloon on a string. Before the Grand Staircase disappeared behind them, she looked over her shoulder at Sean Patrick Ó Loinsigh. His sea-storm eyes seemed to follow her, like a portrait in a haunted house.

Just met you, tall, dark, and dead, and already I'm headed down a dark hall toward a locked door. Why do I think this isn't going to end well?

———

She was wearing breeches. He'd seen them before, on her, on other females, as he roamed the castle he'd once called home, but had become a sort of public thoroughfare, people coming and going, gawking at the furnishings, speculating about ghosts when he stood as he was standing now, unseen, at their elbows.

Women had always worn the most astounding things. He well remembered the first time he'd taken panniers off a woman. The strings holding them up had knotted, and in the end, he'd just ripped them off. The woman had been vexed.

He didn't care to remember that now, if even he could, beyond the barest flicker. He could not, in the wasteland of memory to which God was pleased to consign him, relive the details of any woman he'd bedded. He was grateful for that. It would be an unimaginable pain to remember soft lips and yielding thighs, when his only bedmate was despair and his only pleasure...

Of pleasure, there was none.

Still, to be dead was one thing, but to be a dead eunuch quite another. So, when the sight of the lovely creature walking away from him in breeks lifted his cock like a flag in a stiff wind, he was both amazed and joyful. The first and every sight of her gave him the same happy surprise. He was sure that if he saw her a thousand times, he would be rewarded with a thousand flint-hard pindles. The fact that now he had to contend with cockstands so persistent that it ached to walk —ah, it was no price at all to feel like a man again.

He was that, after all. A man. A man who had, against the odds and in a partial way, survived his own death. Now, though, when he thought of losing the woman he'd just found, the one who might save him from his own accursed salvation, he was shaken by heart-stopping fear. No manner of man, fell or foul, had ever panicked him like this woman who stood no taller than his chest. When he thought of the pit into which he'd be hurled if she was snatched away before he had a chance to hold her, kiss her, make her his own...

He might have survived his first death, but Patrick was certain he could die again, of desire.

Celeste went with the Lytton woman into the small room at the end of the hall. He could follow but wouldn't, now that he knew she could sense him. There was no reason for him to stay just outside, staring at a closed door, but the fact that she was behind it made him want to linger.

He didn't have to be what he was to know what the two women were doing. They were scholars, they'd be at it for a while. Truffling around in the Collection, looking for anything with his name or face on it. They'd find little since there was little to find. His whoreson brother had seen to that. It wasn't enough for him to wipe Patrick bodily off the earth, he'd had to erase every trace of him so that no one in years to come would even know he existed, had lived.

Perhaps, it was just as well. He didn't want the brandy-haired woman to know what he was or what he'd done. Not until he was ready to tell her, and she was ready to hear it.

Could anyone ever be ready to hear such a tale? There were good parts, a page here, a chapter there. Better for the woman to know those first, so that she might not condemn him too thoroughly for the rest.

What would it be like to tell her? To have her on his knee, his arm around her waist, her warm bottom against his thigh, while he told her the good parts? Ireland as he remembered it, a patchwork of green fields and white chalk and blue skies. His mother's smile as she petted her old cat. The smells and sights of Paris, the city that taught him far more than his tutors at the Collège des Irlandais. The dun stone walls of the school, the constant drone of students reciting in Latin, like a hive of learned bees.

And her own life, what of that? He wanted her to tell him of her home, her land. Her schooling as a wee girl, her first kiss—no, he didn't want to know about that.

They might pretend that neither of them had kissed before. Yes, that was the better thing, the right thing. It was true, after a fashion. Certainly, they had never kissed each other. Patrick wasn't sure there had ever *been* a kiss like the one they might have. A woman whose life would never, after that kiss, be the same, and a man whose life was...

The surging crowd in the Great Hall suddenly depressed him. He would go to his bedchamber, have a pipe, look out the window into nothing because, for him, there was nothing to see. At least he'd have the image of the woman to fill his mind and heart. It was enough.

It was everything.

FIVE

On Saturday—well, half past one in the morning, so really, it was Sunday—CeCe had finally shed the last of her walkers. They'd come in a hired bus tonight, the better to get drunk in the Anchor and Bell before boarding. The one-hour excursion had stretched to ninety minutes, mostly because half the group were struggling to walk in a straight line and the rest were asleep standing up. Gone, goodbye, good riddance, especially to the ghost question she hated more than all the others. On tonight's Walk, it had come from a slightly swaying, middle-aged gent.

"Have *you* ever seen a ghost?" A common question from people who believed every old castle, house, graveyard, or motorboat was haunted. She suppressed a sigh. Eunice Tattersall really was barking up the wrong tree with her plan for CeCe to lead ghost tours. The PD should be asking one of the Savannah aunts. Three of the four were loopy-doodle for the paranormal, Aunt Nicole being the worst of all. *Sorry to disappoint you, Eunice. You're stuck with me, not the G Team.*

She gave the swaying man a smile and her standard answer. "Not that I'm aware of."

Now, the question, the man, and the rest of his tipsy friends were gone, and she was alone in the Great Hall. She reminded herself of her answer. Reminded herself that there was nothing hiding in the deep recesses and dark corners of the lofty space. Last weekend was last weekend. She was definitively, blissfully, thoroughly, over it.

Hadn't she walked through the Castle, including the Tower, four times during the week? Only in daylight, true, but she didn't want to have to explain to anyone if she was discovered prowling around at night, when there was no Candlelight Walk scheduled. All four times, there had been no one there who shouldn't be there. Staff, docents, tourists, a plumber sorting the restroom on the second floor—no one else.

Tonight, she'd checked the Castle from top to bottom before her Walk, turning on battery candles as she went. Peered into every unlocked room, rattled the handle on every locked door, Great Hall to Tower, then back to the ground floor. Nothing. No lost tourists, staffers working overtime, or late night carpet cleaners. No one at all, just her.

When she admitted her walkers at midnight, she locked the Forecourt door behind them. Unlocked it to let them leave after the Walk, locked it again when she called goodnight to the last of them. So, unless the intruder from the weekend before could pass through walls, he was barred from the Castle.

The one thing she hadn't done was tell anyone what had happened—what she *thought* had happened—in the Tower seven days ago. Her job was on stormy seas as it was; reporting a workplace apparition wouldn't exactly calm the waters. She'd asked a few docents about security and found, not to her complete surprise, that the Castle didn't have any. Oh, sure, the doors were locked. The front one, the one opening into the Forecourt, was even alarmed, but she would give odds it wasn't monitored. None of the lower windows in the building could be opened, and someone would almost certainly notice if one was broken or jimmied. At the end of the day, docents were responsible for checking everything on their assigned floors. The Head Groundskeeper walked the perimeter of the Castle once a week, to confirm that all was as it should be.

But St. Rhydian's had no security in the armed-guard-with-growling-Doberman sense of the word. Why would it? It was a mostly overlooked historic site in a small town in remote coastal Wales. It wasn't as though the castle's Collection included Michelangelos or diamond tiaras. The most valuable thing CeCe knew of was a huge Mughal wall hanging in the Empire Room. It wasn't very likely a thief would drape *that* over their shoulder and lug it downstairs and out the door. Why would someone break into St. Rhydian's? To hold an unauthorized wedding reception?

So, lame as they were, the Castle's and her own security measures made her feel secure. Sort of. She squared her shoulders, heading for the Tower to begin turning off her candles.

Empty. The room will be empty.

She started climbing the Grand Staircase. Apart from a prickle at the back of her neck when she passed the portrait of Sean Patrick Ó Loinsigh, she didn't have a single uncanny twinge until she got three floors higher, to the fifty-eight Tower steps. Just for a minute, she wavered. Standing at the bottom of the steps, determination warred with the hairs-on-end sensation at the base of her skull. A faint glow made its way around the twisting stairs, and CeCe couldn't tell if it was welcoming or daring her. Either way, she was headed up. *I will* not *be scared off my own tour route.*

She began to stamp up the stairs, making the biggest racket she could, even if she wasn't entirely sure why. Was she trying to scare off a rat, or an intruder? She added loud singing to her stamping.

"Yankee Doodle went to town..." *Stamp, stamp, stamp.*

There'd been nothing up there earlier. Just her and her eleven walkers and their collective G&T breath. "A-ridin' on a pony..." *Stamp, stamp, stamp.* So, why would there be anything up there now? *Because last week, there was a sexy dead man?*

"Stuck a feather in his hat—" She pounded the last few steps, and bolted through the doorway, bellowing, "And no one's in the Tow-er!"

"Just you and me and the moon." A deep voice. A deep, gravelly, Irish voice. A voice attached to a man who was every bit as big, handsome, and strange as the week before. He couldn't be back, but he was. His scent came with him. Tobacco, sea water, peat smoke.

CeCe didn't quite let out the holler behind her teeth, the one that could be heard in Cardiff. The man seemed to understand her readiness to scream the Castle down, though, so he held both hands up in a gesture of, what? Restraint, goodwill, disarmament?

"You stay right the hell where you are," she warned.

"Tcha," the man clucked, and gently added, "You've never a reason to fear me. I'm as harmless as a kitten."

"I had a cat bite once that sent me to the hospital."

"I'm sure the wee moggie had a reason. Did you strike it with something like that?" He pointed to CeCe's hand, and she saw, with a start, that she'd grabbed the Tower's battery candle and was gripping it exactly like she was ready to bash someone with it. Not that it would be much of a weapon against a man the size of the one in front of her. Carefully, keeping her eyes on him, she slid the candle back into its niche, staying close by in case she changed her mind and decided to bludgeon the man to death.

Then, she stared at him. He stared back. He was dressed just as he'd been the first time—breeches, buckle shoes, and all.

She and the man were the diameter of the Tower Room apart, around ten feet. Way too close for comfort.

The best defense was a good offense, as George Washington said. "Sir," CeCe snapped, "you're going to tell me how you're getting into the Castle and what you're doing here. But let's start with the basics. Who *are* you?"

"Ah, but you know who I am. You spent an hour looking at my portrait, did you not?"

The prickle at the back of CeCe's neck spread down her back. "Are you stalking me?"

"*Stalking* you?" Damn, if there wasn't an aggravating amount of humor in his deep voice. "Do you mean as one stalks a deer? No, not a deer. A pheasant, perhaps, or a wee, soft rabbit. Nay, I had seen your lovely self not at all, until some weeks before we met in the Tower that blessed night. Which is not to say I did not hope for you." He shook his head. His hair wasn't tied back tonight. The black fall of it swayed around his jaw with the movement. "Hope is a poor word. Expect is a better one. You were foretold, in a prophecy."

"Foretold. Prophecy." CeCe was fairly sure she'd never said those words aloud, and certainly not together.

"I can explain, though it might take a little time."

I can explain. Wasn't that what every man said when he'd done some inexplicable thing? As for the foretold in a prophecy part... "It's fine. I don't need any explanations." *Or soothsayers.* "It's only that, I just—" *Just what?* What did she need, if not explanations?

She cleared her throat. She'd handled classrooms full of surly undergraduates. She could manage one slightly demented visitor-reenactor-cosplayer who hadn't bought a ticket. "Let me guess. You—not at all stalking—saw me in the Great Hall, looking at the portrait of Sean Patrick Ó Loinsigh. So, that's who you decided to impersonate."

The man threw back his head and laughed. CeCe fought it, but the laugh took her with it, anyway. Free, full-throated, and as big as the man, the laugh carried her away to some place where she laughed, too, held in his arms. The tobacco-peat smoke scent of him wrapped around them both and...

Come back from Neverland, girl.

The man was still chuckling. "I am no capering mountebank who pretends to be what he is not."

"Well, you're certainly *not* Sean Patrick Ó Loinsigh." *Because that's almost as absurd as me standing here, debating with you, when I should turn around and leave.* "We've both seen the portrait, fine. But *I've* seen the sketch the portrait was painted from." She pointed at the man's face. "And *you* got the nose wrong."

Not-Sean Patrick Ó Loinsigh nodded sagely. "Ah, yes. The crayon rendering."

Crayon. The eighteenth-century word for a charcoal or chalk drawing tool. Just like the one used to make the sketch Miriam Lytton had shown her. A nice touch for an impersonator, who was still a trespasser, and still talking in his entertaining, if demented, way.

"The rendering was made before my face met the grip end of a pistol." He ran a finger along his long nose, mostly straight except for a dent in the middle. "The sketch was made in the Spring of 1757, the portrait just after. The pistol made my acquaintance in 1759."

What's happening to this conversation? No, why was she even having a conversation? She should, at that moment, be looking at the handle on the Forecourt door. From the outside. Instead, she couldn't seem to take her eyes off the nose of the man in front of her. As long as she was looking at his nose, she might as well look at his mouth, decidedly one of the most attractive mouths she'd seen recently. His upper lip, with just the right amount of stubble that, against her lips, would feel so...

My God, what was she *thinking*? A few minutes ago, she'd been in charge. Now, she felt like she'd missed a step and slipped into the deep end of the pool. *Keep to the drawing, CeCe, keep it real.* "Sketch or no sketch, you expect me to believe your name is really Sean Patrick Ó Loinsigh?" She pulled herself up to her full five feet, four inches, from which height he still loomed over her. "I'm sorry, sir, but I don't believe you."

"Then I regret to say you'll have to take that up with my mother." He smiled.

The exact, edge-of-a-laugh smile in the downstairs portrait of Ó Loinsigh. The smile, the scar, the hair, the eyes... All exactly and impossibly identical to the portrait of a man that anyone in their right mind would confirm was dead and gone. CeCe covered her rising panic with heavy irony. "I'll try to remember to do that. For now, let's just set aside the name with the sketch and the pistol and your nose. Tell me this, instead. How are you getting into the Castle?"

"I don't need to get in, beautiful inquisitor, because I never go out."

"Right. You hide somewhere. You come in during the day, and then what? Tuck yourself into a wardrobe? A mop closet? Under a bed?"

"That would be...incommodious." The word came out on another laugh, this one low and husky.

He was laughing at her again. She bristled. "So, since you're a man who's been dead for over two hundred and fifty years, help me with a gap in the historical record. When did you—" Cece made air quotes with her fingers, "—die?" Hah! She'd got him with *that* question. Or not.

His answer came without a sign of hesitation. "That was

in 1761. The twenty-first of August. Six of the afternoon, more or less."

No points, Tower Man, since there's nothing in the record to prove or disprove it. Like the rest of his story, it had to be fluff, window dressing, frou-frou. What in tarnation was she doing? Debating historical trivia in the middle of the night with a—housebreaker. A tall, broad-shouldered housebreaker with night black hair, eyes like a stormy sea, and a scent that drew her closer, closer...

With a huge effort, she forced her runaway thoughts back into line with her job. "Sir, this conversation serves no purpose."

She meant to say more. About breaking and entering, the National Trust, and how actions had consequences. But something—anger, fear, attraction, confusion, maybe a mix of all four—suddenly bore down on her like a wave. If she didn't get out of its path, now, it would sweep her away like a scrap of seaweed on the beach.

She pointed toward the doorway of the Tower Room. "I'm leaving, Mr. Whatever-Your-Name-Is. When I next visit the Castle, you will *not* be in it."

As soon as she said it, CeCe realized it sounded like a spell. *Begone, ye noisome phantom! I abjure thee!* Too late to take it back. Without even turning off her battery candle in the wall niche, she stormed out the door and down the Tower stairs.

———

Down the stairs meant halfway. Step twenty-nine, more or less. CeCe skidded to a stop, jamming her right hand against the wall to stop her momentum. Her left arm waved uselessly in space since the Castle hadn't gotten around to installing a guardrail.

Her brain whirred like a flywheel. She had to leave. She

couldn't leave. She was stuck in the place she hated, but kept revisiting. The place between ancient and recent history.

Ancient history was her mother, Gabrielle Gowdie, *Mom*. Who, twenty-five years ago, fell so crazy in love with a man that she had his child out of wedlock even though he was nowhere in sight. And what did CeCe know about that man? *"He just—fascinated her."* That's what Aunt Hélène had said. Either her aunts didn't know any more or they weren't saying. What more was there to say? Four increasingly crazy years after she'd met him, Mom dove off a bridge and drowned.

Recent history, the place where ancient collided with now, was the man in the Tower, the one she'd just run away from.

She could just imagine the online entry for her particular case study in history. "Presumed apparition (disambiguation) in St. Rhydian's Castle, Tower Room." She might have to add a subtitle. "Case study of a dangerously fascinating man wearing knee breeches and silver buckles."

Because that was the problem, wasn't it? If she'd learned anything from the mother she barely remembered, it was that fascinating men were dangerous. Fascination was for snake charmers and hypnotists. For people who lured fish into their bare hands, or put chickens into trances.

For people who got so fascinated they abandoned their child and threw themselves off bridges.

When the words *man* and *fascinating* got together, CeCe had always flown out whatever door was open and down whatever stairs were nearest. Flight landed her in a safe place— the twenty-ninth step. There wasn't a lot of room for joy there, but at least she hadn't taken a dive off any bridges. Yet.

This time was different. She didn't know why or how, but it had something to do with the tingle at the back of her neck. A week ago, in the same place, at the same hour, just before the first time she saw the fascinating man she'd just run away from, her neck had tingled.

And, oh my God, was it tingling now.

A sharp sensation in a different body part, her wrist, made CeCe yank her hand off the wall and shake it. She'd been leaning all her weight on it, as though she could press herself right through the stone and away. Into the night and the fresh air, where she could just magically float down to her car and the Castle road to her flat.

But that won't work, will it, CeCe? The scenery would change on the outside, but on the inside it would look the same. She'd still be twenty-five. Then thirty-two, thirty-eight, forty. Still stuck on the twenty-ninth step.

Or, she could go back up to the Tower Room.

Carefully—in part because the stairs were steep and in part because her self-preservation instincts were screaming so loudly in protest that they made her dizzy—CeCe turned around. She started climbing again.

Six

When she entered the Tower Room, her fascinating man was right where she'd left him. She wasn't sure what to expect. Would he be irritated, even insulted, that she'd huffed away after warning him off? In fact, he smiled radiantly, as though her abrupt trip to the stairs and back was perfectly normal. CeCe had an uneasy feeling it might be normal for her now.

Before she could speak, he did. "Let us begin anew." The deep roughness of his voice licked over her like a cat's tongue. He made a leg, a formal bow in eighteenth century parlance. It was an elegant movement. Nothing elegant about the muscular thigh that tested the fabric of his breeches when he extended his leg, arms out to the sides, upper body lowered. Still smiling, he rose. "Sean Patrick Ó Loinsigh. Your most obedient servant."

"Celeste Gowdie." She took a step forward, hand extended. "Call me CeCe."

For a split second, the man ignored her hand. "Gowdie." He pronounced the word correctly, carefully, his eyes narrowing. Then, he shook himself slightly and took her fingers in his. He lowered his head over them.

His mouth on her hand was no more than the brush of a moth's wing, warmed by his breath, but at the place of contact CeCe's flesh tingled as fiercely as the back of her neck.

"Your forename, *Céleste*." He said it the French way. "A word almost as lovely as the woman who bears it. Will you permit me the intimacy to address you by it?"

Intimacy. A dozen inappropriate forms of it flitted through her brain. She swatted them away. "Of course. What would you like me to call you? Mr. Ó Loinsigh? Sean?"

"Patrick." A solid name, one that went with the voice. A dead man's name, but if it got her new friend talking, she'd use it.

Patrick's extraordinary gaze took in the bare chamber. "I am a poor excuse for a gentleman, to be unable to offer you so much as a chair, Celeste. But if we take our ease upon the floor, we may converse." CeCe's eyebrows rose, and Patrick immediately added, "At a proper distance, as the lady pleases."

A gentleman trespasser—a new combination for her. She lowered herself to sit against the wall, under the candle niche. Folding her legs to one side, she protectively tucked her skirts around her calves and ankles. Patrick settled himself against the wall opposite. A proper distance, as he'd said, though in a fast second he could be—

Don't think that, CeCe.

She stayed put. She'd thought all week about the conversation she'd have with Tower Man if he turned up again. "Why are you pretending to be dead?"

"But Celeste, I am not—"

"Fine, all right, pretending to be alive. You certainly aren't dead. You're—" *Warm.* His breath on her hand, his lips touching her skin. "Let's put dead away for now. We don't have a living history program at the Castle, but we might, someday. Call this an audition. Convince me you're Sean Patrick Ó Loinsigh."

"Primus," he began, and CeCe thought, *Oh, we're doing this in Latin now, are we?* Patrick continued, "The name is not Oh loyn-zee, it is O-lin-shig. An Irish name, meaning 'exile from the sea.' In the case of my own self, I can only call that humor of the blackest sort. I was born—"

"I know that part, I looked it up. 1730."

"I was going to say in Ireland, but you're right about the year."

"You are the natural son of Richard Thomas Alchester DeBlaes, Earl of Trawsgoed and master of St. Rhydian's. The Earl died in 1762—"

"My father breathed his last in 1760."

"History says—"

"History is full of errors. You of all people should know that, Celeste."

He knew she was a historian. Points ceded for researching the Castle staff. "I won't argue, since you'll just insist you were there. So, your father was..." She did rapid math in her head. "Nineteen, when you were born? That's very young. How did your parents meet?"

"Like other noble sons both feckless and sober, my father had been sent to the Collge des Irlandais—"

"In Paris," she broke in. "Founded by Jesuits, when the abbeys and monasteries in Britain were dissolved by Henry the Eighth."

"It pleases me that you know of it."

Point in his favor. Men weren't always pleased by highly educated women.

"The old Earl, my grandfather, had landholdings and tenants in Ireland. When his son completed his studies in Paris, he was sent to assay those lands and tenants. Instead—"

"Instead, your teenage dad was dallying with an Irish barmaid."

Patrick's eyes darkened. It was just a flash, but she'd apparently slandered his mother, or his father, maybe both. How, she wasn't sure. It was just a campfire tale, right?

"Sorry. That was rude." A few awkward seconds ticked by. She would ask the question she'd thought of when she looked at his portrait. "What was she like, your mother?"

Patrick's eyes calmed, stormy seas to quiet ones. He stretched out his long legs, bending one at the knee. His big—really big—foot, in a scuffed shoe, was close enough that she saw the worn patches in the leather sole. He laced his fingers around his bent knee. CeCe's eyes widened.

Patrick's knuckles were battered, enlarged, and his hands were crisscrossed with scars. One began between the last two fingers on his right and ran right up into the wrist, where it disappeared into the threadbare cuff of his shirt. When he spoke again, the gentleness in his voice was at complete odds with the violent history of his hands.

"Aoife Ó Loinsigh was my mother. The only child of a widowed farmer of small means but fine sensibility, she'd been raised as a gentlewoman. When her father died, there were no other kin, and the farm was failing. My mother was just eighteen, sweet, pious, and struggling. A great beauty, as well, and alone. At first sight of her, my father was struck by love as though by fever. He spent months in Connemara, his obligations forgotten, his rank meaningless. Only the death of my grandfather wrenched him from my mother's side. My father could not renounce the title to which he unwillingly succeeded. Only an order of the Crown could have released him, and that was as unlikely as a mouse on the moon."

CeCe was pretty sure there had been a mouse on the moon, caged in some lunar craft or other. It was still a nice touch of authenticity for Patrick—the make-believe eighteenth-century Patrick—to say it was impossible. If the man across from her was an actor, he was a darn good one.

"My father returned to the place of his birth, this place." Patrick tilted his head, taking in the Tower, the Castle, and the vast lands that were attached in the 1700s. "He became, against his every wish and dream, the Earl of Trawsgoed, master of the estate. Its lands, its dependents, its wealth, its enemies—all his, while the only thing he really wanted was left behind in Ireland. My mother, increasing. Six months gone when he left."

It wasn't that rare a story. Country girl seduced by a wild aristocratic youth. Pregnancy, abandonment, heartbreak, et cetera. But there was something in Patrick's telling of it. The pain that visited his face, the emotion thickening his voice. She straightened her spine. *It's fiction. It's fantasy. A yarn.*

So, why could she see it? The green hills, the whitewashed cottage, the young woman standing in the doorway. Black hair whipped around her pale face by the wind, hands folded over her belly and the child within. The woman's eyes, dappled jade, looking to the east with longing and despair.

If she believed it, the woman's son sat opposite her now. He shifted, unlacing his fingers. Stretching out both legs, he crossed them at the ankles, crossing his arms as well, over his chest. The thin linen of his shirt drew tight with the action. CeCe tried not to gawk at his pectorals bulging under the cloth. It was cool in the Tower, a relief after the hot day, but it did things to both their bodies. She could see Patrick's nipples, flat dark circles, pebbled at the centers. Her own breasts responded, and her mouth went dry.

"The years fled. My parents were not reunited. Still, my father never stopped loving the bride of his heart. He supported her and the child they had made, all the days of his life. On his deathbed, he gripped my hand with the little strength he had left, and spoke my mother's name, twice.

Then, he breathed his last." Faintly smiling, Patrick looked at CeCe. His eyes brightened but stopped short of twinkly. "In 1760."

She nodded but stopped short of friendly. "Got it. 1760." Had he found an error in the historical record? It was possible, even amateurs found them. As to his relationship with the Earl... "When you say your father supported you—"

"In the way a man of honor supports his children, Celeste, be they in or out of wedlock. I was sent, at the age of nine, to the Collège des Irlandais just as my father had been. My schooling was as fine as that of any lawful son, though I was rarely favored with the friendship of my betters."

"Did you have to—"

"Trounce the lace-cravated whelps?" He said it with a chuckle, and she had a feeling he might have enjoyed the trouncing. "Most of them came round without a beating. I gained a grudging respect for sport. On the field and off."

CeCe had a vivid mental image of both. The man sitting across from her at seventeen, a brawling youth with coal-black hair and startling eyes and a body like a young Atlas. Pummeling his mates in a boxing ring, drinking them under the table in a Parisian tavern. Pulling a buxom wench onto his muscular thighs, and—

It's a fable, remember? She wrenched herself back. "You ended up here, eventually."

"I did, when I was summoned. I was eighteen years of age."

CeCe thought he might go on, but he didn't. The silence stretched to a minute, and finally she prompted, "When you came here, you—"

"My tale matters not, Celeste. Yours is the one worth hearing."

"I'm a historian from Savannah, Georgia, Patrick. You're the one with the interesting backstory."

He didn't comment, just looked down at his hands. Had he run out of fictional past? Truth or fiction, she had apparently got all she was going to get for one night. She couldn't think of anything more to say, but she couldn't make herself go, either. *Still on the twenty-ninth step, CeCe?*

If only she'd met Patrick on one of her Walks. In street clothes, just a hunky, uncomplicated Irishman on holiday in Wales. And they'd joked, and flirted, and gone for a drink after the tour...

She pretended to straighten her skirts, sneaking glances at the man opposite her instead.

Legs like a footballer. A chest so massive it seemed mythical, the chest of Thor or Odysseus. The impressive span of his shoulders tested the seams of his worn shirt. The collar opened at the neck, showing a triangle of ruddy skin, a faint dusting of dark hair toward the bottom of the gap.

No more looking. It was the looking that gave her little shocks of sensation deep in her belly. Deeper. Pleasant, but risky. They were totally wrong, those feelings—*any* feeling other than determination to get the man barred from St. Rhydian's, fast and forever. In her head, she'd called him demented. What if he truly was delusional? It was cruel to encourage him. Not to misquote Shakespeare, but that way lay madness. His, hers, theirs.

Time to bid her delusional yet *fascinating* buddy goodbye. CeCe wished she could say it in Latin. She gathered her petticoats and stood. Patrick stood when she did. For a few seconds she was speechless, staring up at him. He really was big. And incredibly, dangerously, good-looking.

She finally got a few words out. "This has all been really... informative." A Eunice Tattersall word, sour in her mouth. Patrick took a step toward her and she backed up, alarmed.

He strode right past her, to the faux sentry slit, open to the night. "It's getting on for dawn," he murmured.

Dawn? Couldn't be, they'd only been sitting and talking for an hour.

"Best away to your bed, *cuisle mo chroi*."

"C-cushla makree?"

Patrick turned his one-sided smile on her, and something quivered in CeCe's chest. He leaned slightly toward her, speaking quietly, sharing a secret. "It's Irish, for *vein of my heart*."

Well, then. She would've bet good money Patrick wasn't one of those men who called all women *darlin'*, *sweetie*, or *honeybunch*. If he were, she'd know how to respond, and it would be fast and deflating. *Vein of my heart*, though. That left her tongue-tied.

CeCe edged along the wall, so she could look out the sentry slit, too. The opening was narrow. For them both to look out, they had to stand almost shoulder to shoulder. Actually, her shoulder only came to his tricep, making her feel like she stood in the shadow of a tall tree.

Below them, the Castle gardens were gray sculptures in the mist. The towering three-hundred year-old yew trees bordering the walkway to the Forecourt, were just bunched canopies of dark green. Beyond and above them, red and gold spilled over the horizon. The sea was unseen, but near. It beckoned with a whisper of rolling surf.

Silent and still as a tree himself, the man by her side was seemingly fixed on the daybreak, so CeCe fixed her eyes on him. Her second rude thing of the night, but she might not get another chance.

The man who called himself Sean Patrick Ó Loinsigh was even more striking close up than from six feet away. Dots of fire in his eyes reflected the rising sun on the Irish Sea that he probably would say was "half a league" away. His hair was dark and rich as a seal pelt, straight and smooth. CeCe liked it unbound, falling nearly to his shoulders. The bristles on his jaw and upper lip stood out sharply against his fair skin. His beard was not all the same black, but flecked with russet hairs, and silver.

His scar was toward her, and she fought the same compulsion she'd felt when she saw his portrait. To trace the ridged flesh as it traveled along his temple, the outer edge of his eye, his cheekbone. It seemed impossible that a historical reenactor would go to the trouble of creating such a lifelike scar for—what? To impress her? When he got her hooked on his persona, would he tell her about his idea for museum theater at the Castle? Was all this just a living history version of serious dress?

Reenactors could be extravagantly serious about what they did. But when you saw them up close, something usually gave them away. Eyeglasses or the faint rims of contact lenses. A prohibited cell phone pinging in a uniform pocket. The smell of *Acqua di Gio*, instead of the sweat and wood smoke that a real person of the time would reek of.

She inhaled deeply, taking in Patrick's scent. Like his scar, it seemed authentic. She couldn't just stand back as a historian and appreciate it. This man's smell engaged her. Her, CeCe. Not the historian, but the woman. It captured her, crawled under her clothes. Wrapped her, bound her, infused her lungs and made her want to take it deep, so it would never leave. With his scent came the warmth of his body. It flowed over and into her, too. In bed, on a cold night, he'd be—

Don't even think it. But she couldn't *stop* thinking it. She had a rushing, vivid image of herself under him, his strength and heat covering her, filling her. Standing so close to him, her body came alive with urges. *Touch him, take him.*

As though he knew what she was thinking, Patrick turned his head toward her. Intent burned in his eyes. Desire was in every line of his face, his mouth.

No, CeCe, no, no, no! At best, he was a fantasy, one Aunt

Diane would call "*délicieux*," but utterly impossible. And risky to know, in the way all fascinating men were risky to know. Especially the handsome ones.

She slid her gaze away, quickly, and spoke to the view beyond the window. "What do you see?"

"Not I." Patrick pointed toward the west. His other hand, warm and heavy, came slowly down on CeCe's shoulder, sending arousal so intense through her body she barely heard his next words. "What do *you* see?"

She forced her attention to his question. "I can't see it, but I know it's there. The Irish Sea."

He nodded. "On the seaward edge of Trawsgoed land, there are ruins, the broken remains of a fifth century oratory. It was left derelict for many years, but other monks came. It was they who built the abbey beneath our feet. Benedictines." Almost as though he was talking to himself, he added, "They wore black robes."

She'd studied that part in the Guidebook. "They dedicated the abbey to St. Rhydian. He was unconventional."

"He was. Canonized by local acclaim, and not by Rome. The people here said he could understand the speech of animals and make water rise to his hands. He was killed by Viking raiders in 811. A man of God, he was, but died with a sword in his hands."

That wasn't in the Guidebook. Detailed knowledge like that...CeCe had met academics who had it, but they were usually musty pedants with clicking dentures and overflowing briefcases. Patrick was—not that.

His hand moved on her shoulder, rubbing it, his thumb tracing circular patterns. Her heart raced like a rabbit. The faint rasp of his scarred fingers on the linen of her bodice seemed loud, and everywhere he touched, fires of sensation leaped up. CeCe fought a powerful craving to curl into him, purring. She caught herself before she did, shrugging off his hand and turning to face him. She'd make one more stab at law and order. She owed it to her job. To her sanity.

"You can't come back here, Patrick. I don't know how you're getting in or why, but please, don't do it again. Sooner or later, someone with no imagination will catch you, and then you'll be in real trouble, maybe even get arrested."

She would have sworn on a Bible she said those words. What came out of her mouth, though, was, "Will I see you again?"

His reply was a husky whisper, rusted iron wrapped in velvet. "God willing, *mo chroí*."

He had touched her, twice. Once when he'd grazed her fingers with his lips, and again when he'd rested his hand on her shoulder. She'd obviously lost her mind, since it seemed perfectly logical that now they would kiss.

He reached for her waist and pulled her close. She let him. His hands settled on her hips, and hers went to his shoulders, as though they had always rested there. She looked up and saw infinite yearning in Patrick's eyes, just before he lowered his head and took her mouth in his.

But none of it happened. She didn't tell him to go away. He didn't kiss her. She thought he might. He entrusted them both to God and bent over her, while she closed her eyes...

CeCe opened her eyes and blinked in utter confusion. No kiss. No man. Just her, standing dazed and alone, arms by her sides and empty, mouth tingling the way her fingers had tingled when Patrick bowed and touched them with his lips. Had she fainted again? Was she having seizures?

Sean Patrick Ó Loinsigh had vanished, and she had no idea when or how. One second he was there, his size and heat pulling her into him, his body so near his shirtsleeves grazed her as he reached out. And then...

CeCe squeezed her eyes shut, imagined him back, and opened her eyes again.

Nothing. He was gone, and the light of the candle was gone, too. Just her, in a dawn-lit stone room, with no proof of the man and the night apart from a lingering whiff of peat smoke and tobacco. And she couldn't be sure she wasn't imagining that.

Numbly, she reached into the pocket of her skirt for her keys.

SEVEN

atching her go. It tore him more painfully than the first time. More, because this night he had almost kissed her.

Kissed her! The nearness of it all but unmanned him where he stood. When he had his hands on her, petting her, stroking the cloth between her body and his fingers...he'd wanted to tear the garment away, tear his own clothing away. In that sliver of time, he'd felt her body against his, tasted her in his mouth, and known the instant of fierce rapture when he thrust into her. If it had pleased God to take him in that instant and cast him into oblivion, he would have gone willingly.

Willingly for himself, but not for her. And so, he had pulled back, dragged himself from her at the crucial second before he did something that might have long lasting and terrible consequences for them both.

The worlds of the living and the dead. Only the thickness of a leaf separated them, but for all that, they were closed, each to the other. Granted, there were those among the living who had a peculiar awareness. They could sense the dead, be moved by them, and even, in rare cases, see them. But for the dead to return such an awareness in any real, any *living*, sense? It did not happen. It *could* not happen.

Yet, he saw the beautiful woman in the Tower, and she saw him. Saw him not as a shred of mist nor a flicker at the edge of her sight, but as the man he had been in life. Vigorous. Longing. Filled with a restless, pounding impulse that craved liquid release in her body.

It was more than seeing. He could touch her. She could touch him. The knowledge was torment, it was Hell. A place to which he was no stranger. The grotesquely familiar place he'd known from the first day he'd answered his father's summons to the Castle. The best he could say was that the summons, and the blood oaths Patrick had been called to fulfill, dated to his grandsire. Even farther back, to old jealousies and old disputes. But the sons of sons inherited hatred along with their titles and were obliged to avenge their fathers' fathers.

He pushed his own darkness aside to peer into the wider darkness of the Castle road. The road disappeared into the night, and he could no longer see the woman's coach on it. By now, she was driving out the Castle gates, the limit of his world. Beyond the gates, there was a town, one that surely had changed beyond recognition since the village of his lifetime. The woman would have her own life there. A dwelling. Friends. A shop where she bought ribbons. A baker who sold her bread.

Left behind, there was nothing for Patrick but the long gray and the compulsion to count the minutes until her return. Until the woman, his world had not had a clock in it. Oh, to be sure, there was one in his bedchamber, one he'd not wound in decades. Its ticking drove him mad. What was the point of marking the hours, the minutes? Eternity was not measured with a timepiece.

But now, there was a reason to watch the slow sweep of the hour hand. A week until they were together again. A day. Six hours. An hour until breath filled his lungs, until his heart beat again.

Céleste. He whispered her name, and it calmed him. She was everything he'd not been in the last third of his life, the third that was all horror and sin. Her perfection rent the cloth of that sin. Rent and discarded it, leaving him whole and good as he once was, before murderous necessity turned him into the mockery of life and death that he was now.

Could anything save him?

She could. He doubted she herself knew why, but his angel, his Celeste, had given enough of her living self to create this glorious moment for them both. Glorious and fragile. She might, she should, withdraw her gift. He would be unable to follow. The door between worlds, now standing open, would disappear, and the threshold with it. Every sweet promise of life and love would be snatched away in a terrible second.

Even worse, he could take too much, pull her across the narrow divide, wrench her from the vital condition that was hers by right, and land her in the long gray with him.

No. He would not let that happen. His strength had come with him into the gray. He would hold her, hold them both, on the border between worlds. He would keep their feet on that slim margin, and there, they would find their joy. It would not be the joy of the living. But he would exhaust himself to give her something that would make even an angel sigh with pleasure.

He might never truly have her, but he would never let her go.

EIGHT

"Miriam, have you run across any inconsistencies in the file on the DeBlaes family?" CeCe gestured at the computer on Dr. Lytton's desk. "In particular, the death date of the Earl? Richard Thomas, I mean, the one whose death is recorded as 1762. I've just run across a secondary source, and, uh," she stumbled on the words, thinking of the source's claim to be primary, "it suggests the date may be wrong. So—"

"Truly, Miss Gowdie, on Mondays I don't have time to do my own research, much less yours. Now, if you don't mind, I'm quite busy."

Well, that was unexpected. Miriam hadn't looked up as CeCe entered. She'd responded to the knock on her door and CeCe's cheery greeting with a curt "Come!" Now, she dismissed CeCe like she was a freshman arguing about an exam grade. The Collections Manager had been so gracious last week.

CeCe bit back her surprise and an apology. Instead, she looked hard at the woman seated at the desk. Miriam Lytton was so pale she might have been marble instead of flesh.

Watching her thin hands on the computer keyboard, CeCe saw them tremble. Maybe Miriam had dodged the question about the Earl because she couldn't stand up long enough to find the old paper files in the cabinet.

Despite the waves of rejection wafting in her direction, CeCe stayed where she was. The only sound in the small room was the faint clicking of the keyboard and Miriam's breathing. Her inhales sounded labored, her exhales hitched.

Finally, CeCe spoke, softly. "You're not well, are you?"

"I'm perfectly fine," Miriam snapped. There was another awkward pause.

CeCe kept her voice soft. "I'm sorry, Dr. Lytton. My research bloodhound got off the leash. I'm terrible when I'm after something. Please forgive me."

Miriam looked up. Her smile was faint but genuine, and she kept her faded blue eyes on CeCe as she spoke. "I shouldn't have reacted that way. I'm the one who should apologize." She pointed at the chair across from her desk, a stack of books on the seat. "Just put those anywhere and sit down." CeCe moved the books to a corner of the desk and sat.

"Would you care for tea?" Miriam gestured toward an electric tea kettle on top of the filing cabinet.

"Thanks, Dr. Lytton, but no. I had three cups this morning and I'm a bit waterlogged. Tea-logged, I guess."

"Call me Miriam, please. Tea is a dreadful habit and I'm as much of an addict as most Britons are. I tried to switch to herbals. You know, chamomile, lemon. I was climbing the walls in under a week." They both laughed. There was barely a beat before Miriam spoke again. She still smiled, but pain clouded her eyes. "I have CML."

Chronic myelogenous leukemia. A nasty disease, life-shortening, often fatal. CeCe schooled herself not to show the shock she felt. "Have your doctors here been in touch with Mount Sinai, in New York?" The pain in the Collection

Manager's eyes turned to surprise. "My Aunt Hélène is a physician. She's board-certified in the treatment of blood disorders, including CML."

"Thank you for calling it a disorder." Miriam picked up a paper, shifted it to another spot, then looked at CeCe again. "It sounds so much better than cancer. I've been ill for years and am no longer responsive to treatment. It's just a matter of time."

CeCe didn't insult the woman opposite her with platitudes. *There's always hope. New cures are being discovered all the time.* "How long...?"

Miriam shrugged. "Any day now, I imagine. I try to keep working. Some days are better than others. Today is..." She lifted one of the books CeCe had shifted, opened it, then closed it and put it back. Her gaze, pale eyes in a pale face, rose again to her visitor. "Not one of the good ones."

CeCe didn't smile at the mild jest. "What can I do to make today better?"

The Collection Manager's sudden grin transformed her. For a few seconds, she looked like an eager professor greeting a new class. "Do you know The Lark, on the High Street?"

"I do. It's the quintessential English tearoom. Fabulous crumpets."

"It is, and they are! Both are all the more unlikely since The Lark is so far into Wales it's almost in the Irish Sea." Miriam opened the top drawer in her desk and extracted a handbag. "To indulge in an Americanism, let's do brunch."

———

The Lark lived up to its reputation and they had a delightful meal. They talked about history, of course—the Castle's and Wales'—then wandered off onto sideroads like the War of the Roses. Somewhere in the mix, CeCe slipped in her question about the death date of the third to last DeBlaes, but Miriam couldn't offer a contradiction to the date on file.

"Isn't there a grave or a tombstone or something?" CeCe asked.

"The DeBlaes came to Wales from Sussex. Your Earl is buried there, in a family vault with his father and the rest of the family. I've never seen it, but there's no reason to suspect a plaque or inscription—if there is one, and there's not always —which differs from the recorded date." Miriam stirred her second cup of tea. Her eyes came up, suddenly sharp. "Did you say you have a source for your concerns over the date?"

Yes, but not one I'm willing to tell anybody about. "No, not really. I must have read something somewhere."

Miriam's gray eyebrows lifted, but she didn't say anything. CeCe changed the subject, and they chatted happily for another hour.

CeCe had driven them both to town in her battered rental Mini Cooper, so, after brunch, she brought them back to the Castle. Figuring she should pick up one of her skimpy paychecks, she waved goodbye to Miriam in the Great Hall and headed for the PD's office. Eunice Tattersall was out. That left her to the tender mercies of Mrs. Hopkins, her secretary.

The only positive thing CeCe could say about Mrs. Hopkins was that she was consistent. Consistently unpleasant. Worse, she was a doormat. If the PD told her to gun down tourists with a semi-automatic, the secretary would be loading rounds before the order was out of her boss's mouth. It was no secret why everyone called her Eunice Lite behind her back.

"Mrs. Hopkins," CeCe began, standing, since the frowning secretary hadn't offered her a seat. Or a greeting. "I'm concerned about security in the Castle."

Eunice Lite didn't bother to look up from her desk. "You'll need to take that up with Ms. Tattersall when she returns," she clipped out. "Thursday."

CeCe nodded, took her check, and left. She went back to the car park, as always, by the long paved walkway that sloped down from the Forecourt. The walk and the double row of ancient yews that flanked it—CeCe loved them. She usually fell into a sort of happy trance under the leafy canopies, visions of strolling women in panniered skirts and men in embroidered waistcoats filling her brain. Today, she was distracted, eyes lowered, remembering how the tops of the trees looked from the sentry slit in the Tower Room, Patrick at her side, dawn breaking. If the young man walking toward her hadn't spoken, she would have crashed head-on into him.

"*Prynhawn da*, Miss Gowdie." It was Alun Jones. Like her, he was a recent addition to the Castle team, saying *prin hown dah*, good afternoon in Welsh.

"Oh, hi." *Perk up, CeCe.* Nothing that was wrong in her life was Alun's fault. She should at least try to be pleasant to a colleague about her age, one who beamed restrained but very male interest in her snug jeans and trim jacket. She put on her brightest Candlelight Castle Walk smile. "Please call me CeCe, Alun. How's the work going?"

"Not too bad, thanks. We're down to the early eighteen hundreds in the Library."

"Oooh, Jane Austen wallpaper." Ha ha, a history joke.

"Who knows? Maybe one of the rooms is papered in an undiscovered novel."

"Keep scraping, Alun. You might find the handwritten draft. It'll be worth a fortune."

"Help me with the work and I'll split the profits with you."

There was a thought. Not Jane Austen, but helping Alun. Why not? CeCe had more spare time than she knew what to do with, and Alun could use the extra hand. She didn't even care about getting paid. It would be real history, and about as far from ghosts as she could get. Before she could say, "Count me in!" Alun went on about his project.

"It's really quite exciting. I'm nearly done stripping the Hellenic Room, and I'll start plastering in a week or two. It's slow, of course. Once I recover whatever was on the walls in 1747, I'll fabricate a reproduction distemper, though I can't use white lead—oh, sorry, sorry! I'm nattering, aren't I?" Alun grinned, white teeth flashing.

CeCe laughed again. Tante Diane would call him *beau*, too, with his ready smile and blue eyes under a mop of auburn curls. Even in paint-splattered overalls and a faded T-shirt, he managed to look and smell fresh, like the cool air rolling off the Welsh mountains toward the sea.

"Natter away," she reassured him. "If it makes you feel any better, I'll bore you some time with my research mania, George the First and the building of Hampton Court Palace."

"I'd forgotten! You're a fellow historian. Everyone talks about you like—er, that is, I meant to say you're not just a tour guide, you're..." Alun's fair face turned red. He waved a hand toward the Forecourt where CeCe's little bands of ghost hopefuls gathered on Saturday nights.

Thud. Back to earth, the place where she *was* just a tour guide. "No problem." She widened her smile until her cheekbones hurt. "Enjoy your day." She turned away and strolled toward the car park with what she hoped were nonchalant strides.

Daft American. That was what Alun and everyone else at the Castle probably thought about her. Would attitudes change when she started dragging ghost hunters around? Yes, they would get worse. Very, inconceivably, embarrassingly, worse.

At the car park, CeCe dug in her bag for the key to the Mini. Just before she got in, she looked over her shoulder at St. Rhydian's. The sight made her feel a little better. It always did.

From her first visit, she'd loved everything about the Castle, even the moment when a docent corrected her pronunciation of the name. *"It's ruhd ye-an, dearie, not 'rye' like the bread."*

The Castle's height alone was thrilling. The medieval abbey foundations on which it was built raised St. Rhydian's high enough that it was almost fully visible over the giant yews. She loved the way it dominated the landscape, gray stone walls taking on the color of each time of day. Rose in the morning, gold at midday, red when sunset fired the single western tower with its crenelated top. A veil of ivy clung coyly to the façade, and its multi-paned windows shattered the light into a thousand bright lances.

Outside the walls, famously lush gardens circled the Castle in tiers, like liveried footmen arrayed for service. Even the wild parkland across the road, with its small herd of roe deer, seemed there just to provide scenic views for noble eyes gazing out the Castle windows.

She imagined the grounds as Patrick would have seen them, had he really lived in the eighteenth century. No elaborate landscaping, the lawns dotted with sheep. Well-stocked stables. A kitchen garden with an irascible chef—French, of course—snipping herbs and cursing his English employers. All fantasy, of course, like Patrick's story, but it fit pleasurably into her own fantasy of the Castle.

Her Castle. Did her new friend in the Tower feel the same way? Maybe that's why he was haunting the...

Haunting? *Oh no, CeCe.* Malingering, maybe. Loitering, skulking, prowling around.

Disappearing in an eye blink.

All right, the disappearing part troubled her. She sighed and wedged herself into the Mini. It was just a stunt. She'd seen a video of a David Copperfield show where he made the Statue of Liberty disappear. Enough was enough. No more time devoted to figuring out the sleight-of-hand Patrick was using to make himself seem like a grand mystery instead of an interloper. No more time devoted to *him*. She had worse troubles.

As she drove her rent-a-heap toward the front gates, resignation settled onto her shoulders like a heavy cloak. Resisting the PD's ghost walk scheme was a waste of time. She loved St. Rhydian's too much to leave, and Eunice Tattersall knew it. Without a work visa, her passport only allowed her to stay for a couple more months. Then, unless something radical happened, she'd have to leave the U.K. She didn't have the resources to wander around Europe hunting for history jobs, so she'd have to crawl back to Savannah with her tail between her legs.

The PD was right. Ghost walks were her only viable path to stay, and CeCe would take it. She drew the line at making up ridiculous tales like Jasper Marcotte did, but if staying at the Castle meant finding ghosts...

She'd just have to find them.

NINE

Patrick fought a burning sensation in his gut as he watched them from a second-floor window. The Welshman, in a lively fashion, was speaking with Celeste. He didn't much care for either the speaking or the man. Particularly the man. Him with his quick smile and sky-blue eyes and smooth face. Smooth, unscarred face. It made Patrick's teeth grind. Not to mention, the man was a lot younger than himself. A quarter millennium or thereabouts.

He didn't care for the young man's voice, either. That Welsh lilt. Vowels rolling with the unhurried cadence of oars pulling a boat or a seashell tumbling end to end in the surf. Patrick didn't care for the way that voice pleased Celeste's ears. He didn't care for it at all.

And that thatch of red-brown hair on the man's head. Patrick had never trusted ginger-haired men. They were widely thought to be sly. To be sure, the man's hair wasn't a true ginger, more like a fox color. You couldn't trust foxes, either, though, could you? The foxy hair was fetching to women, he would wager, and not a speck of gray in it. Patrick had been only thirty-one when he died, but he'd warrant his life was harder than anything the younger man had seen. It had given him some pewter hairs among his black. Perhaps, Celeste would think them distinguished, call them silver.

She'd offered to help the Welshman in his labor on the Castle walls. Aye, she would. She was the sort of woman who would stoop out of kindness to assist anyone who asked for help. He'd seen how she was with the drink-addled prats she led around the Castle. They deserved, more often than not, to be pitched off the roof, but she never lashed out at them or their crackbrained chatter. Of course, she would help the Welshman. Patrick was agreeable to that, as long as the Welshman comported himself with respect. If he didn't, he'd be a dead Welshman.

Besides, the man was betrothed, was he not? Some woman in London Town. Odd name, the woman had, Carina, Caro. Patrick had heard him speak of her to La Tattersall, awe in his voice. Perhaps, the Welshman was a fortune hunter, and the fiancée had a large dowry, in which case he was right to be awed. Certainly, her suitor hadn't two shillings to rub together, or he'd not be slaving away on the Castle walls like a common laborer. If that was so, if he had a dowry waiting, then he should hie himself to London, make his marriage bed, and lie in it. There was nothing for him at St. Rhydian's other than his pails of paint and a trowel or three. If only Patrick were alive, he'd cheerfully put the man on a horse and point him to the turnpike. He might even buy the horse.

Celeste Gowdie was not for the Welshman, nor he for her. Patrick knew the man for her. He knew it in his blood, in his bones. Did she? Not yet. It was on his list.

Best get on with it, then. You've stalled at the first item. He had, with good reason. It was a delicate business and fraught with peril. Delicate as the business of romance always is, and perilous because of the history that his enticing historian, surprisingly, did not know.

Still...*Qui onques rien n'enprist riens n'achieva.* Nothing ventured, nothing gained. She would be his. They would belong to each other. It would be so, even if he had to drag archangels from Heaven or the Devil from his fiery den to make it so.

Besides, it had all been foretold by the *banfháidh*, the seer.

It was long ago, during his living years. He'd almost forgotten it entirely, but when the beautiful woman with the tawny eyes came to the Castle, the prophecy rushed back with all its power and strangeness.

The *banfháidh* had arrived at Samhain, at his mother's cottage. Unbidden, winded, gasping, she'd barely made it to the door. Even at eight years of age, Patrick knew it must be a matter of grave importance for a crone of so many winters to hobble on her stick up the steep path. His mother made her welcome with a lavishness that told her son their visitor was no ordinary one. Mamaí several times used the honorific *máthair chríona*, wise mother, as she gave the old woman the good chair by the fire and stirred up the stew in the kettle so she might hand her a steaming bowl.

After their guest ate, his mother poured her a deep dram of whiskey—good grain whiskey, not the raw *poitín* from potatoes the neighbor made. Then, the two of them, Mamaí and Patrick, sat for an hour in respectful silence while the whiskey went down, and the sun began to lower outside the cabin. It was nearly dusk when the *banfháidh* spoke.

She began by pointing a bony finger at Patrick. He saw the shock and a flutter of disappointment in his mother's eyes. She had hoped, he was sure, for a prophecy regarding her own future. Her very tenuous future. No husband, provision for her and her bastard son arriving only at the pleasure of his father.

The finger curled once, twice, snagging Patrick's attention like a fishhook. Why beckon to him? Who was he to merit a prophecy? Prophecies were for statesmen and nobles, for those like his mother who consorted with them.

"*A Phádraig, a mhic.*" Patrick, my son. The old woman addressed him in Irish, her voice as weathered and dry as the hand that wavered in his direction. "*Goitse!*" Come here, she ordered. So, to her side he went, shaking almost as much as the crone's hand. His eyes darted toward his mother, hoping she would stop the *banfháidh*, tell her no, her foretelling was not for her small son, be away with her and her raven croaks.

But his mother said nothing. As soon as Patrick was within reach, the crone took his wrist in a grip like iron. Hers was a shaking hand no more. Instead, she clutched him like a wild thing, a fey thing, a thing with a grip as unyielding as a mighty man's. Patrick struggled but could not break away. The old woman's eyes gripped him as her fist did. They were milky orbs that smoldered and commanded, for all they were sightless. Then the *banfháidh* spoke, fast but distinct, close to his ear. He understood the Irish words, even though his mother spoke to him mostly in English now.

"*Over the black robes, broken the one,*
Torn by the brother to venge the other.
Under the tower painted red,
No hearth nor hound, no home nor bed.
Lost to the salt sea, lost to air,
Lost to all but Heaven fair.
'Til witch's gold be bound to wife,
Among the dead, un-live thy life."

At the last line, Patrick gave a violent wrench to free his arm. Then, he ran from the cottage, ran and ran into the trackless hills. An hour later, his fright faded with the sun. He made his way home and found that the *banfháidh* had departed in the full dark. Glad of her going, he was yet amazed she had refused a bed and gone out as she came in, muttering and tapping with her stick, feeling her way along the path that to her blind eyes looked the same at night as in daylight.

By the next morning, he laughed at her and her rhymes and stories. The caws of an old crow, what were they to him?

His mother did not laugh, not then and not for many days. Instead, she wept. Patrick did not understand her derangement. His mother was no ignorant cotter. She spoke well, both Irish and English. She read books, tutored him in literature. Taught him the penmanship of a learned man. Taught him how to make a proper leg, to address his betters with the manners and art of gentle folk. Why had she let some blatherskite of a crone make her uneasy?

Patrick coaxed her to make light of the words spoken by the *banfháidh*. But each time he jested, she scolded him, then put him aside, weeping harder. Or took him in her arms and held him so tightly he could scarcely breathe. Over and over, she moaned through her tears, *"Rachaidh tú cibé bealach a dtabharfaidh an chinniúint thú, mo mhac."* Fate goes as she will, and you can but follow, my son.

Too late now to tell his mother that she was right all along. Right where he was wrong, wise where he was a young fool.

He must try to make his beautiful woman understand the inevitability of what lay ahead. He would begin when next he saw her. She might fight it, might argue against it in her mind, as he had done so many years ago. But she could no more turn aside from it than could the autumn leaf refuse to fall from the tree. No more than he could, from the hour the *banfháidh* told him his future. His, and hers.

Fate goes as she will.

TEN

What a pathetic lump of compromise CeCe was. After all her resolve, she'd only made it to Wednesday night before she was standing in the Forecourt in eighteenth-century dress again, holding a list of questions to ask a screwy, trespassing, historical reenactor. Pathetic.

But she'd spent Monday afternoon until the town's library slash museum closed, and then all day Tuesday there again, failing at what she usually did best. Even with her formidable research chops, how much Castle ghost lore had she found? Nada, zip, zero, goose egg, *pas un mot* as her aunts would say, not one word of the stuff that would make Eunice Tattersall do a happy dance. Eunice would only put on her dancing shoes for ghost stuff, and the historical record didn't offer any.

That was absolutely the only reason she was standing in the dark of night in the Forecourt. The man calling himself Sean Patrick Ó Loinsigh might be a reenactor gone barmy, but he'd clearly done his homework. Deeply, and exhaustively. It wasn't strange in itself. She'd known obsessed historical reenactors who spent decades studying a single battle, a person, a place.

She looked again at the list of questions getting damp and wrinkly in her hand. St. Rhydian's resident obsessive might be able to give her what the library couldn't—the Castle's bleak history, and the bleaker the better. Bleak enough to be mashed and tweaked into spine-curdling ghost stories.

Was that also why she'd dressed like Molly Pitcher tonight? A bid for solidarity with her new living history nutjob friend? She'd changed clothes three times before she left her flat, reminding herself over and over that it didn't matter what she wore. A cotton dress with a pullover, a cashmere cardigan with jeans, a silk blouse and a skirt. Nothing felt right. In the end, except for the cap that always itched, she dressed like she did for her Walks, like somebody who lived at the Castle in the 1700s. For some reason, it felt right.

Because you're the other *demented living historian?*

She lifted her thick hair off her neck and blew out an irritated breath. She certainly was *not* standing outside the Forecourt door at midnight because she wanted to see Patrick again.

He probably wouldn't even be in the Castle, anyway. That was a good thing, wasn't it?

A light came on. Not one in her head but—surprise, surprise—in the slit window of the Tower, a weak golden gleam that barely penetrated the night. A few seconds earlier it wasn't there, and now it was. More lights winked on in the Castle. Top floor, second floor, first floor, Great Hall. Not brash overheads, but soft, flickering lights. Someone was turning on her battery candles, one by one.

This is such a bad idea. Her common sense, her aunts, Sister Mary Eustace, who was her favorite elementary school teacher—they were all telling her that. So, why was she punching the disarm code into the door keypad with an unsteady hand? Why was that same hand depressing the handle of the door and letting her into the Great Hall? Why were her feet heading for the Grand Staircase?

She stalled at the bottom step next to his portrait. Behind the big oak finial, Sean Patrick Ó Loinsigh's image was half visible and completely unnerving. A familiar prickle at the back of her neck made her turn her head and look up to the first landing.

The man himself stood there. Just as he was in the painting, dark blue jacket and waistcoat, white linen, broad shoulders. Eyes like the deepest ocean, making her want to drown in them.

Oh, yes. That's why.

———

Over the course of a minute, everything went to smithereens. She didn't know if she ran up the stairs to him or he came down to her, but suddenly she was being carried in his arms. She might have been a six-pack of beer for all the effort he showed in sweeping her up and against him.

At least, she had the presence of mind to protest. "Stop it, stop it! Sean Patrick! Mr. Oh-linn-sig! Put me down! Now!" She bleated and struggled ineffectually for three floors.

He did finally put her down, but the way he did it...she was held in his steel embrace, pressed against his chest, squawking into the buttons of his waistcoat. Then, she was being carefully, slowly, allowed to slide down his body until her feet touched the floor. There were things she felt as she slid downward that snatched protest out of her mouth and air out of her lungs. *My God, he's big. Warm. Hard.*

She jerked away from him and stood, panting. At the top of her brain was shock from meeting his arousal with the whole front of her body. Under that was confusion, since she had no idea where she was. She hadn't paid much attention to geography as he carried her. She'd been too busy trying to decide how she felt about their relationship going from zero to abduction in two weeks.

While she reeled and panted, Patrick waved a hand at the room and answered her unspoken question about location. "You know this chamber, I think. It had no particular name when I spent hours by the fire here, but now I believe it is called the Hellenic Room. For obvious reasons, as you see, and kindly do not blame my century for *that*." He pointed to the seam where the wall met the ceiling.

CeCe looked up at the deep border that ran around the room, just below the crown molding. Nude Greek athletes posed and scampered with lances, shields, and a discus or two.

"It's Victorian," she began. "Hand-painted and—wait. Did you say *fire*?" Sure enough, the ornate Italian marble fireplace behind Patrick framed a roaring blaze. "Oh, my God! What are you doing? You can't build a fire in here, it's a Listed Building! And none of the fireplaces have been used in—"

"Calm yourself, Celeste. This chimney and I are old friends. I assure you it draws better than any other in the Castle."

"Put it out, put it out, put it—"

He had her in his arms before she could finish. "Will you trust me?"

She wasn't about to say anything to that. She couldn't say anything at all since her mouth and her brain stopped working when he wrapped his arms around her. He was still hard, she felt the size and jut of him against her. The man might be handing her fiction about his past, but his body was a hundred percent fact.

CeCe's mouth opened, then closed. She fixed her eyes on the middle button of his waistcoat. Pewter, or maybe silver. It had something incised on it, a fleur-de-lis?

"P-pu-put out the fire. Please," she choked.

He released her as quickly as he'd embraced her. She backed hastily away.

"As the lady pleases," he said as he had when they first sat together in the Tower Room. He crossed to the hearth and began carefully moving logs around with an iron poker.

At least when CeCe told him to do something, he did it. Probably a sign he wasn't going to assault her. Though, she supposed it might be called assault to hoick her into his arms and carry her up three flights of stairs. *Holy Moses, he's strong.*

"Why did you light a fire, anyway? It's—" She fumbled through the Fahrenheit-Celsius conversion in her head. *Subtract thirty from Fahrenheit, divide by two...* "It's summer," she stammered.

He didn't look up. "You were trembling."

No argument there. While Patrick kept poking at the fire, CeCe looked around. The room was indeed called the Hellenic, but apart from the weapon-waving Greeks on the wall, there was no Ancient World splendor in it. Instead, it displayed the sad recent history of the earldom in a nutshell. After a century of selling off what had once been a vast estate, the household furnishings had gone on the block, too. Finally, the ancestral home went to the National Trust in 1987. By then, most of the rooms were like this one. Eclectic and mismatched furnishings, almost dowdy. Some treasures, more odds and ends. A moth-eaten Aubusson carpet in faded taupe and blue covered about half the floor. A Second Empire French *escritoire* with ormulu trim perched by the door, looking down its nose at a pre-World War I Rennie Mackintosh chair. No bed. Not a good room for seduction, if that's what Patrick had in mind.

He finally finished prodding the fire and stood on the hearth, looking at her. With one hand resting on the marble mantle, he seemed totally at ease. Unlike CeCe. She'd gone past trembling into, what, vibrating? Something on the spectrum between anticipation and blind panic.

With a cough, she assumed a tone of authority, not that a part-time American tour guide should be ordering anyone around. "Patrick, you really can't just, you know, *live* here. In the Castle, I mean."

He raised one hand, palm outward. "I swear by St. Brigid, lass, I am not living here." He smiled. *Oh, please no, not that.* It was the smile that made her want to slap him. Right after she kissed him.

Before she could think her way out of *that* quandary, Patrick distracted her. By taking off his clothes. Not all of them, but he started by shrugging off his jacket and draping it over the back of a chair. Then, he unwound his cravat and tossed it over the jacket. His fingers worked at the top buttons of his waistcoat, opening them. The button and loop at the neck of his shirt were next, and his fingers spread the placket. Several inches of manly chest appeared, along with a shadow in the crevice between his pectorals.

CeCe swallowed. She was having a hard time not looking at his chest. He knew it, she could tell from the sinful tilt at the corner of his mouth. The mouth she was sure had almost taken hers in the Tower Room.

She forced her eyes up, into his, and tried to sound firm. "Let me be clear. Do *not* take off any more clothing."

He didn't, but it was too late to stop her body from sending her all sorts of signals about how fine it actually would be if Patrick took off more clothes. All of them. She swallowed hard and decided to stroll over and inspect the French *escritoire*. Maybe it would be cooler on that side of the room.

It wasn't. She ran her hand over the satiny wood of the little desk. Nice, but not as special as it seemed from the other side of the room. *Seen one escritoire, you've seen 'em all.* Same with men, right? *No.* There was something different about Patrick.

What was it about him? He wasn't the only good-looking man she'd met. His parts—the ones she could see and the others she could imagine—were fine on their own. The body like an ad for a boxing gym. The night-black hair, with one stray lock that had come out of his queue and was hanging, a dark, silky comma, over his ear. The confident pose, muscular but unselfconscious, natural. Not the posing hero on the cover of a romance novel, but a legendary warrior in repose. Sunday morning in Valhalla.

She suddenly realized she'd turned away from the *escritoire* and was rooted like a shrub, staring at him from the other side of the room. She whirled around, lunging at the Mackintosh chair like she'd never seen one before. Imagine that, a thing you can sit on! It has four legs! Even facing away, she could feel Patrick's eyes on her.

If you know what's good for you, CeCe, you will stop this right now. There was no future for her with any man for whom knee breeches and buckle shoes were business casual. Her job tonight was to pick his brain for a ghost walk script, nothing more. Where was her darn list? She must've dropped it on the floor. Backing away from the chair, she scanned the rug.

And backed straight into a very big, very solid, male body.

CeCe spun around, too startled to even scream. He was so close that her sudden about-face lashed her skirt against his legs. Thoughts of her missing list whooshed away, replaced by such an acute awareness of Patrick that she clenched her hands to keep from grabbing him. Focused on that, she got double the shock she might have gotten at another time, when he opened his arms and spoke in that rough velvet voice of his.

"Come to me, Celeste. By Mary, Queen of Heaven, I vow to do you no harm. Crave answers as you will, as you must. All can be found in the space between the beats of my heart. Take that heart from my breast. It is yours."

Had any man ever spoken like that to her? Never. Maybe a man wasn't speaking to her like that now. Maybe she was drunk, or drugged, or hallucinating. A week and a half ago, on a perfectly normal Saturday night, she'd gone up a flight of stairs to turn off a battery candle. From the top step, she'd dropped into another century, into a ballad of courtly love. Parts of her said she belonged there. Other parts of her said to run away. The door was right behind her. She should shake her head, make some excuse, and leave. She should forget about Patrick Whoever-He-Was, his voice, his eyes, his mouth. All of him. She should—

Her options dissolved because Patrick didn't wait. Or maybe he read—rightly—the catch in CeCe's breath and the jumping pulse in her throat. In one smooth motion, he pulled her into his arms and brought his mouth down on hers.

How did a man who made regal bows and spoke like a courtier kiss? This kiss was no flutter of lace, and the kisser was no courtier. He was earth-bound, carnal, fierce. He tasted of whiskey, cinnamon, and hot desire. His mouth was firm and yielding at once, a trace of beard burning against her lips and chin.

Patrick kissed her with all his attention and absolute possession. He consumed her mouth as though she was the only woman he had ever kissed, ever wanted, ever taken. To CeCe, it was all firsts. The first true kiss, the first tongue to penetrate and stroke her, the first lips to drink her, swallow her, leaving nothing behind but an ache for more, more.

His hands went to the back of her head, cradling it so he could claim her mouth more completely. Whatever fantasies she'd been having about him went up in flames, burned to cinders by the reality of his single-minded ravishing. Nothing held back, nothing studied, Patrick simply owned her mouth as he clearly meant to own the rest of her. He growled low in the back of his throat, and she sagged against him.

Helpless. She was helpless in his arms. If he stopped holding her, her knees would buckle, and she would slide to the floor. She wanted to. She wanted to fall where she stood and let him cover her, take her. The speed of her surrender was frightening. *Stop, stop…*impossible. It was like stopping the sun.

The kiss spread downward from their mouths. Heat flared and coursed through her body, filling her breasts, her belly, her thighs, her core. She whimpered her joy, sharp as pain, into his mouth, and he gave a deep rumble in answer. CeCe put both hands behind his neck, pulled at the ribbon trapping his hair until it loosened, then flicked it to the side. She thrust her fingers into the smooth strands and raked her nails along his scalp.

Patrick's hands left her head and dragged along the length of her back. Strong fingers stroked the muscles down, then up, then down again until he cupped her buttocks. Murmuring in some language she didn't understand, he pulled her close and tight. She almost soared into release as he rocked her against him. He was iron hard and urgent. She felt the heat of him right through their clothes.

Against and above and around her, he was all size and strength. Hers for the asking. She was molten, wet submission. His for the taking. She opened to him, pressed into him, while every nerve in her body ignited. The room and the world dissolved. There was only him, his mouth, his breath, his body. Outside him, outside them both, a potent mist began to rise. Omens, signs, pagan gods. They flickered in the mist, each one a message and a warning.

Too late. Nothing could turn her away now. She was his.

———

He'd finally rendered her speechless. Good. Patrick needed her to stop talking or they'd never get to the next part. And every part of him wanted every part of that.

But still, she did not believe him, and without belief there wouldn't be a next part. Damn to hell the world that had put blinders on the eyes of her soul! Sharp edges and astringent viewpoints had sharpened and narrowed as the decades went onward. The Old Way faded and lost power, year by year. Once the witch burnings started, it was only a few decades before magic became something in which no one dared to believe. Fear shored up with the pasteboard certainties of science and logic. Those were to blame, not the woman in his arms.

Nevertheless, here she was. Here was where he must make her understand that nothing she had been taught contained a mote of truth. Not truth about what they were. What *she* was. For the magic he embraced wasn't the world's, nor was it his. It was hers. Magic that poured from an ancient source as unstoppable as a flood. He had felt it ripple the first moment she was near, it sang from her blood. How odd that she did not feel it in herself.

She would. It was just a matter of time.

Gowdie. From the Gaelic word for *gold*. Even when he was alive, he hadn't heard that name for years. All of that had taken place nearly a century before his time. Not that he thought it had disappeared since then. Magic of that magnitude might go to ground, but it never disappeared. Not the needles of the Inquisitors, nor the rack, the wheel, the flames —none of those could vanquish it entirely. It tumbled through Isobel Gowdie's line, each of her descendants as full of worth and power as she had been in her day. Had some suppressing charm been turned against Celeste, she a golden heiress of the force that had so dazzled the Inquisitors they could think only of extinguishing it?

He had known too little of that in his life, charms and magic and hidden powers. He'd mocked the women who wouldn't fling wash water out the door for fear of drenching the Little People and incurring their wrath. He'd doubled with laughter when he saw farmers drag their plows in roundabout circles rather than cut down the enchanted tree in the center of a field.

The pooka, the banshee, the trooping fairies and ring-dancing fairies and water fairies. He cursed himself now for his ignorance of them and their ilk. Now, with his arms encircling magic, he knew the deep fear of losing it, her, everything. If she took fright before she had a chance to understand what he was, what she was, what they were to each other...

'Til witch's gold be bound to wife.

It was blasphemy to think of all that when he had his mouth on hers and her body riding his cock. His loins screamed for discharge every time she bucked against him. But he must not lose control. Thinking about leprechauns instead of the torturous pleasure of her breasts and hips—that, at least, kept him from following the command of his aching balls. If not for that diversion, he'd drag her to the floor and mount her like a stag.

'Til witch's gold be bound to wife.

He could *not* lose control. He and this woman teetered upon a fearsome edge between known and unknown. He was not simpleton enough to think he could hold them there forever. He was increasingly sure he could not hold them there a minute longer. Sooner or later, he would stumble and slip, or be lured or dragged away from the safe and narrow bar where now they stood. But the way was formed, wherever it led they must walk upon it, together. Best her eyes be open when that happened. He must open them, now.

It took all his might, but Patrick tore his mouth from hers. Breath heaving with effort, he held her close, his chin resting on top of her head. Her cheek was against his chest, her breasts warm on his stomach. He felt her heart vibrating like a sparrow's. It took long, difficult minutes before he could speak.

"One always hopes," he whispered hoarsely into her rose-fragrant hair, "that faith will pave the way for knowledge. But yours is a questing, agile mind. I can but praise you for it. As well, you are a daughter of the modern world. That world has lost its way."

CeCe lifted her face. Confusion was written all over it. "What—what are you talking about? Patrick?"

A lush brown curl had fallen into her eyes, and he brushed it gently away. She could barely have felt it, but she inhaled sharply and her eyes wavered.

Patrick steadied himself and his voice. "Celeste, *mo chroi*. We must talk about my being a ghost."

ELEVEN

creee-arrwk. Just like that, the conversation veered from garden variety weird to very insanely weird. As though the man holding her had started speaking in Elvish or Klingon. The room went into a three-martini spin.

CeCe didn't even try to stop the shaky laugh that burst from her. Instead, she pulled out of Patrick's arms and walked unsteadily around him to the fireplace. Just before her legs gave out, she sank into a padded Louis Quinze armchair.

For a long minute, she fought for self-control. Finally, she won enough of it to push a couple sentences out through clenched teeth. "No, not really, Patrick. I mean, we can if you want, but it'll be a short conversation beginning and ending with the fact there's no such thing as ghosts."

He took the matching armchair facing hers and stretched out his long legs. Why did he have to look so completely at home in a castle where he was squatting?

"It is the mark of a gentleman," he began, "to affirm whatever a lady says. In this instance, though I risk your calling me a quarrelsome brute, I must beg to disagree."

"Based on?"

"I could say based on the evidence of me before you, but somehow I think you will require more impartial proof."

Here we go. He wanted to have an irrational conversation about ghosts? Why not? It wouldn't be any more irrational than the ones she had with her Candlelight Castle Walkers. Of course, she hadn't kissed any of them. "Impartial, empirical, concrete. Any of those would be good."

"Concrete. I see. So, Celeste, did you, with your own lovely ears, concretely hear Julius Caesar proclaim, *'Veni, vidi, vici'*?"

"No, of course not—"

"You accept Plutarch's version of events, then?"

"Well, yes, as a secondary source—"

"Something more direct? Tacitus describing the Ancient Celts, then."

"That's generally acknowledged to be reliable, insofar as—"

"I'm cheered by your acquiescence. I'll presume upon it to give you more of the same where ghosts are concerned."

"Now, wait just a minute—"

"'*What wicked thing have I done to thee, that thou hast laid hands on me?*'"

She'd never backed down from a challenge to her scholarship; he probably knew that. Eyes shut, she searched for the memory file labeled *Funerary Customs of the Ancient World.* Summer Term three years ago, Dr. Adrian Hoffman. Got it. "Letter left in the tomb of an Ancient Egyptian. He believed his dead wife had haunted him to death."

"'*Don't slack, don't soften, don't surrender to weary mind-lessness of what I suffer.*'"

"The ghost of Clytemnestra, urging revenge for her murder." CeCe wriggled irritably in her chair, trying to remember the Aeschylus play. "*Seven Against*—no, that's wrong, it's..."

"*The Eumenides*. That and the Egyptians are a bit remote in time, I'll agree. What think you of Dante? '*Però che quindi ha poscia sua paruta, è chiamata ombra.*'"

What CeCe thought was that her Italian wasn't just remote, it was non-existent. Did he know that, too? If he wanted to dash water on their kiss, Patrick was doing a terrific job. The water turned icy when he translated the quote.

"'Like the flame that follows the fire wherever it shifts, by this semblance henceforth it is called a shade.'"

Shade. The fourteenth-century term for ghost. Only in Italian, which CeCe didn't speak. With difficulty, she kept her voice level, but it had a bite to it. "It's just words."

"Oh, let us not dismiss words, my beauty. We've not yet brought Shakespeare into our proofs." Patrick pressed his hand to his heart, eyes turned to the ceiling. "'*Alas, poor ghost! Speak, that I am bound to hear!*'"

Control left her in a shout. "*Hamlet*! It's not even—"

"I agree, not the Bard's strongest effort. I much prefer *Richard III*. '*Methought their souls, whose bodies Richard murder'd, came to my tent, and cried on victory.*'"

"Stop quoting plays, Patrick!" CeCe sat forward, gripping the arms of her chair. "They're literature, not proof."

"Ah, it's proof you want. Tell me this, Celeste. What proof do *you* have of the world beyond life?"

"None. Because there isn't any."

"Absence of proof being proof of absence?"

"You're twisting things around. You haven't given me any reason to believe anything you say." Suddenly sullen, she sat back in her chair, crossing her arms. "It's not *real*."

Patrick's infuriating smile didn't waver a millimeter. If he told her she was beautiful when she was angry, she'd kill him.

He got close. "Such a lovely skeptic. You've not been to distant planets, but you believe they exist, do you not? You will argue that they can be seen with reflecting telescopes, and you are not wrong. But you, yourself, have you set foot on these distant planets? You have not. You believe the men who describe, from a safe distance, the ghostly reaches of the cosmos. Yet, you will not believe the ghost who sits before you."

That was it. Enough. Too much. She sprang to her feet, and Patrick immediately stood, too. CeCe brushed her skirt, tugged down the hem of her bodice. Despite the heat of her anger, her words came out raw and cold.

"I believe that a *man* might think he's a ghost and, if he does, then I feel sorry for him. Honestly and truly, I do. Or maybe a *man* thinks I'm like the fatuous people on my Castle walks. They look for ghosts around every corner, so of course they'd believe there's one in front of this fireplace. If a *man* thinks I'm like those idiots, then I don't feel sorry for him at all. I feel insulted and angry and—" *Hurt. Because, despite knowing better, I started to fall for a fascinating man.* "Goodbye, Mr. Ó Loinsigh. Stop trespassing on this site. If I ever, *ever*, see you here again, I'll call the police. You can entertain them with your folktales."

She didn't exactly flounce out of the room, but it was the next best thing. One foot in front of the other, not looking back. Chin up, shoulders squared, she jogged briskly down the stairs. Her car keys were out of her pocket before she reached the Forecourt door. She banged it shut behind her and savagely punched numbers into the keypad. *Reenactor Weird Shakespeare- quoting Opportunist Kissing Man.* He could leave St. Rhydian's the same way he got in, by whatever secret passage, priest hole, or unlocked window he was using. She didn't care anymore.

———

Thick fog had rolled in while she was in the Castle. The Mini's headlights were good as far as they went, which wasn't very far. It was three miles to the Gates and better lighting in town, and the voice of her high school driver's ed teacher was telling her to drive slow, or at least slower. Instead, she bore down on the accelerator. She needed speed. She needed escape. She needed to outrun the humiliation of letting herself get to First Base with a lunatic.

What, what, *what* was she thinking when she let that happen? CeCe felt like she'd been thrown off a wild horse. When they'd kissed, as odd as everything had been so far, she thought she understood where she was. It was different, of course. Everything about Patrick, from her first sight of him to their kiss, was different. But it was also familiar, in a way that made her want to trust him. As though they'd been together before, and were just now being restored to each other. Not a kiss, but a homecoming.

Then, afterward, he'd told her he was a ghost, and followed it up with Trivial Pursuit, Phantom Lit Edition.

Damn him. It just confirmed the wrongness of ever getting off the twenty-ninth step. The rightness of never allowing fascinating men into her life. Moderately attractive, that was the best she could hope for, if she didn't want to end up like her mother. Jasper Marcotte had been an edgy choice, what with the way his pseudo-historian aura drew her in. The man she just left in the Hellenic Room? He was way beyond edgy, with his exquisite eyes and his fluent Italian and his hot mouth.

Holy shit, it's foggy. The road sloped gently upward toward the town, but before the last incline it sank into a low patch, crowded on either side by thickets of tall trees. Fog collected in the hollow like froth on cappuccino. *Slow down*, her brain begged again, but all she could think of was getting off the grounds and away from the Castle. She shot forward and—

A flash of shining eyes, a jagged crown of antlers, a blur of tawny flank. *Deer!* CeCe stomped hopelessly on the brake pedal. She'd never stop in time, and if she swerved into the trees it would kill her. She braced for the impact.

Patrick. He hurled his body into the buck, then faced her, squarely in the path of the car.

CeCe hit him. Head on. Brakes screaming, her screaming, no earthly way to stop three thousand pounds of metal hurtling at fifty miles per hour. She squeezed shut her eyes and wrenched the wheel.

The car shimmied and smoked as it slid on screeching tires to the side of the road, front tires churning twin gashes into the sod. CeCe's arms locked straight, her hands clamped rigidly on the steering wheel. Her eyes opened but her senses had shut down, her mind a vacant field of shock.

Seconds that felt like hours went by. Thought and sensation slowly returned. She dimly registered a hiss from under the Mini's hood, along with metallic clicks, a hundred tiny parts rattling to a standstill. Pain throbbed in her shoulders. Bile rose in her throat and she wanted to vomit.

I hit him. I hit him. God, forgive me, I hit him. But she couldn't have. The crash would have been devastating. It would have killed him and possibly her, too. The impact...

There was no impact. *How was there no impact?*

Céleste. Her name. His voice. She heard it and didn't hear it, as though it arrived in her mind without ever passing through the air. She turned her head to the left.

He was there, a few yards away, standing in the road. She stared, her brain and body frozen. Stared, and saw the deer behind him, down on its front knees in the grass at the edge of the asphalt. It got to its feet jerkily. With a shake of its antlered head, it bounded into the woods.

She saw it all. Through Patrick's body, as though through a cloudy pane of glass.

CeCe's throat moved, but she couldn't form words. She could only keep staring as Patrick slowly became opaque and solid in front of her eyes. The fog swirled around him, a sudden breeze shredding it. The breeze raised his hair and tossed it around his face. Clouds in the night sky broke, and a full moon illuminated that face, handsome, scarred, infinitely sad. He didn't speak again, didn't move. Just watched CeCe while her reality shattered and blew away like the fog.

She had driven her car directly and at deadly speed into a man. It should have killed him. But it didn't. Couldn't. Because he wasn't a man, he was a—

Her arms suddenly liquid and weak, CeCe fumbled the Mini into reverse and backed it onto the road. She shoved the shifter into drive, pressed the gas, and roared forward. She didn't look in her rearview mirror to see who or what was behind her. Once out of the hollow, the fog lifted. She drove at a safer speed up the road and away from whatever had happened. It went pretty well for the first minute. Then, her whole body started to shake uncontrollably. It shook all the way back to her flat.

———

Patrick watched her from the edge of the trees. Watched as every cord that secured her world to its moorings unraveled and fell away. He reached into his waistcoat pocket and withdrew the half sheet of paper she'd dropped when he'd swept her up and carried her to the drawing room on the top floor. He read the list, then shook his head. Would Celeste have any interest in such trivial things now? Now that she'd seen, now that she knew?

"That was a bit dramatic."

He turned to the thin, pale woman who'd just arrived at

his side. She had the faint luminosity of the newly dead. "I didn't foresee the deer, Miriam."

"I know, Patrick." Miriam's brow furrowed. Her glow limned slightly. "You *are* Patrick, aren't you? Sean Patrick Ó Loinsigh? From the painting?"

The poor hen was struggling with the sudden omniscience of the afterlife. Patrick well remembered the shock of it. "The same," he told her.

"Celeste is confused." Miriam waved a hand at the road where the deer and the car were long gone. "By all this."

"Her family was remiss. They should have told her about the Gowdie."

"They were trying to protect her, the way families do. But you're right. She should have been told. She'll find out soon enough, I imagine."

"Aye, she's sharp as a needle. T'won't be long before she knows all."

Miriam nodded. "She's good at finding things. What she does with it all...I suppose it's best if she comes to an understanding of herself, by herself." Miriam seemed distracted by her cardigan. Frowning, she ran her fingers across the pilled navy wool and worried at a loose button. "If I'd known I was going to die this morning, I'd have worn something nicer."

Patrick smiled. *One can never outlive one's vanity.* Hadn't Lady Montagu said it?

The Collections Manager returned her hand to her side and her focus to Celeste. "She may not like what she finds, Patrick. That's when she'll need your wise heart and your broad shoulders. That's when she'll need you."

"I'll be here." Minutes went by as they watched the moon, bisected with clouds. It had passed its zenith and was beginning to lower. Finally, Patrick spoke again. "You might be a friend to her, to us."

"I shall always be a friend to you both. But I think..." Miriam's form blurred, then sharpened. "I think I can't linger here. I'm not one of those who...I'm not like you."

"And you've someone waiting."

"My daughter." She paused. "At least, I think she's—"

He smiled as he put his large, solid hand on her shoulder. "She waits, Miriam. Godspeed."

"And to you, Patrick."

TWELVE

CeCe didn't sleep the rest of that night, not an hour, not a minute. Once she made it to her flat, she sat on the bed, fully dressed, and quaked from head to toe like Jell-O on a plate. The night was warm, but she was freezing. She finally got up, went to the radiator, and rotated the dial until the heat came on. Back in bed, she wrapped the duvet around her, and quaked some more.

It was five o'clock in the morning before she calmed down enough to take off her clothes and crawl under the covers. An empty gesture. Sleep didn't come just because she was in the right posture and place for it.

Thought didn't come either, not in an organized way. Over and over, she asked herself what she'd seen and felt in the Castle, on the road. She couldn't come up with a single answer that made sense. One thought hammered away at her, a tuneless chant on an endless loop. *He saved my life, he saved my life, he saved my life.* Exhausted and lulled by the tropical heat in the flat, she finally slid into unconsciousness just before dawn.

Except it wasn't sleep. It was a twitchy, dream-fractured coma in which she was driving through deer, a herd of them. The car and the deer burst apart each time they collided, turned into wisps of fog, and drifted away. Then the herd reformed and bounded across the road in twos and threes, while she drove at them, through them. Again. Again.

At nine, she awoke feeling like she hadn't even had the three hours of sleep between dawn and giving it up as a waste of time. She went to the bathroom and stared at herself in the mirror over the sink.

Peur bleue, scared blue. It was one of Aunt Diane's favorite French expressions. CeCe didn't look blue, but her brows had a tense crease between them and her mouth was strained. Screaming or crying: it could go either way.

She showered and dressed, barely feeling the water on her skin or the jeans and T-shirt she pulled on afterward. The tuneless chant in her head was replaced by another one. *Now what, now what, now what.*

Her eighteenth-century clothes lay in a heap on the floor where she'd dropped them in the middle of the night. She never did that. With no pressing iron in the flat, she'd have to borrow one, or take the costume to a laundry. She spread the wrinkled clothes on the kitchenette counter and went over them carefully.

No traces, other than faint smells. Her own perfume, Chanel No. 5. Her mint hand cream. A whiff of wood smoke from the fire in the Hellenic Room. Patrick. He was there, on her clothes. She lifted her forearm to her nose. There, too, on her skin.

In her heart. *Damn him.*

CeCe hung the clothes in the compact wardrobe at the foot of her bed. Then, she switched on the kettle and made tea so strong the spoon could probably stand up in it. The mug barely warmed her fingers as she held it in both hands, watching a patch of cloudy sky through the flat's one window over the sink.

Should she tell the Programmes Director? *Right, CeCe. Tell her what?*

"Last night, there was an intruder in the Hellenic Room, where I wasn't supposed to be on Wednesday or any other night. The intruder kissed me with my consent, but then we had an argument, and I drove away. Actually, I drove into the man, but he was made of fog..."

Or, *"Last night, there was an intruder in the Hellenic Room. One who looks exactly like a portrait in the Grand Staircase Gallery. He and I exchanged a kiss, but when I left, he followed me, pushing a deer out of the path of my car. I drove my car into him, which was fine, because he was transparent..."*

Maybe, *"There was a supernatural entity in the Hellenic Room..."*

Sure, CeCe, do any one of those. Telling Eunice Tattersall about Patrick the Intruder would bring police, paperwork, and the perception that CeCe was a time-wasting trouble-maker. Telling her about Patrick the Ghost, even leaving out the deer rescue, would probably mean Eunice would rethink her decision to hire an unhinged American tour guide. Worse, CeCe might have to explain herself to a psychiatrist before she was encouraged to pack her suitcase and return to the United States.

She couldn't accept any of that. She couldn't accept anything as real that had happened on the Castle road. But she couldn't ignore any of it, either. She started shaking again when it occurred to her that she might be losing her mind, but she forced herself to admit that was at least a possibility. Her mother had committed suicide. CeCe didn't even know what was wrong with her to have gotten to that point. CeCe had just turned five when it happened, and she didn't remember much about her mother at all. It was such a taboo subject among her aunts. None of them ever talked about it.

Maybe it was time for the daughter of the suicided mother to look her past in the face. The thought made her so queasy she wanted to sit with her head on her knees, but maybe it was time to find out if she'd inherited crazy along with brown eyes.

———

A half hour later, she was at the health clinic in town. She registered as a non-NHS patient and waited patiently to be seen, which happened in an impressive fifteen minutes. Either it was a slow day for disease, or the novelty of an American patient got the clinic's attention.

Her exam was careful and thorough. At the end of it, Dr. Ramanujan looked quizzically over her half-glasses. "I can't find a thing wrong with you, Miss Gowdie. You seem perfectly fit."

"Are you sure? I briefly fainted about ten days ago and fell on a stone floor. Maybe I injured my head?"

The doctor dutifully scrutinized and palpated CeCe's skull. "Does this hurt? Tenderness here? Here?" She kept cool fingers on CeCe's neck while she asked her to turn her head from side to side, up and down. "How about this? Any pain? Stiffness?" Finally, "Nothing I can find externally. Do you have blurry vision? Dizzy spells? Vomiting?"

CeCe shook her apparently healthy head. "No, nothing like that. What I had was, well, there was a—I mean, I had this —waking dream." That was it, a waking dream. Sounded so much better than calling it a psychotic episode.

"Hmm. Did it involve your work?"

"Er, yes, you could say that."

"Ah, well, then. Are you sleeping?"

"Mostly." *Except, last night I was kept awake by thoughts of a dead man.*

"Try some warm milk before bed," Dr. Ramanujan urged gently. "It'll relax you. I'll draw some blood and we'll see if the lab tells us anything we need to look at more closely, but you appear quite well now. Just be sure to come see us if you faint again, all right?" She patted CeCe's hand like she was consoling a toddler. "It's probably nothing. Everyone has work-related stress."

Yes, Dr. R, but not everyone has a work-related ghost.

———

Fine. The doctor couldn't find anything outside CeCe's head, but maybe someone should look inside it, and she didn't mean with an MRI. Her finances didn't allow for private counseling, but there was another choice. She walked from the clinic up the High Street and stood outside the Town Hall, where she peered critically at a flyer taped on the building. She'd seen it before and it had only fleetingly caught her interest—until now.

SELF-HELP GROUP
Are you troubled? Having negative thoughts? Experiencing difficult conditions?
Join us in the Town Hall on Thursday afternoons for tea and talk, led by
counseling professional, Cecil Whyte, MSW.

The session started in an hour. Just enough time for lunch, if she could force something down.

————

Cecil Whyte's self-help group gave her pretty much the worst two hours of her life. Everyone—except CeCe, who declined the Talking Stick—spent ten or fifteen minutes mumbling, sobbing, or, in one case, shouting their troubled lives at the group. After the domestic abuse, abandonment, bereavement, life-threatening diseases, and dead pets, there was no way on Earth she was going to blurt out her tale of a possible ghost who'd saved her from a fatal collision with a deer last night at the witching hour.

Witching hour. Half listening to a man talk about his teenage son's drug problems, CeCe thought witchcraft would be her last, desperate recourse. She remembered the magical goods shop she'd discovered on her first day in the town, hopelessly lost as she tried to find somewhere to buy cards to send home to her aunts. What was the name of the shop? Bubble, Bubble? Cat and Cauldron? Local scuttlebutt had it that witches—real ones, not the sexy Halloween costume ones— hung out there.

CeCe shook her head, hoping her fellow self-helpers thought she was expressing sympathy for the teen addict's father, who was now openly weeping. *Sorry, Sabrina. I'm not desperate enough yet to consult the village healer/midwife/conjure woman.*

The session finally ended. While everyone else swarmed the table for tea and cake, CeCe shook Cecil's hand, commenting vaguely on how helpful the session had been. Then, she left the room, trying not to run.

Outside the Town Hall, she stood on the sidewalk for a while, taking deep breaths of diesel-acrid air from High Street traffic. She struggled to get her bearings. Not in the town; she knew where she was. She needed to get some bearings in her life, the place where she was abruptly and depressingly lost.

Everything that had roared into her life in the past couple weeks was completely off the radar screen of her plans. She'd thought they were good plans. They were meant to end up exactly as good plans should. A good staff position at a good historic site. Education Director. Curator. Someday, if she played her professional cards right, Executive Director. Really good.

The plans would give her the distance she needed between her and her personal history. Between her and her mother. Pregnant and unwed at eighteen. Dead at twenty-three.

Her story, not mine. Something uncanny had happened in the Castle, but CeCe was not losing her marbles like her mother apparently had. She didn't know if Dr. Ramanujan, or Cecil's session, or her own stubbornness had convinced her, but she just didn't see how, after twenty-five years of sanity, she would go stark raving bonkers in a week and a half.

Unfortunately, the possibilities that were left after she eliminated insanity were almost as—no, way more—frightening. CeCe shook herself. She needed to get some backbone. She needed to stay grounded.

She needed a double espresso at the Costa up the street, so she headed in that direction. Once she got her coffee, she'd sit with a pile of paper napkins and her pen, making good, solid, team player notes on a ghost walk for St. Rhydian's Castle. It was time to forget everything she thought or imagined or conjectured had happened in the past couple weeks.

Forgetting Sean Patrick Ó Loinsigh, whomever and whatever he was—that would be hard. So hard she wasn't sure she could do it. She wasn't sure she wanted to, even though wanting to forget him had to be the first step in returning her life to normal. It was just that when he'd held her, kissed her...

With him, she'd felt safe for the first time in her life.

Safe? Okay, maybe safe wasn't the right word. But if she couldn't figure out what he was, and she couldn't tell anybody about him without them thinking she needed to be sedated, then there was no part of him she could keep in her life. Nothing. Not a touch, not a look. Not even a memory.

A wave of loss hit her so hard that she had to sit on a bench outside Costa and get herself sorted, before she went inside and blubbered all over a teenage Welsh barista. *Why the hell are you grieving, girl?* She'd just met him. Two weeks ago, he was nothing more than a painting of a long-dead man with a handsome face.

His face. His hands. His singular ferocity. His melting gentleness. His warmth, his size, his touch, his smell, his impossible, beautiful eyes. He'd been right there, hers, a treasure in her hands, and then—gone. If only she could have kept him a little longer.

Maybe that was why her mom's loss was still so hard to accept. It shouldn't be. CeCe was so little when it happened, she almost didn't know her mother. She didn't see her die. Her body was never recovered, so there was no traumatic funeral with a flower-heaped coffin. CeCe's four fussy and wonderful aunts had stepped up to mother her afterward.

But there was something about the brevity of her time with her mom. It left her with so many questions. Too many for the wound to ever truly close. If her mother had lived, what school plays would she have watched from the audience? Would she have cheered when CeCe won spelling bees or debating contests? Would every Christmas and birthday present have a *To CeCe from Mommy* tag?

Why didn't you love me enough to stay, Mom?

So many questions, no answers. And now, Patrick and his question remained.

"Will you trust me?"

She should have answered him. Even if she'd lied, she should have said something. Words that gave him, gave them both, something to hold on to, to remember. But she hadn't. And now, their time apart would be so much longer than their time together, would be nothing but questions, spoken to the dark, unanswered.

Thirteen

CeCe was as ready as she would ever be to launch her St. Rhydian's Team Player Agenda. *Bullet Point One: Support Your Teammates*. On Friday morning, she asked Eunice Lite where Alun Jones was working, and was relieved almost to giddiness when she was told he was in the Library. It might be a while—or never—before she could face the Hellenic Room again.

On her way there, she realized she had no idea what her duties as an unpaid forensic conservationist would be. Whatever they were, they'd include some sort of real history, the kind she'd hoped to interpret at St. Rhydian's or somewhere like it. The kind that had no drunk tourists, profit-fixated administrators, or paranormal encounters in it. *Lead me to it, Alun.*

———

After four hours of cataloging the books Alun stripped from the Library shelves to get at the antique wallpaper beneath, they stopped for lunch. He drove them to town, where they snagged a lucky space in front of The Lark.

The meal flew by, a whirl of good food and professional humor. Tales of loopy professors, madly disorganized museums, clueless boards of directors—all the quirks of public history. Alun talked about his fiancée, Carin, who worked at the Victoria & Albert Museum in London, and might be coming for a visit on the weekend. "I'm sure she'll want to take your Candlelight Castle Walk."

CeCe squirmed without comment. The last thing she wanted was for a fellow historian, especially one working at the venerable V&A, to watch her lead a half-dozen boozy tourists around the Castle.

Apart from that slight awkwardness, lunch was fairytale perfect. With his quick laugh and charming Welsh accent, Alun was good company, so good CeCe almost forgot what had happened on the Castle road. Then, because that's what happened in fairytales, the spell broke.

"You knew about Miriam Lytton, didn't you?"

"I—what?"

"Dr. Lytton, the Collections Manager."

"Yes, I know her. We had lunch here just last week. Is she…has something—?" She couldn't make herself finish the question.

"I'm so sorry, CeCe. I should have guessed no one would think to tell you. I don't suppose anyone knew that you knew her. And it's only been a couple of days. But she passed away Wednesday morning. She'd been ill for a very long time, of course, and…"

Alun kept talking, but CeCe didn't hear a word he said. She just sat, nodding, and nodding some more. Her hand mechanically stirred her tea.

"CeCe? Celeste?" She looked up, startled to hear Alun's voice. His blue eyes were kind, concerned.

"I'm fine. It's just—I thought she might have more time." *Isn't that what everyone thinks?* Sean Patrick Ó Loinsigh died at thirty-one. He probably thought he had more time, too.

CeCe wrestled with her thoughts. She finally took her hand from her teacup. "Uh, I should go back to the Castle, Alun. I need to visit Ms. Tattersall's office."

———

As she stood in the PD's outer office, waiting to be admitted to her exalted presence, CeCe thought it wasn't a bad thing she'd drunk so much tea at The Lark. She was a wired combination of shock, energy, and the determination to lie as no one had ever lied before.

"I've done it!" she announced when she finally stood in front of Eunice Tattersall. "I've got ghosts!"

The PD's grin would have done the Croc in *Peter Pan* proud. Every tooth showed as she chirped, "Why, Celeste!" *We're on a first-name basis now, are we?* "I'm so glad you've come around to the idea. That's lovely!" Lovely, lovely, lovely —the PD's favorite word. After *auto-da-fé*, maybe.

"Yes, I'm feeling very positive about it. The thing is, I really would like the kickoff to be something special, you know? I thought we could hang a banner over the front gates. It's an expense, I realize, but I really believe it's worth it. And maybe get a little local press? Put something on the website? Make lots of social media posts?" CeCe pressed her hands together, her eyes pleading like a little girl asking for a pony.

She rattled on, growing more earnest by the second. "In fact, so we can get a totally great launch together, I'd like to cancel this weekend's Candlelight Castle Walk. I mean, with numbers being so small. There aren't even any advance ticket purchases this week. It would give me more time to devote myself *completely* to getting the ghost walk polished and crowd-ready for opening night!" A big, toothy, ear-to-ear smile. *You're not the only one who can do crocodile, Eunice.*

It worked and she wasn't sure why, except that the PD was so happy to finally get her coveted ghosts that if CeCe had asked for a TV crew from the BBC, she probably would have gotten that, too. *Lovely, lovely, lovely.*

———

She left the PD's office in mingled dread and elation. She'd gotten her Saturday off and wouldn't have to face humiliation in front of Alun Jones' fiancée with her V&A Staff lanyard. But all she'd gained was a reprieve, not a pardon. And she'd told Eunice she'd have ghosts for her the following week. She could do it, she had to. She'd gotten one ghost, hadn't she?

Not funny, CeCe. For a minute, sadness hit her so hard it nearly sent her to her knees. She wouldn't give in to it, she couldn't. But it frightened her, the way she was holding herself together with the toxic glue of denial. A few months ago, she would have been thrilled at being asked to create a new historic program, even a silly one. Now, work felt like a distraction from the only thing she really wanted—to be back in Patrick's arms.

Ghost. Man. Despite the Career First orders she handed herself, the truth was that she didn't care what he was, only that she might never see him again.

What was happening to her? She was an emotional house of cards, teetering. Any second, she'd collapse, right there in the Great Hall, sobbing and beating her fists on the floor. *That'll look good on your performance review, girl.* She dragged her hand across her wet eyes and took a deep breath, trying to look anywhere but into the Hall. Because in the Hall was the Grand Staircase. The Portrait Gallery. The painting at the bottom of it.

She jerked her head to the right. The branching hallway stretched to its end at Miriam Lytton's office. That was painful, too, seeing Miriam's door, so definitively shut. CeCe thought about the scholarly clutter behind it, the books and files and computer and electric tea kettle. She crossed herself and whispered. "May Holy Mary, the angels, and all the saints welcome you now that you have gone forth from this life." It was all she could remember of The Prayer for the Dead. Was she saying it for Miriam—or Patrick? She crossed herself again, pulled back her shoulders, and walked into the larger, brighter space of the Hall.

She was halfway across when she ran into a docent. Actually, the docent ran into her, which was typical for asthmatic, nearsighted Poppy Norris.

"Oof!" Poppy wheezed, pushing her glasses up on her nose. "There you are!"

Poppy Norris, hands down, was one of CeCe's favorite things about the Castle, and not just because the docent let everyone know she thought the sun rose and set on "our pretty American tour guide." Plump, forty-something, always cheerful, and kind, Poppy reminded CeCe of one of the Fairy Godmothers in *Cinderella*. She deserved a lot better than her work assignment. Eunice Tattersall had put her on the third floor which, with Poppy's asthma and all the stairs, was cruel.

CeCe clambered out of her dark mood to greet the docent with a smile. "Hi, Mrs. Norris. What's new on Three?"

"Oh, please, dear, call me Poppy. I'm so glad I caught you. It was just lucky my friend Mairead saw you go into Ms. Tattersall's office, since she knew I was looking for you. She ran up to tell me—" Poppy took in a wheezy breath, "—because I found this yesterday on a hall table outside the Hellenic Room, and I was sure it must be important. Plus, after all, it has your name on it. Such a lovely thing, too, and very historic looking. I didn't want to leave it in case some visitor made off with it. You know how some of them are."

"I do. Larcenous is what I'd call them."

Poppy handed CeCe a journal of sorts, its cover a tri-folded piece of soft leather the color of tobacco. It was encircled several times with thin leather thongs and knotted at the front. Tucked behind the knot was a scrap of heavy paper, inscribed with her name in French. *Mlle Céleste Gowdie*. It was written in graceful script, with rusty brown-black ink.

Oak galls, CeCe thought as soon as she saw the writing. Ink was made from it in the eighteenth century. She brought the journal to her nose with trembling hands. It not only had the color of tobacco, it had the scent, mingled with others she would never be able to forget. *Patrick.*

"It *is* yours, isn't it?" Poppy wheezed on. "I wouldn't want to take something that..." The docent trailed off, her worried gaze turned toward CeCe.

"Yes, it's mine." CeCe kept her voice as calm as she could, even though her heart was pounding so loud she was sure it was audible outside her body. "I can't thank you enough, Poppy. I must have left it when I was—" *Kissing. Arguing. Dodging deer.* "Scouting locations for the new tours. Sorry you had to bring it all the way down here."

"Not at all. I'm done for the day." Poppy took an inhaler from a pocket in her Forties-style pinafore, one of several the docent wore at the Castle. CeCe was surprised the PD hadn't prohibited them as unauthorized whimsy. Poppy sucked hard on the inhaler, then put it back in her pocket. She patted CeCe's wrist, grinning.

"We, the docents, I mean, we're all so excited about the ghost walks."

Well, well. The PD had been so certain that CeCe would cave that she'd leaked the ghost walk news before her "pretty American tour guide" had even agreed to it.

Poppy kept effusing. "The Castle will be famous, and you, too!"

CeCe just smiled. *Please, God, don't let it be true.* She felt sick when she thought of Dr. Grisham-Chu seeing her on YouTube.

———

Patrick smiled at the same time as Celeste, though he kept his smile and himself hidden. *Well done.* The sweet-tempered biddy had found the folio and handed it over. Of the witches who would be so important in what was to come, Goody Norris was the one Celeste should meet first. No one could be put off by her, with her soughing breath and twinkling eyes. There were other witches who would frighten the skin off Celeste, off anyone.

Patrick thought again of the *banfháidh*, with her rheumy blind eyes and rasping predictions. The old woman wasn't a witch, at least he didn't think she was, though what was the difference between a prophetess and a witch? Patrick was no scholar of the many forms of magical creatures. He could tell an elf from a banshee, but beyond that...

He worried about Celeste, worried about them both. She had to survive this. If she didn't, if she fled from herself the way she'd fled from the Hellenic Room, from him, they might as well both walk straight into eternal night. Even so, if they went hand in hand into the dark, he could resign himself to it. Anything was better than him going on in some hopeless form after failing to see her take her rightful place in the order of things. He knew his crimes in grotesque detail, but he would swear by God's right hand he had done nothing so foul as to deserve that.

Celeste was ignorant of everything. It was both her highest virtue and her deepest flaw. Unknowingly, she held enchantment in the palm of her hand. She must either learn to see and live with it, or accept a half-life as shadowy and insubstantial as his. If he did nothing else for her, he must help her make the right decision. Right for her. Right for them both.

Celeste took the folio and waved goodbye to the cheerful witch. How he hated and loved to see her walking away. Hated every time she left the Castle and grounds, went somewhere that he couldn't keep her safe. But, rakehellion that he was, he loved to see her beautiful body from the rear.

Breeches again. Cockstand again. The sight of her tidy hips and pouting buttocks, her round thighs, the small notch between them at the top just below the seam of her arse—they were all perfectly outlined by the garment. When she was his, truly his, God willing, he would prohibit those breeks. She would either stop wearing them or he would have to kill every man who looked at her. Starting with that Welshman she'd spent half the day with, him and his twaddle about wallpaper. Then, they had gone off in his coach to God Knows Where for hours, while Patrick envisioned separating each of the man's limbs from his body after he'd gouged out his eyes for looking at Celeste's delicious arse in a pair of breeks. In his day, a betrothed man who showed such attention to another woman was simply asking for violence to his person, and Patrick was inclined to—

He inhaled deeply, clearing his thoughts. He was trying to leave all that behind, the limb-ripping, the eye-gouging. It wouldn't suit to have Celeste's fashion fancy drive him to wholesale murder. Again.

When she was his. And when might that be? He knew the question to be folly even as he craved the answer a hundred times a day. *Patience,* the well-ordered part of his mind advised, but, by Zeus! Had he not been patient enough? His patience was Biblical. It made Job look like a fidgety boy waiting for a potato to roast in the fire.

There were those, he supposed, who might say that patience should be easy for him. He had nowhere else to be, after all. But anyone who ascribed to such a pea-brained notion did not know that once Celeste had appeared, the long gray lost its smooth and featureless qualities. It became more than a place where, if nothing interesting or blissful happened, at least nothing happened at all. One simply and barely *existed* in the long gray.

Now, Patrick burned. Every mote of his being was on fire, every sense twisted and suffered. His heart shot like an arrow into joy, then fell into a pit of despair so deep he knew he would never emerge. He had forgotten, in the two and a half centuries of his penance, the devastating power of a single word. *Need.*

FOURTEEN

By the time CeCe got back to her flat in town, her hands were icy with nerves and anticipation. She forced herself to make a cup of decaf Earl Grey. Then, she put the mug and the leather-bound journal on the kitchenette counter. She stared at them both for a while.

"Just do it, you coward." She took a big gulp of the tea and began untying the leather thongs of the journal. She would read it standing at the counter, taking notes on scrap paper to the side.

The standing only worked for ten minutes. After that, she had to sit down. Or fall down, since what she was reading was so shocking it made her Candlelight Castle Walk script sound like *The Cat in the Hat*. From the outside, the journal was a piece of leather covering twenty-seven unbound sheets of Edwardian high-rag paper—paper she'd last seen in the writing desk of the Castle's first-floor Morning Room. But on the inside...

CeCe took the journal to the nook where her single bed was shoved against the wall. Spreading the pages out on the duvet, she sat cross-legged next to them. After a few deep breaths to steady her nerves, she went back to reading.

———

Two hours later, she stretched and went to the counter to retrieve her cold tea, wishing she had some Jim Beam to add to it. She didn't, so she dumped the tea into the sink and tried to sort out her whirling thoughts on what she'd just read.

It was bad. Really, really bad. Twenty-seven pages, twenty-seven violent incidents, each one worse than the one before it. The stabbing and choking and bleeding and dying—bad enough just to read about. But to accept, as she had to, that such terrible detail could only result from first-hand experience...

It meant that Patrick was in the thick of it, spattered with the gore of it.

It was some comfort that not all the carnage was from Patrick's lifetime. The Castle and the abbey on which it was built were apparently dotted with people who had met grotesque ends—God, there was even a rabid dog bite—as early as the thirteenth century.

"A serving wench who concealed her belly until, of a night, she birthed in the stables, then strangled the babe and threw its corpse in the cesspit...

"Tom Gisley, a smuggler, who, with his fellows, rowed to a foundered Spanish ship, killing all aboard to seize the cargo. When found out, the lot were beheaded in the Forecourt, save Tom, who was drawn and quartered. The bodies swung in iron cages along the Castle road until they rotted away to ribbons...

"Brother Heylin, a lecherous monk, run through ninety-one times by the father of a maid despoiled and got with child. This was done in the Chapel, so that blood ran like a crimson river along the nave to the altar steps..."

Those were just the secondhand reports, according to Patrick. He hadn't actually met the ghosts. *Met them?* He'd only heard about them from people living in the seventeen hundreds, his time. His time as a living man, not the quarter millennium from then until now, when he appeared to CeCe, bringing along some serious baggage.

He knows. He had to know how it would devastate her to read those twenty-seven tales. To know there might be twenty-seven or ninety-seven more that he hadn't put to paper.

Come on, CeCe. History is full of violence. She was a historian, she knew that. She said it aloud, to the kitchen counter. "The past was violent." Maybe if she heard it enough, she could accept it. The trouble was that it had all been in books before. Other than a couple of Vietnam War nurses whose oral histories she'd recorded, she hadn't known anyone who'd actually *lived* any portion of it. Lived it as Patrick said he had. And, if he had, where exactly was he when the journal horrors took place? Was his the hand on the sword, or the pistol, or the twisted rope?

In the grand scheme of things, those were the small questions. There was a bigger and much more frightening one. CeCe looked at her empty mug in the sink. Maybe she should make a run to Tesco for a bottle of wine. She settled for switching on the kettle to make another cup of tea. Not that tea or wine or Jim Beam would help with the big question.

Who was Patrick, really? On the evening they'd been trading literary quotes and arguing about ghosts, he was an attractive but unbalanced person with a gift for breaking into historic sites, telling good stories, and showing off fake facial scars. By the next morning, after the deer-in-the-headlights event, he was what he'd said he was all along. The bastard son of an eighteenth-century earl. A warrior. A gentleman. A scholar who spoke Latin and Italian and Irish and French. A warm, strong, embracing, sensual...

Dead man. CeCe's world tilted on its axis. Saying she didn't believe it now, after everything, was like singing "You are my lucky star" while the alien slavered within the walls of the spaceship.

The tea kettle whistled and CeCe nearly shrieked with it. She poured water into her mug, then realized there was no tea bag in it. She didn't need tea, anyway. She needed something real she could hold on to. But holding on to the only reality Patrick brought with him was like grabbing lightning with her bare hands.

He's a ghost.

Singular. Believing in just one ushered in a whole army of beliefs. Beliefs that dropped her in a universe that defied logic, reason, and maybe sanity. Now that she knew about that universe, she couldn't un-know, just as she couldn't un-read the journal.

She walked the six steps to her bed, looking at the open journal on it. A memory from her middle school years flitted through her brain. When she was thirteen, she'd read Ray Bradbury's *Something Wicked This Way Comes*. It scared her so much that when she finished each chapter before sleep, she closed the book, shoved it in the drawer of her bedside chest, and put another book on top of it before she shut the drawer. Locking it up, just in case something might escape from the book in the night.

Left open, who knew what things would crawl out of Patrick's journal while she slept? CeCe shuffled the twenty-seven pages into order and put them back into the leather wrapping. She tied it shut. Then, she hid it inside the drawer of her nightstand, just like she'd done with *Something Wicked*.

The scrap of paper with her name on it, though—she couldn't bear to lock that away. The thick, slightly rough paper was irresistible under her fingers. She tried to stop it but couldn't hold back a painfully sweet image of Patrick. Just after he'd kissed her, his large, scarred fingers brushed aside a lock of her hair. Those fingers had touched the paper. He'd held a pen or a quill and written her name. Slowly and precisely, but with dash. Each letter glided like a swan on a white paper pond. The *M* of *Mlle*, two spiking towers between lush curls. The *C* in *Céleste*, double loops at the top like the tendrils of a young plant. The *G*, fat-bottomed and florid. He had taken his time with her name, poured something into the writing of it that was both more formal and more intimate than penmanship. What an astounding—man?

She took the scrap of paper to the windowsill over the sink, propping it against a juice glass of wilting wildflowers from the edge of the Castle car park. Then, she stood for a few minutes, looking out the window at the bit of town, mostly treetops, that she could see from her second floor flat.

The sun was going down. It was dark enough in the flat already that she should turn on some lights. Outside the window, though, the trees were still brilliantly washed in golds and reds by the setting sun. She'd never thought about it before, but wasn't it all magic? The sunset, the light-painted trees, the birds wheeling in nest-seeking flocks against the indigo sky.

People just accepted it as natural, a daily spectacle they believed someone, somewhere, had a logical explanation for. But every explanation depended on trust, if not in the explanation, then in the thing that came before it, or the thing that came before that.

Will you trust me?

The last shred of CeCe's disbelief left her with a grudging over-the-shoulder opinion. *What's natural is that people should wilt and die, at the end of their lives, like flowers. Not stay around for lovers in another time.* But here was Patrick. Here she and Patrick were. Together.

She hated to admit it, but it was probably time to consult a specialist. Tomorrow, she'd go to the magical shop in the town.

FIFTEEN

The next day, Saturday, was mockingly cheerful and bright. After her dark homework the day before, CeCe wasn't sure she was ready for buttery sunshine, marshmallow clouds, and flags pirouetting atop the Town Hall. It certainly wasn't the sort of day she would have picked for her mission. For that, shouldn't the day be gray and stormy, with a cutting wind and pelting rain?

No wind, no rain, no peals of thunder. Just a great day for hunting unicorns, or the Keebler Elves. Instead, she was on a mission to find a witch who could help her with her new dead friend.

It didn't surprise her much, as she hiked up the long incline of the High Street, that she couldn't stop thinking of her Aunt Nicole's conversion to paranormal fandom. It was really Aunt Nikki—lovable but obsessed—who'd helped turn her niece against The Beyond.

Right from the beginning, Nikki's magic mania had seemed out of character. She started out just like the other aunts. All of them normal. All on the fringe of middle age. All hat and dress-wearing, Mass-attending, nicely spoken,

Savannah women. A doctor (Hélène), an interior designer (Sophie), a realtor (Diane), and Nikki, the grade-four schoolteacher. Couldn't get much more normal than that. But somehow, about eight years ago, Nikki had swerved onto the road less traveled. She started buying afterlife books and normal went right off the map.

"You have got to read this," she insisted to anyone who got within reach, shoving *A Pyramid of Souls* at them. "CeCe, this book will change your life," she'd said. And *Angels Call Your Name* went on the coffee table.

Harmless, at first. But like addicts everywhere, Nikki eventually dipped into the hard stuff. A year after *Pyramid*, she was going to séances twice a month and chatting with Great-Uncle Maurice, who'd been dead since 1989, and a deceased clairvoyant named Jeanne Mersault, whom her aunt swore advised her every Tuesday from the top of the chifferobe in her bedroom.

"But truly, they are *real*," Nikki protested to anybody who tried to talk her off the ghost train. Her belief, or maybe her persistence, was alarmingly infectious. One by one, her sisters Sophie and Diane bought tickets on the same railway. Now, they all went to séances, though thankfully Nikki was the only one talking to a chifferobe. The sole hold-out was Aunt Hélène. Her medical training made her invulnerable to hoodoo, though CeCe thought maybe her doctor auntie was harboring secret beliefs. Before she left Savannah, CeCe had seen a dreamcatcher dangling from the rearview mirror of Hélène's Lexus.

CeCe was halfway up the High Street. She stopped, heart pounding, for a breather. The light cardigan she'd put over her tank top this morning felt like a fleece parka, so she pulled it off and tied it around her waist. Somewhere around here was a mews, aptly called Puzzle Lane, that branched off from the High.

There it was. Ten paces took her to the ancient stone archway leading into the mews. She peered through it. Puzzle Lane was so narrow she was sure that if she stood in it with her arms outstretched, she'd touch both sides. Cobbled paving sank in the middle, and a trickle of greenish water ran along the depression toward the High Street. There was hardly any light in the lane. It beckoned dismally, the place that every horror movie audience yelled at the heroine not to go.

CeCe plunged under the arch.

———

The Broom & Bottle was painted in faded gilt letters over the door of a shop nearly at the end of Puzzle Lane. Below the shop's name was *Jana Smithbury-Tewkes, Proprietor.*

CeCe paused at the shop window. She'd seen worse. Pickled innards in jars. Victorian obstetric tools. Some people, like Aunt Nikki, would love this display. Heaps of crystals on black velvet, two stuffed owls, a dry tree branch with amuletic jewelry hanging from it, a dozen books with pentacles and astrological signs spattering their covers.

CeCe sighed deeply. She, who'd spent Wednesday night snogging an otherworldly being, had no right to cast stones at a few pentacles. She put her hand on the door handle of the shop, Nikki's voice twittering in her head. *"Today is the first day of the rest of your life."* God forbid.

The door stuck, and when CeCe finally shoved it open, it set off a discordant jangle of bells and rattles somewhere. She froze on the doorsill, wondering if she'd triggered an alarm, and looked down. The doorsill was painted black. It had pentacles on it, too.

Limen. The Latin word popped into her head. It meant 'threshold.' *Liminal.* A quality of ambiguity that occurred in the middle stage of a ritual. She knew the words and their meanings, they were tossed around in cultural anthropology all the time.

Was that where she stood now, in the middle of some magical act? CeCe shook her head and entered the shop.

It took about thirty seconds and ten paces to realize Jana Smithbury-Tewkes had done everything she could to make The Broom & Bottle a place you wouldn't go unless you really, really needed to. For one thing, the lighting was so low it was a while before CeCe could see anything at all. When her eyes adjusted, she gawked at an alchemist's lair bred to an antique store, totally unlike the shop Aunt Nikki's séance buddy, Leonora, owned in Savannah. Leonora's shop was a sort of Spencer's New Age Gifts. Candles, incense, handmade soaps, Tibetan prayer flags attached to the ceiling.

CeCe couldn't see the ceiling in The Broom & Bottle. Above her, dozens of herb bunches were tied to the rafters by their stems. Crackly dried foliage brushed her head as she passed under the bundles, though she had no idea where she was going. Meandering paths led through tables, desks, bookshelves, and disorderly piles of goods—metaphysical, Wiccan, astrological, divinatory. Even Harry Potter. The smell of herbs was overpowering.

She took another few steps and froze again. Maybe she should just stand where she was and hail the proprietor. Surely, they must be somewhere close.

Hssst. A cat, CeCe was sure of it. She cautiously peered into the gloom, toward the hissing. A large Victorian parrot cage on curved iron legs was to her left. The cage door was ajar. Instead of a perch, there was a pillow. On the pillow was a big, black Persian cat.

CeCe glowered. "Hiss all you want. I'm here and I'm not leaving until I see your owner."

"That would be me." A woman suddenly appeared in front of her, looking at her customer with suspicion and...

more suspicion. CeCe couldn't figure out how the woman got there without making a sound, since she certainly didn't look like someone who padded silently around.

What she looked like was the daughter of Jove and a burlesque queen. Tall and round and buxom, she had a strong jaw and thick arms, like a lady wrestler. Her hair was platinum on the sides, bright blue on top, and piled into a Sixties beehive over a face of smooth alabaster. Her robust body was snugly packed into a black sheath dress with no sleeves. Enormous silver earrings the size of teacups swung from her earlobes.

Was she a witch? CeCe had no idea what a real one looked like, though she wasn't an idiot. She knew they didn't look like the Wicked Witch of the West. This maybe-a-witch wore vivid blue lipstick; was that typical of her kind?

"Finally here, then," the woman barked from her cobalt lips. "Come in. Sit." Jana Smithbury-Tewkes swept a pile of books off a wooden chair onto the floor, then disappeared into the recesses of the shop.

Finally here? Had she been expected? CeCe sat, dropping her shoulder bag next to the chair. She faced a small table. There was a stack of calendars on it. The top one was titled *End of the World Day Minder.* Seemed like an oxymoron.

She barely got settled when a gray striped tabby appeared and began rubbing against her ankles. After the hissing black cat, CeCe thought she shouldn't try to make friends. But the tabby kept rubbing and twining, so she reached down and gave it a tentative head scratch.

"Good kitty." A Persian, like the black one. Curious. CeCe didn't think there were any striped Persians.

Jana Smithbury-Tewkes returned, plopping into the chair across from CeCe. "What's your problem?" she asked curtly. "Talk fast, I've got a past lives regression in a half hour."

CeCe peered over the calendars on the table. "My name is—"

"I know who you are."

"How do you know who I am?" Was Smithbury-Tewkes a witch and a psychic, too?

"Small town."

"Oh, right. Well, I don't really want to be here. In your shop, I mean, not the town. But I just don't know where else to go."

"Always flattering to know I'm a last resort."

"No offense, it's just that I have a history with the..." CeCe waved her hand, taking in everything from a two-volume set of *Spell-Casting for Beginners* to a rack of Hogwarts tea mugs.

"And yet, you're here." Smithbury-Tewkes began rearranging the calendars into two stacks in front of her, leaving a clear space in the middle. She whistled tunelessly through her teeth as though her customer wasn't, in fact, there.

CeCe didn't know what to say. The striped cat had gone away, but another one was sitting next to her chair, tapping its paw on her thigh for attention. The cat looked like a mochaccino. Chocolate-bodied with cream paws, ears, and muzzle. Long silky fur—another Persian. She wondered if the shop owner bred them.

Hearing a *thwack*, CeCe looked up from her cat fancying. Jana had cleared the table and slapped a small wooden box in the middle. She lifted the lid, removing a deck of cards. The witch—if that's what she was—started shuffling the deck, keeping her eyes on the cards as she spoke. "I'm not going to ask again *why* you're here, since we'll waste more time while you pretend not to understand me. I'll tell you why. It's the ghost."

CeCe felt the blood drain from her face. "You *know*?"

The woman said nothing, just pointed to a small, engraved

sign on top of one of the calendar stacks. *Jana Smithbury-Tewkes. Divination.*

So, small town or not, witch or not, the woman *was* psychic. Psychism. Crystal balls. Tea leaves. Table-turning abracadabra hocus pocus communing with the dead from chifferobes.

CeCe shot to her feet. "Ms. Tewkesbury-Smith, I—I'm sorry. I've made a mistake. Thank you for your time, but I—I mean, this really isn't for me, this is—"

"The name is Smithbury-Tewkes. You may call me Jana. Or Reverend High Seer, whichever is easier. Sit down. We have work to do." The witch—*she'd earned that title, yessiree bob—*kept on shuffling and cutting the cards.

CeCe sat again. She decided she was more afraid of what was happening with the man in the Castle than anything that could happen in The Broom & Bottle. Something touched her knee and she looked down just as another cat jumped into her lap. *Does that make four?* Not surprisingly, a Persian, but this one really was spectacular, tawny and spotted like a long-haired cheetah. CeCe knew she shouldn't interrupt Her Reverence, but she had to say something.

"This is the most beautiful cat I've ever seen. What's its name?"

Jana didn't look up from the cards. "No Name."

"No name? How could you have such a beautiful pet and not give it a—"

"That *is* its name."

"You mean—"

Jana smacked the deck down on the table so hard CeCe bounced in her seat. Neither of them spoke or moved for a slow count of ten. Jana, eyes closed, appeared to be meditating. CeCe couldn't bear the silence.

"Well, it certainly is a lovely cat," she squeaked. "How many do you have?"

Jana opened her eyes. "Just the one. Now," she fanned the cards into a half circle, faces down, "pick a card. Don't touch it."

Touch it? The last thing CeCe wanted to do was touch any part of fortune-telling with any part of her body. Finally, since it was obvious Jana wasn't going to let her off the hook, CeCe reached out an unsteady finger and pointed to a card in the middle.

Jana turned the card over and slid it across the table. "There's your trouble. The Knight of Pentacles. Black-haired man. Ruled by duty and justice. Rides a black horse."

"He's not on horseback. He's—"

"Dead, I know. You did hear me the first time when I said he was a ghost, didn't you?"

Yes, she'd heard. Now, Jana was mumbling to herself, chanting, praying, incanting or something, her electric blue lips moving. She waved at the cards. "Pick another one."

This time CeCe actually had to hold her wrist with her other hand to control the trembling, but she managed to point at another card. Jana flipped it over and slapped it down next to the Knight of Pentacles.

The second card did and didn't seem to belong to the same deck as the Knight. The border was the same—pentacles in gold circles—but the central image was a woman from the waist up. Her skin was ivory, like CeCe's, and her eyes were like hers, too, large and amaretto brown. She wore a white, close-fitting cap of some sort and a dark shawl over her shoulders. *High Priestess*, the card read.

"There you are." Jana's words had an 'end of story' tone.

"That's it? Are we done?"

"I *said*," Jana's forefinger, the nail blue like her lipstick, hovered over the card, "there *you* are."

CeCe's mouth drew tight. "I am not a Tarot card."

"Take it now. Take them both."

CeCe still didn't want to touch the cards. What she wanted was to leave the shop. But Jana's glare pinned CeCe to her chair. She gingerly lifted the cards off the table, holding them by their top edges between her forefinger and thumb like they might detonate.

"Keep the Knight." Jana swept up the deck and returned it to the wooden box. She stood, still talking. "Send the other one to those who know you, because there's a lot you *don't* know."

"What? Those who know me? You don't mean my aunts, do you? I really don't want to drag them into this. What do they—"

"Not my tale to tell." Jana turned away, picking a route sure-footedly through the clutter and toward the back of the shop.

"Wait! Don't I pay you? I broke up the Tarot deck. Isn't there a fee or—"

Jana waggled her fingers over her shoulder and disappeared into the gloom.

CeCe picked up her shoulder bag and put the two cards in it. Unnerved and piqued at the same time, she wondered if she would have been better off with the Keebler Elves. When she found her way back to the door, she glanced at the Victorian parrot cage. No Name Cat was inside, on the pillow.

He was totally black again.

Sixteen

CeCe glumly surveyed the empty Forecourt. On a normal Saturday night, there'd have been at least a handful of Candlelight Castle Walkers milling around. But she'd canceled the tour, so it was just her, gripping the Forecourt door handle and feeling a mixture of excitement and disgust with herself. She'd stayed away as long as she could, and how long was that? A few days. She'd had to lecture herself not to arrive at sundown.

Two weeks ago, she would have said *adios, Tower Man*, and been happy about never seeing him again. Him, the intruder, the stalker, the don't-know-what. Two weeks ago, she was ready to chalk the whole thing up to a blip on the green screen of her metabolism. Tummy upset, maybe, like Ebeneezer Scrooge seeing Marley's ghost. *An undigested bit of beef, a blot of mustard, a crumb of cheese.*

Even a few days ago, she'd stood in front of Costa and resolved never to think of Patrick again, much less see him. She'd told herself he was everything she didn't want in her life. Distracting, dangerous, unbalanced, *fascinating*. A short cut to her mother's madness, a washed-out bridge in her career, a huge *Wrong Way* sign on the highway of her life.

Now, though, she'd been standing—in eighteenth century dress because, as before, nothing else felt right— at the Forecourt door for ten minutes. Her hand had been glued to the door handle for five. What if he wasn't inside? What if he wasn't on the Grand Staircase or in the Tower or the Hellenic? What if he wasn't in any of the forty-seven rooms plus kitchen and cellar? If he wasn't, she'd—

She had no idea what she'd do. All she knew was that she had to see him again. If she could find him. How did you summon a ghost? A séance? That wouldn't generate anything but disgust from having to hold the sweaty hands of strangers on either side of her. An incantation? No. Patrick wasn't the sort to come running because someone called him with bell, book, and candle. She didn't know how she knew, she just did.

She knew other things about him, too. Maybe didn't know, exactly, but sensed. The way he caused the back of her neck to prickle when he was near. The way something darker, sadder, hid under his rakish smile. The way he touched her with such care, as though she was made of glass, while under the gentleness his body coursed with savage heat and desire.

Was she really having this unhinged chat with herself? Would she be having it if she'd studied the Other Side, like Aunt Nikki did? Maybe it wasn't too late for that. She could buy a few books from The Broom & Bottle. *The Afterlife For Dummies. Ghosts For Beginners.* Maybe there were online courses. A TED Talk.

Or maybe she was just stalling again. She should mail Jana's Tarot card to her aunts and call it a day.

Was that why she was stalling, her aunts? No, not them. What they knew. "*Because there's a lot you* don't *know.*" That's what Jana had said. CeCe should've told the witch that there wasn't much she didn't know about her four aunts, who'd been underfoot all her life. There were years and years when they'd all lived together in the three-story yellow and white house in the Starland District, the house her aunts bought after coming to Savannah from Moniac on the edge of the Okefenokee Swamp after CeCe's mother died.

CeCe saw the big old house in her mind, as she had seen it this afternoon when she'd spent an hour at the kitchenette counter in her flat, trying to write to her aunts, a few words, at least, to go with the High Priestess. Addressing the envelope was the easy part, so she'd done that first. *Hélène & Diane & Nicole & Sofie Gowdie.* Two of them were married (one widowed, one divorced), but they all kept the surname Gowdie. As had her unmarried mother. As did CeCe.

It was when she'd started on the note to go in the envelope that things screeched to a halt. After several false starts, she'd studied the one piece of paper she had left, inhaled, and written across it. *Y'all want to explain this?* No signature; they'd know. Then, she'd folded the note and put it in the envelope with the Tarot card. Unsealed, the envelope was still on the kitchenette counter.

Before she mailed it, before she did anything, she had to talk to Patrick. CeCe put her shoulder to the Forecourt door and pushed open the heavy oak slab. She'd search the Castle from top to bottom if she had to, and she'd find him. She was afraid of what she, what he, what they both might do, but there was no one in the world she needed more than the Knight of Pentacles, *her* Knight of Pentacles, and she needed him now.

———

He sat in an armchair before the fire, in a bedchamber now called the Prince Regent's, waiting for her. His brave, beautiful woman. Any other woman would have disappeared after what had happened in that accursed Hellenic Room. And on the road. Any other woman would have fled in a whirlwind of screams and fear, never to return.

Celeste Gowdie was not any other woman. When they kissed...there was so much in that kiss. Surprise, pent-up longing, the taste of desire.

And shards, brittle as broken glass. The edges and slivers of Celeste's disbelief were working their ways out of her mind and heart. He had felt the broken pieces go, tearing them both a little. They left a faint tang of blood that, to him, made the kiss all the sweeter. The loss before gain, the sacrifice before bliss. He had given everything to be where he was in that moment, but he would give it all again to have her. She had given, too, and the pain of it would go on for a while. He would make her forget. But first, she would have to remember.

Patrick leaned back in the chair, letting his head fall back, and stretched his legs to the fire. His adorable little dragoness had eaten the head off him about the blaze in the Hellenic Room. He smiled to remember it. She didn't understand that he could make the Great Fire of London in the Castle and it would scorch nary a brick, nor leave even ash in the grate. She'd learn, if she hadn't already.

She arrives. He heard the groan the Forecourt door made when she pushed it open, and the thud of her leaning against the oak to shut it behind her. He pummeled down an almost over-mastering urge to leap from his seat and race down the stairs, to lift her into his arms and carry her away like some Sabine captive. This once, at least, he must let her come to him. He must know that she came of her own will, of her own desire.

After this one time, though, he fully intended to have his unfettered way with her any time she'd let him. As long as he didn't lose control of the joining. He must never do that. He must hold himself in check, and he could.

Couldn't he?

Patrick sat up, ran his hands through his hair, and stared at his fingers. There was a slight tremor in them. Christ on the Cross, his nerves were in tatters, and she wasn't even in the room. What a fool he was to think he could manage this. To have waited so long and now have her so close...

He made fists and thumped them hard against the arms of the chair, making it shudder.

He would not weaken. He couldn't.

SEVENTEEN

It was easier to find him than she thought it might be, even with just the *Exit* signs—green in the U.K., with a walking man image—and her cell phone to light the way. CeCe simply followed the tingle at the back of her neck. It was like a Geiger counter. The stronger the tingle, the nearer the source. With hardly any hesitation, she ran up the stairs to the third floor, where most of the former bedrooms were located. Three doors down, on the right. She walked to the door and hesitated, her hand on the jamb. The door itself was open a few inches, a dull, wavering glow in the gap. *Wonderful, another prohibited fire. Why don't we just make s'mores?* The prickle at the top of her spine was strong now, so strong she reached back with her other hand and rubbed at the spot. She looked hard at the door handle, just as she had in the Forecourt. Not ready to go in, not able to go away.

She knew the room. It was the Regent's Bedchamber. So-called because George IV had stayed the weekend at St. Rhydian's for a shooting party, not long after he'd become Regent in 1811. There was a whole page in the Guidebook devoted to the room. The then-Earl had done a décor upgrade prior to the Prince's stay, and it had cost a whopping eleven hundred pounds sterling. Wall coverings, art, rugs, drapes, furniture, the lot. All for a few days hosting the squirrel-cheeked, curly-haired Regent who would be King in another nine years, since his father was barking mad. No wonder the estate went bankrupt.

CeCe looked down at her fake Georgian walking shoes. Her toes just touched the doorsill as they had at The Broom & Bottle. Another threshold, another liminal moment. Her instincts made one last feeble attempt at sense-talking. She could leave the Castle, right now. She could drive straight to the Heddlu, the police. They would come over and listen to whatever historical fantasy Patrick spun for them. That was their job. Hers was to be a tour guide.

The trouble was, the tour guide believed the fantasy, too. She pushed open the door.

First impressions, all mind-boggling. Patrick looked, if possible, bigger and more handsome in dark breeches, waist-coat, and white linen shirt. A loosened cravat. Hair free and swinging around his jaw.

Furniture in the room was sparse, most of the better bits having been sold or moved to other rooms before the Castle went to the National Trust.

Not the bed, though. It was against one wall, on a raised platform. And it was enormous, as big as any bed before the words 'California King' entered mattress catalogs. The head-board was taller than CeCe, lavishly carved from mahogany and surmounted by a gilded coronet. It screamed *Royalty Sleeps Here*. Red brocade drapes fell from the coronet, held back by gilded bronze tie-backs. A bronze satin spread covered the mattress.

CeCe's eyes darted from the bed to Patrick and back again. The Hellenic Room hadn't seemed right for seduction, but this room was made for it.

If Patrick was planning to seduce her, he wasn't in a hurry. He didn't rush to embrace her, pick her up, or carry her off as he had before. He stood by the Georgian fireplace, still as the statue of a mythic warrior from Ireland's past. Finn MacCool, maybe, or Cú Chulainn. Still and waiting, with those arresting eyes and that enigmatic mouth.

CeCe spoke first. "On the road. You saved my life. And yes, I will trust you." Patrick opened his arms, and she threw herself into them. He enfolded her as she relaxed against him with a sigh. *In for a penny, in for a pound.* Some time later, when their hearts had slowed from racing greyhound speed to something like normal, Patrick unwound his arms and sank into the prince-sized armchair in front of the—of course, briskly burning—fire. Beeswax candles in silver candlesticks flickered on the mantel, bathing them both in soft, golden light and filling the room with the scent of honey. There was a matching chair opposite Patrick's, but he took hold of CeCe's hands and pulled her onto his lap. His thighs were as large and hard under her as she thought they'd be. She lay against his chest, her head nestled in the hollow between his jaw and shoulder. His arms belted around her, one wrist clasped in his other fist.

The feeling of homecoming washed over CeCe again. Even though it was the first time they'd sat this way, it felt familiar and domestic, like they sat this way every evening. Evenings at home. Him, relaxed, embracing her. Her, leaning into his warmth. *How was your day, sweetie?*

But that was the biggest, falsest fantasy of all, wasn't it? The one that absolutely never could come true. Sadness squeezed out of CeCe's heart, like a tear. They'd hardly begun whatever it was they had with each other. She couldn't say where it was going, but she knew where it could never end.

She wasn't ready to talk about the road incident, but Patrick was. He gently pushed her away from him, so that she sat upright on his knee. The pose and the way he looked at her made CeCe feel like a child about to be fussed at. She wasn't far wrong.

"You could have been killed." Quiet censure darkened his words.

Like the child she felt, CeCe lowered her eyes to her hands, twisting in her lap. "I know."

"What were you thinking, to drive your coach that way? Did you not appreciate the peril?"

"The deer are supposed to be fenced."

"Deer go over fences. Where the stag leaps, the others follow."

CeCe nodded, still focused on her hands. "I wasn't thinking. I was...upset."

"Did I upset you?"

"Yes. No." She lifted her gaze. The worry in his sea-green eyes made her melt with shame. "I'm sorry. I won't do it again. I won't run from you. Ever."

He pulled her down to him. CeCe worked her hands around his chest so she could lay her body tight against his. They were quiet that way for long minutes. Finally, CeCe's inner Southern girl poked her in the manners.

"Thank you so much for the ghost stories."

"The history, you mean."

"Eunice Tattersall thinks I'm making it up."

"As long as it oversets the besom and her scheming, it matters not what she thinks."

Besom. An unpleasant, troublesome woman. CeCe's eighteenth-century vernacular wasn't vast, but she knew that word. "I'm grateful, anyway. The tours I'll be leading, I mean, the people who go on those sorts of tours are—"

"Soft-headed nincompoops?"

"They're not all—"

"Gabbling lack-wits?"

She giggled. "Just some of—"

"Chuckle-headed gundiguts?"

Her giggle burst into a guffaw.

Patrick pinched his nose and gave a high-pitched approximation of an English aristocrat through it. "I *say*, Miss Gowdie, *frayt*-fully impertinent to *awwsk*, but *maynt* you please tell me, is the caw-sel *hawnnn-ted*?"

CeCe howled with laughter. They both did, which somehow became kissing, which somehow went on for a while. The kissing subsided into another embrace. Patrick rocked her gently in his arms, and CeCe closed her eyes with happiness. She knew she would never be as happy as when he held her. She didn't want it to, but her mind kept returning to the last time they were together. The kiss. The after-kiss. The after-after-kiss.

"Patrick, when you're not with me, where do you go?"

He stopped moving, and the smile left his face. His fingers ran over her back, tiny sparks chasing them. "There is a place with no name. None that I know. I call it the long gray."

"Is it Hell?" CeCe bit her lip when Patrick paused. Out loud, it sounded like a stupid question.

He answered, anyway. "It is not Hell, *mo chroí*."

"Is it Heaven?"

"No, not that." He kissed the top of her head, then whispered into her hair. "Though a far better place than I ever expected to go. Better than I deserve."

She thought for a minute, idly fingering the buttons on his waistcoat. "You're very nicely dressed today."

"I made an effort. Not that I ever lounge about in the nude."

CeCe tried not to linger on *that* image. "The place you are, when you're not with me. Are there—well, *others*?"

"Ghosts, you mean, or nude ghosts?" Patrick laughed at

the expression on her face. "You've read the accounts, have you not? This house is full of ghosts."

"No one can see them, though, right?"

"No one but you, my beauty."

Well, that made her feel special. "I can see you. I don't want to see the others."

"You won't."

For another minute, she thought about that, then about the question she really wanted to ask. "What I meant was, are there..." *Say it, say it.* "Lady ghosts?"

He lifted her chin with his forefinger, bending his head to brush her lips with his. "None that hold any interest for me. None like you, celestial woman. No one in the here, or the hereafter. Only you."

CeCe's pleasure faced off with her apprehension. "The long gray. I—I don't think I want to go there, Patrick."

His kiss and his whisper returned to her hair. "And so you shall not." Abruptly, he stood, gathering her easily in his arms. "But you shall come to bed." His tone didn't invite disagreement.

Not that she would have disagreed. She was boneless in his arms, her will dissolved along with her bones. Patrick could roll her down the stairs and she wouldn't resist him. What had happened to Celeste Gowdie, staunchly independent woman? Dedicated historian and career-driven professional? Maybe she could call this research. Field work. *Ghosts of the Eighteenth Century: A Sample.*

She landed with a squeal on the gigantic bed. There was just enough time to register that it had a real mattress, not the plywood slab many historic house museums install on their beds, before Patrick landed atop her. Not fully atop, thankfully. Two-hundred pounds of male muscle would have crushed her. But deliciously atop, weight on his elbows and knees. Knees that were pushing hers apart.

CeCe panicked. "Wait just a hot minute, your lordship!"

"Don't call me that, Celeste. You know I'm a bastard."

"As long as I can call you mine, Patrick, that's all that matters. Are you...mine?"

He answered her with kisses. Kisses warm and growing warmer as they moved from her mouth to her neck. Sucking and nibbling at the skin above the edge of her bodice, his tongue pushed aside the gathered edge of her chemise to delve into the hollow between her breasts. All the while, his hands were busy with his clothing. CeCe came out of a sort of swoon, to see him on his knees, pulling his waistcoat off his shoulders and dropping it alongside the bed. His cravat was gone, too.

"Uh, wait, Patrick! I—we—maybe we shouldn't..." Speech deserted her as he put his hands on either side of her head, supporting his upper body. She stared at the muscled chest inches from her face, visible in his unbuttoned shirt opening. A hysterical voice in her head was shouting about safe sex, and an even more hysterical voice was saying an STD was the least of her worries if she was in bed with a ghost. Patrick chuckled. God, even his chuckles were sensuous.

"Why? Are you wed? A match you never wanted, I'll vow, but now you're saddled with an inconvenient husband. Some bandy-legged dotard, with a sagging lobcock and breath like a privy."

Whomp. Just like that, Serious Patrick became Jolly Patrick.

"Or some common rogue who rolls home in his cups and switches your lovely round backside with hazel withies just to make you cry. I'll not torture him, my flower, though he deserves it. I'll dispatch him quick; he won't know a thing."

"I'm *not* married," she huffed.

"Ah, but you were, is that the trouble? Widowed, and still grieving for your man. I'm sure he was fine, and I'll not speak ill of the dead, since I hope there were tears in the eyes of a fair few women when I myself left this earth. I'll console you, dearest, I'll ease your pain, I'll—"

"Not married! Not widowed!"

"Well, you're never a virgin. *I am but a poooor spinster,*" he moaned in a falsetto, *"Bereffft by my solitary state..."*

CeCe shocked herself by tittering like a preteen.

"Mind you," Patrick went on, "I've no objection to a woman who's indulged herself. Maidenly restraint is highly overvalued, in my considered opinion. It's merely an impediment to a woman's pleasure. And mine, as well." He pushed his hand under her skirts. With a gasp, CeCe pushed it back down.

"Nay." He came up to his knees again. In one fluid motion, he yanked his shirttail out of his breeches. CeCe's breath caught at the flash of muscular stomach when the cloth came up. "You're no virgin, so don't be trying that fable on." He rolled away from her and sat back against the massive headboard, legs outstretched, hands behind his neck. "It's been a wee while, though, hasn't it?"

CeCe wasn't sure how long a wee while was, but it had been a lot longer since Jasper Marcotte. Blood rushed into her face. She turned on her side and stared up at Patrick. She was far from a virgin, but something about him made her feel like she was. Like she was seeing—really seeing—a man for the first time.

The fine linen of Patrick's shirt fell in soft creases across his shoulders and chest, his massive arms. A slight smile danced on his lips. His eyes were deep green in the dimly lighted room, and a very evident erection tented the front of his breeches. A musky blend of lavender and man wafted from him, making her feel slightly drunk. The memory of his kiss in the Hellenic Room turned the drunken feeling into a kind of delirium. That kiss, the way his mouth, his tongue, his body, had all urged her toward wet surrender...

Panic grabbed her again, and she sat up hastily. Her brain said things were moving too fast. Her body said they weren't moving fast enough. She plumped a satin-covered pillow and propped it, and herself, against the headboard as far away from Patrick as she could get without falling off the bed. Her shoulders twitched defensively.

"I had a boyfriend in Savannah. That's Georgia. In the...Colonies."

Patrick tsked. Even his tsking was sexual, a deep catch in his throat. "You're not implying, I hope, that I'm unaware of the Colonies and their various names. I may be dead, but I'm not a rattlebrain. So, tell me about this friendly boy in Oglethorpe's colony. A tender youth of ten or twelve?"

"Don't be silly. He was, he *is*, twenty-seven. Well, twenty-eight, now. A grown man."

"And was he a raging fire between your legs, this grown man?"

She didn't answer. Patrick tsked again, deeper and more sexual than before. "A tragedy, that is. A man of twenty-seven years came to your bed and left you unsated. To be sure, he's twenty-eight now, nearly a graybeard. Advanced age is often to blame in a case like that."

Why were they having this conversation? CeCe rolled onto her other side, facing away. "It wasn't—he didn't—"

"He didn't, that's the God's truth. Didn't, wouldn't, and couldn't."

He was behind her, then, in that swift and noiseless way he had of moving. CeCe's mind raced. *Get off the bed, stand up, leave the room.* She didn't do those or any of the other things common sense told her to do, just like she hadn't refused to let him kiss her in the Hellenic Room, and she hadn't run away and called the police an hour ago.

Why did paralysis seize her every time she was with Patrick? She became a rabbit in the presence of a wolf, afraid to move. Afraid not to.

Behind her, he gently lifted her hair. The slight tug, the sense of her thick curls filling his hand—they wiped away thought and sent responsive jolts down her legs.

His head lowered and he nuzzled the back of her neck. Breathing her scent in, breathing words out in the language CeCe didn't understand, while his body spoke with perfect clarity. Spoke to her skin, her bones, her sex.

Reaching under her arm, he ran a finger along the top edge of her bodice. She expected the finger to thrust underneath the cloth, but instead he brought it, and the finger next to it, to her lips. Instinct and desire made her open her mouth to admit them, and she gripped his wrist to keep his hand in place. Her eyes closed at the taste of him, the thought of how the rest of him might taste. Shameless with excitement, she nursed at his fingers, making hungry little noises.

Again, Patrick read her thoughts, not that he'd have to be a psychic like the witch on Puzzle Lane. "When what's between my legs gets between your lips," he breathed into her ear, "you'd best have a thirst, my girl, because you'll draw a pint of Ireland's finest." She laughed, giving him a chance to withdraw his fingers and *then* thrust them into her bodice.

Her laugh turned to a sharply indrawn breath. Strong but gentle, Patrick worked his hand under her stays, to her nipple, tweaking and tugging it with his moist fingers.

CeCe's moan was lost in the deep timbre of his question. "Do you like that? Tell me what you like, Celeste. Tell me now."

Telling would require speech, and she was past that already. She nodded, her breath coming in little pants. He pulled harder on her nipple while a rush of wetness went to her core.

Slowly, he closed the few inches between them until he pressed against her. His size, his hardness—they drove away what was left of CeCe's capacity for rational thought. She wanted them both naked, skin on skin, hands and legs and mouths seeking, stroking. His length pushed against her backside—a promise, a threat—and she spoke his name.

Patrick groaned a response. Keeping one hand in her hair, he brought the other below her waist. Strong fingers fanned across her belly, pulling her into him, tight.

"Say it again," he murmured hoarsely, and CeCe did. He rewarded her with a sharp little bite on the side of her neck, where it joined her shoulder. She shuddered, her breath coming fast and shallow, a storm of fear and hunger gathering under Patrick's hand.

"Again." It wasn't a murmur this time, but a command.

She moaned and, after he nipped her neck again, begged, "*Please.*"

He began moving against her. CeCe arched her back, matching him thrust for thrust. His hips spanned her entirely, and his hand pressed her against him with every thrust.

Wild thoughts and images raced through her. Was this what coupling with him would be like? Patrick's body, huge, unyielding, driving into her. Her senses narrowed to one, the sensation of a man taking her right through her clothes.

God, she wanted him to take her! Her deepest parts flooded, and with faint whimpers she pushed back at him, harder, craving the thick bolt he rubbed in the crease of her backside. Could he come that way? Could he come at all? Would he lift her skirts and take her from behind, like a stallion? What would he feel like, pounding, emptying into her?

Desperate, she stuttered, "I w-want—I want—"

Patrick hushed her softly. "All for you, my treasure, all for my Celeste." No more laughter in his voice. Now, it was thick and wicked as night. "Let me lose myself in pleasuring you."

In one smooth action, he clutched her skirt, petticoat, and shift, hauling them above her knees. Then, with an oath, he reached between her thighs. His broad, hot hand cupped and kneaded the mound barely covered by thin panties, the only concession to modern-day dress in her costume.

CeCe was drenched and ready. She knew Patrick could feel it through the cloth, knew it drove his lust. Groaning, he massaged her sex until she nearly screamed with need. She reached above and behind, burying her fingers in the silk of his hair. Patrick pushed his head under her arm and lay it next to her cheek. His stubbled jaw rubbed and prickled, as he watched himself work her with his hand.

"I'm not a friendly boy," he whispered harshly as he seized the crotch of her lacy briefs in his fist. One tug, hard. Another, and he ripped the cloth in two. The tearing sound unleashed something in them both, something ancient and animal.

"Whatever else I may be," he hissed, "I'm a man. Yours, entirely, completely. Today, tomorrow, always." His fingers went unerringly to her center, parting the tender folds. CeCe whimpered, unable to form a single word. Patrick's breath came hot against her ear. "And make no mistake, vein of my heart, you are *mine*."

She shut her eyes and gave herself to his touch, to the friction against and inside her. To *him*. He was instantly attuned to her response. Again and again, he brought her just to the edge of release, then stopped the movement of his fingers while he kissed the back of her neck and crooned words in English, in Irish. The second she subsided, he returned his attention to her yearning sex, while CeCe lost her hold on sanity. She strained and arched into him, begging, weeping—

One second, she trembled as his fingertips circled the swollen bud at her apex. The next, she cried out, once, twice, and flew over the edge. Patrick bit into the soft flesh at the side of her neck at the instant she peaked. The long, searing spasm tore and shook her with its force. After, in the space of a breath, she fell into a sweet, sated sleep.

———

A minute—or two, or five—passed before she felt consciousness return. Her climax was so shattering she hadn't even felt Patrick's hand withdraw. Still gasping and quivering on the bedspread, she opened her eyes.

He was gone again.

CeCe jackknifed to a sitting position. She jumped off the bed, eyes wide, and stared at the room. Still the Regent's Bedchamber. Same as before, and yet totally, ghastly, different. Stripped, now, of everything that had been there when Patrick held her in his arms.

It wasn't even a room. It was a shell, a husk. Musty and cold, cobwebbed in the corners, floured with dust that the cleaners had missed on chairs and tables. No fire, no candles, no light apart from the ceiling, where an old electric fixture flickered.

CeCe turned to the bed. Heartbeats ago, it had been rumpled and warm, full of desire. Now, it was tidy, flat, and dull. Museum furniture, in a staged room where no one had lived or loved for a hundred years.

Not totally vacant, though. One solitary, very confused woman stood in the middle, wondering if she'd seen her dead man for the last time.

"Please," she whimpered, "please come back."

EIGHTEEN

Please come back. It was what Patrick had whispered on the night Celeste first saw him in the Tower, then fled, afraid. As she had done then, he fled this night because of fear. He dared not stay abed with her a minute longer. When she came apart in his arms, he knew he had only seconds before he rolled atop her and took her like a beast.

It tore him now that she felt cast aside, at the time a woman should feel most cherished, most adored. He deserved to be flogged for that, a knotted lash across his back, drawing blood. Twenty strokes, fifty. Someday Celeste would understand, but she didn't understand now. Now, she felt pain. Pain he'd caused.

Compared to the shame of that, his suffering was a trifle. He watched her return to her coach and leave the Castle grounds. Then, he went back to the cold room, where he sat in the cold chair by the cold fire. He gripped himself through his breeches with a fervor he hadn't felt since he was fourteen. Gripped and pined. Celeste's scent was on his shirt, his hands, torturing him.

He couldn't go on this way, and the fact that he'd brought

it on himself was no balm. He must be more careful. A room with a bed in it defined "occasion of sin" more eloquently than any of the Holy Fathers at the Collège had.

Holy Fathers. That's it, he would cool his lust with thoughts of Father Augustin, his Latin tutor. The priest had a wart on his nose the size of a hazelnut, with hairs sprouting from it. How often Patrick had sat in his class, ignoring the declension of *concedo, concedes, concedit.* Musing, instead, on the breasts of the stable master's daughter Françoise, while he got harder by the second. He had only to stare at Father Augustin's wart in order to rise at the class's end without shaming himself in front of the world.

Or, he could think about matrimony. That had always been a quelling thought. In the past, the mere consideration of it had reduced him to wilted celery. Not that he'd ever been trapped in the parson's mousetrap. He told himself that was because no woman had so taken his fancy that he felt compelled to court her. In fact, no marriage-minded mother in the Known World would have thought of dropping her daughter at his feet.

Putting aside reluctant mothers and maidens, he could think of a handful of trollops who would also have laughed themselves silly at the thought of looking at him over the breakfast table for decades. And the widows. Any number of them would've worn black for the rest of their lives before seriously considering the altar by his side. That, before any of them really knew what he was, what his duty to the earldom of Trawsgoed had made him.

Face it, Patrick. You weren't much of a bargain in the marriage market when you lived. Dead, you must assume your stock has fallen.

But courting Celeste...

He would deal with the impossibility of marriage later. For

now, for her, he must woo. He owed her that, at least. Flowers and—what were the other parts of wooing? *Think, Patrick.*

Poetry. Wasn't that part of it? He knew some rhymes. "*A swain and a maid under the moon did lie...*" No, probably not that sort of poetry. Shakespeare, maybe, or that other fellow, Horrick. No, Harrick. "*A sweet disorder in the dress, kindles in clothes a wantonness...*" Hell's bells, that was as bad as the shepherd swiving the milkmaid. He should have applied himself more energetically at the Collège, not that love poems played a large part in the curriculum.

If he made it through the courting, he would have to tackle the proposal. How did it go? "*Most estimable lady, I beg to offer you the protection of my title* (non-existent), *the fulsomeness of my fortune* (at the time of my death, two shillings sixpence and a small gold cross), *the conviviality of my family* (one mother in Ireland, plus a cat), *the income* (?) *of my lands* (?)..."

Still and all, and even having so little to offer, if he successfully went about a proposal in the usual way, they would arrive at the next damned part. The part where she looked over his head (since he would be on one knee) and spoke to a distant candle sconce.

"*You do me too much honor, Mr. Ó Loinsigh. But I think we would not suit.*" After which, just to drive the blade to the hilt, she'd add, "*Nonetheless, I shall for all time cherish in my heart the memory of your affection.*"

Bollocks.

None of that mattered, anyway. What mattered was that he had to make Celeste understand that if he *could* marry her, he would. He would marry her onboard a ship, in a chapel, in Gretna Green, in Canterbury Cathedral with every bell ringing. He would put a diamond on her hand or a plaited ring of dandelion. He would take her to Paris, or he would buy Paris and bring it to her. He would give her children and, with her, watch them grow, watch them marry and make babes of their own. He would grow old with her, old and rickety, and lie by her side as they—

No. None of it. They would have none of it, not if things went on the way they were going now. Somehow, they must turn. Patrick must turn them. Somehow, the foreseeing of the *banfháidh* must come to pass.

He'd been terrified when the young stag in the road nearly killed her. He'd stopped it, frightening Celeste half to death, anyway. The closest he'd come to losing his life in a fight had been with Geoffrey Urquhart, Lord Somerset, who'd ripped his face in a duel. On that day, Patrick had known fear for the first and only time in battle. Somerset was a fabled bladesman, and Patrick saw death rushing toward him in the seconds before he drove back his opponent's *pattinando*, then sent his own rapier into the man's heart. In those seconds, Patrick had not been so terror-struck as he'd been by a fucking deer.

What if something like the deer in the road happened to Celeste again, somewhere else? Somewhere he was not near, was not watching? Unthinkable. Celeste must live. She must live for her own sake, for his, for them both. The *banfháidh* said...

He bent forward, scrubbed his hands through his hair again. Was it madness to put all his coins on that one wager? What did the croaking beldame know? He was thrice a fool for believing her. And yet...

'Til witch's gold be bound for wife.

Seven words. It was the flimsiest of foundations on which to build hope, but better that than no hope at all.

Nineteen

"Patrick is a ghost."

It'd been four days since the night in the Regent's Bedchamber, and CeCe had said it at least a hundred times. Out loud, under her breath, in her head, over and over. In her flat, in the shower, drinking tea, while she was driving, entering the Castle, leaving it by the yew-lined slope to her car.

After a while, she practiced saying, "Patrick is *my* ghost." It didn't take a hundred repetitions to accept that. Of the things that had happened in the Regent's Bedchamber, that was the final sum, the bottom line, the complete and unarguable takeaway. Her heart had accepted it. Now, it was just a matter of getting her rational mind on board. No more waffling, shilly-shallying, hemming and hawing. Patrick was a ghost, he was her ghost, and she was—

What *did* that make her? His human? His live person? His un-undead? CeCe was almost maybe potentially willing to nearly possibly say she would accept all of them. She wasn't ready yet to say she was happy with any of them. Maybe she'd get used to it.

She supposed somewhere—maybe in those books and

online courses she hadn't perused—there were things to ask a ghost, if you had one nearby. But for the life of her, CeCe couldn't figure out why she would ask Patrick any of them. She'd already surmised that the afterlife was more like Atlanta International Airport than a small tea party, so there was no point asking her ghost if he'd run across Great-Grandma Micheline or Sister Mary Eustace. The deer in the road had answered in the affirmative the only question worth asking.

The other questions? They could wait until she got over the shock of the first answer.

There was plenty to distract her, anyway. When she arrived at the PD's office on Wednesday afternoon to check the online ticket purchases for the debut ghost walk, the numbers stupefied her. Fifty-seven advance tickets—four times the number of people she'd had on any of her Candlelight Castle Walks. It irritated her, but at the same time she couldn't help feeling a little excited. With the ticket buyers who were bound to show up unannounced, she'd have to open a second Saturday night tour slot, ten o'clock maybe. She might even have to add a tour on Friday.

The rewards of team playing. And to think, all she had to do was fling her principles off the ramparts.

Saturday, and everything was ready for the premiere. The Castle staff were dizzy with anticipation. CeCe was just dizzy. Her excitement over the early ticket rush had faded. Now, there was only grim fact. Once she strolled down this particular career path, there would be no turning back. The Candlelight Castle Walks had been bad enough, but at least those were historical, not hysterical. Her old script about the nobles and common folk who did everything from ruling the earldom to scrubbing the privies—a little boring, maybe, but straightforward history, not a single ghoulie in it. But this?

Ghosts of the Castle! The brand-new banner over the gates screamed it. CeCe had asked for Internet publicity, but she wasn't prepared for the lurid images on the St. Rhydian's website. Writhing people in Georgian attire (a period sketch of Bedlam, which wasn't anywhere near Wales) and a Grim Reaper (really?) on the Castle ramparts. Below those, a blood red caption: *Who haunts these halls? Find out each Saturday at the stroke of midnight!*

She pleaded guilty to some sensational Web content of her own. Why couldn't she have kept her mouth shut when she went to the PD's office on Wednesday? Eunice Tattersall asked where her reluctant guide had found the Castle ghosts.

Ambushed, CeCe blurted out the truth. "I have a collaborator. He's dead."

Eunice threw back her head and laughed, a sight as blood-curdling as anything in CeCe's script. Even Eunice Lite laughed, a mute baring of the gums that resembled an enraged senior Pekingese ready to take a bite out of someone's hand.

"Brilliant!" Eunice crowed, actually clapping her hands with joy, then making a frame of them like a marquee. "The real ghost walk created by a real ghost!" The slogan was up on the website before CeCe could say *html*.

Despite feeling sick about the whole thing, she'd spent the remainder of the week playing like a goal-scoring member of the St. Rhydian's Ghost Team. First, she laundered, mended, and pressed her eighteenth-century wardrobe. In a charity shop in the town, she found a broad-brimmed straw hat with a shallow crown. With a ribbon tie behind her head and a modish downward tilt to the front edge, the hat made CeCe the cover photo for *Vogue*, April 1747.

In the same shop, she snagged a square of plain white silk. Folded diagonally, it made a modesty scarf, a delicate cloth napkin that rested across her shoulders and tucked into her bodice at the front. It was fine for Patrick to leer at her 36C-pluses, but there would be photos snapped by ghost walkers. The last thing she planned to look like on Instagram was a mead wench, bosom amidships.

Then, she organized Patrick's journal into a script, written neatly on three-by-five cards. The tour would begin in the Castle Solar, a sort of parlor passage with tall windows at the back of the first floor, where Patrick had given her spectacular details about the knifing (eighteen wounds inflicted by an aggrieved husband) of one Gregory Miles Fortenoy. "A cuckolding swine," Patrick had called him.

From the Solar, CeCe would take the group through the locations and details of various homicides, gruesome accidents, lopped-off limbs, and disgusting, ultimately fatal ailments. Bonus extra: two suicides. She would be careful not to claim there actually *were* ghosts at any of her stops, just that there *could* be, or that conditions *suggested* them. In her experience, that was enough for fans of the Unseen to dissolve into puddles of belief.

She was immovable on one point. The tour would not include the Tower. Eunice was disappointed, but CeCe dug in her heels. "All those people crowding up fifty-eight steps? They're narrow and steep, and there's no handrail." CeCe wagged her head somberly, like a physician asked if the patient would survive an operation. "It's up to you, Ms. Tattersall, but in the States, we call that a lawsuit waiting to happen."

The PD wasn't gracious about it, but she agreed. No Tower.

Personally, CeCe was past caring if every one of her tour-takers fell on the stairs and broke their ghost-craving necks. But the Tower had become sacred space for her. She'd be damned if she'd let tourists spoil it with their cameras and stupid remarks.

By a quarter to midnight, CeCe was as ready as she would ever be. Parking in the crowded lot was difficult. She might need to ask for her own space. *Reserved for Executive Ghost Director.*

When she walked into the Forecourt, she was stunned by the crowd. She should've anticipated it, since she'd seen the preorders. But sales at the ticket window were so brisk that the flustered volunteer handling them ran out of paper tickets. She had to ink paid visitors' hands with the only stamp she had behind the wicket, *First Class Post.*

Facing the mob of seventy people in the Great Hall, CeCe knew her guess was correct. The Castle would have to add one, maybe even two, more ghost walk slots. CeCe would never get groups as large as this one through the narrow passages and doors of the Castle, at least not without damaging furnishings, or people at the back complaining they couldn't see.

She did quick math in her head. *Ghosts of the Castle!* was making an absolute killing, pun intended. *So, why aren't you happy, Ms. Team Player?*

CeCe felt a tug at her sleeve. She turned around and found herself looking at Plaid Tam O'Shanter Lady and her plaid-hatted Purse Pooch. Only this time, both were wearing steampunk mini-toppers.

"I knew it was haunted." The woman smirked, and even the dog looked smug. CeCe forced her face into a rigor mortis smile. She headed for her first stop.

She peeled the last ghost walker off her at nearly two in the morning. She was wrung out, as much or more by the Q and A at the tour's end as by the walk itself. Rattling off the script in a convincing way was easy and didn't require any real engagement on her part. Knife in the gut? *La-di-dah*. Arms hacked off? *C'est la vie, bruh.*

But the questions at the end—*What's your ghostly collaborator like? How well do you know him* (nudge nudge, wink wink)? *Is he your first ghost? Doesn't he scare you? Do you let him touch you?* Er, uh...

Did her audience really buy the phantom collaborator story? Some did, some weren't sure, some didn't care. Who cared, as long as they bought tickets? That was the PD's goal for the whole humiliating exercise, wasn't it?

The testimonials were worse than the questions and took longer. Every second person had seen a ghost, knew someone who'd seen a ghost, wanted to see a ghost. The debut tour was fairly global. CeCe heard about ghost sightings in Copenhagen, Miami, Toronto, and one heavily Scottish story from a friend of Purse Pooch's owner. That one was about ghosts, or maybe pastries, in a Glasgow tearoom.

When Eunice looked at the numbers, she'd be doing her happy dance, for sure. Even on a dead—*oh, funny*—night like Friday, when the grounds hitherto had more wild foxes than tourists, CeCe knew she could drag dozens of ghost gogglers from one end of the Castle to the other.

High-fiving was in order. The Yank tour guide had done it. Week after week, month after month, the Castle coffers would fill. *Cha-ching.* CeCe was box office gold, indispensable. Her cultural worker visa was in the bag, because what clown would deport a cash cow?

So, why wasn't she happy dancing, too?

CeCe sighed miserably as she locked the Forecourt door behind the last walker. At least, she didn't have to trudge up and down the Castle, dousing battery candles. Now that she was a celebrity, the job of turning them on and off was given to a docent.

The docent solved one problem, but created another.

CeCe couldn't loiter around the Castle after the ghost walk to see *her* ghost. On Friday, she'd put a cryptic note on the Tower Room floor. *Wednesday*. She had no idea if Patrick would find the note, but they hadn't exactly worked out a way to communicate. It wasn't like she could text him. The opening night of *Ghosts of the Castle!* made it clear that all their meetings would have to be on weeknights. CeCe would be too worn out after thronged ghost parades for dallying with any kind of lover, dead or alive. Hopefully, she and Patrick could come up with some sort of schedule.

Mary, Mother of God, what was she doing? Filling in her Google Calendar with paranormal staff meetings?

One tired footstep at a time, CeCe stumbled to the parking lot, thinking nonstop of a hot shower and a waiting bed. She tried not to think that she wouldn't even be able to take a useful reference away from all her trouble and embarrassment. Useful references didn't come from ghost walks. Not unless her next job was at Walt Disney World.

She wanted Patrick. More than wanted, she *needed* Patrick. Needed his deep voice, alternatingly rough and tender, his laughter, his warm, enveloping arms, his hard body pressed against hers.

She got to the Mini, key in hand, and was just about to press Unlock when she saw them lying on the roof of the car. Red roses, a dozen at least, and among them bluish purple delphiniums. Their stems were wrapped in a narrow length of white linen—Patrick's neck stock. The stock he'd untied before he shed his waistcoat, pulled his shirt out of his breeches, pressed his body against hers, and claimed her as his own.

CeCe gathered up the bouquet and dipped her face into it. Sweetness and Patrick, mingled together. She'd seen the great beds of roses, the narrow borders of delphiniums, in the Castle

TWENTY

Over the next few weeks, CeCe's life turned into a variant of the game where a kid pulled petals off a daisy. *He's real, he's not real.* All she could say for sure was that when she was with Patrick, he was the only reality she knew, the only reality she wanted.

They talked. He told her about Paris in the mid-eighteenth century, his student years at the Collège des Irlandais. Still decades away from the firestorm of Bastille Day, Patrick's Paris was intoxicating, half elegance and half squalor. Through his eyes, CeCe saw the hanging meat and heaped fruit of the street markets, the floating baths off the *quai du Louvre*, the startling inventions of the day. Some were huge, like the thousand-worker factories producing paper or printed fabrics. Some were small, like the umbrella that opened with a button on the handle.

In Patrick's stories, she walked the halls of the Collège, dodging cuffs from monks and priests, laughing at the jokes played on them by the students. "Never me, of course," he protested in mock innocence. "I was a perfect angel."

The more he told her, the more she wanted to know, but

Gardens. Hugh, the head gardener, would wonder on Monday what happened to his finest blooms.

Some alien emotion wound around her heart, like Patrick's cravat wound around the roses and delphiniums. It was alarming, exhilarating, and almost lethally problematic, but CeCe knew it for what it was. She was falling in love. Her beloved was infuriating, irreverent, lusting, possessive...

Dead.

there were more immediate lessons. His mouth on hers, his touch roaming across her body, his murmured desire against her throat, her cheek, the yielding flesh of her breasts as he coaxed them out from her bodice and held them in his large, warm hands, suckling them until she nearly fainted from the want of him.

She still wore her eighteenth-century dress for their meetings. It went with the Castle rooms that were so different, sometimes even looking as they were in Patrick's day. She never asked why or how. It was enough that everything seemed right when they were there—the rooms, the touching, the clothes. His clothing became as familiar as her own. She knew every stitch, every button, as he knew hers.

He never stripped her, but found every ingenious way of caressing her, dressed, in the firelight and candle glow. She never stopped aching to see his body naked, in the light, to take what they were doing to an explosive end. Patrick always stopped her when she tried.

"No, my jewel. There are limits, there are dangers."

Limits. CeCe understood those pretty well. Limits came from the real world, the world without a ghost whose mouth and hands drove her wild. A ghost she couldn't say a word about to anyone because of a torrent of repercussions.

The dangers... "Is that why you disappear?"

Patrick took his time in answering. First a kiss and a caress. Then, he wrapped her in his magnificent arms, held her with his magnificent eyes. "I keep us on the slimmest of margins, *mo chroí*, a narrow strand between two raging seas. It takes all my strength."

"I'm sorry, I didn't know, I—"

He put a finger on her lips. "That's of no import, Celeste. But you so unseat my reason that I fear, at times, to lose my footing."

"And so, you go away."

In response, he kissed her. One kiss became two, became many, a chain of kisses, the lightest and most fragrant of bonds, while night passed into dawn.

The dangers hovered, though, just out of mind. Whispers half heard, half understood. Darkness building in the corners each night, dissolving in the sunrise of laughter.

In her more sober hours, CeCe knew that everything was fleeting and fragile. She knew it, hated the knowing, and pushed it to the back of her mind. Somehow, someday, the whispers would become roars, and the darkness would rise up like a dragon, breathing fire. Then, she and Patrick and all they had would be burned alive. Like witches.

But not this night.

———

She hadn't expected an immediate response to the one-line letter and Tarot card she'd sent her aunts, but their answer was a long time coming. Long enough that CeCe was working on a pretty good burn. Her aunts were old fashioned, but they knew about texting and email, and that newfangled thing called the telephone. Apart from checking her cell and her emails daily, CeCe peered twice a week into her pigeonhole in the ground floor break room at the Castle, where staff and a few docents got mail. Finally, four weeks and three days after she'd mailed her aunts, she received their reply.

It was early afternoon and the break room was empty. She sat at a table and tore open the envelope with the Savannah GA, USA, postmark. Inside was a letter, typed, probably on Aunt Nikki's vintage Royal manual typewriter. "Always write letters," Nikki had said more times than CeCe could count. "It's the polite thing to do."

Four sheets of paper, neatly folded. There was also a

smaller folded square of light gray newsprint paper. CeCe put it to one side and opened the letter.

Single-spaced typing. Good grief, the letter was three times longer than the Gettysburg Address. Alarm made goosebumps rise on her arms. She'd figured nothing good would come from the Tarot card, but what in the bejeezus did her aunts know that took four pages to tell?

My dear sweet CeCe,

I'm sure angels watch over you. I have seen them in my dreams and feel them in my heart. Every day, I send clouds of positive energy to surround you, as I have since you were a baby. We all looked after you when our sister Gabrielle, your mom, went away (Hélène and Diane will tell you more about that, sweetheart, and I'm sorry we waited so long). I was living at home and Sophie was too young, so it was the natural thing for me to babysit you more than the others. You forgot, I'm sure, but when you were little, you called all my sisters Auntie but you called me Momma. And so I feel some Great and Loving Universal Intelligence put your little hand in mine. It stays there still.

There is something else about your life, the time when you were about four to six, that you may have forgotten. We all sort of hoped you would forget. It reminded us too much of Gabi and what happened to her.

You were a very advanced child in every way, so it wasn't any surprise that the second you started drawing pictures, you drew them very well. But you only ever drew one thing. Other children made dogs and cats and flowers and sometimes even houses, but your houses had towers and flags and those zigzag walls at the top. I say houses, but I really mean one, always the same one. Even somebody with no imagination could see it was a castle. First, you drew it with crayons or markers, or whatever you got into your fingers, and then with a set of colored pencils I got you for Christmas. Your Aunt Hélène was ticked off about those pencils; she said I shouldn't encourage you.

For a while, Hélène took your pencils away, but it didn't stop you. You just drew your castle at school. I wasn't teaching yet (I was still in college, then), but I always went with Hélène to the parent-teacher conferences at Sacred Heart, and that's how I found out. Ms. Gonzalez and Sister Mary Eustace both told us. Sister Mary Eustace gave us some of your drawings (I have enclosed one with this letter). The drawings were really amazing, CeCe, almost professional. Sister Mary Eustace said you were artistically gifted and just needed to "branch out more," but Ms. Gonzalez was a little less enthusiastic. She suggested we get you into some other things, like ballet or Brownies (Like we hadn't tried that).

The reason Hélène was so upset about the drawing was because when your mom was just four or five, she also started making pictures. She didn't draw a dog one day and a tree the next. Only one thing, one big house, the same as you drew one castle. Your Grandmomma Louise thought at first it was nothing. You know, like some children have an imaginary friend, and Gabi had her imaginary house.

Then, one day, one of your Grandmomma's friends, Rosalie Fourcette (you won't remember her, she's gone now), came by our house. Gabi was sitting on the floor with some paper, drawing you-know-what. Rosalie said, "Well, look at that! It's a picture of Two Rivers!" And, "Oh, I know that place, it's on the St. Mary's," and so on.

That Fourcette woman never could keep her mouth zipped about anything, CeCe. She blabbed around about "this little girl who's drawin' the old plantation down Moniac way that everybody knows is haunted, and that little girl ain't never seen it and, after all, what can anybody expect from those Gowdies who are related by blood to..."

Well, Sophie and Diane will tell you more about that. I was

little when the Rosalie Fourcette business happened, so I can't say I remember it, but the story got told over and over until we were all sick of it.

You drawing your castle—it went on for a while. Finally, just like your mom, you stopped, and everything was fine. Until now, I guess. We were all a little concerned when you ended up where you are, but we wouldn't have said anything except you sent that Tarot card. Anyway, I'm sorry, CeCe. I'm so, so sorry about everything. Angels will hold you in their arms, I'm sure of it, so don't be afraid.

Aunt Nicole

When she finished reading, CeCe was as cold as if she'd been standing on the rocky beach a mile from St. Rhydian's, the sea wind lashing her. *Everything was fine. Until now, I guess.* What the *hell*?

Maybe she should make a cup of strong tea before she opened the other enclosure, the folded square of newsprint. While she was thinking, two docents bustled noisily into the room. One she didn't know, but the other was Mairead, a friend of Poppy's.

"Hello, there!" Mairead was Poppy's opposite, tall and thin and athletic. Someone said she ran 5K races every weekend.

"Hi, Mairead." CeCe didn't think she was hiding her mail, but she folded her hands over the papers on the table. Mairead saw.

"Letter from home?"

CeCe nodded, smiling. After a beat, the other docent asked about chocolate biscuits. Mairead turned to her.

"Top shelf. Next to the instant coffee." She turned back to CeCe. "I heard your ghost walks are a grand success."

CeCe was pretty sure everybody from the Board of Trustees to the groundskeepers had heard. She forced a bigger smile. "Yes, it's gratifying."

Mairead smiled, too, but her eyes had a look in them. A dying-to-know-more look.

"Do you want some?" The other docent held an open packet of chocolate HobNobs out to Mairead.

"No, I don't eat that stuff. Nora, this is Celeste Gowdie. She's the one who—"

"Hi there, Nora." CeCe's right hand shot out like a Moray eel before Mairead could finish pinning the ghost walks on her. "Nice to meet you. Please call me CeCe."

Nora beamed and shifted the cookies to give her a quick handshake. "Oh, what a lovely American accent!"

Lovely. Was Nora a friend of Eunice Tattersall's? CeCe couldn't think of something to say about her American accent or anything else. She just sat, hands covering the letter again, wishing the docents would go away. Mairead finally got the hint.

"Come on, Nora. If you've had your sugar fix, let's get back to work. This is the third break you've taken in three hours." Mairead grabbed her friend's arm, tugging her toward the door. "Cheers, CeCe."

CeCe waved as the two women went out, leaving uneasiness that seemed somehow bigger than the room. She lifted her hand from Aunt Nikki's letter and glared at it. Finally, she folded it up. There were important things in it, things that beckoned behind the mystifying narrative, but first she needed to examine the enclosure. With hands that felt clumsy, not quite her own, she unfolded the creased square of newsprint and looked at it.

St. Rhydian's looked back. Drawn in crayon with the earnest clumsiness of a child, but completely, frighteningly, recognizable.

The box in her mind was so secret she didn't even know it existed until the drawing dragged it out, like a trunk someone had discovered in an attic. *"Oh, look! Wonder what's in this?"*

It hadn't been visible a decade ago, a year, last week, but now, suddenly, CeCe saw the box in three dimensions. It was square, deep, locked tight for twenty years. Now, bursting open with a snap and a clang, the box was breached, its contents flying up and out. Images, sounds…

She was six. She sat at a school desk, a crayon in her hand, a sheet of paper waiting. She began to draw. It was so delicious to make every line. In her head, CeCe and the lines were talking. No. They were *singing*. Singing together as they became walls and ramparts, became the castle, became the song. Stone on stone, word on word. If she tried, she could remember…

Hey, ho, nobody home
Meat nor drink nor money have we none
Yet we will be merry-o
Hey, ho, hey.

But somebody *was* home. At home in the castle that appeared under her hand. A man. She never drew him, but she always knew he was there. Striding the halls with his long legs, saddling a black horse in the stable yard, staring into the fire with a book in his hand, looking toward the sea from a west-facing window in the tower. The only window in the only tower in the only castle CeCe ever drew.

She blinked and the vision vanished. In its place, the reality of the break room arranged itself like a Surrealist painting. The table, a woman sitting at it, a piece of paper in her hands, the image of a castle on the paper, a torn envelope to one side. *Still Life with Madness.*

Her cell phone pinged and CeCe jerked violently. She dug it out of her shoulder bag, swiping the screen. There was a text, a long MMS, from Aunts Diane and Sophie. Dread formed a cold ball in her stomach.

Bonjour, CeCe,

Though maybe it's not morning for you. We're not actually sure what time it is where you are. Sophie says it's late afternoon.

It's a hot morning here. We hope this text makes sense, though it may not.

Our cousin, Andy, and your Aunt Hélène—they never got along. So, when Andy did the family genealogy, he wouldn't share. Sophie and I never had a problem with Andy (though I think he's still mad that I wouldn't marry him), so we asked him for his notes and he mailed them to us. Here's what you need to know and probably should have known for years. We're of French extraction, just like we told you all along. But we're also related by blood to Isobel Gowdie, the Scottish witch. The blood runs through her sons. After she ran away from the witch trials in Auldearn, Scotland, in 1662, she disappeared. Or so most people thought. But she actually came to America, to the Colony of Georgia. She had several children (no one is sure if her Scottish husband died or she just took up with a second one). Where she went after that, nobody could say. Isobel's family were known to be soulers, but we're not entirely sure what those are. We don't know any more, honey, only the connection and that word. It may be important or just one of those family stories. Sophie and I think you should have known sooner and we would have told you, except Hélène didn't want us to say anything after the way we lost Gabrielle. I think she felt there had just been too much upset, not to mention the witch connection and all. Please take good care of yourself. We pray for you every day and hope we can all be together soon. Don't worry.

Love from your Aunts Diane and Sophie

Were all her aunts insane, or just the three she'd heard from today? *Known to be soulers. The witch connection. Don't worry.* How could she not worry, after two messages that flipped her world upside down and inside out? What did Diane and Sophie mean? *The way we lost Gabrielle.* Her mother went off a bridge. She drowned in the St. Mary's River near Moniac when CeCe was five, her body never found. That was what happened.

Wasn't it?

How had her life gotten here? Just weeks ago, there were a few ripples of aggravation rocking a castle-shaped boat. Now, a tidal wave of secrets threatened to capsize her, the Castle, and everything she thought she knew about her life. Not just secrets. *Lies.* Lies of omission, maybe, but her aunts had omitted them for more than twenty years.

What would her aunts think about her own enormous lie of omission? The one called Sean Patrick Ó Loinsigh.

Okay, be calm, be objective. She closed her eyes and took several deep, slow breaths, willing her pulse to slow. *In on five, hold for five. Out on five, hold for five.*

She opened her eyes. She was a trained researcher; she could handle this. There was nothing she could do about Patrick, but she could address the steaming mess her aunts just dropped in her lap.

What data did she have? Not a lot. The text from two aunts. A letter from a third. A drawing by her six-year-old self. A song that she didn't know she knew, but had apparently been stuck in her head since preschool. Isobel Gowdie, Scotland, and soulers.

CeCe cleared her phone and went to the Transport for Wales website. She needed a train ticket for early tomorrow morning.

Twenty-One

CeCe was in the Sydney Jones Library at the University of Liverpool, where her ID from UGA got her visiting scholar privileges. She'd been at a long worktable for two and a half hours, long enough to finish three coffees and get thoroughly disoriented and alarmed.

Long enough to pick up a study buddy, too. She noticed him first because, even though he was the only other person at the table, he kept edging closer. Now, he sat directly opposite. Second, he kept staring and wasn't very good at pretending to contemplate the wall behind her with scholarly abstraction. Finally, he cleared his throat and asked her what she was working on.

Not so bluntly, of course. After the edging and staring and throat clearing, he ran a hand through thick sandy hair and blinked his large hazel eyes a few times. "I see you're reading *Britain's Ritual Beginnings*."

Nice voice. Educated, upper class-ish. To say CeCe was reading, however, was optimistic. She'd grabbed a copy of the book off the shelves because it, along with most of the others she'd dumped on the table, was on the References page of what she *was* reading: "Redeeming the Dead," an article in *The Journal of the Royal Anthropological Institute.*

When she didn't respond immediately to his pitch, her new buddy added, "Are you a post-grad?"

CeCe recognized a flung academic gauntlet when she heard one hit the floor. She snatched off her computer glasses and stuck out her hand. "Celeste Gowdie. M.A., Cultural History. University of Georgia, U.S.A."

The man across from her stared at her hand for a couple of seconds, then took it. His palm was a bit clammy, but his grip was firm.

"Duncan Ross. Winding up my doctorate in Anthro."

CeCe could hardly believe her luck. A doctoral candidate in the exact field she needed. Like digging aimlessly for buried treasure and being approached by someone with a metal detector.

"I only mentioned the Whitmore book," Duncan went on, "because it's really dated. And not entirely reliable. You might be derailed by some of the mistakes in it. May I ask what you're researching?"

In response, CeCe turned her laptop around so Duncan could see the image filling the screen. She'd seen all she wanted to of it, and she wouldn't be likely to forget it when it was no longer in front of her.

It was a grainy black and white photograph of three people. According to the caption, the photo was taken in Wales before the First World War. The caption didn't say and she couldn't guess if the people were men or women, because they were all wearing grotesque costumes. Two of them had oversized masks, the kind that covered the whole head. They looked like giant, rotting potatoes with mouth and eye holes. The third wore an equine costume, a scary one. A painted shroud covered the wearer's body to the ankles. Atop it was a mask, one that appeared to be made from a genuine, defleshed horse's skull.

The author of the article bearing the photo had more accolades after her name than even Dr. Grisham-Chu. She was Felicity R. Throckmorton, D.Phil. Anthropology, Fellow of Magdalen College, Oxford. Distinguished Professor in British History. Rhodes Scholarship, Bodley Medal, British Academy Medal. Author of *Britain's Solar Rites Before 1600*, *Harvest Customs of Britain's North Counties*, and *Folklore and Magic in the Isles*. Chair of this, Dean of that, Emeritus of the other thing.

Duncan had fewer merit badges on his sash, but he apparently knew his stuff.

"Yes, of course." He turned the laptop back toward her. "Throckmorton on souling." He waved a hand at the empty chair at CeCe's right. "Do you mind?"

She didn't, so Duncan stood—he was a stretch, CeCe realized, as tall as Patrick—and came around the table. When he folded his lean body into the chair, she caught his scent, a comfortable blend of soap and Caswell-Massey aftershave. It went well with his button-down shirt and corduroy trousers. CeCe slid the laptop over so they could both view the screen.

"It started in Scotland, or so we believe," Duncan began, idly scrolling through the article, but not slowing to read it. "Without knowing more about its origins, it's impossible to determine the *terminus post quem*."

Time after which. Anthropology jargon for the earliest date of something. CeCe was going to have to stay on her toes with her newfound colleague.

"It definitely had spread throughout the British Isles by the sixteenth century. Most people performed the rite on All Souls' Day, but it could happen anytime from just before Samhain—that's Allhallowtide, what we now call Halloween —to November second."

Halloween. Of course, it would have to join the party.

"Over time," Duncan continued, "it got pushed by the Church farther and farther from its heathen roots. Closer and closer to Christianity. Still on the move, actually."

"How is it you know so much about souling, Duncan?"

"It's just one of the rabbit holes I went down when I was researching something else."

"Which was?"

Duncan smirked, glancing dramatically around the huge room. He lowered his voice to a whisper. "Morris Dancing. But if you repeat that to anyone, I'll deny it with the fervor of an accused witch. Besides, I've a family connection of sorts."

"With soulers, Morris Dancing, or witch hunts?"

He laughed loud enough to raise glances from some nearby researchers. "Just soulers, thankfully. I've a very proper Scots granny." His expression turned wry, like someone admitting there was a cattle rustler in the family. "Gran refuses to have anything to do with it. Work of the devil and all that. But she admitted her parents and grandparents observed it. In fact, her father played *that*." Duncan put his index and third fingers, nails slightly chewed the way overworked academics often chewed them, on the horse-headed figure in the photograph. The laptop screen wobbled. "The Mari Lwyd."

It sounded like *Mahree Loyd*. "Is that Scots Gaelic?"

Duncan shook his head, adopting a broad Highland burr. "Nay, lassie. 'Tis Welsh, but we dinna remember what t'was called in Scotland before the hell-spawn English came. Anyway, it's a figure that appears in a number of folk rituals, but it turns up most in souling."

CeCe put her readers back on. To gain time, she pretended to study the photograph. She didn't want to know more, but she needed to. "The Mari Lwyd, what does it do?"

"By itself? Very little. A lot. Different things, depending on the region. In souling, it's part of a parade of sorts. Small groups of people in costume go from house to house, begging for food and drink. Money, even. They can be quite assertive."

"In the States, we call that a shakedown."

Duncan laughed again. "It'd be exactly that, if the take was for the people demanding it. But it's not. Or at least, they say it's not. It's a price set in the afterworld, you see. A ransom for the rescue of souls who are trapped between here and hereafter."

Here and hereafter. Patrick had said that. "As in dead, but not dead? Like vampires?"

"More like ghosts."

CeCe's brain braked to a standstill. Her heart sped up, then thumped so fiercely she was sure, if Duncan looked at her wool pullover, he would see it jumping. He didn't seem to notice, just scrolled back to the start of the article and kept talking.

"To me, the whole thing smacks even now of pre-Christian ritual. At some early point, virginal young women were sent to an isolated spot with the goods from the soulers' rounds. The souls came and collected them."

CeCe found her voice. *A* voice, one that skittered upward like she'd sat on a tack. "The *women*? The souls collected the *women*?"

Duncan shrugged. "The women, the goods. I can't say which. That part's not done any more, anyway, and hasn't been for generations. Strange bit of business, though, isn't it?" He turned to look at her, grinning.

Think it's funny, don't you, Mr. Caswell-Massey? Just a quaint sampling of cultural anthropology, a fieldwork transcription, a bucket of pottery shards. She took a deep breath. What else would it be to Duncan? What else would it have been to her, before Patrick? She let out her breath with her next words. "So, Duncan, let me recap this. If the, uh, ransom, that the soulers collect is sufficient, then the souls are released from their limbo between worlds."

"They are."

"Because people believe in them."

"Because people believe the souls deserve a second chance at life everlasting. Or maybe just life. Any road, they're released. Rescued. Restored."

That part, she understood. Soulers paid to bring back the dead.

Duncan bent conspiratorially toward her. His face had the smug expression academics got when they were about to impress someone. "Here's something I actually remember from my gran, when she wasn't denying that souling existed at all. She said the end of a visit by soulers is always the same. A man lies still as death on the floor and a rhyme is sung over the body." He put on his Scottish voice again and chanted. "*Tak a bit o' my nick nack, get ye up an' walk, Jack.* Foolish, I know. But it has a fell sound, doesn't it? Eldritch, I guess, is the word."

Terrifying is the word. "Duncan, this is a *non sequitur*, but do you know anything about Isobel Gowdie?"

He didn't answer for a brief interval, just stared with a lifted eyebrow. *He probably thinks I'm dragging him into another silly folk magic byway.*

"I know that if, as your name suggests, you are related to her, then you've got witch royalty in your veins. Like being descended from William the Conqueror, only with a broom and a black cat."

Very funny. CeCe smiled but she couldn't quite manage a laugh.

Duncan wasn't laughing, either. He was leaning forward to look at the time display at the bottom of the laptop screen. He muttered under his breath. "Bloody hell." Then, louder, "Sorry! For my sins, I've been cursed to lecture on Indo-Aryan migration, and I've got just five minutes to get there." He unfolded his long frame from the chair and walked around to the other side of the table. As he picked up his briefcase, he smiled. "Say, Celeste Gowdie from Georgia in the U.S.A., may I buy you a pint later?"

Stand up, CeCe, readers off. She could at least be polite to this stranger. Whether from kindness or self-importance or the urge to hit on her, he had saved her hours of research.

"That's really nice, Duncan, but I'm seeing someone." *Sometimes I see him. Sometimes I don't. Sometimes he's there. Sometimes he's not.*

"My loss." Duncan chucked his chin at the laptop. "Good hunting." He gave her a little wave and strode off into the Library.

CeCe sat, pinching the bridge of her nose. No matter how *eldritch* it got, she couldn't back down from her research now. She'd just started. There had to be more to souling than what Duncan told her. *Let's put that another way. There has to be more* sense *to it than that.* Sense or nonsense, she had no choice. Somewhere, there would be proof that this souler business was *not* relevant to her life. She could find it. She was a good researcher, even though she didn't have as many letters after her name as ThrockOxford, or even Duncan Ross.

Before she forgot about him, she had a stray thought. Why couldn't she have a man like Duncan in her life? Pleasant, helpful, moderately hot, uncomplicated.

Alive.

CeCe put her readers back on and plunged into the online catalog. She hadn't even begun researching Isobel Gowdie.

———

Six hours, another coffee, eleven journals, a dissertation, and two theses later, a lot of what she'd read was as muddy as the coffee, but CeCe understood why she'd never heard of souling before. The practice was like a suburban housewife who worshiped Satan on Saturday night but covered it up with bake sales and yoga classes during the week. Souling had hidden in plain sight, camouflaged for centuries, lurking just behind harmless customs that seemed on the surface to be similar. Mummers, molly dancers, guisers, rhymers, goose-dancers, plough-jacks, tipteerers, galoshins, and *yes, Duncan,* Morris Dancers.

Souling. If she'd thought she would find a reason why she, CeCe, had no connection to it, her day in the stacks was a dead loss. These creatures, these *soulers*...they led her down roads and up alleys and round and round in circles, finally dumping her violently at the place she'd started.

Herself. Celeste Gowdie. A name that wasn't a name—she'd conceded that, too. It was a trapdoor, a portal, an infernal time-hopping machine. It shot her hundreds of years into a past she hadn't even known existed a few days ago, but that was suddenly, horribly, hers. She hadn't pulled any levers or punched any buttons, but she'd landed among people who wore bony horse heads and believed one could buy back the dead, like used textbooks. A time, the seventeenth century, and a place, Scotland.

Where grim-faced Inquisitors asked her ancestor, Isobel Gowdie, *"Have you conversed with the souls of the dead?"* To which, she answered, *"They have gone in the Devil's name, they have come back in the Lord's name."*

Was that why Isobel Gowdie escaped death at the Inquisitors' hands? Because she wasn't only a witch, but a souler, too? Did the fate of certain souls, souls known and loved by some of the Inquisitors, hang in the balance of Isobel's gift? The gift she might have passed to her descendants?

CeCe stretched in her spine-crimping chair at the table. She hadn't looked away from her work in hours, and her head pounded like the bass beat in a techno dance club. There hadn't been time for breakfast before her train, and she was sure she'd missed lunch. Not that she was hungry now. The four cups of coffee she'd drunk since she arrived in Liverpool felt like they were still in her stomach, soured and heavy, a sludge of anxiety and caffeine.

She yanked off her glasses, shut her eyes, and pressed her fingers to the lids. It didn't help. Behind them, images still burned. People in bizarre costumes. Masks out of nightmares, dark holes where the eyes should have been. Scottish housewives threatened with needles and hellfire. That grotesquerie was what her aunts wanted her to believe was her ancestry, her heritage?

It's a mistake. Some freakish coincidence. History was full of them. *Gowdie. It's just a name.* CeCe's name, her mother's and her aunts' name, the name of the kin she had in Savannah, in Moniac on the St. Mary's. All perfectly normal people. None of this mytho-magico-mumbo jumbo was connected to any of them. *Can't be. Impossible. Please let it be impossible.*

But if it was, her ghost lover was impossible, too.

CeCe sighed and opened her eyes, looking around the vast, bright room. This university library was like every one she'd ever been in. It was quietly busy with serious scholarship, the pursuit of learning, *gravitas.* It was what grounded her. Her world, the world of dates and events and places and persons.

Bonfire of the Vanities, Savonarola, 1497.
Coronation, Elizabeth the First, 1559.
Witch Trial, Isobel Gowdie, 1662.

Why, oh why, did everything keep coming back to the witches?

TWENTY-TWO

When she'd walked out of The Broom & Bottle the last time, CeCe was pretty sure she never wanted to darken its door again. But here she was, after eight hours and less shut-eye than she'd have gotten on an overnight transatlantic flight.

Not a lot had changed at the shop since her last visit. The door still made a noise like a dropped silver tea service when she pushed it open. No Name Cat was in the Victorian cage. He meowed and turned a deep pink. It was a marker of how offroad CeCe's life had gone that a begonia-colored cat didn't seem all that strange.

Jana stood in the middle of the shop, stacking books on the table where she'd read CeCe's fortune. The witch looked up when the door clamored. She was wearing black toreador pants with matching stiletto heels, and a long-sleeved turtle-neck. A half-dozen black knitting needles stuck out of her blue-platinum beehive, like porcupine quills. Her lipstick was a savage crimson. She looked like a Fifties beatnik whose motto was Make War, Not Love.

Another witch stood next to her. At least, CeCe thought

she was a witch. If not, she was about the witchiest looking non-witch CeCe had ever seen. She wasn't an inch over four feet eleven, and her hair was in a single, very long, iron-gray braid. The hair and the wrinkles around her bluish gray eyes suggested she was seventy, but her expression had the innocence of seven. Her dress was an explosion in a scarf drawer, a flowing, multi-layered chiffon tunic in a riot of colors and patterns, brushing her ankles at the hem, with fluttering sleeves to her fingertips.

Jana introduced the second witch as Selene. CeCe got Selene's full, slate-colored gaze. The gaze said it would take no effort at all for Selene to walk into and around CeCe's mind. That was apparently true.

"Just in time, granddaughter." Selene's voice was whispery and faint, as though any second tiny moths would flutter out of her mouth. She took CeCe's hand, stroking it gently.

Jana spoke bluntly, as she usually did. "Here you are again."

"It's not like I want to be here," CeCe grumbled.

"What makes you think the universe cares what you want?"

Finally, something she and her magical life coach agreed on.

Even after all she'd been through with Patrick, the messages from her aunts, and her best stab at research, she still wasn't sure she believed in magic. She said as much to Selene, who'd kept hold of CeCe's hand and was examining it carefully, one finger at a time.

The older witch's mouth turned up in a smile that on a young woman would be called coy. She lifted chalcedony eyes, direct and glowing like those of No Name Cat. "Some choose magic," she told CeCe, "and some are chosen by it. Some *are* magic. For them, there is no choice."

Everyone's entitled to an opinion. CeCe gently disengaged

her hand and reached into her shoulder bag. She'd brought Nikki's letter and handed it to Jana, who held it at waist level so the smaller witch could read it, too. Jana had a pair of cat eye readers parked in the neck of her sweater, and put them on. Selene had a small magnifying glass on a chain around her neck. She held it over the pages. Jana turned each one when Selene nodded.

CeCe gave them a few minutes to get to the last page, then took out her cell phone and held it so they could see the MMS from Diane and Sophie. Jana read the text aloud to Selene, who closed her eyes to listen.

"There are some images in the phone." CeCe took back Nikki's letter and handed her phone to Jana, who swiped through the images as she held the phone out for Selene. The witches took their time looking at the old photographs of soulers that CeCe had lifted from books and her laptop screen in the Sydney Jones Library. CeCe looked away. Seeing the images once was enough. When Jana handed back her phone, CeCe shoved it and Nikki's letter quickly into her shoulder bag.

The Knight of Pentacles card was also in her bag. She extracted it and held it out to the two witches. It surprised her, how hard it was to let it go. At first, it had seemed like a piece from a board game. *Do Not Pass Go. Advance to Boardwalk.* Now, she felt attached to it, possessive. When Jana took the card, CeCe almost snatched it back. She forced down the urge and spoke to both witches. "Is all this stuff connected?"

Selene didn't answer. Jana spoke obliquely. "Intention is the heart of all ritual, and all ritual is a journey. Since you've arrived, you might want to consider what you were thinking when you set out. Or did you intend to arrive arse over teakettle? Because that's where you are, daughter."

"Excuse me, are you blaming *me* for this?"

Jana went on as though CeCe hadn't spoken. "It's probable that what you have here," she tapped the Knight of Pentacles with a scarlet fingernail, "is a leathling."

It sounded like *lathe*-ling. Selene, who let Jana hold the card and didn't seem to want to touch it, explained in her mothwing voice. "It comes from the Irish word, *leath*, meaning 'half.' A leathling is a soul neither truly dead nor truly alive, trapped between one condition and the other."

"How, exactly, does that happen? I mean, why would a person end up in..." CeCe waved her hand. She would not name the long gray.

Jana answered, "As my gran put it, 'Some there are that's too bad for heaven, but too good for hell.'"

Wonderful. Another wise granny. Was she Scottish, too?

"Did you bed him?"

Whoa, Nellie. Selene's question took CeCe completely by surprise. She went mute for a few seconds, then changed the subject. "My name, Gowdie. My aunts think it has something to do with the souler thing. Do you know anything about that? Or a song? Apparently, I used to sing it when I was a child, and I don't think my aunts taught it to me. I only remembered it after I read what they wrote. Something about hey ho, and money, and nobody home." The look on the witches' faces drained any more words from her.

Jana spoke to Selene. "We'll have to bring in the others."

The older witch nodded gravely. "Oh, yes, most certainly. All will need to be present to discuss this."

To CeCe, Jana said, "Morgana's in Glastonbury for a conference, so it won't be for a few days, a week perhaps. I'll get a note to you when we have the date and time, so you can—"

CeCe threw up her hands. "All right, wait a minute! You're holding a, what, tribunal or something? You still haven't explained what any of this has to do with me." A finger of fear touched CeCe's spine. "Are you saying I'm a *witch*?"

"Witchcraft can be learned, daughter. What you are comes in the blood."

The finger on CeCe's spine turned into a claw. She recoiled from it. "Listen, you two. Until I came here, to Wales, to this place, I never ran into *any* of this stuff. Until I came here, my life was perfectly normal and—"

She halted mid sentence. Her life *was* normal, wasn't it? The lid of the box in her head rattled. She sat on it, hard. Dark things forced their way out, anyway. Crawled around her brain, tongues flicking like lizards. A child drawing the same thing over and over, a mother taking secrets to her death, the neighbors talking, Isobel Gowdie, who created whirlwinds and soured milk. *Have you conversed with the souls of the dead?*

She rallied. "You know, this is ridiculous. My childhood was just like everybody else's. There was no black magic in it, okay? Not a single cauldron, jinx candle, or rooster with its throat cut. I had American Girl dolls, not magical poppets. On Halloween, my crafty aunts Diane and Sofie made me a princess or a ballerina costume, and I went trick-or-treating like all the other kids. I'm totally certain that if I'd dressed up like a dead horse, or a potato man, I'd remember."

"You didn't remember the song, though, did you?" It came from Jana, and the razor wire look in her eyes stopped CeCe cold.

Selene was at her elbow, jogging it lightly. "Did you bed him?"

CeCe snatched the Tarot card back from Jana. She spoke as she turned toward the door. "We're done here."

TWENTY-THREE

After her visit to the Broom & Bottle, CeCe's brain turned into a superhighway of contradictions at rush hour. She could stay on the road, barreling toward a head-on collision, or...

Denial 5.1. Her heart gave her one set of facts. Her rational mind gave her another. So, she simply stuck her fingers in her ears and hummed her rational mind away.

Wednesday night, the night when she came alive in Patrick's arms. They were in a second-floor salon, the Blue Drawing Room. It got its name from the watered silk wall coverings that must have been enchanting when they were new in 1840. Now, the walls had faded to a pale blue. *Marian,* CeCe had heard the color called, as it supposedly resembled the Virgin Mary's cloak. The saintly connection made her giggle. She was sitting on a tasseled Victorian hassock at Patrick's feet, her eyes traveling up his body as she thought about kissing her way to his groin.

Her giggle faded when her gaze reached Patrick's face. He was acting oddly. His kiss when he met her at the door of the room was scorching, as usual. But then, he'd abruptly released her and retreated to the fireplace, resting his forearm on the mantel. There was a pewter tankard and pitcher there. Apart from a long quaff from the tankard—beer, she could smell it from her hassock and wondered where he'd gotten it—he'd barely moved a muscle in five minutes. A figure silent and grave as granite, the familiar quirk of his mouth gone, replaced by a grim hyphen.

He'd shown shades and tints of mood before. Even in his brightest moments, there was something beneath, a toxic stream CeCe could almost hear flowing in his veins. Acheron, the river of sorrows.

Tonight, his mood was different, darker. She rose and went to his side. "What's going on, Patrick? What's wrong?"

He stroked her cheek, his touch featherlight. "Sit." His voice was granite, too. Not a block, but fragments, jagged pebbles, sharp under the Irish lilt.

CeCe lowered herself to the hassock again. "Sitting." She tried for a laugh. "Little Miss Muffet sat on her tuffet..."

"It's about John Knox, the rhyme."

"Knox? The religious fanatic?"

Patrick nodded, once. "The spider. He named Queen Mary as a witch, the tuffet being her throne. His demand was that she and all accused witches be tortured until they recanted—or died. All on the strength of hearsay."

CeCe squirmed. Knox probably wouldn't look kindly on Isobel Gowdie's descendant, however far removed in time. Somehow, though, she didn't think Patrick's mood had anything to do with sixteenth-century theologians.

She reached out, touching his knee to get his attention. "Is something bothering you?" He didn't answer, and alarm clutched at her. She shut her eyes, trying to feel its source. *There.* Under Patrick's skin. The dark river flowed over its banks. Water, cold and oily, immersing her as well as him. Her eyes fluttered open. "You want to tell me something, don't you?"

His laugh held more pain than humor. "Want to? No. Need to? Yes."

CeCe thought of the journal, his Bible of blood. "If it's something you've done, Patrick, something in the journal you gave me, it doesn't matter. I—"

"It matters to me, Celeste!" His shout rang out in the empty room. When he spoke again, his voice was softer, apologetic. "Of what I shall tell you tonight, not one word appears in what you call the journal. The sins of others—to write of those took no effort at all. But to tell you of my own..." His voice trailed away, then strengthened. "It matters not just to me, but to both of us. It matters that you know what manner of man stands before you. It matters that you know what his hands, so bold to touch your flawless skin, have done."

CeCe's anger rose, pushing tears into her eyes. "Please don't make this about me! I haven't asked what you did to end up here, have I? I've taken you just as you are. I've taken you as a *ghost*, Patrick."

"You have, *mo chroí*. But before I was a ghost, I was a living man. I must tell you of that, for it gnaws at me day and night. I bid you to listen now. If what I say..." He took a step away from the fireplace, ran his hands through his hair, then dropped them to his sides. "If you go from me, Celeste, it is no more than I deserve. But I will have you love me, if you love me, in the light of truth. There will be no lies between us."

I will have you love me. They'd never spoken of love, not really. Lust, affection, the joy of each other's company. Those were in the air every time they touched. Not love. Not until now.

She'd known for some time she loved him. Patrick. The ghost. The man. Whatever he was, she loved him. Only now, for the first time, she had to consider what it meant if he loved her back. Maybe, on some level, she'd supposed he couldn't. Or maybe she was the problem. Maybe she couldn't wrap the word itself around two people who lived—no. One person who lived, and one who hadn't lived since the last third of the eighteenth century.

'Til Death do you part. The marriage vow leaped unbidden into her mind, mocking them. Death had already parted them. Death had brought them together. CeCe spun out of control just thinking about it, but Patrick didn't give her time to stop the carousel.

"I don't know what you think it meant, when I was summoned by my father to this place, to St. Rhydian's. I didn't know myself. My life from the age of nine was spent in the Collège. The space within its walls and the city of Paris were all I knew, apart from my youngest years in Ireland. When my studies ended, I was given a month to travel there, to say farewell to my mother. Then, I crossed the Irish Sea again and landed here," his long arm stretched in the direction of the coast, "as battered and drenched as a body can be without being drowned entirely.

"The crossing was ill-omened. It was February, and a gale churned the waters into green foam and ice. A corbie, a raven, blew into the mast of the ship. It was like Calypso herself had slapped it out of the sky. The bird fell senseless on the deck, and the crew sent up wails and prayers to see it. None would touch it but myself, while the ship rolled and bucked with men's hands clinging to the rails instead of working the lines." He began to pace. Three strides one way, turn, three strides back.

"I took the raven and tossed it into the air with all my might. Lightning struck it as it hurtled upward. It gave a scream like a woman, flapped its wings, and hung above me, glowing and sparkling. Its eye was a black bead, and its mouth opened and shut, for all the world as though it spoke to me.

Whether it praised me for bringing it back or cursed me to Hell for snatching it from rest, I could not say. But the crew muttered and spat. They crossed themselves, looking slantwise at me with fear and hate in their eyes.

"The corbie flew back into the storm, but I knew I would see it again. As I did." Patrick took the tankard from the mantel and held it against his mouth, tilting back his head to drink deep. The tankard went back on the mantel with a heavy thud. CeCe wondered how long he'd been drinking before she arrived. His eyes had a glazed look, like a man unable to bear the burden of sober sight.

"T'was in the Year of Our Lord seventeen hundred and forty-nine, and I was eighteen. Eighteen years before that, my father left off being 'Dickie maneen,' my mother's pet name for him. He was dragged back to Wales to become the Earl of Trawsgoed and forced straightaway by his station in life to perform like a dancing bear. First, for the sake of an heir, he wed a high-born chit with the manners of a queen and the intellect of a teaspoon. There were two sons from the wife. They were but stripling youths when the Earl's wound laid him low. When there was a need to deal with the treachery and challenge that had always assailed Trawsgoed, the need was filled by the bastard half-Irish son. The son with a strong body and unquestioning obedience. The Earl, my father, was but forty-four when he died, his life cut short by Edwin Annesley, he who later became Marquess Burleigh. Annesley had so insulted the DeBlaes name when both were younger men that they dueled over the matter. The match was called when the two drew blood at nearly the same instant. Annesley's wound healed in good time, but the blade he drove into my father was tainted and its poison spread, slowly."

CeCe remembered the Earl's portrait in the Staircase Gallery. Now that she knew Patrick, she could see him in his sire. A broad-shouldered man, with jet hair and light eyes, a well-modeled face, with a proud nose and a strong chin. A commanding man, soon to be enfeebled.

"As duty broke my father, so it bloodied me. I became the sword my father no longer could raise, the arm of justice for those who plotted Trawsgoed's ruin. Not all fell by my hand, thank God and St. Brigid. Some fell in war, some in peace. Some at home, some abroad. Some were killed by cuckolded husbands or by jealous wives, as well they deserved, the fornicating scum. Some died when their cheating at cards or horse dealing was found out." Patrick raised the tankard again and took a long draught. He wiped his mouth against his sleeve. "Many, I killed. Edwin Annesley, whose filthy sword had been the ruin of my father—he was the first. Then, Riordan Fitzgerald. Next was Geoffrey Urquhart," Patrick touched the scar along his eye, "who gave me this. Simon Gordon Seymour, middle son of the Duke of Montrose. François Sans-Souvielle, Comte de Toulon—a spy, so I suppose that was patriotism, not murder, but it was my hand that made the garrote and twisted it round the traitorous fop's neck. Andrew Poole Barnett. Rudolf Heide-Ansbach. Bertrand Allsworthy. Philip...Philip..." Patrick laughed, low and mirthless. "'Tis a measure of my wickedness that I cannot remember all their names."

Tears welled in CeCe's eyes, and she clenched her fists so hard the nails dug into her palms. She reached for something irrelevant. "Did you—were they all killed here, in the Castle?"

Patrick shook his head, his unbound hair swaying. "Nay, there were many, as you now know, who perished within these walls by misadventure or design. But here—" His head fell back, and a terrible groan came from his throat. "Here, I've killed only one."

Only one *here*. A flickering filmstrip of deaths elsewhere played at lightning speed in CeCe's brain. Patrick armed with a sword, a pistol, a knife, a rope. In dark, in light, in a forest, on a hilltop, in a valley, on the sea. Striking, slashing, lunging, choking...

She jumped to her feet, pressing her hands against Patrick's heaving chest. "You didn't choose that life," she rasped, then had to cough before she could go on. "It was chosen for you. And we can't know where our actions will lead, ever."

"Aye, we cannot." He turned his head to stare into the fire. "And there are no second chances, more's the pity. But if there were..." Patrick grasped her shoulders so hard it hurt. His eyes burned into hers. "Ah, if there were, sweet Celeste, I'd not have obeyed my father's summons. I'd have stayed in green Eire, worked the land around my mother's cot. Or spent my life in Paris, the city I love. Above all, I'd never have come to this house and the sins awaiting me." He enfolded her, fiercely. CeCe felt his heart kicking against his ribs, a drumbeat of war and pain.

You'll recover, she wanted to say. *You'll forget*. But after nearly three hundred years, how likely was that? Now, his wounds were hers, and would never heal as long as his did not.

Finally, Patrick opened his arms and held her away from him. Their eyes locked. His were drowned bodies of grief in a deep sea. "I won't blame you if you think me a beast, now." He brushed hair away from her forehead, stroked her cheek. "I think myself one. A man with the blood on his hands that I have—by the Cross, that man has no right to put those hands on you."

"Patrick—"

"No more tonight, Celeste. Brief enough is the time we have together." He pressed her hands between his. "Pray with me, my love."

My love. He had spoken the words. Her heart spoke them back. *My love, my love*.

"*Deus meus*," he began, his voice thick with emotion, "*ex

toto corde paenitet me omnium meorum peccatorum." The Act of Contrition, the prayer of confession and remorse. CeCe fumbled the Latin, so Patrick changed to English. "And I detest all my sins because of Thy just punishments..."

The fire glowed and crackled beside them, the only sound besides their hushed words. Patrick prayed them through devotions CeCe had forgotten. She remembered them now from childhood. Her aunts, their nice dresses rustling and their colognes blooming like a garden, flanking her on a pew at Sacred Heart or St. John the Baptist. Their musical voices echoing the words of a priest from Atlanta, from Ireland, from Ghana.

Time went by, there was no tracking it. She and Patrick clung together, begging mercy for a soul. Half damned, half dead, all hers.

Twenty-Four

Four hours. That was all the sleep CeCe got by nine o'clock in the morning, when Eunice Lite phoned her to come into the PD's office at ten.

As she stumbled to the shower and then into her clothes, gulping a scalding cup of tea between the two, she tried to figure out why she was getting a summons from On High. She didn't think she'd done anything recently to get sacked. Not now, with *Ghosts of the Castle!* raking in bushels of cash. Maybe the PD had come up with another non-history gambit for her American historian. Staging a fashion show? Running a St. Rhydian's Casino?

She'd find out soon enough. CeCe stuffed the night before, and Patrick's agonized confession, into the box in her head with everything else. She drove to the Castle.

Eunice Lite came from behind her desk in the PD's outer office the second CeCe entered. The secretary wafted a hand toward the third person in the room, the one CeCe hadn't noticed—for good reason.

She was almost an optical illusion, a pale, slender woman on a white bench, blending into the cream wallpaper with her ash blonde hair, gray eyes, and a suit the shade euphemistically called champagne. Even the woman's Louboutin ballet flats looked bleached, like oyster shells left in the sun.

"This is Savin Bloom," Eunice Lite bit out, cheerlessly. "She'll be joining us here at the Castle. Ms. Tattersall would be obliged if you'd show her around."

The blonde woman stood and smiled thinly without parting her lips. She was wearing taupe lipstick that almost matched the suit, and her smile went nowhere near her eyes.

Bloom, huh? Freeze-dried lily, maybe. Despite not enough sleep and too much black tea, CeCe switched on her team-player grin and beamed it at the woman. "Absolutely! My pleasure." Then, to Eunice Lite, "The Castle proper? The Gardens? The staff areas?"

"Everything." The secretary went back to her desk.

Bloom and CeCe stared at each other, two cats with politely retracted claws. CeCe blinked first. "Right! Let's start at the top, shall we?"

She set off for the Grand Staircase, Bloom in tow. *Joining us here at the Castle.* What did that mean? Trustee, docent, secretary, ticket sales, third gardener specializing in hedges? Probably not a gardener. One look at Bloom's expertly manicured hands (pearl nail polish), and CeCe knew they'd never touched compost.

———

After an hour, CeCe was ready for the company of her noisy and nosy ghost walkers. She'd tried with all her might to make conversation with Savin Bloom but got only polite syllables in return. *Yes, no, perhaps, hmm.* Direct questions didn't get much out of her, either. She wasn't just colorless, she was impenetrable. A blonde brick.

CeCe gave up on repartee and stuck to the script. Since a

Castle and Grounds tour only lasted an hour and a half, she had plenty of free time after she returned Miss Congeniality to the PD's office. She wasn't wearing anything she cared about getting paint or plaster on. Why not offer a pair of hands to Alun? He was working away at the walls in the Hellenic Room, which at first gave her a shiver.

Get over it, CeCe. She stood in the doorway, taking it in. It was nothing like it was when she'd seen it with Patrick, when she'd been in a ghost trance, or an interdimensional time warp, or whatever. Now, it was a wet dog-smelling space draped in plastic sheeting and canvas drop cloths, booby-trapped with large cans of paint, open ladders, and troughs of gluey plaster. The only thing that was the same was the painted border of nude Greek athletes, waving their lances—both types—along the top of the walls.

Despite CeCe's insistence that she didn't care about her clothes, Alun looked skeptically at her jeans, knit Henley, and canvas oxfords.

"Your show," he shook his head. "But I'll only let you keep helping if you take something from my stipend. That way, you can buy some charity shop clothes to work in."

"Deal." CeCe grinned. "I don't have to be forced to shop with someone else's money."

Two hours later, she and Alun were elbow deep in plaster, joking and laughing at everything from politics to television archeology. The only time the chuckles faded was when CeCe asked about Alun's family.

"If you can believe it," he said, "my father is a rector. Holy Rood, a small Anglican church in an equally small parish in Denbighshire."

"And your mother?"

"We lost Mum six years ago."

CeCe froze, paintbrush in hand. "Oh, Alun, I'm so sorry."

He nodded. "Thanks. She had a very serious heart condition. We knew she could go any day."

Any day. Wasn't that what Miriam Lytton had said, inadvertently predicting her own death? CeCe missed the drily humorous scholar. *Go in peace, Miriam.*

The minute of sadness fled. CeCe went back to the messy, gratifying work. Contentment crept up on her, and she welcomed it. She'd take Alun's conservation chores anytime over her tourist-herding job. What was she at the Castle, after all? A cowpoke. An over-qualified sheepdog. When she and Alun knocked off for the day, she'd ask him to put her on the schedule for as many more work sessions as he could.

———

That tore it. The Welshman with the trowel was a dead man. It wasn't that Patrick blamed him for making an arse out of himself over Celeste. What man above or below ground wouldn't? But the fact she actually *liked* the plaster-slathering gob, smiling and jesting and encouraging him to talk about his family...

Which, of course he did, the gob. Bringing tears to Celeste's big, beautiful eyes, tender doe that she was. She'd weep for the Welshman's dead mother, and the gob knew it. He probably didn't even have a mother. An orphan, probably, raised in a workhouse. Apprenticed to learn the trade he was applying now to the Castle walls. Gobshite.

Celeste pitied him, that's all it was. What else could it be? The Welshman was a bit younger, to be sure, but Patrick was in his prime. The other had a decent build, and why wouldn't he, working man that he was? But Patrick could take him with one hand, no question. One hand and sitting down. Blindfolded. It was only that...

She'd make a fine mother, his amber-eyed beauty. Patrick

let himself see their children. Sturdy sons, black-haired like himself, waving wooden swords and shouting like berserkers. Fair daughters, masses of brandy hair lifting and blowing in the wind as they rode their ponies, whilst he—

Ah, but there was no *he* in it. No father to her children. No children for her. Not with him, anyway.

The Welshman would be only too pleased to put a babe in her belly. Three or four, as many as she wanted. And what pleasure he would have in the doing of it, pounding away at her night after night. The babes would all be ginger-haired, then, like him and her both, since she had red in her rich brown curls. Not a black-haired pup among them.

Patrick looked at his hand, made it into a fist. He could break something. He wanted to. It helped with the anger, sometimes. He'd done a lot of that in the beginning, the last part of the eighteenth century and half the nineteenth. He'd brought a smashing plague down on the Castle and everyone living in it. Nor had he always waited for nightfall. In the broad light of day, he'd hurled every pot from the kitchen into the scullery yard, more than once. Overturned beds. Chucked linens out of chests and cupboards. Slammed every door, tore one right off its hinges. Shattered more than a few window-panes. Curses and prayers had flown upward from dozens of mouths, servants ran screaming from the house, a priest was called in, Holy water was flung around like sea spray.

It hadn't changed anything then, and it wouldn't change anything now. The Welshman was alive and a hand's breadth from Patrick's woman. While Patrick was dead, still dead, always dead. Unless...

It wasn't a question of daring, nor of self-preservation. He didn't care to preserve his half-life for another hour. And daring was easy enough when care for oneself was absent. But *her*, his treasure, his love. He quailed at the thought of what must befall her if they stayed as they were. They could not.

They must either step off their narrow ledge and chance the fall into darkness or lose the fragile joy they borrowed from their own—from her—tomorrows.

Every day she aged, every day she slipped farther away, while he stayed the same. She did not see it yet, but she would. Patrick saw it already. The faintest thinning of her substance, the topmost layer of her being. The depth of a sigh, no more. No more than her natural displacement in time. No more than the future taking her away.

Her future. He had none. He could not move so much as an hour, he was fixed to the endless moment of the long gray. She must leave him, answering the tug of things to come. If she tried, if either of them tried, to stay that force, she would be torn in two, leaving not enough of herself to live in either her own tomorrow or his perpetual today.

All that would happen, unless he deciphered the *banfháidh*'s accursed rhyme, unless he discovered how to stop the engine of time that was drawing them apart.

Unless, unless, unless...

TWENTY-FIVE

CeCe wriggled in her stays, trying to get comfortable. For almost two hours she'd been dragged around the Castle by the photographer from *Wales Alive*. She planned to give him thirty more minutes, and then say she had an urgent appointment. An interview with the PM of Canada. Lunch with Camilla Parker Bowles.

"Almost done!" The photographer moved her a few feet so she wasn't blocking the Earl's portrait on the Grand Staircase. CeCe looked up and over her shoulder. The Earl's somber countenance radiated scorn. *"Makin' a circus of my house, are you, gel? And tumblin' my bastard, too! Daggletail! Lightskirt!"*

"One more!" the photographer ordered from behind his camera. "Try to look like a ghost."

Like a ghost? Clearly, this photographer didn't know what a ghost looked like any more than did the four other papers and magazines that had made her pose for photos to go along with articles on *Ghosts of the Castle!*

"Let's move to the kitchens, Miss Gowdie." Oh, right, the kitchens. The editors must have heard about the typhoid fever carrier found working in the kitchens in the 1920s. No one died, but the idea that a vengeful cook was still haunting the Aga gave her a nice bit in her ghost walk script. She was actually rather proud of it, since she'd ferreted it out from her own research and not Patrick's journal.

An hour later, *Wales Alive* had enough photos to illustrate a war, much less a two-page feature on St. Rhydian's. The photographer left CeCe in the kitchen, not even lingering to help her put the meat cleaver back on the wall rack. What a photo. Her standing on a low stool, cleaver raised overhead as though she could give someone typhoid by whacking them with a kitchen knife. Her academic standing would be a memory once that went into circulation. And as for Dr. Grisham-Chu—

"Celeste."

"Patrick!"

"Hush, *mo chroi*."

Where was he? She could hear but not see him. She started as his breath brushed her ear. "Go to the butler's pantry."

CeCe looked warily around the kitchen. It was sketchily furnished and not a favorite stop for day-touring groups, though cookery enthusiasts sometimes asked about it. In one corner, a door opened into a deep butler's pantry, empty except for some china salvaged from the Castle's glory years. She darted inside, pulling the door shut behind her. She'd barely turned from the door before Patrick had her in his arms.

Their kiss went on for minutes. Toe-curling, spine-melting minutes. When their mouths finally disengaged, they were both panting. The room was dim, but there was something inexpressibly wicked and wonderful about kissing Patrick in daylight, even just the thin bar that came in under the pantry door.

The naked hunger in his voice caressed her. "I couldn't wait."

"I can never—"

His fingers touched her lips. "Don't speak, poppet. I cannot be heard, but you can. It wouldn't do for someone to enter and find you talking to—" Patrick pointed to the shelves along one wall, "—a row of tureens."

CeCe suppressed a giggle. He kissed her again, and she turned into more liquid than a roomful of tureens could hold.

"Follow me," he said into her ear when his mouth was free.

Follow him? How was she supposed to do that? Follow a man no one but her could see? Up the stairs and down the hallways of a historic site where a few dozen tourists were strolling around? Not to mention the six docents and that many staffers trotting hither and yon.

Apparently, that was the plan. CeCe's skin crawled the whole way. Several docents and all the tourists shot startled looks at her eighteenth-century garb as she passed. A handful of tourists hastily grabbed their cell phones and took pictures of the costumed character. It was a miracle no one asked her to pose for a photo, but she moved fast, with purpose, ready with excuses. *Sorry, some other time, on my way to an execution.*

Execution? What on earth had made her think that?

———

"I was sure you didn't sleep on the floor, like a spaniel."

"No spaniels. Wolfhounds. My father kept two of them."

They were in his bedchamber, after Patrick led her along a confusing, twisted route. Up from the kitchens beneath the east wing, then across to the west wing and down again, into the Castle's heart. The walls CeCe saw every day changed to rough stone, lit at intervals by candle lanterns on iron hooks. Even the smells changed, from old house smells in the upper floors to beeswax and wood smoke in the lower ones.

She figured they were now in the oldest part of the Castle,

the bit that remained of the thirteenth century abbey. An iron-banded wood door at the end of a long narrow hall opened into a stone-flagged chamber roughly twenty feet square. There, the smells were different still. Peat in the hearth, parchment, ink, leather, tobacco. Patrick's own smell of lavender and man. CeCe would know it anywhere.

He walked to the center of the room, opening his arms wide. "Not very impressive as a gentleman's bedchamber goes."

"It's yours. That'll do." Like his scent, CeCe would always have identified the room as Patrick's. While he lit a fire in the small hearth, she made a slow circuit of the space, touching this, examining that. On one wall, a window, a thick-glazed double casement with a curved iron handle in the middle. Beneath, a broad oak table with barley twist legs and a plain wood stool to one side. A litter of writing things a gentleman in the eighteenth century would use every day were arranged on the table, so it must serve as Patrick's desk. A red pottery pen holder was stuffed with quills, some white, some barred, and horn pens with delicate brass nibs, stored upright. A packet of powdered ink, the flap open, a few dark grains spilled onto a stained dish. A stack of bound books, and atop them, a brass astrolabe on a stand. Sheets of thick paper, edges curling, held down by a carved wood weight in the shape of a winged griffin.

Patrick hadn't rated much furniture besides the table and stool. An armchair of leather and wood stood in front of the hearth, on a striped rug of coarse wool. CeCe went to the chair and ran her fingers across the plain armrests and well-worn back. *Here, he sits and reads a book.* Beside the chair was a small table. On it, a pale yellow candle had dripped wax onto a silver candle holder. A white clay pipe rested in a blue and white saucer. *He smokes his pipe here, watching the fire.*

There was a bed. It was against one wall, at right angles to the armchair, and covered neatly with wool blankets. A thick sheepskin lay on the floor next to it, and a squat, iron-bound trunk crouched at its foot. CeCe lifted the lid a few inches, and a strong smell of lavender escaped. Used in the past to protect clothing from pests, it was the scent she'd smelled on him.

The bed was clearly made for Patrick's long frame, but it was narrow, built with no expectation of a wife to share it. The bed of a warrior who might also be a monk. CeCe sat on it, absurdly happy it didn't squeak.

Patrick left the fire and came to her. He bent to kiss her, but she stopped him with a hand to his chest. There was no need to be coy, to beat around the bush about why they were where they were and what they were going to do. She'd waited long enough, they both had.

"I want to see you," she told him. "All of you."

He didn't deny or mock her command. CeCe looked at what he was wearing—the same as when she'd first seen him—and knew it would be the last time she'd have to imagine the body beneath it. The cuffs of his loose linen shirt were already unbuttoned, the sleeves rolled to his elbows. He grasped the hem of the shirt in both hands and pulled it over his head and off.

Her gaze shot instantly to a scar across his chest, just below his left nipple. Long, four inches at least, it was jagged and dull red, as though it had never properly healed.

Patrick caught her eyes and held them as he spoke. "My death wound."

Three words, said without emotion. Three words, and CeCe couldn't imagine three she wanted less to hear. Hot tears blurred her vision and her throat closed. Patrick's chest was as magnificent as the rest of the body she'd explored so far, but the brutal scar was all she could see. What had she expected? That a man like him would die in his sleep? A peaceful exit, exempt from the bloodshed that was his whole life?

"How did you—"

He sat beside her, the bed depressing with his weight. The heat of his naked torso against her drove answering warmth into CeCe's center. Taking her hand, he kissed the knuckles softly. "I killed my half-brother, John Herrick."

"The heir to the earldom."

Patrick nodded, looking down at her hand. He stretched out her fingers, stroking them, lingering on each nail with his callused thumb. "He violated my half-sister. She was eleven years of age."

CeCe stopped moving, stopped breathing.

"Her name was Margaret. Maggie. Sweet and innocent as a lark, she was. I found him on her. I cut off his head."

"Good."

The faintest quirk of his mouth acknowledged CeCe's comment. "My other brother, James Hugh, did not think so. I was a fugitive from the Castle and his wrath for many months. Then, he threatened my mother. So, I returned and took the blade that was waiting for me.

"That was the day the corbie returned. It flew to the top of the Tower, its black eye turned upon me. T'was the last sight of my eyes."

For CeCe, it wasn't the raven but the hideous rip in Patrick's chest that was the end of the story. She bent, bringing her lips to the scar. Rough under her mouth, it tasted of Patrick's skin and, faintly, of coppery blood, of salt. A memory surfaced, Aunt Nikki kissing CeCe's knee when she'd fallen as a child. She heard herself murmuring, as Nikki had done so long ago, "*All gone, now. All gone...*"

When CeCe finally pulled away, she and Patrick both caught their breath with shock.

The scar wasn't there. Erased, wiped out, the skin where it

had been was now smooth and unmarred. As they watched over several seconds, the wound slowly returned. CeCe ran her fingers over the ugly ridge of it. Something shattered in her heart, some last stubborn barrier to belief giving way. Grief and anger clouded her voice.

"I'll kiss it every day, Patrick. Every day and every night, a hundred times a day, a hundred times a night. Until it's gone and it stays gone. Until everything that gave it to you is gone, until everything you did, everything that was done to you, everything—"

He pulled her into his lap and stopped the flow of words with kisses. They sat silent, wrapped in each other, for a long while. Finally, CeCe asked, "Will I be with you when I die?"

A low chuckle escaped him. "Until recent weeks, you've hardly admitted you're here with me at all. Now, you want to know how we'll fare in the afterlife." He went serious again. "There's dead, Celeste, and there's dead and gone. Dead and gone is the better state, because then you know, so to speak, where you are."

"Except, you aren't."

"You're where you should be, where the natural order of things has put you. The last thing you want is to be something like me, neither dead nor alive."

"A leathling."

He pulled away a little, black eyebrows arching. "So, you've been talking to the witches, have you? Aye, that is something you don't want to be."

"Is it—catching? I mean, from our being together, will I..."

She'd hoped for denial. *Oh, no, my love, that's not possible, you are safe.* Instead, Patrick said nothing at all for a space. Then, "I cannot tell you how the thing goes, for I don't know, truly. But I know we are at—no, we *are* a doorway of sorts, where powerful magic happens."

"*Limen.*"

He nodded at the Latin word. "A threshold, yes. I'm an unnatural thing, Celeste, a creature neither of light nor dark. Fixed, immobile. While you are moving, carried away by the stream. That's all to the good, that's as it should be."

"No!" She gripped his arm. "I don't care about thresholds, I don't care about streams. I won't leave you, Patrick. Are you listening? No matter what happens, I won't leave. I don't care."

"You must care, my love. It is your life."

Her laugh was so harsh it hurt her throat. "My *life*?" Life without Patrick. Life as it had been before him. Pointless, lonely, driven, goals chosen by convention, or fear, or her own shallow sense of attainment.

And her future? What future? No dreams, no passion, just relentless, marching sameness, while she grew older and less hopeful year by year. The long gray, her own edition.

"Patrick," she breathed, cupping his jaw in her hands, "without you, I have no life. And every time I walk away, I don't have you. I'm already a leathling, aren't I? Alive when we're together, dead when we're not. Our pasts—they're blanks, no matter what we tell each other about them. I think we both believe we won't have a future. All we have is now. A now you tell me we're losing, hour by hour. So, in the now that we have left, all I want is to know you. Really know you, body and soul. Please, Patrick, please."

He turned his face away, his mouth set in resistance. "You are asking me to lead you into danger."

CeCe put her hand alongside his chin, turning his face gently toward her again. "I'm asking you to let me set my own course. It's my life. If I can't say where I want to take it, then I might as well not have it." She lay her head against his shoulder, sighing into the warmth of his skin, the strength of his chest. "No yesterday, no tomorrow. Let me have today. Let me have you."

He started to reply, but she captured his neck in her arms. Her lips pressed to his, and his response was immediate: mouth, tongue, hands, cock. Pulling his mouth away, he growled into her hair. "If you come to harm…"

CeCe laughed, eyes bright and dancing, lips curving in joy just for him. "Strip," she ordered, and they both laughed.

For the first time in months, she felt fearless. No more sticking in place, paralyzed by consequences. No more struggling like a pup, dragged by its collar. She would be, *they* would be, free.

TWENTY-SIX

Patrick stood by the bed. Slowly and deliberately, he removed the rest of his clothes, folding each garment and laying it on the trunk. When he was bare, he stood before CeCe without shame or shyness, arms relaxed at his sides, letting her look her fill.

My God, he's big. That was her thought the first time she saw him, in the Tower. But now, so close, and naked... He was carved like a statue, but with fair and lightly freckled skin in place of cold stone. He wasn't just big as some men were, big without definition, bulky and stolid. Patrick was defined by muscle from head to foot. Not protein-shake-gym-session muscle, but that of his era, created from hard training with blade and cudgel, long years on horseback and on foot in the hills and fields of Wales and the Continent. His shoulders swept wide, and his biceps and forearms spoke to exceptional strength. His chest was deep, and a rippled torso stretched to taut hips and powerful legs. As they had looked and felt in breeches, his thighs were mighty. Better. Carved and defined with the bunched thews a man got from horsemanship and sword fighting. Between them, his manhood was thick from the excitement of stripping before her.

That part was as big as the rest of him. Big and as ready as a man could be for what was coming next. CeCe felt a jolt of excitement shoot straight down her thighs. Suddenly shy, she flushed. She couldn't just sit there staring at him, at *it*. Lifting one hand, she twirled her index finger. Patrick understood and turned around.

She bit her lip to keep from saying something stupid about the beauty of his backside, but a helpless sound escaped from the back of her throat, anyway. She'd never seen a man like him. The sweep of his back, the mounds of his buttocks. He was like sculpture, like the pictures she'd seen of Hercules fighting the Laocoön or the Fountain of Neptune in Rome. Patrick's back would have been as smooth and unmarked as sculpture, too, were it not for a dozen scars. She wanted to kiss each one, know its history, mourn it. A thin dusting of dark gathered in a triangle at the base of his spine. She leaned forward and put her lips there, and his sudden stillness stopped her own movements. After a second, he turned, slowly, to face her. The fire in his eyes made her want to throw herself down at his feet and worship, as before a pagan god.

He reached back to the leather thong holding his hair, untied it, tossed it aside, and shook his head. Black waves fell over half his face.

"Now you," he said huskily, pulling her to her feet.

CeCe was sure Patrick knew, more or less, what was under her clothes. They hadn't caressed and fondled for so long without him learning her body by touch. But this, disrobing her in an almost formal fashion—it was maddening and delicious at once.

He took off her garments one by one, kissing each before he folded it and placed it atop his own on the trunk. Was it sacrilege to think of the priest kissing his stole as he put it over his neck in the Mass?

After he'd deftly untied her petticoats, it occurred to her to be jealous. Her ghost was clearly familiar with women's clothing, therefore women. But he was here, now, with her, giving her his full attention. Besides, any woman he'd disrobed before her was almost three hundred years in her grave.

Patrick removed all but her shift, then paused. He closed his eyes and slowly, lightly, ran his hands over her body—thighs, hips, belly, buttocks, flanks, shoulders. Nothing but thin muslin between his fingers and her flesh. CeCe had never felt anything like it. Her pulse raced. She was sure Patrick could feel the fluttering under his hands.

He paused at her breasts, held them for a minute. Uncertainty pushed blood into CeCe's face. He'd touched her breasts before, but never so completely. Did he truly like them? Were they too small, too big, not firm enough?

"Your breasts are perfect," he groaned, and her heart soared. He circled her nipples with his fingertips, coaxing and tugging until they sprang forward and pressed against the cloth.

CeCe whimpered as liquid response flooded her. "Oh God, yes, *yes...*"

Her reaction added to his cockstand, and the warm length of it pressed against her. She opened her eyes and stared down at it, then lifted her gaze to its owner, who smiled. CeCe was pretty sure she blinked a few times.

He put his fingers under her chin and tilted it up. "I will not hurt you." Bending to her lips, he took them tenderly, but with arousal that was barely leashed. CeCe could taste the musk of it in his mouth, feel it in the tautness of his body. When he pulled back, his eyes had gone dark, complex, the gentleness in them warring with savage instinct. For the moment, gentleness won. "Don't fear me, my love, never fear me. I will be slow, and you will be ready."

CeCe thought she might be ready now. Her sex was clenching and wet, swollen with need. She reached for Patrick's shaft, but he took her hand away and kissed the palm. "Not yet," he murmured. "Not there."

As he promised, he took his time. First, he lifted her shift and pulled it over her head, folding it carefully as he'd done the other garments, then pressing it to his lips before he placed it with the rest. The combat CeCe had sensed in his body raged in hers as well. A blind, desperate ache made her want to wrap her arms around his neck and her legs around his hips, bucking against him until they both screamed their release. But Patrick's slow undressing of her, the languorous way he handled her clothing, handled *her*...forever was too little time for that.

Patrick sat on the bed again, but when CeCe tried to straddle him, he held her away, moving her slightly so she stood a foot from him. He touched her again, never rushing, never giving in to the arousal that pulsed so visibly between his thighs, only stroking, examining, tasting. His mouth grazed the skin of her shoulders, her arms, her hands, her stomach and hips. Turning her, he did the same for her back, cupping her buttocks in his hands while he dragged his lips along the long cleft of her spine, kissing her from the dimple at its base to a place at the back of her neck that gave her an electric shiver when his tongue slid over it.

By the time he lowered her slowly to sit on his thighs, facing outward with her legs outside his, the trembling in CeCe's belly had spread to her whole body. Her bottom fit between his cock and his stomach. He surged against her cleft, but didn't try to enter her. Instead, he allowed her to fondle him, to rub herself against him, coating his length with the flood from her sex. Between kisses, his breath came warm and fast against the back of her neck. CeCe couldn't hold back another second. She fisted his member, thick and silky, and stroked it once, hard. He cursed, low and filthy, into her hair.

Thinking, reason, the whole outside world: everything fled except the breathless, quiet universe they were crafting from ritual and desire. She reached behind to stroke his shoulders, then down his arms to cover his hands with hers, making them partners in his slow, thorough taking of her. When he held her breasts, her fingers moved with his while he kneaded and pulled, tugging at her nipples until she nearly wept with need. He slid one hand between the angle of his cock and her body, his fingers parting her folds while she panted and begged.

"Please, please, Patrick, please..."

His mouth came down on the tender flesh of her neck, where it joined her shoulder. He licked her there, then used his teeth, just hard enough to make her gasp, at the same time his fingers circled and flicked the swollen bud at her core. CeCe did weep, then, tears of frantic love and want streaming into the words. "Patrick...I'm..."

The wave took her and she shattered, flying into a hundred pieces, each one winged with pleasure. Her legs shook so hard they wouldn't support her weight, but didn't need to, as Patrick rolled them both gently onto the bed. They lay spooned, on their sides, panting. Patrick's hand cupped her the whole time, rubbing gently as aftershocks made her twitch and moan.

Slow bits of CeCe's reason limped back. "We should—if we're going to—" *Come on, brain and mouth, get online again.* "Should we talk about pregnancy?"

He stilled behind her. After a few seconds, he went back to his slow petting, while her explanation floundered like a fish in the bottom of a rowboat. "I mean, there are things I can do. I suppose we should...it's not that I'm worried about STDs." *Because those are diseases of the living.* "But I don't have any idea whether—I mean, should we use a—" *Christ, try to be a historian, CeCe. What did they call condoms in the eighteenth century? Sheaths? French letters?*

Patrick spoke softly, his hand never ceasing its gentle caress. "I think I cannot get you with child."

"Oh." That was good, right? So, why did it not feel good? Why did it feel like another item tacked onto the list of things they couldn't do, couldn't have?

Patrick lay back on the bed, stretching out. Then, he pulled her atop him, her back to his front again, and positioned her so his formidable cock could penetrate her from underneath. Just barely. Even the crown filled her. Using one hand to squeeze and fondle her breasts, Patrick used the other to stroke her slit.

Despite her convulsion of pleasure just minutes before, readiness rushed to her sex, and CeCe nearly sobbed with it. Stretching up and behind, she combed her fingers through Patrick's hair. He turned his head to one side, then the other, placing a slow kiss on each of her wrists. All the while, he nudged by inches into her, while she helplessly shook and gasped.

Hoarse with arousal, his voice was hot and low in her ear. "Do you feel my cock against you, inside you? I'll take you now, for I can't hold back any longer."

He didn't need to. CeCe cried out as another spasm tore through her body. As she crested, Patrick used both hands on her hips to push her down onto his shaft, burying himself deep. He held her that way, while shuddering pulses made her arch and moan. Only then did he withdraw. Great arms flexing, he raised CeCe and shifted from beneath her. In a single second, she lay breathless on her back. He reared atop her.

It was the thing she had dreamed of, him above her, intent, inflamed. Patrick parted her thighs roughly, like a man who owned her. But then he slowed, entering her by smooth degrees, while she lifted her knees to ease his passage. When he was fully inside, they both held motionless, joined in the ancient way. He pulled back, thrust forward without haste, then waited for her to accept him. Again, and this time she felt herself shaping to him, taking and gripping him along his length and girth. He answered the change with a heavy groan and another slow thrust.

"More," CeCe whispered, sliding her hands down to grasp his powerful buttocks. "Give me more." His low laugh dissolved into a sharp intake of breath, as she constricted her sex around him. Once. Again. Set free by her response, he began to plough her, regular and strong. She lifted her hips to meet him. Both fragile under his charging body and wanton as a wildcat, she answered his every plunge with a rise of her own. One knee braced against the wall, she let her other leg slide off the side of the bed, touching her toes to the floor so she had leverage to push her pelvis up and against the man who took her.

Fully open, she still wanted more. He'd wanted her to say his name and she did, over and over, begging and then screaming for everything he could give her, everywhere he delved, remorselessly, into the secret places of her body. All that was inside her, all that she was...hers to give entirely, his to capture, to keep.

She felt her climax coming, a dizzying fall into a fathomless sea of surrender, the sea she'd sensed the first time they'd kissed. "Take me," she pleaded. "Take me, Patrick. Take me with you."

They spent together, sobbing into each other's mouths. Patrick's body shook atop and inside her, a gush of hot seed overflowing her cleft as CeCe arched and held against him.

Deep waters closed over them both.

———

Sound was the first of her senses to return. Patrick's breath above her, ragged and harsh. The tiny rustle of the blanket as her shoulders shifted. The low hiss of smoldering peat in the hearth. From the window, a muted rattle, as wind pushed against the panes.

Patrick's arms, bracketing her, still trembled. Carefully, he collapsed to one side, so as not to crush her. He lay his rough, large hand against her cheek, and CeCe felt the tremor in it. Stark truth, that tremor, of what three hundred years of longing did to a man.

And, God help them both, what longing might have done to the single soul they now shared.

———

Hours later, she woke. Patrick still slept, his face smoothed by the contentment she had wondered if she'd ever see.

Her own sleep had been troubled. She'd been dreaming, or at least she thought she had, and the dream followed into her waking mind. It was the same sweet and hopeless vision she'd had after the deer in the road incident, when she'd sat on Patrick's lap in the Regent's Bedchamber. The man by her side asked her to marry him, or she asked him. Perhaps, they just agreed to it, without needing to ask. It was the day of their wedding, and they were joining their hands and lives here, in a rite at the Castle. The docents, the witches, her aunts from America—all were witnessing, all laughing and applauding. There was music, drinking, dancing, all night long.

The vision changed, and instead of noisy nuptials, she and Patrick sneaked away to Ireland. They were marrying in an ancient chapel, then coming home to a stone cottage in Connemara. Years were passing, like pages flipping over in a calendar. CeCe saw children, dark-haired and smiling, healthy and loved. Perfect, as only dreams could be.

A high, faint chiming somewhere in the room woke her fully. Five bells. Dawn coming, dreams flying away, leaving something bitter in her mouth. She sat up and looked around for the clock. Found it, small and brass, on the oak table. "Is that the real time?"

Patrick still lay on his back, but his eyes were open. He stroked her spine with the back of his hand, sending sparks up and down her skin. "Do you mean, is it your time? Yes, I keep it that way."

She turned to smile at him, and he smiled back. Their first night in bed. Sleeping. Some sleeping, anyway. Patrick had suggested there would be a price to pay for it, but CeCe didn't care. Whatever the price, it was worth it. *And besides,* a small nervous voice inside her said, *you can't take it back now.*

She looked down at her body, glistening with the dried outcome of their coupling, then ran a hand through her hair and moaned. "I have to go, Patrick. I need a shower and clean clothes, and I told Alun I'd help with his wall coverings."

"The Welshman can wait." Patrick pulled her back into the bed. She forgot showers and clothes and wall coverings. There was something subtly new in their caresses. Sharp urgency was bone-deep certainty now. Why fantasize about impossible futures, good or bad? Here, in Patrick's arms, there was a gloriously real present.

Finally, with one last wistful caress of Patrick's stiff member, CeCe clambered out of the bed, ignoring her ghost's laughing grab at her ankle. She snatched her shift from the pile of clothes and pulled it over her head, then dug for her skirt and bodice. *Forget the stays, forget the stockings.* She'd make herself just decent enough to get to her car.

Patrick grumbled, rising, and retrieved his breeches. "I can't believe I'm competing for your time with a paperhanger." She gave him her raised eyebrows and he wisely changed tacks. "I'll take you back. I know a way where you won't be seen until you're nearly to that mechanical coach of yours."

"Wait, this room," She struggled into her bodice. "Does it still exist? In my—in the other world? Where is it?"

"Oh, aye. It still exists. It's Eunice Tattersall's office."

CeCe laughed, banishing the last tinge of her dream.

———

It was full daylight by the time she got back to her flat in the town. As she let herself in, she found an envelope shoved under the door. Hand-folded brown paper, smelling strongly of herbs.

Unfolded, it was a handwritten letter from Jana Smithbury-Tewkes. The writing was a little hard to read, but the message was clear. The witches were meeting on Friday, six o'clock, at The Broom & Bottle. *Your presence is required. JST.*

Hadn't the witches ever heard of Zoom? CeCe was frankly fine with ignoring Jana's directive. Who were these people, anyway? A gloom and doom chorus, warmed-over wisdom and unsolicited advice. She could've stayed in Savannah with her aunts if she'd wanted that.

Just before she obeyed the urge to wad up the herb-drenched paper and toss it, CeCe remembered what Patrick had told her, his eyes shadowed with worry. *"You must care, my love. It is your life."*

All right, she would go to the meeting. She would do it for him.

TWENTY-SEVEN

What had he and Celeste done? It wasn't a question, not really. *What they had done.* A statement, declarative, frightening.

Patrick ran his hands through his hair, still disordered from lovemaking. Returning to his bedchamber had dropped him straightaway into a hornets' nest of contradiction. The disheveled bed, speaking of incomparable pleasure. The empty room, warning of the void into which that pleasure might have propelled them.

They had done the thing he'd sworn not to do, the thing that might have pulled them right over the border between worlds, his and hers. She'd begged, she'd pleaded. Pleaded with eyes and words and hands. Soft, loving hands that would bring any man to his breaking point.

All true, but he couldn't blame their fall on anyone but himself. His fault, like all the rest. Another sin to heap upon those that already damned him. He'd vowed to protect her, he'd *sworn* it. And what had he done? Ravaged and rutted upon her like a mad beast, losing all control. Even now, the thought of her body, the wet, plump rose of her sex, the triumph of himself buried in her to the hilt—even now, if she were within reach, he'd take her again. Again and again and again, until they both lay dead of pleasure.

Except, you're already dead, Patrick, boyo. Dead before you took her. Is that what you want for the woman? That she join you in the long gray? That you both wander, hopeless, for as many years as it takes to hate the sight of each other? He ground his teeth with self-loathing, throwing himself into the chair before the now-cold fire.

She'd wanted to know about his death wound, and he'd told her the truth. Half of it, anyway. The half before his brother ordered the corpse rowed away from shore and dumped over the gunwales. He might still need to tell her that part, if she asked about his grave. But nothing could ever compel him to tell her the rest. The loathsome part in which his body had washed back to the beach the day after, and his brother, in a fury, ordered it cut into pieces and fed to the pigs.

All was seen by the old Earl's steward, Collum—*God grant him eternal peace!* Collum well knew what blots on the escutcheon both lawful sons were. He salvaged the corpse's bones, the only parts the pigs wouldn't eat. Stuffing them into a sack, he rowed westward a mile, then emptied the sack over the side. Perhaps, in the end, some bits of Patrick had gone on the tide to Ireland. It would be a fine thing, to go home.

But Celeste didn't need to know that particular truth. Not all truths, he'd found, stood up well to the light.

Light. The way Celeste looked with candlelight dancing across her ivory brow, painting gold in her hair. The love-drenched scent of her, the naked presence of her at his side. Perhaps, there'd been no harm. She'd seemed well when she awoke. Smiling with her pink, well-kissed lips. Eyes soft and drowsy with repletion. Her body was just as warm and smooth and full in the right places as when he'd first undressed her. Perhaps, for once, the red and punishing eye of fate had been looking the other way. In that hour of blindness, they'd had their joy, but if they were wise...

Wise? Where was the wisdom in any of it? Perhaps, there was a different wisdom, a defiant one, born of the certainty that Celeste was for him and he for her. He was stupid as a sheep for grasping at it, but for the hundredth time since he'd first seen her and she saw him, Patrick picked through the words of the *banfháidh*'s rhyme.

Over the black robes. That part was simple enough. The Castle, built on the ruins of an abbey where black-robed monks once worked and prayed. *Broken the dove, torn by the brother.* The innocence of Maggie, shattered by her demon brother, John Herrick. *To venge the other, under the tower painted red.* Himself, the other, waiting in the Forecourt at sunset, for the death he'd earned by striking the demon's head from his shoulders. *Lost to the salt sea, lost to air, lost to all but Heaven fair.* So he had been, cast into the sea, never to rise until Celeste brought him closer to the surface than he deserved.

'Til witch's gold be bound to wife, among the dead, un-live thy life. That was the part that confounded him. The most essential part, the key. He must divine its meaning. If he could not, then he would have only one recourse. To let Celeste go.

They could meet a while longer, share that, at least. They could have conversation, laughter, and embraces. He would be attentive to the hours in her presence, would store them all together and relive them in memory. For years. Forever. They would be all he'd have of her, of them. They would have to be enough.

Too restless to sit any longer, he pushed to his feet. He'd remembered a few more of the incidents Celeste craved for her ghostly excursions. He had some blank paper; he'd write them down. Crossing to his desk, he rummaged through his quills, couldn't find one that didn't require trimming, and scowled.

In a sudden blaze of frustration, he swept the lot of them onto the floor. He bent over the desk, hands flat on the old oak, head bowed.

Celeste would go on without him, as she should. Alive and vibrant, glowing with the life and future that were rightly hers. She would go to the arms and the bed of a husband—if not that fox-haired Welshman, then some other. Patrick would twist from the gibbet of despair when the other took the joy of her body and the years of her life.

It would be his right, though, the man's. He would be there to love and cosset her, to stand next to her in the day and lie next to her in the night. While Patrick would go on as he had before Celeste, before a single spark of hope lighted his black condition.

Still, the spark flickered in the old seer's prophecy, if he could only breathe it into flame. If not, what could he give her? Less than nothing. The dust from a grave. Nay, not even that. Salt water, sand, and the bottom of the sea.

TWENTY-EIGHT

Friday afternoon, six o'clock, The Broom & Bottle. The shop looked different, more open, less cluttered. The hanging herbs had been harvested, apparently, since CeCe could now see clear to the rafters. No Name Cat was installed in his cage, the door latched. CeCe said hello. No Name meowed and turned an impressive magenta.

She took a deep breath, ready to walk into something solemn and ritualistic. People in pseudo-Egyptian robes, blurred by clouds of incense. Or a business meeting. Power-Point slides on a screen, laptops clicking around a table.

Instead—except for the magical goods stacked everywhere—the gathering looked like a book club on *Pride and Prejudice* night. A handful of women milled around, chatting. The center of the shop had been cleared for a long folding table. It was dotted with water glasses and plates of cookies.

Jana saw her and waved her to the table. The witch was wearing retro satin lounge pajamas, black with orange piping. Her lipstick and nail polish matched the piping, and a large orange silk hibiscus wobbled in her beehive.

The shop owner reeled out introductions. Selene, she

already knew. The tiny woman had gone dress-up boho with a tiered, printed gauze skirt and a bell-sleeved voile blouse in parakeet green, set off with a dangling necklace of old buttons and brass bells. Her steel-gray hair was straight, loose, and fell to her knees.

Two witches CeCe took at first to be twins, but who turned out to be domestic partners, were named Rowan and Wren. They were slim, fit, and tanned like farmers, which it turned out they were. They wore jeans, with matching black tees emblazoned in red. *'We're the granddaughters of the witches you couldn't burn.'* Their identical short, spiky haircuts stood up like brushes, and when they hugged CeCe (doing it together, four arms enfolding her), they smelled of thyme and honey.

"Organic farm," Jana told her after Rowan and Wren said, "*Welcome!*" simultaneously and drifted off. "Basil and Bee. Herbs, bees, goats, hens. A fine place." She beckoned over a conservatively dressed (rust-colored twinset, pearls), woman in her fifties. "Here's Morgana." To CeCe, the woman looked more like a Cindy or a Sharon. Did witches have stage names?

Jana rested her hand on Morgana's shoulder. "This one's a genius with potions, oils, unguents, and elixirs."

"Goddess has blessed me," Morgana dipped her head with its neat cap of ash-blonde curls. She looked like one of the nice Savannah ladies who attended Sodality meetings at Sacred Heart. When Morgana raised her head, however, CeCe saw something rare, wise, and wild flash in the witch's brown eyes. "Potions run in my family," she told CeCe.

CeCe smiled politely. *Secrets run in mine.*

"Nothing beats your astrology oils, Morgana," Jana effused. The two began chatting about those, along with zodiac face creams and mood lotions. They beamed like they were talking about their grandchildren.

After a few minutes, Jana bustled off. Still beaming,

Morgana turned to CeCe. "Such beautiful skin." She scrutinized CeCe's face like an aesthetician. "Don't let me forget to give you a jar of Marigold Mud. It'll keep you looking twenty when you're sixty."

Sixty. CeCe couldn't think that far ahead. She was just hoping to get through the meeting.

"All right, sisters!" Jana trumpeted from the other side of the room. "Let's be seated."

The witches pulled the table away from the center of the room, replacing it with chairs. Halfway through the furniture moving, a chorus of cheery hellos went up, and CeCe goggled to see Poppy Norris enter the room. Poppy made the rounds, greeting and being greeted by the others. She ended her tour at CeCe's side.

"Hello, Miss Celeste," Poppy patted CeCe's cheek.

"Hel-*lo*, Poppy. I, uh, I never would have pegged you as, well, as—"

"A witch? Oh, that doesn't surprise me. Many people don't think you're a historian, either."

Touché and ouch.

Finally, the chairs were in place and the witches sat. Five chairs, each with a witch bottom in it, arranged in a half-circle facing the only non-witch. Poppy stood behind the seated witches. Maybe she didn't have her degree yet? Jana pointed to a single empty chair opposite the occupied ones. Nervously, CeCe took it.

The witches began by talking about, instead of to, her. First one witch at a time, very calmly, and then all at once. Just like the Savannah aunts did, when they got together to discuss something. A show of parliamentary procedure before disintegrating into all-out quarreling.

It didn't take long to see the six witches didn't agree about what she should do, or even if Patrick was a leathling. Rowan and Wren surprised her. She was sure they would agree with each other, but they didn't. Rowan thought her ghost was just a ghost, but Wren was sure he was a leathling. Morgana, whose strong suit seemed to be folk magic of the British Isles, gave a short lecture on souling. The others were riveted. CeCe had already learned most of it from her brain-bending day at the Sydney Jones Library. That made her a little smug. Not a witch, but not a total newbie, either.

The potions mistress ended with an emotional plea for everyone to remember that if souling died out, those spirits trapped between worlds would be trapped forever. CeCe fell straight out of smug into downright scared.

Even though she was the only one who actually had a dog in the fight, nobody in the room asked her for input. Not that she could add much to the conversation from her lofty perspective of having seen *The Ghost and Mrs. Muir* twice, plus *The Craft*, during which she was pretty sure she fell asleep. Still, she was the only one in the room who had their own ghost.

The witches droned on, and her attention wandered. She wished No Name Cat was free to socialize. She could use a friend, even a color-changing feline one.

Sudden silence jerked her attention back to the meeting. Selene's hand was raised, palm outward. A subtle gesture, but it stopped everything cold. All eyes were fixed on the older witch. Selene lowered her hand and addressed CeCe, her voice low and wispy as always, but as always asking the same question. "Did you bed him?"

A collective stare locked on CeCe. It stayed locked for the full ten seconds it took her to answer. "I don't believe that's any of your business."

All eyes swiveled back to Selene, like a witchy Wimbledon. Selene held out her water glass. Rowan jumped up for the pitcher, brought it back, and poured water into the glass.

Selene drank. Then, her voice, thin but clear, rose in an eerie song.

"Soul, soul, come will a soul
Only if the coin be whole
Then we will be merry-o
Hey, ho, hey."

It was the same tune from CeCe's childhood, but with different words. The cold that had coursed through her when she first remembered it came back, spreading like frost under her skin. She struggled to speak. "I—I only remember the other part, the first part, I guess."

Why was everyone so quiet? Why were they all looking at her?

Selene explained, carefully, as to the child CeCe had been so long ago. The child who sang and drew castles. The child to whom all this should have been explained, but wasn't.

"You are the coin, granddaughter. For your leathling to exchange his half-life for a whole one, the tribute must be all of a piece. Blood alone can work the magic."

She heard Aunt Sophie's voice, speaking through her text. *"...we're all also related by blood to Isobel Gowdie."* Not just any blood, then. Isobel Gowdie's. And now hers. It hadn't really hit her when she got the MMS. How could it? She hadn't even known who Isobel Gowdie was, when she was hiding in the staff break room while messages from her aunts turned reality upside down.

Selene's blue-gray eyes hadn't left her for an instant. They sharpened, glittered. She seemed to grow larger and younger, a strong young sibyl, a seer, unlocking CeCe as she'd done when they first met. CeCe felt the witch enter her mind, without permission and without CeCe being able to stop her. Selene moved around its furnishings as though they were no more than chairs and tables in a room.

"Yes," Selene breathed out as she returned to herself, a tiny old witch in a room full of them. "You are the coin of the song, child. But you have joined with your ghost in full measure, hearts and bodies unrestrained, and now you must answer to the laws of his world. Your earthly self, the only tribute you have to offer, will begin to fly away, bit by bit, like wisps of smoke."

Morgana's voice shrilled in distress. "Oh dear, oh dear! This is what comes of forgetting the Old Way!"

CeCe was speechless. What had they just told her? Patrick had warned her there would be risks, but...coins and blood and wisps of smoke—what did they mean for her, for him? She couldn't lose him, she'd just—

Jana abruptly stood, brushing off her satin pajamas. "What's done is done," she announced.

There was a low chorus of assent, and everyone else rose. They began putting chairs away, folding up the table, setting the shop to rights, saying goodbyes.

The meeting of the witches was over.

———

Shock kept CeCe stuck in her chair until Wren prodded her out of it so it could be folded and put away. Standing in the spot where the chair had been, she rehearsed what the witches said. Scrabbled to find ways around it. It was just their opinion, after all. While she was as broadminded as the next person, she didn't have to believe it, them, any of it.

I mean, really, I'm standing in a shop that sells Gryffindor neckties.

By the time all the witches but Jana dispersed, CeCe had ignited a small flame of defiance and an even bigger one of denial. "Jana, I know they mean well, but everything will be fine. Besides, my personal life is just that, mine. I'm not comfortable with strangers messing around in it."

Jana ignored her comment completely. She had her cat-eye readers on and was bent over a stuffed-to-overflowing Irish dresser, rummaging in the lower cabinets and muttering. "No, not those. Um, no, don't think so. Oh, so that's where that went. Right, then, here we are." She straightened and handed CeCe two glass bottles, one red, one blue. They were around three inches tall, the height of mini-bar liquor bottles, but larger in diameter. They had narrow necks, and their tops were sealed with black wax.

The shop owner pointed at the red bottle. "That one opens the door." Then, at the blue. "That one closes it."

CeCe laughed as she held up the red one. "Shouldn't it have a tag that says *DRINK ME*?"

Jana's face, under her orange hibiscus, showed no sign of amusement. "You're laughing now, daughter. But when you need them, it won't be a laughing matter."

Open the door. Close the door. Don't laugh. What in tarnation was Jana talking about? CeCe peered dubiously into the red bottle. She was sure she could see tiny things swimming inside, like pinprick tadpoles.

"Mind you, don't shake either one before use. One drop on your tongue before you sleep." Jana shoved a spill of loose objects back into the cabinet and pushed a knee against the door to shut it. "Off you go, then."

———

Back at her flat, CeCe sat on the edge of her bed. She held Jana's bottles, one in each hand. If she drank from them, even once, it would be as good as saying she believed in magic. Not the rabbit-out-of-the-hat kind, but the kind Jana and the other witches practiced. The kind with a 'k' at the end. *Magick.*

The kind that her aunts were now, after all this time, telling her was embedded in her genes.

Why believing should be so hard for her, she couldn't say. After all, apart from heredity, she was romantically involved with—*say it, girl*—a supernatural being.

Maybe she had trouble saying it because, even knowing what she knew, Patrick didn't *seem* supernatural. He seemed completely and exuberantly natural. Warm, virile, hard-bodied, deep-voiced. His smile, his laugh, his touch—they were as real and solid as anything in the flat where she was now. CeCe rolled the witch bottles gently between her fingers. As real as them.

There were inconsistencies and gaps, she admitted that. Breaks between the world she and Patrick shared and the one outside it. They unsettled her; she'd admit that, too. The Castle bedchambers and salons that, with Patrick, looked as they had decades and even centuries in the past, then reverted to carefully staged rooms during the day. The ale she could smell in a pewter tankard and taste on Patrick's tongue, though she knew he didn't eat or drink. The glowing hearths that were dead the next morning, their fireboxes as cold as any that hadn't had blazes in them since George VI's reign.

Reluctantly, she revisited the insanity option. *Let's say I'm hallucinating. Mad as a hatter, cuckoo, looney tunes, elevator goes nowhere near the top.* That was a possibility, though she couldn't imagine how she could be psychotic with regard to Patrick, yet still be sane enough to carry on with her tours, with daily life, research, interactions with her ghost walkers, the PD, Eunice Lite, Poppy Norris, Alun Jones.

And psychosis didn't explain what her aunts had told her. Didn't explain CeCe's suppressed memories, confirmed by her aunts. Didn't explain Patrick's journal.

She put the two bottles on the nightstand and pulled out the drawer, removing the journal. Not to open it, just to hold it on her lap while she thought. There were hallucinatory states that more than a few people thought were paranormal, not insane. Automatic writing. Speaking in tongues, or in dead languages. Past life regression, in which subjects under hypnosis minutely described events and people from bygone eras.

She supposed she could have written the journal herself, in a hallucinatory state. She opened the leather cover, ran her fingers over the fine thick paper and the elegant lines of script. She barely knew what eighteenth century Round Hand was. The idea that she could come up with twenty-seven grisly tales spanning five centuries, then write them out in penmanship as different from her own as a horse-drawn carriage was from her rented Mini...it boggled her mind.

And where would she have gotten the ink? She'd scraped through high school chemistry. The notion that she could make *ink*—organic, dark brown, from ground oak galls with their characteristic scent...

Scent. She closed the journal and brought it close to her face. If she shut her eyes, Patrick was there, next to her, as real and fragrant as when he kissed her. *Peat smoke, sea water, tobacco, man.*

She put the journal back in the drawer of the nightstand. After a second's hesitation, she put the witch bottles there, too. Cold and exhausted, she peeled off her clothes and pulled on her old UGA sleepshirt. Then, she crawled under the duvet and brought it up to her ears, curling sideways in the bed.

Too many questions. At the end of them—as at the beginning—only one answer mattered. Patrick, always Patrick.

TWENTY-NINE

Monday morning meant it was time for a well-earned paycheck. Saturday's *Ghosts of the Castle!* had been one for the history books. Two dozen walkers, all Japanese. The group had an interpreter, but CeCe was fairly sure a lot of her script got lost in translation. Everyone seemed happy, though, and she posed for photos with each of the walkers. And the interpreter.

She snagged her check and ducked into the staff break room to look in her pigeonhole. A poly mailer with an international label was jammed inside. The mailer had the Savannah house's return address. She clucked her tongue. Now what?

Don't be snippy, you know you love them, and they like to surprise you. It wasn't anywhere near a holiday, but her aunts frequently gave her gifts out of season. Nikki sent Christmas presents in June. *"Halfway to Yule!"* Birthday stuff came all year from Sophie. *"It's a few months early, I know. But I saw this and thought of you."*

CeCe found scissors in a drawer under the tea bar and

clipped open the mailer. Inside was a small cardboard box like the kind for a ring or a pair of earrings, but when she opened it, there was a wad of bubble wrap crammed inside. In the middle of the bubble wrap, a tiny memory card. Puzzlement knitted her brows. She hadn't brought her laptop, but she didn't have any more errands today at the Castle or in town, so she could go right back to her flat with the card. It must be something pretty interesting for her technophobic aunties to put it on an electronic storage device. And then mail it to her. In Wales.

The letter and MMS from her aunts—those had taken her aback. But they'd already disclosed the worst. Hadn't they? Whatever was on the memory card, she needed to find out now. Before one of the witches saw it in a Tarot card.

———

For the first minute, she couldn't hear anything on the recording but scuffling and squeaking noises. Finally, two speakers: her Aunts Hélène and Nicole. For a few seconds, they just mumbled unintelligibly, then Hélène's loud, authoritative voice made CeCe scoot back from her laptop.

"CeCe, I was hoping we five could get together and discuss this in person." Aunt Nikki muttered something in the background. "But that isn't going to happen anytime soon. And I think...well, we all think, there are things you need to know now." There was more muttering from behind Hélène, who said something indistinct. When her eldest aunt spoke into the microphone again, though, she sounded strong and determined.

"What I'm going to tell you will seem like a fairy story. But it's not. It's our story, the story of our family. We should have told you all this sooner, but we didn't know how. And, well, I think we were hoping we might not have to. But we sort of know what's been going on with you in Wales, and it's time you knew the rest."

"Past time." That was Aunt Nikki's voice. After what sounded like chair casters squealing, she went on talking. "You know you were born in Moniac, on the St. Mary's. But before that we were living in Savannah. Your grandparents had a house in Forsyth Park, then. One summer when Gabrielle, your mother, was seventeen, she went down to Moniac to visit her cousin Yvonne and the family. And she got herself in some trouble. Your Grandmomma Louise thought maybe she should go down there until it all got sorted out.

"First, it was just Momma and Hélène who went down there, but Momma said she wanted more help, so I went. After a few months, Diane and Sophie went, too, right before you were born."

Moniac on the St. Mary's. CeCe had a few faint memories of it. Hot. Humid. Live oaks so gigantic they seemed to brush the clouds. A wide and sluggish river, alternatingly bright blue and dull gray, depending on how bright or stormy the sky was.

Hélène's voice again, booming as she sat too close to the mic. "When we got down to Moniac, we found Gabi was in a bad way. She'd started walking out in the swamp, always to the same place. It was that old plantation house, the one they call Two Rivers.

"It was nothing but a ruin, that house. Everybody, not just us but other people, told Gabi over and over." Hélène put on a thick Georgia accent, "'Don't go 'round there, girl, 'cause somethin' gonna fall on your head. Or some convict might be livin' in that ol' heap an' you gonna git yourself killed.' We could have moved out of Moniac, I guess, but every time Momma brought it up, Gabi had a fit. Momma thought that if we moved, Gabi would just keep going there, even if she had to take the bus, or walk ten miles or worse. Maybe Momma was wrong about that, it's too late to say now."

CeCe could see her aunts in her mind, sitting shoulder to shoulder. Where had they been when they made the recording? In Hélène's home office, probably, with her desk computer and her floor-to-ceiling shelves full of medical books. Outside, it would have been late Savannah summer, hot and sticky, but that one room was always cool and dark, because Hélène kept the blinds shut to protect her books. Nikki spoke again, not quite as loud as her sister but loud enough.

"Gabi was walking over to Two Rivers all the time, every day. Your grandpapa, back in Savannah, he sort of broke off from Gabi when she got pregnant with you. I think what made him mad was that she wouldn't say who your daddy was. After that, Papa didn't say much of anything about Gabi, or at least nothing I'm going to repeat.

"Now, Gabrielle wasn't doing anything wrong, I don't want you to think she was. She was a good mother to you, even though she was so young. But she was just—I don't know, sad all the time. And she wouldn't stop going over to that old house, it was like she had a fixation. Your grand-momma didn't know what to do with her. She prayed a lot, and we had Father George from the chapel in Moniac over and he prayed over Gabi and even put Holy water on her head. She didn't fight or argue with anybody about it, but she wouldn't explain herself, either.

"Some of the cousins weren't very kind, CeCe. They said right to our faces that we needed to get a psychiatrist for Gabi. A couple of them even said she needed an exorcism. What a bunch of stupid, backwoods..."

Hélène took over again, and CeCe's spine jolted at her aunt's words. "It was the drawing and that Scottish witch business, honey. That's why people were talking the way they were. Even before Andy did the genealogy, I think some folks must've found out about Isobel Gowdie. Or maybe Andy blabbed. And that Fourcette woman, well, you know how people talk.

"Anyway, your grandmomma wouldn't let doctors touch Gabi. She said God would heal her if we just—I mean, there was nothing else wrong with her and we were so sure she'd snap out of it..."

There was a long pause in the recording. Just when CeCe thought her aunts were going to leave her with a half-finished family horror story, Nikki came back on.

"It was right around Halloween. I remember 'cause it had cooled off and the rains had stopped. Gabi was sitting on the porch with you. You were about four and a half, then, and, oh, sweetie, you were so cute! You were wearing a fairy costume Sophie made you. You and your mom were talking up a storm and laughing. We all thought, oh, that's fine, Gabi's back to her old self. But, all of a sudden, she got this look on her face, like she'd seen a—"

There was another pause, not as long but a lot scarier than the one before. Nikki started talking again, her voice thick.

"Gabi started running, not walking like she'd been doing, but running off toward the river. I hollered and we all went after her. Well, except your grandmomma, she had that bad hip. But all us sisters, the four of us, ran after her because we just had a feeling that this was different and, I don't know, worse than what she was doing before.

"Gabi ran like a bat outta Hades, right into the swamp and up that long dirt road to Two Rivers. She got right up to the house, in a little clearing in front of the veranda, with us all behind her."

Hélène spoke again, her voice uncharacteristically soft and cracking. "She s-stopped running and stood there, like a statue. Her arms were stretched out and her eyes were shut tight. We were afraid she'd start running again when she opened her eyes, so we made a circle around her, the four of us. We thought we'd get ahold of her if she came out of her trance, or whatever it was and..."

Hélène's voice faded away. Nikki's came closer. "But, then —CeCe, honey, I know this is going to be hard to believe, but it happened. I was there and I saw it, we all did.

"We had our arms out and we were looking right at her. One second Gabi was there and then..." Nikki trailed off into faint sounds of crying, but CeCe wasn't sure which of her aunts was making them. With a loud sniffle, Nikki continued.

"We did everything, CeCe. Everything except tell what we saw because who was going to believe that? Who was going to believe us? Sophie and I were just teenagers. We'd all get sent to psychiatrists, then. That swamp is huge, but we did search all the Two Rivers part of it, for two weeks. We had the police and boats out on the water and dogs and trackers and all. The Sheriff's people went through the old plantation house like they were combing fleas out of it. Finally, the Sheriff told your grandmomma, 'If she went on deeper in the Okefenokee, ain't nobody gonna find her, 'cause, you know, the gators.' Well, he was another backwoods Cracker."

CeCe reeled. Her mother had committed suicide, she'd always been told that and had believed it. Went off a bridge in a fit of depression, body never found. The wild story of a plantation house in the swamp and her mother vanishing while her sisters looked on...

Her mind blanked.

Into the blasted field of her shock came Nikki's voice, stronger than before. "Your grandmomma took it very hard. She just sat in her chair, rocking and saying, 'I knew she would do it, I knew, 'cause there's no way to stop it when one of them wants her and she wants them back.'"

When one of them wants her. Just who did her grandmother think, or know, 'them' to be?

"I swear, baby girl," Nikki continued, "we didn't plan to

lie to you. But after we couldn't find a trace of Gabi in Moniac, we all came back to Savannah and then it just seemed like everything happened at once. Papa died, heart attack, but he'd been sick for a long time. And then your grandmomma passed a year after. You might not remember that, you were pretty small, and Momma just went into the hospital and passed there."

No, Nikki. I don't remember any of it. Not her mother disappearing into the woods. Not her grandparents dying. Maybe she just didn't have a very good memory. She hadn't remembered the song or the castle drawings, had she?

Her Aunt Hélène was back on the mic. She'd seemingly pulled herself together and sounded like her usual take-charge, big-voiced self.

"CeCe, you were a good little girl, you didn't even cry. Of course, we cared for you like you were our own, like we'd been doing, anyway, with Gabi being so—distracted. After our parents passed, the Forsyth Park house came to us all, but we talked about it and decided to sell. That's when we got the house on Bull Street."

Nikki spoke again, her voice as gentle and kind as always. Aunt Nikki. The reliable, mommy-stand-in aunt. The one who always told her the truth. Or so CeCe thought, until now.

"I know we let you believe your mom drowned herself in the St. Mary's, CeCe. Well, at first, we told you it was an accident. Later, we got afraid you might look for records. Suicide was what the police wanted to call it. We didn't like it, but we went along, because it seemed best at the time, with you being so little and all the rest of it.

"But now you know, CeCe. Now, you know everything."

Hélène came in again with a breaking voice. "Please forgive us, CeCe. We love you."

And, finally, Nikki. "We do, sweetheart, we truly do. And you shouldn't let any of this bother you."

There was a stretch of dead air and the recording ended, along with everything CeCe had ever, in her life, believed to be true.

THIRTY

If she'd really had been thinking straight, she would have realized she wasn't. But it somehow seemed perfectly fine not to do anything about the information she got from her aunts. The letter, the MMS, the audio file. Especially the audio file. What they described, what Hélène and Nikki told her...pretty strange. But it was her mother's, or maybe her aunts' kind of strange. Not CeCe's.

After all, lots of people had strange things in their families, and lots of people chose not to dwell on them. She'd known her childhood bestie for years before she learned that when Felicia was three, her parents had joined a cult and vanished in South America, leaving their daughter to be raised by the aunt and uncle that Felicia always introduced as Mom and Dad.

CeCe didn't think her family was any stranger than Felicia's. She certainly didn't think other people had the right to an opinion. The witches would probably have one about the audio file, especially after the way they reacted to Nikki's letter and the MMS. Not to mention the dressing down they gave her at the so-called conference in Jana's shop. There had been a lot of opinions flying around that night. But whose business was her family history, really? Hers. Hers, and Patrick's.

So, it definitely wasn't straight thinking that she didn't say anything to him.

———

They went on meeting every Wednesday and often on Sunday, too, since they couldn't keep their hands off each other for a full week. They made love everywhere in the Castle; the Ward Room, the Alexander Room (both named after late eighteenth century peers), the Victoria-Louise Room (named after the Prussian princess), and even the billiards room (not a huge success).

The stables were her favorite. Gone for almost a hundred years before the Castle opened to the public, in Patrick's day they'd housed several dozen horses. Powerful jumpers for hunting, elegant ladies' hacks, sleek and stylish carriage horses, even ponies for carts and children. Deep in a nest of fragrant hay, she gave herself to Patrick again and again, and he to her, while the horses—one of them a black stallion—snuffled and stamped quietly in the dark.

The weeks flew by, fast, faster. The things her aunts disclosed, the things CeCe remembered, the warnings from the witches...she put more distance every day between them and her. What they'd told her was all past tense, anyway. The witches' warnings had a tense of their own. Future magiciple, maybe.

October and November were filled with programs and events CeCe used to impress Eunice Tattersall. Maybe, just maybe, if her job performance was over the top, Eunice would have an epiphany. *"Wait! Why am I wasting such a brilliant historian on ghost walks! She belongs on staff!"*

The not-yet-a-staffer didn't expect miracles, but the PD's

response was so faint it was almost invisible. A nod here, a smile there. The pinnacle of the Director's praise was a casual comment after CeCe's wildly successful Halloween History Scavenger Hunt. "Well played, Celeste."

At the end of November, Christmas decorations went up in the town and the Castle. Obligingly, the weather changed from *Wind in the Willows* to *Pooh and the Blustery Day*. Did the falling thermometer cool ghost walk fever? Not so CeCe noticed. Numbers didn't thin, but the walkers got thicker. First, they turned up in windbreakers, pullovers, and mackintoshes. By what would have been Thanksgiving in America, they were swaddled in quilted jackets and coats. Getting her well-padded groups through narrow passages in the Castle was harrowing, made worse by the miasma of Fisherman's Friend and damp outerwear.

Other than her weekly Fight with Fleece, the Castle was the same old, same old. Her hope that the PD would agree with Alun Jones that she wasn't "just an actor" went into Sleep Mode. She'd become exactly that, an actor, starring in a long-running movie about tormented ghosts. *Beetlejuice*, in Wales.

She should never have mentioned her Savannah tour guide experience when she interviewed at St. Rhydian's, she knew that, now. She should've been close-mouthed and wanly polite like Savin Bloom, though Savin's business envelope personality didn't seem to be getting her anywhere. The woman still slunk around the Castle with no visible duties while CeCe, doggedly team playing, still tried to be friendly.

"Hi, Savin. How are you today?" And, "Hello! Good to see you. Oh, my God, I love those shoes." Savin never responded with anything more energetic than a stiff smile or a nod.

CeCe was over it. British reserve was one thing, but Savin Bloom was a Dove Bar at the back of the freezer. Honestly,

CeCe couldn't figure out what the woman was doing at the Castle at all. Then, late in November, Poppy dropped the blonde brick into their weekly chat in the third-floor hallway.

"Savin Bloom and Eunice Tattersall. They were at university together."

Old boys. Or maybe, as they were called back home, good old boys.

Poppy went on. "Mairead wheedled the connection out of Eunice Lite. Cambridge. Trinity College, I think."

"What degree did she take? Savin, I mean."

"None. I don't think she's aware she needs any advantages beyond Mummy and Daddy's money, and maybe she doesn't." Poppy's voice lowered. "They're quite wealthy. Father's a peer."

Money and privilege and Who You Know. Nothing pegged CeCe as American more than thinking she wouldn't see them in Wales. Things hadn't really changed at the Castle since Patrick's day. Fewer swords, maybe.

THIRTY-ONE

Two and a half months since her meeting with the witches. Time and denial whispered sweet lies, saying the meeting was no more than a video on cultural anthropology. *Folk Magic of Old England*, narrated by Lucy Worsley. The witches meant well, but, honestly. Color-flipping cats, mood lotions, and rhymes about souls and coins?

The red and blue bottles from Jana were still in the drawer of CeCe's nightstand. They could stay there until she found a discreet way to dispose of them. Maybe she'd send them to Aunt Nikki, who might enjoy some pixie dust from abroad. She could tell the chifferobe about it.

There'd been no more contact from Nikki or the other aunts. Embarrassed, probably. They should be, with their confused recollections, their doomsaying tucked into endearments. *Don't worry. Don't be afraid. You shouldn't let any of this bother you.*

It didn't bother CeCe because it didn't matter. Georgia was a long way from North Wales.

In winter, North Wales was monochromatically pretty, a

bumpy landscape in gray and white. St. Rhydian's charmed. Snowdrifts on the steep roofs and crenelated ramparts made it a gingerbread house with icing. It was even better inside. Electric logs glowed in all the hearths that visitors saw. Garlands of artificial holly spiraled around the Grand Staircase to the second floor and garnished every mantle. Huge arrangements of evergreens and seasonal blooms filled vases in the Great Hall. The Castle looked and smelled like an Aspen ski lodge.

Patrick's bedchamber became the perfect winter nest. More, it was the cabinet of curiosities CeCe had always yearned for, the place her childhood self must have known was at the hidden heart of the castle she drew. Patrick did Show and Tell better than any first-grader. He taught her to use his astrolabe, sighting out the single window in his room. Let her examine a beautifully bound volume of Alexander Pope's *Essay on Man*—a gift, Patrick said, from his principal tutor at the Collège when he left.

One night, he put his childhood catechism in her hands. It was a tiny book with a faded rose pressed under its cover. "My mother plucked the rose from her garden on the day I left home for Paris."

A folded paper was tucked a few pages behind the rose. Carefully, CeCe removed and opened it. It was an ink drawing, also faded, of the front of a thatched cottage. A striped cat sat in the open door. Patrick belted his arms around her, his low laugh warm against her ear. "My mother made the sketch. That was her cat, Fergus."

CeCe folded the paper and returned it to its place. Then, she closed the little book and kissed it.

Lying in the narrow bed after making love, they had long, lazy conversations about history, art, philosophy, natural sciences, medicine. Pretty much everything CeCe thought she knew about eighteenth century learning was wrong. When it came to things like geometry (which Patrick called 'Archimedian principles') or algebra, she was a blithering idiot compared to her ghost. In philosophy, as long as it was prior to the late Enlightenment Era, he bossed her from -osophy to -ology.

As for languages, Patrick recited long passages of the *Iliad* in its original tongue. He smoothly gave her the First Tale of Boccaccio's *Decameron* in Italian, and CeCe retired from the field.

When the talk was done, what followed was the most wondrous wonder of all. She'd thought their early kisses were a homecoming, but they'd only taken her to the front steps. What followed their first complete union in Patrick's bed—that was the homeland of souls made one, over and over. While a cold rain beat on the window, they twined and soared, always kissing, always murmuring of eternal love.

Two things mattered, and only two. They were happy. They were together.

———

CeCe hated to admit it, but even Eunice Tattersall delivered rainbows to her happy place. Poppy Norris handed them over during their last weekly chat in December. After a couple of good pulls on her inhaler, Poppy got it out in one breath. "The Castle is doing so very well for funds due to your ghost walks being such a huge hit, that the Trustees have approved another staff position, which I think is positively brilliant, don't you?"

"Another staff position?" *Calm down. Only a rumor.* "Do you know what sort of position?"

Poppy put her finger alongside her nose. "There's talk of an Education Director."

Education Director. *Oh, please God, let me have that job.* She had the right training, the right tools, the right experience.

And the spectacular work she'd done in recent months—*let's not forget that, Eunice.* On top of everything else, she'd just about given herself a football injury being a team player. She'd *earned* the new job.

She hoped Poppy wasn't offended by the lightning-fast thanks she got before CeCe raced back to her flat and her laptop to refresh her CV. At the bottom, she packed a round into her resumé's big gun: a published article she'd written for the U.K.'s small but prestigious *All About History Magazine.* The article, about Alun's forensic conservation at the site, included a witty interview and photos. The editor loved it. CeCe would bet her bottom dollar the PD hadn't seen it, busy as she was with champagne brunches, administrative conferences in five-star hotels, and schmoozing the Board. CeCe couldn't wait to wave the magazine in Eunice's face.

Her career, her dreams, her heart—they were all on the same exhilarating page.

So why, when she closed her laptop and put the kettle on for tea, did she suddenly have itchy feelings? She'd never had premonitions, but then, she'd never thought of herself as being descended from soulers. Or from Isobel Gowdie, infamous witch. And a mother who disappeared in plain sight.

One thing she could say without consulting a crystal ball. People were behind whatever itched under her skin. People were always behind itchy feelings.

Facts were reliable. People were not. They slipped and slithered, shifted and swayed. They were illogical, tricky, and opaque. They hid things that looked really ugly when a light shone on them. A couplet from *Macbeth* floated uncomfortably through her mind as she poured hot water into her mug, one that reminded her of the scary book her middle school self had hidden in a drawer.

By the pricking of my thumbs, something wicked this way comes.

THIRTY-TWO

After three tries, CeCe got Eunice Lite to put her on the PD's appointment calendar. Thankfully, it was on a morning when she and Patrick hadn't been cavorting all night beforehand. She was fresh and perky when she entered the PD's outer office, wearing the suit she'd worn to her first interview at the Castle.

What a wide-eyed innocent you were in those days, girl. Before ghost walks, Sean Patrick Ó Loinsigh, witches, double double toil and trouble, and the question 'did you bed him'?

"Go in." Eunice Lite spoke almost without moving her lips.

———

As job interviews went, it wasn't bad. It wasn't good, either. Short, polite, inconclusive—that's what it was.

Yes, the PD admitted, the rumors of an Education Director sailing up to the Castle dock were true. Indeed, congratulations were in order. The increased staff would make a big difference to the Castle. No, the job opening had not been circulated. National Trust hoops to jump through, blah blah blah. Of course, the PD would like CeCe's updated resumé. Yes, the article in *All About History* was delightful, and thanks for the copy. No, sorry, unable to chat more at the moment. However, CeCe was a *lovely* addition to the Castle. How *lovely* it was to have her at St. Rhydian's. *Just lovely*.

What wasn't so lovely was going out of the office without any more information than when she went in.

———

Patrick's opinion of Eunice Tattersall being what it was, CeCe couldn't expect him to say anything positive about the interview. He didn't, though his grumbling barely distracted her from his naked body, lying alongside hers in the hay of the stables.

"She's not to be trusted." His breath fogged. The lofty space was only partially warmed by the horses in their stalls. "Why you wish to be in the employ of a devious shrew like—"

"You just detest her because she's English."

"Not at all. I detest her because she's a devious shrew. I merely scorn her because she's English."

"Oh, I see." CeCe trailed her fingers down Patrick's stomach, savoring the texture of downy hair atop muscled flesh, the way the hair darkened in a narrow path toward his groin. She was getting even more distracted, but couldn't quite let the job interview go.

"Patrick, I can't just push visitors around the Castle for the next five years, or however long it takes Eunice to remember I'm a historian and not a hostess." CeCe had a sudden, horrifying vision of herself at fifty, a middle-aged tour guide in Colonial attire. Sure, if things were different, she would leave St. Rhydian's. She would find a job at another historic site, a museum, something, somewhere. But Patrick couldn't leave St. Rhydian's, and she would never, for any reason, leave Patrick. "You do see, don't you?"

"I see," he murmured, taking her hand and wrapping it around his erection, "that your bubbies are standing up from the cold, saucy dames that they are." Patrick cupped one breast in his hand, then lowered his mouth to it. "I shall give this one a thorough lashing."

He did, and then she did something for him, which led to something else for her. Eunice Tattersall was just so much breath misting in the cold.

THIRTY-THREE

In the theater, no one said the name of the play aloud. It was "the Scottish play," if anyone needed to refer to *Macbeth* at all, and even that was considered bad luck.

Maybe CeCe's fleeting recall of the "something wicked" couplet had somehow jinxed her. Maybe her whole life was jinxed, starting with a witchy ancestor. Maybe the jinx started before that, in some distant era when her forebears didn't pray to the right gods or sacrifice the right livestock. All she knew was that the next chapter in her jinx book began on the first Saturday night in January, with a *Ghosts of the Castle!* that sheared off into disaster.

At the tour's start, she didn't spot the problem walkers. It wasn't like they were wearing tan coveralls with proton packs. While everyone milled around her in the Great Hall, a man in his thirties introduced himself. Short and pudgy, carrot-orange hair, freckles. He shoved a pale, chubby hand at her.

"Hello, there, I'm Ian." He gestured to about twenty people behind him, all ages, all staring fixedly at her. "We're from the Source for Paranormal Incident Transparency."

SPIT? Had he really just said that?

Ian's people kept staring at her, so CeCe stammered something welcoming. They looked all right. Dressed just like everyone else. Padded jackets or coats, some with knit caps, flat caps, or floppy tweed hats, at least half with glasses. Sensible shoes. They did seem a bit laden down with hefty shoulder bags, cross-body bags, camera bags, backpacks, or even, she noted with a shudder, fanny packs.

The walk began in a normal way, if anything about a ghost walk could be called normal. CeCe gave a brief history of St. Rhydian's, all the while thinking about SPIT's ridiculous acronym. Not that Ian's was the first odd group to join the tour. In September, the Quidditch Club from Oxford had arrived. October brought the Bristol Bell Ringers and the British Fuschia Fanciers. SPIT seemed to have more luggage than the other groups, but lots of people carried bags, stuffed with cough drops or snacks or hand sanitizer.

Ten minutes into the walk, CeCe wished the Castle had embraced the almost universal prohibition against carriers of any sort in public venues. Everyone in SPIT began hauling things out of their bags and packs. If she really were a ghost guide and not a historian blundering her way through notes, she would've been quicker to recognize what they were unpacking. EMF meters, digital thermometers, thermographic cameras, several sets of night vision goggles.

Ghostbusting gear.

She tried to focus on her script, but it was difficult when all the machinery went into play. Distraction turned into disruption in the Solar. Ian suddenly yelled, "Nothing here!"

"Zero on the EMR!" woofed a tall, gangly man in the back.

Something like a loud gargle came from a heavy woman with a video camera obscuring her face. "Argh! Camera's working now, Ian! Nothing on the monitor."

"Uh, excuse me," CeCe began. Before she could say more,

a half-dozen SPITers shoved past her to the row of long windows along the Solar's south-facing wall. They were all talking at once, and the three in front donned night-vision goggles. They jostled and jabbered and pushed toward the windows, but the three goggled ones began waving their arms and shouting.

"False alarm! Just a reflection, people! Not an orb. Repeat, not an orb!" Instead of returning to their places, they clogged the middle of the passage, loudly chattering. CeCe fought to get the rest of her walkers through and beyond them. She raised her voice, a notch or two below actual bellowing.

"Could you clear the passage, please? Hello, there! Make a hole!"

The SPITers were slow, but finally CeCe managed to part them and shepherd the other walkers through. Equipment-laden, they still talked among themselves, falling in behind.

Why couldn't that have been the end of it? But, no, it was just the beginning of *Ghostbusters V*. She got the group to the second floor without incident, but in the hallway, an agitated SPIT woman in a Bogner ski jacket and matching cap yelled loud enough to be heard in the car park. "Point five four! I've got a cold spot!"

The rest of the group rushed toward her like ducklings.

The non-SPIT walkers clustered on her side of the passage, looking helpless. One man, bless him, a short, tweedy, spectacled gent who looked like a headmaster, actually tried to intervene on her behalf.

"See here," he called above the SPIT gabble. "We'd like to get on with the tour, *if* you don't mind!" SPIT paid him about as much attention as the *Titanic*'s captain paid to the big ice cube looming over the deck.

The Bogner jacket woman wailed. "*Sor*-ry, my mistake! Read the thermometer wrong. No cold spot, repeat, no cold spot." Someone took the thermometer from her, and a loud argument ensued as she didn't want to give it up.

A diversion, CeCe needed a diversion. "Let's just pop into the Empire Room!" She stretched out her arm and moved quickly in that direction. They would have made it, but the non-SPIT walkers were touch-averse and polite Britons. They straggled behind, murmuring *Oh, pardon me* and *No, please, you first* until they were trampled, almost literally, by the SPIT herd coming up from the rear.

CeCe clenched her jaw. Why couldn't she have a dozen New Yorkers along tonight? They'd put up a fight. Instead, the SPITers charged through the other walkers and nearly pushed her into a glass display case as they rushed into the Empire Room. Surprisingly, they stopped moving and talking once they were inside. CeCe found herself returning the direct stares of people who'd ignored her since the tour's start.

She should have guessed their silence and focus was a trap, but she didn't. Utterly relieved the disruption had ceased, she dove into her narrative with renewed confidence. "This room," she gestured at the display-encrusted walls, "has been a repository of treasure twice. First, in the late 1700s, it housed globes, maps, and curiosities acquired by the DeBlaes family. These demonstrated the worldliness of the family and its role in Colonial expansion. Inheritors of the earldom conducted business or exploration in India, Africa, and the Far East from the late 1800s until World War Two, and relics of that period are housed here.

"In between those two periods, the space was called the Music Room. Here, family members or invited artists gave small concerts. At one such soirée in May of 1862, a guest, Sir Oliver Faraday, removed a loaded pistol from his evening jacket. He held it up and shouted, 'For Andrew!' Then, he shot himself in the head. He fell to the floor and died on the spot.

"Sir Oliver had lost his only child, a son, the year before in China, in the Second Opium War. He never recovered from the loss. His ghost is believed to haunt this room and is—"

"Wrong! Wrong, wrong, wrong, *wrong*." It was Ian, the SPIT leader.

In the shocked pause after Ian's outburst, CeCe began, "I'm sorry, did I misunderstand you, or—"

"Faraday didn't kill himself here or anywhere. He died in Nanking, from cholera. So, his *spirit*," Ian made air quotes with his fingers, "couldn't be in this room." Upper lip curling in a sneer, Ian spoke over his shoulder to his group. "Unless our guide here took a *really* wrong turn and we're actually in China, not Wales."

The SPITers giggled and hooted. A bald man at the back raised his hand. "I'll have the fried rice!" Two others piped together, "Do we get an eggroll with that?" The two laughed like hyenas.

They were all laughing, except Ian. Hands in his jacket pockets, he rocked back on his heels, smirking. "See, this is the problem with all you ghost walk guides. You just fabricate stories and have absolutely nothing to back them up. But you get away with it, don't you? I mean, no one challenges you. Look, we all have to pay British Gas, but don't you think fleecing people by promising them ghosts and then unloading a cartful of lies is a bit underhanded? Well, the more fool us for paying you."

Thirty seconds. A long time when forty people were boring holes into you with their eyes. Finally, CeCe spoke, in a voice she hardly recognized as her own. Level, flat, and cold. "I know a ghost who would tear your head off for that, you stupid little man."

———

Disasters tended to come in pairs, like shoes or handcuffs. CeCe was so upset by the implosion of *Ghosts of the Castle!* that when she got back to her flat, she grasped at the most ordinary thing she could think of to calm herself down.

Making tea. Filling the kettle, flipping the switch, waiting for the water to boil, lifting the kettle—the very definition of ordinary. It made the shock that much greater when she closed her hand around the teakettle's handle...and realized most of her fingers had disappeared.

Middle finger, ring finger, pinkie on the right hand—all gone.

Not gone in the molecular sense. She gripped the handle with what felt like her whole hand, but she saw right through where the fingers should have been, to the capacity markings on the side of the kettle. Two cups, four cups, six cups.

Somehow, she got the kettle back on the heating element without dropping it. She held out her right hand. The kitchen counter was perfectly visible through it.

She stumbled from the kitchenette toward her bed. Before she even reached it, she was shaking from head to foot. Wrapping herself in the duvet, she rocked from side to side, remembering everything the witches had warned her about, everything Patrick had warned her about. Remembering her mother, who might have lost her mind. Had she lost it before or after she disappeared?

Eventually, she stopped rocking, and curled herself into a tight ball. Around dawn, she finally slept.

THIRTY-FOUR

I t took until Monday morning for the curtain to really fall on the Saturday night tour.

Not surprisingly, she was called to the PD's office. For ten minutes, she waited in the outer office, sitting mutely on a chair like a schoolgirl about to be scolded by the vice principal. Her brain numbly reviewed the previous twenty hours.

After her two a.m. tea kettle discovery, she'd stayed in a drug-like sleep for most of Sunday. She woke with her arms folded across her chest and her hands—her disappearing hands—tucked tightly under her armpits. Maybe she'd subconsciously anchored them in place. Somehow, she got up, but only to visit the bathroom and return to bed. She didn't shower, eat, or dress, just sat cross-legged on the sheets, numb with horror, until she slid into sleep again.

This morning, when her cell phone chimed, CeCe had no choice but to pick it up from the nightstand. Her fingers seemed to be all there when she grabbed the phone. It was Eunice Lite, telling her the PD wanted a word *"as soon as possible, if you don't mind."* Shakily, she dressed and went in as ordered.

Now, she sneaked glances at her hands. Her fingers were back where they belonged. *Stay there, please. Just—stay there.* What scared her more? That they'd disappeared for a while, or that she might have imagined they did?

One crisis at a time. The PD opened her office door and gestured CeCe to a chair. Briefly, Eunice showed a flash of humanity. Or was it triumph?

"Celeste, you look awful." The PD sat behind her desk. "Of course, I can understand why you might."

"I, uh, I think I might have the flu."

"That would explain a lot, of course. You do look very peaky. I won't keep you long, and then you can get right back to bed. I'm sorry to have called you in at all, now that I see how ill you are, but..." Eunice let the sentence trail off while she consulted a piece of printed paper. "I think, all things considered, that we are very lucky. Thus far, only half the participants in Saturday's ghost walk have asked for a refund of their ticket purchase. Many complained, but some were quite apologetic. They liked you and believed a gang of ruffians had somehow got on the tour. As one of them wrote," the PD read from the paper, "'some people were very ill-mannered and rattled the poor girl.' Then, of course, your comment about knowing a ghost who—well, knowing a ghost. After that, some of the participants wondered if you were quite well."

No, I'm not. Not well at all, Eunice. I'm vanishing like— Selene's words came back with awful clarity—*wisps of smoke.*

There was a little more meaningless chat, and then she left the PD's office with the verbal equivalent of a head pat and a cheek slap. A trifle, considering CeCe didn't know at the time how *not* finished the affair was. She learned that over the next few days.

No one from SPIT asked for a refund. From their perspective, the tour was brilliant. The group created a fuss and threw attention on their ghostbusting agenda, which was just what they had come for. Most of all, they collected material for a substantial exposé, one they posted exhaustively on social media. Pro- and anti-ghost groups all over the world viewed the posts. Saw the photos made with SPIT's thermographic cameras. Clucked over the readings, all negative, from the EMRs and digital thermometers. Read the accounts of what SPIT did *not* see, as opposed to what CeCe's script suggested they might.

Worst of all, the Castle was a sitting duck for Ian's hateful sniping. He thinly disguised it as concern for "our heritage sites, so tragically underfunded that they must resort to this sort of chicanery and dross to make ends meet."

Cockeyed irony made the fracas worse. When Eunice had first proposed the tours, CeCe insisted that she didn't believe in ghosts. She did everything but beg on her knees for the Castle not to chase after the paranormal. The PD forced the ghost walks on her, anyway. Then, when the paranormal turned around and grabbed them all by the throat, the guide who tried to warn the Castle away got the blame.

More repercussions would come, CeCe was sure about that. For the Castle, for the ghost walks, for her. But those were in the future. All she could think of now was how to tell Patrick she was literally coming apart at the seams.

THIRTY-FIVE

Denial hadn't really worked before, so there was no point trying it again. As it turned out, denial, like choice, was irrelevant. She was in the Hellenic Room, sitting with Patrick on the rug in front of the fire, trying to get an explanation started. She didn't want to start. She wanted the world and everything in it to stop, stop moving, stop changing.

She and Patrick were naked, facing each other. CeCe sat between Patrick's bent knees, her legs over his, wrapping his hips. His arms encircled her shoulders, and she curled her hands against his chest. Patrick's chin rested on the top of her head, and his breath moved her hair. She was safe. With him, she would always be safe.

Except, she wasn't. Not since a humble tea kettle had shown her the terrible truth.

"Patrick," she whispered to his chest, unable to look into his face, "I need to tell you something. I mean, something is happening to me, and I—"

"Did you think I'd not noticed, *mo cuisle*?" So sympathetic, the voice, so tender, but CeCe cringed to hear the words. "I've learned and loved every inch of your body. I know when you crave a tup, and when you need sleep instead of sporting. When you want food but are too vain to eat. When you've been out in the weather too long and are taking a chill. When your breasts are aching, and your courses are about to start. How could I not see the loss of you, even a single particle like the tiniest grain of sand? And I, the wretched creature who brought this curse upon you. I, the cause of—"

"You're not the cause. You're not!" She'd sworn not to cry, but her eyes burned and flooded. She wiped at them roughly, angrily. "It's not your fault. None of it is your fault. The witches warned me. You warned me."

"Musha, now, girl. There was nothing you could do."

"There was, there is! If only I...it's my fault! This wouldn't be happening if I were better, if I were stronger—"

"If not for your virtue and strength, my jewel, I would not be here at all. Every minute of every hour we've had together is because of you. Your love called me from the void. I came for it. I came for you."

CeCe reached through his arms and clasped her hands around Patrick's neck, trying without success to keep desperation out of her voice. "We'll figure something out. I'll go back to the witches. I'll do anything, I'll do..."

Do what?

Patrick didn't say it, didn't say anything, but the question hung in the air, mocking them. He pulled her tight while she caved in on herself, a crumpled leaf of despair. Caressing her, he murmured comfort and love, kissing away the bleak destiny that was enveloping them both.

Thirty-Six

He wasn't ready. He must become ready. Cruel, his punishment, that allowed him no peace, no sweet retrospection, when she left his arms. Fear and guilt rushed in, and no room in the Castle was large enough to contain them. He paced the chamber Celeste called the Hellenic, wanting to put his fist through a wall, heave a chair at the windows, anything to relieve his torment.

Heavenly saints, don't take her. Take me.

How had he ever thought he could save them from the runaway horse of their fate? Arrogance. It would be added to his other sins.

I'm already damned, doubly, thrice, a hundred times. She is beauty and goodness, passion and wit. I am less than nothing, a mistaken birth, a mistaken life. Hurl me back into emptiness, it will cause not a ripple on the waters of time. But spare her.

To be so powerless—that was the worst of it. Patrick clung to the thin hope they might still gainsay their fate. It was his mistake that had brought their woe, the mistake he'd made with the *banfháidh*'s prediction. If he'd been a wiser and better man, he could have interpreted it. Properly interpreted it, not with the eager folly that led him to believe he knew what it meant, when in truth he hadn't and didn't.

He still might. He must. Eternity would not be long enough to mourn his failure if he could not discover the meaning in time. *Brigid, patroness of Ireland, hear me.*

His aimless strides had brought him to the hearth. Bracing his hands on the mantle, he stared into the fire and racked his brain for understanding.The *banfháidh*'s rhyme was as stingy with revelation as a miser with ha'pennies. It nevertheless pricked at recollection, prodding him with the sharp end of regret. Where had his translation gone awry? He was only a child at the time, he might not have understood the antiquated Irish the old woman used. Had he heard it wrong or twisted the meaning of the words?

'Til witch's gold be bound to wife.

Christ, the useless things he remembered about wives and husbands and weddings and marriage! The penny brides and the Beltane beds and the fire leaping. The foot washing and drams and horseshoes and silver sixpences.

Why could he not remember the one thing that might bind Celeste to his side, and the both of them to life? *Brigid, saint of the troubled, voice for the weak and weary, hear me.*

What, *exactly*, were the words the *banfháidh* had used? He fixed his gaze on the fire, stilling his active mind, dropping his passive mind into the well of memory.

Bound to wife. Bound to...

Something in the deep well stirred, then rose sluggish and slow toward the surface. The word, that English word, *bound*. Destined, pledged, committed.

By God, it was not *bound* in the sense of destiny, that was wrong! He had heard the Irish words wrong or remembered them wrong. *A bheith ceangailte.*

Tied. The Irish phrase meant tied. As *bound* could also mean in English. Bound from the Old English *binden*, to tie up with cords. Cord, from the Old French *corde*, meaning string, rope, strap. *Bound to wife*, not as in destined, but as in *tied together*.

It might be. It *must* be. *Brigid, saint who brings light to the darkness. Save her, save us, even though in my prideful desire I have taken our souls to the edge of night.*

THIRTY-SEVEN

In the weeks that followed, CeCe watched helplessly as the disappearing became worse. It wasn't consistent—a mixed blessing. For days on end, she would feel and look completely fine. Then, she would go to brush her teeth and find she could see right through her hand to the toothbrush. She prayed, believing illogically that she could pray the phenomenon away.

But it returned, again and again. Each time, she hoped it wouldn't spread. Maybe she could conceal it, if it never progressed to more than her fingers. And toes. Once, her right forearm, through which she saw her face in the mirror as she was pinning up her hair.

It got worse, in a different way. In the beginning, despite parts of her being invisible, they were still *there*. They had mass, just as they'd always had. Then, they began wavering, shuddering, like the surface of a pond. What had been solid flesh before was now, when transparent, less solid. Every day, it grew more like the smoke Selene had warned her about.

She knew how it would end. At some point, she would simply fade away. The grim certainty should have unhinged her, but it didn't. What terrified her was eternal separation from Patrick. What had he told her? Dead and gone. *I'll be dead and gone.*

She clung to a thinning sliver of hope. As long as she lived, as long as she stayed intact, there was still a chance for them. Her mother had taken that chance, CeCe had to believe that. Not suicide, not a meaningless vanishing, but stepping through some door to reunite with her otherworldly lover. CeCe would go through that door, too, when it opened. If it opened. If Patrick or magic or fate or whatever strange force was orchestrating all this called her through it.

Only if the coin be whole...

She sent a message through Eunice Lite, telling the PD that she did indeed have influenza and had been advised by her doctor to stay home for at least two weeks. *Ghosts of the Castle!* went on hold. After the SPIT fiasco, CeCe knew a leave of absence would put her on very thin ice as far as her job, not to mention the new staff position, went, but she couldn't dwell on that now. After everything that had happened in past months, she had trouble remembering why a staff position at an out-of-the-way Welsh castle was so important. Was it what she'd really wanted? Or was she driven to prove to the world, prove to *herself*, that she was more than her mother's interrupted life?

At any rate, her career hopes, her goals: they hadn't evaporated, just been put on pause. When and how she activated them again was something she'd have to deal with later. If there was a later.

But Patrick was the beating heart of her life, now and future. Patrick and her, the two of them together. Nothing else mattered. From the moment she'd begun drawing castles with a nameless prince inside, nothing else ever had.

Thirty-Eight

They had three desperately happy weeks. Happy, because they were with each other every night. Desperate, because they stopped pretending the inevitable was not. They let it in, into their kisses, their embraces, their coupling. Joy and sadness were with them, always.

The worst thing was the pain lodged in Patrick's eyes. So many times, CeCe was sure he would simply vanish, that minute, as he'd done when they were first together. That, or tell her to walk away and not look back. She knew he thought of doing one or the other, but he always stopped before he said the dreaded words, or disappeared the final time.

She couldn't leave him, and he wouldn't leave her. They kissed, and joined, and laughed, and talked, making each night like the first one, even though each night could easily be their last.

The last night came, of course, as they knew it would.

They were in a small, attic room. In the Castle's Victorian era, it had been an upper servant's bedchamber. For a governess, maybe. CeCe had seen it before. It stored old files and neatly labeled boxes of surplus Castle furnishings.

Now, the room was nearly empty. One small window, high on the wall, gave weak moonlight to an iron single bed, shoved into the corner. A musty mattress on it, no sheets. A burning log glowed in the tiny fireplace.

They made love, tenderly and long, while the room grew warm from the fire in the grate and the one in their bodies. Then, Patrick sat, propped against the head of the bed. His knees were drawn up and CeCe sat facing outward between them, leaning back against his broad chest.

"I've a story to tell you, my love," he began.

She pulled his arms around her and reached her own up and back, her fingers lacing behind his neck. "Once upon a time. You have to begin that way."

"As you desire, mistress of my heart. Once upon a time in Ireland, there were very few priests or monks."

"Because the Penal Laws of 1691 outlawed them."

Patrick kissed the top of her head. "Clever girl."

"Is this a story about religion?"

"It is a story about love."

"I like love stories. They have happy endings." The silence that followed was deep and cold, like the sea. "Please, Patrick." Her voice came out as thin as the thread that remained of her hope. "Please tell me the story has a happy ending. The handsome prince and his lady love got married. They had a dozen beautiful children, and they all lived happily ever—ever—"

There was no longer strength in her to stop the tears. She'd held them off for weeks, but now they came in a torrent, and her hands slid down to cover her face. Patrick held her tight as she broke into a thousand pieces.

When the worst of it passed, she curled sideways against him. The thud of his great, strong heart was under her cheek, the rumble of his deep voice against her ear.

"Every love story is happy, Celeste. To have loved at all is the only happiness that matters."

She sat up, shifting her body away to look out the window. A full, risen moon threw shining ribbons onto the clouds and she spoke to them, not to the man behind her, but the moon. "Why can't things just stay as they are?"

He pulled her back into his embrace. She closed her eyes and breathed in his scent, letting him enclose and shelter her. His arms were a wall against time. If she didn't open her eyes, if the two of them stayed just as they were this instant, nothing would alter. She and Patrick would remain. Unchanged, embracing. The world would go on without them. A year, a hundred years, forever.

He answered her question, but not the way she wanted. "My treasure, if we remain as we are, we will not remain at all. We will be parted eternally by death, as we each have been parted from others we've loved. Give me your hand, now."

She didn't move, couldn't. He gently took her hand and held it up to the moonlight, spreading her fingers. The great pale orb was perfectly visible through the center of her palm.

CeCe roughly pulled her hand back, cursing it silently. She had tried so hard. She still had to try. "No, Patrick, no. We can stop the—we just won't have, you know, the touching. We'll promise each other not to—"

"How long do you think we would keep to that vow, Celeste? Everything in our blood burns to join as it has, as it does, as it always will. The wasting of your sweet body—it's worse each day. How long before you slip away in my arms and leave me to howl in anguish for the rest of time, knowing what I did?" He shook his head, moonlight casting silver glints onto his loosened black hair. "Nay, we took our joy. Now, to pay the price of it, we must part."

Fearful and trembling, CeCe looked up. The sadness in

Patrick's eyes settled into her heart like a stone. "You're sending me away. Don't you want me anymore?"

He pulled her to her knees, shook her. "Never think that, not for an hour, not for a second! Listen to me, Celeste." One hand gripping her shoulder, he used the other to lift her chin so he could look into her face. His mouth was set in a fixed line of resolve. His voice had the same set, inflexible as steel. "There is nothing that could make me leave you or ask you to leave me, save to preserve the wholeness of your life. And even that, I do only because I believe in a future that brings us together again." He cupped her face with both his hands. She rested her cheek against his rough palm, bathing it with her tears.

Patrick's voice softened, becoming almost a whisper. "There is no future without you. Nor would I want there to be. Without you, bride of my soul, who will teach our sons to speak French with a terrible American accent?"

She laughed a little through her misery, cradling his hands with hers.

"Who will teach our daughters to speak up for themselves in any language, Celeste? Who will debate me like a priest, and seduce me like a wanton? Who will lie down by my side each night, and give me a reason to wake each morning? Who will make my home, my bed, my life? You. You and no other. So, we part, but only for a while. Each rising of the moon and setting of the sun make but one day closer to our reunion. You are mine, Celeste, now and forever. Mine until that moon fades away and that sun is a cinder in an empty sky."

"But what will you do?" she cried, her voice thick with pain. "Where—where will you go?" A lock of her hair had fallen over her forehead, and Patrick tucked it gently behind her ear. Such a small, familiar gesture. CeCe's heart broke entirely to realize she didn't know when, if ever, she'd feel it again.

"I'll return to the long gray. Not a tree, nor a hill, nor

another's face to look upon. There I'll stay, until it pleases God to release me to your arms again. Or, he damns me to the hell I no doubt deserve. Much will depend on what we do now, this hour. Give me your petticoat."

Startled, she hesitated, then reached over the edge of the bed to the floor where she'd dropped her clothes. She hauled up the plain, white linen underskirt. Patrick took it from her, grasping it in both hands. The sound of ripping was loud in the empty room. CeCe watched, confused, as Patrick shredded the garment, ending up with a long strip of white cloth from the hem.

He spoke, steady and full of purpose. "Come, let us return to our story. The lack of priests and monks in Ireland."

She nodded. "After the Penal Laws."

"Those religious who remained, hid under the cover of night, in stables and caves. Ancient ruins and hedgerows sheltered christenings and masses. Consecrated wafers smuggled from France were shared. But marriage—"

CeCe remembered Morgana, calling up the past. "It went back to the Old Way."

"The Old Way, aye. When lovers bound themselves together without the Church or the law. It is called handfasting," Patrick explained, reaching for her right hand. He pressed it against his left, her palm to his. Their fingers entwined, the insides of their forearms touched. Slowly and deliberately, he used his other hand to wrap the torn linen strip around their joined hands. Around and around in a figure eight, while he spoke without ever taking his eyes from hers.

"I, Sean Patrick Ó Loinsigh, take thee, Celeste Gowdie, to wife, as my heart wills it. To thee I pledge my troth, by this oath and binding, that we never will part, not on Earth nor in Heaven, for all time." He inclined his head toward her, and she took up the vow, her voice breaking and desperate.

"I, Celeste Gowdie, t-take thee, Sean Patrick Ó Loinsigh, to husband, as my heart wills it..." She stumbled over the next words. He helped her, and when the vow was done, he lifted their clasped hands, pressing his lips to the place they were bound together.

"Once before, *mo chroi*, I asked you to trust me. I ask again." His deep voice hoarsened with emotion and his eyes darkened with longing, as though he would pull the sight of her into the wasteland that beckoned him. "Trust me, Celeste, and I swear to you by all I hold sacred, we will be together. Kiss me now, my dearest, my eternal love."

She raised her tear-ravaged face. Their mouths came together and she fell deeply, blindly, into the kiss as she had the first time, every time, while her stunned mind chanted a prayer.

Please don't go, please don't go, please don't...

The linen binding, still warm from their conjoined hands, slid limply to her elbow. CeCe looked at it, her mind blank. Then, she fell face down in the empty bed, lifeless, breathless, alone. Her heart still beat and each beat killed her again, again.

A tide of grief came and washed her away.

THIRTY-NINE

A week. That's how long it took for her to become as whole as anyone else she knew. Absurdity heaped on top of loss. All she was, all she and Patrick had been together. The talk, the laughter, the touch, the completion.

All gone in seven days.

She locked herself in her flat, weeping. Weeping? What a colossal understatement. A storm surge of tears rolled over and through her. She wept in the dark, not sleeping. She wept in the light, not eating. She wept at dawn and noon and dusk.

There were so many things to weep for. The worry she'd caused her aunts. The lies they'd told her. The shocking truths she'd learned about her mother and her heritage. The counsel the witches had given her, that she'd thrown back in their faces. The humiliation she'd suffered at the Castle, the lost opportunity, the lost credibility.

She couldn't spare a single tear for any of those, even though she shed millions. Millions, all for Patrick.

And she couldn't tell anyone about any of it. Her aunts were four thousand miles away, so she couldn't bury her face in Aunt Nikki's bosom and cry her eyes out. No ride-or-die friends to get drunk with, to say *he didn't deserve you, he's a dick, you can do way better, girl, c'mon, we're doin' shots.* Who could possibly understand what she was going through?

The witches. On the fifth day, two of them came calling. At first, CeCe didn't want to answer their knock at the flat door. She was in no fit state for company. Wearing the same UGA hoodie she'd pulled on three days ago, she couldn't even remember when she'd last showered. Were her sweatpants clean? She knew she hadn't washed her hair in a week, and it stuck out in all directions. Her eyes were so red and swollen she could barely open them. As she struggled to unlock the door, she thought it was a good thing Patrick couldn't see her as she was. Naturally, that started her crying again, so when she finally got the door open, she was blubbering into the faces of Jana and Rowan.

Like a two-witch disaster recovery team, they entered with bags and boxes and a plastic cage with a handle. Was that No Name Cat?

CeCe watched silently as they unpacked and explained. Rowan brought cheese and honey from the farm. Jana brought Guernsey bean stew and, yes, the magical cat.

"I'm leaving him with you for a few days. He's an aggravating creature, but he has a great gift for healing." Jana dumped No Name's bowls, his litter box, his cans and bags of food on the floor, then let the cat out of his carrier. He immediately twined around CeCe's legs, changing to azalea pink. Trotting over to the bed, he leaped onto it and began grooming himself, as though he'd been living in the flat for months.

Rowan hugged her shyly. "Wren is doing a heart's ease ritual every day for you, sister. She's powerful, is our Wren. Her magic will help." She gave CeCe a final squeeze and went out the door.

Jana followed, but on the doorsill, she spoke in a very kind voice, one CeCe hadn't heard before from her. "Daughter, you didn't mean for this to happen. None of us wanted it to happen. We're all deeply, deeply sad that it did."

It was the nicest I-told-you-so CeCe had ever heard. She had no idea how the witches knew that everything they feared came to pass. But they'd known everything from the beginning, hadn't they? Known and feared and forgiven her defiance of it.

It took her a couple more days, but she finally felt ready to leave the flat. She bathed and dressed, left No Name sleeping on her bed, and went to the Castle. No question that she looked as bad as she felt, but she didn't give a blithering bucket. All she needed to do was keep it together long enough to grab her mail and get her pre-sick leave paycheck, the one missing half due to the refunds after the SPIT debacle. Alun was probably working, but she wasn't going to torture herself with the Hellenic Room. A new Ice Age might arrive before she'd visit that room again.

Wobbly and indecisive, she stood in the Great Hall, trying to get her brain to function. It was balky and rust-locked, like a piece of machinery left out in the rain. The lighting in the Hall, low as it always was, still seemed painfully bright. A strange woman walked toward her from the side hall, the staff offices. She was tall, slim, and fair, wearing universal museum admin garb—tailored suit, silk blouse, three-inch heels, dark blonde hair in a tidy cut. The smell of expensive cologne came with her. *Infinissime* by Dior.

CeCe could just imagine what she looked like to the woman. A tangle of barely brushed hair falling to her shoulders, old jeans and her faded blue *I Heart Savannah* tee, a paint-splattered fleece jacket, running shoes that needed a good scrub. And her eyes, puffy, red, and miserable.

"May I help you?" The woman addressed her crisply, with a *Do I need to call security?* expression.

Belatedly, CeCe remembered she had left her ID card on the kitchenette counter. "I—I work here."

Incomprehension blanked the woman's face. "Are you a docent?"

"I'm Celeste Gowdie." Continued blankness. "I lead the tours on Saturday night." Still blank. "*Ghosts of the—*"

"Oh, yes, of course!" The woman extended a well-manicured hand. "I'm Charlotte Lewin, the new Programmes Director."

The new PD. Her new boss. As she shook the proffered hand, CeCe had an abrupt thought. "Where's Savin Bloom?"

"The Education Director? She's sharing my office for the present. We're a bit cramped, but I've been told a space is being converted to an office for her. Did you need to see her? Or perhaps Ms. Tattersall? She's in the other wing, now. The Executive Director's office."

No, she didn't need to see either of the women. Though, she wouldn't mind seeing them walk into the Irish Sea, weighted with stones. "Thanks, no. Just keeping track of staff changes." Suddenly, she couldn't wait to get out of the Castle. Her paycheck could wait for a few days. Her mail, too.

"Nice to meet you," she told Charlotte Lewin, who murmured something and smiled. The new PD bustled off, obviously still confused about how the odd young woman with the wild hair slotted into the Castle's order of things.

CeCe took a deep breath and began walking up the Grand Staircase. She wasn't sure why, especially since her gut told her to cut and run. Did she really want to go into the bedchambers, touch the beds, run her hand over the places where she and Patrick had lain? Or was she rubbing salt in her wounds, forcing herself to see them as they were now? Empty of life, empty of him.

She only made it to the second floor. Poppy Norris stood in the hallway as though waiting for her, which she probably was. Poppy, dear Poppy, who had given her Patrick's journal, and had been at the meeting of the witches. Poppy, who, when CeCe was halfway up the hall, opened her arms wide. CeCe ran into them.

After the sobbing slowed, her coworker took a handkerchief from a pocket in her apron and handed it over. As CeCe blew her nose and wiped her eyes, the witch grasped her wrists with both hands. Poppy's compassionate but steadfast gaze met CeCe's tortured one.

"It was the right thing, Miss Celeste. It was the *only* thing. And now, you must go on as we do, broken heart and all."

CeCe nodded, since she couldn't speak. She tried to give the hanky back, but Poppy waved it away. Taking CeCe by the shoulders, she turned her around and gave her the smallest of pushes toward the stairs. CeCe retreated down them.

Back at her flat, she fed No Name, then put soap and water in a bowl in the kitchenette sink and laundered Poppy's handkerchief. It was a square of good white linen, well cared for, old. A cluster of shamrocks was embroidered on one corner in green thread. So, Poppy was Irish, despite the very English surname. Then, something another docent had mentioned drifted back. Poppy was widowed a year ago. She volunteered at the Castle to fill her life after loss.

An Irish widow witch. If anyone could understand what CeCe was going through, it was Poppy because...

CeCe was a widow, too. The realization struck her wordless. She stopped what she was doing and stared through the window over the sink. There might be somewhere she could go. Grief counseling. A support group.

No. She wasn't really a widow, because Patrick wasn't really dead. He was just suspended. Adrift somewhere, nowhere, apart, alone.

Like her.

———

After her first awful return to the Castle, she forced herself to leave the flat every day. A trip to the grocery store or the butcher shop. A stroll up the High Street, looking in windows and not seeing anything. Tuesday in the Library slash Museum, where she volunteered at the front desk, forcing a smile at visitors. Or helped archive the Collection, with its smattering of Roman, Viking, and Celtic artifacts. A trip to the launderette on Wednesday. The bank on Thursday. Jana badgered until she got CeCe to come into The Broom & Bottle two afternoons a week. Shelving goods, sorting books that customers had replaced out of order, pasting on price stickers.

Anesthetized by busy work, she hardly noticed when February roared in, bitterly cold. *Ghosts of the Castle!* went on hiatus since visitor numbers were so small. On the one hand, she was glad of the reprieve from her gothic monologue about Castle ghosts. On the other, the empty day and night in each week, like every other empty hour, immediately filled with sadness.

The worst thing was how life went on around her, in spite of her. In her world, there had been a global disaster. *The sky has fallen! The sea is empty!* No one but her noticed.

A Valentine card came from Savannah, signed by all her aunts. They seemed to have reached a silent consensus on their revelations. Isobel Gowdie, their sister's true disappearance, castle drawings, soulers—her aunts had decided, once again, to just not talk about them.

She was angry with them for a while. They'd hidden so much from her. If only she'd known earlier. *Don't be stupid, CeCe, what difference would it have made?* Probably none. She would still love Patrick. She would still be mourning him, unless she'd never met him at all.

Was there any sort of trade she'd be willing to make for that? To never have seen Patrick that first time, in the Tower? To never have loved the ghost whose loss was killing her by inches? Definitely none. And she'd give anything at any price, including life as she now knew it, to have him back. For a day. An hour.

When the roads were open and they could drive into town from Basil and Bee, Rowan and Wren left baskets for CeCe outside her flat door. Goat cheese and jars of honey, bunches of herbs with little notes attached. *Chamomile, for comfort. Oregano, for joy. Sage, for wisdom.*

Never *Rosemary, for remembrance.*

Morgana sent her, through Jana, a jar of the Marigold Mud she'd sworn would keep CeCe looking twenty when she was sixty. When she looked in the mirror now, CeCe barely recognized her own face. She was anonymous, unmoored, a boat that had drifted away from everything she'd ever known or been. Face, body, name...all strangers.

Selene sent her a letter, a short one, mailed to her in care of The Broom & Bottle. CeCe opened it in her flat, sitting on the bed where she'd read Patrick's journal months earlier. She read the letter, then put it aside and pulled the journal from its place in the bedside nightstand, inches from her pillow.

The scent was almost gone. *Peat smoke, tobacco, sea water, Patrick.* She had to press her face against the leather to bring it back. She folded Selene's note and slipped it between the pages. She knew the words the old witch wrote, they were from Antoine de Saint-Exupéry.

It est très simple; on ne voit bien qu'avec le coeur. It's very simple; one only really sees with the heart. And below that, in Selene's spidery hand, *Courage.*

FORTY

Patrick had been gone for exactly six weeks. She knew, since she'd kept track of every day. The weather marginally improved, and the new PD wanted *Ghosts of the Castle!* to restart. CeCe agreed, with conditions. Just Saturdays, and just one ghost walk per week. If the new PD wanted another guide, she could hire one. Her current, no-longer-a-team-player guide would even hand over her script. Gladly.

In between Saturdays and her other odd jobs, she helped Alun Jones. She liked the work. It wasn't the career she'd hoped to find at the historic site, but it was respectable and interesting. She even began to think about picking up the threads of her future. Maybe become an archivist, or a conservator, like Alun. He promised to write her a glowing letter of reference.

"Alun," she protested while painting, "I haven't done anything any local laborer couldn't have done."

"Oh, no! That's not true, not in the least. I'd have been scuppered if I'd had to oversee Lob Lumpkin the carpenter and Sam Soppy the painter."

CeCe laughed, a little robin of happiness greeting the New Year. The robin chirped away for a few minutes, but the song grew darker as she worked. Happy? Yes, she was happy about the work she did with Alun. But try as she might, she couldn't find anything else to be happy about. The Castle job she'd thought was the road to success was nothing but a rotary. Now, she drove around and around, unable to find an exit, unwilling to stop the car.

Work wasn't lifting her mood, but she wasn't ready to return to her empty flat, either. Maybe it was time to brave the cold and the memories in a part of the Castle she'd not visited for a month and a half. Putting on her padded jacket, she waved goodbye to Alun, then headed—not down to the car park, but up—to the Tower.

With no heat and one window open to the elements, the room at the top of the Castle was the fabled brass nail in a latrine lid. But no one would disturb her there, and she needed to be alone, to think. She zipped her jacket to her chin, pulling the hood over her head. Then, she crossed the room to the sentry slit and gazed into the foggy distance. Just as she and Patrick had done, an eternity ago. Two people, one not quite alive and another who'd never known what life could be until the man at her side showed her.

As in those fated, early morning hours, she couldn't see the coast, but she knew where it was, beyond the limit of her sight. The sea, the rocky shore, the bluff with its ruined oratory and a jagged cluster of ancient tombstones. The bluff and the rocks and the stunted, broken, grave markers—they were all covered with snow, now.

Maybe it was time to bury her loss under the snow, with the graves. Maybe when spring came, the rain would wash it away. Maybe.

She slid down the wall and sat under the sentry slit, the stones cold against her back and her hands curled into her armpits for warmth. Desperate for distraction in the past few weeks, she'd done a lot of research. Even on the night SPIT had poisoned her tour, she'd known something was fishy about Ian, about his and the group's contradiction of her, of Patrick. She'd scoured the historical record until she validated her hunch.

Ian was the one who was wrong, wrong, wrong. Rushing to make fools of ghost hunters in general and her in particular, Ian had confused Sir Oliver Faraday with Sir Oliver Brandon. Brandon had indeed died of cholera in Nanking, China—two years after Faraday's suicide at the Castle. Patrick was right. Ian was wrong. So, what? Was it really that important that Patrick or Ian or she have the right answers, to be the expert who said which parts of history were true and which were false?

Something struck her, all at once. If she'd persisted with her obstinate plan to make her mark as a historian, she might have succeeded. But she probably wouldn't have enjoyed it much, because by the time she lost her chance at it—at least her chance at St. Rhydian's—she'd already realized, on some deep level, that interpreting history wasn't for her.

Now, though, there was a whole new world of possibilities. She revisited the hours she'd spent working with Alun, and her thoughts that maybe she'd like to be a conservator, like him. Or a librarian. A primary grades teacher, like Aunt Nikki. A doctor like Hélène, a designer like Sophie, even a realtor like Diane. It would work out, she told herself. She'd forge ahead and be successful, be happy.

"It's all right, it's fine." She'd said that dozens of times since Patrick left, and it still didn't ring true. What rang true was that she was a vase that someone had dropped on the floor, but it hadn't quite shattered. So it was picked up, and the person who dropped it said, *It's all right, it's fine.* And the vase went back on the table, and water was poured into it, and flowers were arranged, and no one noticed that there was a crack in it, nor that it was slowly and steadily leaking its contents onto the floor. But it was, and no matter how often it was filled, it would always end up empty, empty, empty...

The tears came, painful as shards of glass. She didn't know how long she cried this time—fifteen minutes, twenty—but she suddenly realized she was freezing. Not one of her best ideas, to sit on a stone floor in an unheated room with a window open to icy weather.

Time to go before she got hypothermia. She scrambled to her feet. Too fast, apparently, because she immediately slithered back down the wall, her jacket scraping on the rough stone and her bottom landing hard on the floor.

Sick washed over her in a dank wave, a tide of malaise that started in her midsection and surged right up to her head. Her ears rang so loudly she could hardly think, and her mouth went dry. Suddenly, a clenched fist of nausea punched her in the stomach. CeCe clapped her hand over her mouth. If she could just keep from hurling long enough to get to a restroom—

Nope. She doubled over and heaved, painfully. Luckily, there was nothing in her stomach except a breakfast glass of apple juice. It was a lot less tasty going out than it'd been going in.

Goddamn. She was as queasy as if she were on a rolling ship, mid-ocean. She struggled to a seated position again. Did she have the flu, for real? An intestinal virus? Couldn't be food poisoning. She hadn't eaten out in a week, and what little she had in the flat's small fridge was fresh.

Her stomach bucked and twisted. CeCe fell over, away from the wet patch, her belly convulsing again. When the spasm ended, she decided to stay where she'd toppled, breathing through her nose. Better. If she lay on her side, perfectly still, the urge to vomit receded. It was absurd and uncomfortable to be curled up like a beetle with her cheek against the icy floor. But if she tried to stand, she had a strong instinct she'd toss up the last of the apple juice.

After five minutes, she didn't feel any better. If anything, she felt worse. Head to toe exhaustion. Muscles hurting. Breasts hurting. A dull ache in her abdomen. Mouth as parched as a heap of November leaves.

She'd probably caught something from her pack of mouth-breathing ghost hunters. Or maybe it was seasonal. Most of the docents were coughing and sneezing.

Thank goodness for the clinic in the town. It was time to visit Dr. Ramanujan.

———

She'd felt woozy in the Tower Room, but it was nothing compared to the way CeCe felt when she heard Dr. Ramanujan's response to her symptoms.

"Could you be pregnant, Miss Gowdie?"

She didn't answer the doctor's question. What sort of answer could she give? The next half hour was a blur. As she waited for the damning little stick with the double red lines to take her to the Land of Oz, she punched numbers into her cell phone. Train to Liverpool, flight to New York, flight to Savannah. She'd be back in the house on Bull Street by next Thursday.

———

Saying goodbye to the Castle was a challenge. How could she say goodbye to something that wasn't finished yet? She put her ID card in her pigeonhole in the break room and said a few words to the docents and minor staffers who'd been kind to her. She said a few more to Poppy, who was wheezing her way up between the second and third floors. Poppy was cheerful and positive as always, though her eyes behind her glasses showed concern. CeCe wrote out her Savannah address and gave it to the docent, who tucked it into the pocket of her blue-flowered pinny.

Poppy reached out for her, and they hugged. "Remember, CeCe, you can always reach me through The Broom & Bottle. Letter, phone, email—anything, anytime."

CeCe nodded and smiled, fighting tears. Then, she turned away and walked toward the stairs, trying to keep her head high and her shoulders straight. Trying not to scream. If she started, she didn't think she could stop.

Downstairs, in the Great Hall, she considered asking to see Charlotte Lewin. Instead, she stood outside the PD's office and texted her resignation. After four revisions, she managed to compose a five-sentence, rage-free note.

Before she left the staff offices hallway, she walked to the end. A new plastic plaque was stuck on the door of the office that had been Miriam Lytton's. It had Savin Bloom's name on it. CeCe scowled at the door. "Bad cess to ye," she hissed under her breath, directing the curse to Bloom, Charlotte Lewin, Eunice Tattersall, and St. Rhydian's in general. A blessed moment of closeness to Patrick lightened her soul. He'd had a very bad time at the Castle, too.

Forty-One

Years later, if someone had asked CeCe to say what she did between leaving St. Rhydian's and the birth of Aoife Gabrielle Gowdie, she couldn't have told them in much detail. *Post-traumatic amnesia*. She'd read about it somewhere.

After Aoife was born, things got easier for a while, mostly because of her aunts. Hélène, semi-retired, was already living on Bull Street, so she was there to help. Aoife drew the others to the house like bees to a blossom. Nikki, who'd retired from teaching, was the first, making over a room so she could market Leonora's New Age goods online. Sophie had always been in and out a lot, but she finally moved her design business into her old bedroom, computer, swatch books, and all. Diane made some excuse about saving on rent, and next thing CeCe knew, her realtor aunt was selling houses from Bull Street.

An emotional sleepwalker most of the time, CeCe pretended everything was fine. Mostly, she focused on Aoife. By her sixth month of life, Aoife's eyes changed from infant blue to a beautiful and familiar aquamarine. CeCe couldn't begin to describe the joy and torment of holding the baby in her arms, marveling at those eyes and the black hair that curled around her child's smooth forehead.

After what her aunts went through with their sister Gabrielle, Aoife's birth must have seemed like a frustrating sort of *déjà vu*. They asked about the baby's father, of course, but CeCe, like her mother, wouldn't tell. She hadn't said anything at all to them about Patrick, so she couldn't blame them for believing—or wanting to believe—that she'd gotten in trouble in the normal way with a normal man. Still, did they really think history hadn't repeated itself? As far as it went, was CeCe in a position to know more about it than her aunts did? It wasn't like her mother had put a name on her child's birth certificate or left a note or—

Poor Mom. It hit her all at once one morning while she was bathing Aoife. As the baby splashed and cooed in her yellow plastic baby bath, an unexpected stab of remorse struck CeCe so hard she almost called one of her aunts to finish up so she could hide in her bedroom and let out a flood of tears. *Poor, poor Mom.*

Eighteen, pregnant, alone, silenced by fear and secrecy. Gabrielle Gowdie hadn't had the University of Liverpool library, or a study buddy with a doctorate in Anthropology, or a bunch of helpful witches up the street. No letters, texts, or audio files—however delayed—from her sisters. The oldest of them wasn't much older than Gabrielle was at the time, and still years away from learning about their shared souler legacy. Even now, with the access CeCe had to all those things, the legacy was almost too much to accept. She'd wasted so much of her life in anger and resentment toward a mother who was plunged into it without a clue.

She picked up Aoife, warm and smelling of baby soap, and clutched her to her shoulder, not caring if her T-shirt got soaked. "I'm sorry, Mom," she whispered against Aoife's velvety cheek. "I'm so, so sorry."

———

Alun Jones emailed her twice in the months before Aoife was born. Then, she didn't hear from or about him until Poppy Norris sent her a letter, tucked inside a National Trust photo card of the Castle. It arrived a few weeks after Aoife's first birthday and was full of Poppy's run-on sentences. CeCe sat on the back porch steps to read and reread it, while Aunt Hélène's suburban chickens clucked and scratched in the yard.

Dear CeCe,

We are all so happy about the baby turning one! Warm wishes for you both.

Everything here is the same only I have a bit of news about Alun Jones. After his work at St. Rhydian's was done, he took a job in France, some old church that was undergoing restoration, and apparently it was far enough away that his fiancée Carin (you remember her, she was working at the V&A) thought she'd lose him to some mademoiselle if she didn't get serious so she followed him and they were married in Paris. Ooh la lah!

The new Programmes Director (well, she's not new anymore, I guess) went through several actors to lead Ghosts of the Castle! *before she stuck with one from Cardiff. Nobody likes him, he vapes. Always has a funny smell if you know what I mean and he's unfriendly. Mairead says he's a poncey arse. She's blunt, our Mairead but no one disagrees with her on that point.*

Anyway, we all miss you and wish you were back, the Castle's not the same without you. Jana and I and the others send blessings and all our love.

Poppy Norris

She was weeping on the porch steps when Nikki found her. Eyebrows raised in silent query, her aunt pointed to the letter, and CeCe nodded. Nikki took the letter, read it, then put her arm around her niece, holding her but not speaking. She waited for CeCe to say something, or nothing, as she needed to. Finally, CeCe did.

"Before you ask, Alun Jones is not Aoife's father." Her nose was running, and Nikki handed her the dishtowel she'd brought outside. CeCe swiped her nose and went on. "It's just, well, I don't know. I'm glad for Alun, really. He's such a good person. And he wasn't my lover, but he was my friend." Nikki nodded. CeCe had told her about working with Alun when she got the gushing reference he'd attached to his first email.

"Are you sad because he's married?"

"No." *Yes.* She kicked herself for being conventional and naïve, but she wanted what Alun Jones and so many other people had. A future with a spouse and a cottage and a picket fence and a dog. A future that might stretch for years, for decades. After Patrick, that just wasn't possible. Sure, she could find some man and try to build something with him. But he would have to, every minute of every day, share her with a ghost. What kind of man would agree to that?

She rubbed the dishrag across her nose again. "I'm happy for him, really. But it's just—it's like—"

"Like you'll never have that kind of happy?"

It hurt too much to talk, so CeCe nodded. Nikki took her hand. "I felt that way for years, doll baby. Before I met Leonora."

The two of them sat shoulder to shoulder for a long time, watching the chickens do chicken things. Nikki alternately squeezed her hand and patted it. "Any chance you can marry Aoife's daddy?" she finally asked.

A jagged bark of laughter burst out before CeCe could stop it. She answered her aunt's question with another one. "Did my mother marry her daughter's father?"

What CeCe expected was silence. Or maybe platitudes and excuses. *She would have, it was his fault, if he'd only married her, she'd be alive today, maybe you should try harder with Aoife's father, he probably doesn't even know he has a child.* What her aunt said next was not expected.

"We think...we think she might have. But not in this time."

CeCe stared at Nikki like she'd grown rabbit ears. *They know. They knew then, and they know now.* Her world tilted on its axis again, the way it had when she'd finally accepted that Patrick was a ghost.

She should have seen it sooner. It was absurdly simple. No one had told her before because she hadn't asked. She hadn't asked because she hadn't known what to ask *about*. Isobel Gowdie. Soulers. Leathlings. Lovers—hers, her mother's—across time. All the *facts* of her life. Her aunts had known—maybe not everything, but something— about those facts and had made her life a dam against them. A dam made of tragic but less dangerous fictions. Unbalanced mother, unknown father, suicide, abandonment. Right there on the back porch of the house where she'd grown up, the dam broke.

"Diane!" Nikki yelled so loudly, CeCe nearly fell off the steps. The chickens squawked and scattered. Her aunt explained, "She's the one who got the genealogy on our family, you know, from Andy. And she did some work herself, on the Two Rivers family."

"Families," Diane pushed open the screen door to the porch. The door slammed behind her. "There were several."

"Okay, families. CeCe is asking what you know about the man Gabi might have, you know, gone to."

Diane sat on the step, the other side of CeCe, and the three women wriggled together to fit. Diane looked at everything but her sister and her niece. The sky, the yard, the fence, the chickens. It took a few minutes before she began talking. "There are several candidates."

Were they really sitting on the back steps, watching chickens and talking about the ghost lovers in her family? Apparently, they were.

"There was Forrest Hatherly. He was a descendant of one of the settlers who came to Savannah on the Good Ship *Anne*, with Oglethorpe. Or it might have been his brother, Thomas. He was older by a year and a half. Their father founded the Two Rivers plantation in the mid-1700s, and both sons died before they were forty."

Nikki piped up. "That was how the plantation changed hands, since the heirs both died childless. It went to Émile Boudreaux, then. He was a French immigrant, and—"

Diane cut her sister off. "Now, listen, I can't be a hundred percent sure, but I've always had this intuition—"

"Trust that, sister. I've always told you that angels reach into your heart, and what you call intuition is really the touch of an—"

"Right, thank you, Nikki. Anyway, if I wasted money gambling, which I don't," Diane looked pointedly at Nikki, who bought lottery tickets every time she went to the grocery store, "I would put my dollar on Jacques-Antoine Boudreaux. He was the youngest son of Émile Boudreaux and what they called the factor. He bought and sold goods for the plantation. Jacques-Antoine was no saint, I gotta say."

Too bad for heaven, but too good for hell.

"Y'all wait, now." Diane went into the house, the screen door slamming behind her. She was back in a few minutes and sat beside CeCe again. In her arms was a book on Georgia history. Opening it to a bookmark, she handed it to her niece. "There he is."

It was a full-page photo of a portrait painting. A peculiar shiver walked up CeCe's spine. It was the same shiver she'd felt at St. Rhydian's, standing on the bottom step of the Grand Staircase and staring at a portrait of Sean Patrick Ó Loinsigh, dead since 1761.

The painting in the book was captioned *Jacques-Antoine Boudreaux, 1785-18(?)* Its subject was a young man of almost Greco-Roman good looks. He had tawny skin, a strong aquiline nose, chiseled cheekbones, and dark, soulful eyes. His mouth was sensuous, curved upward in a slight smile. Deep brown, artistically mussed curls fell across his high forehead and above his ears. He was shown from the knees up, seated in an ornate chair and looking trim and fit in a black double-breasted tailcoat. His shirt was brilliant white, with a collar that nearly reached his ears. Under the collar, his cravat was elaborately knotted.

The artist had done an especially good rendering of Boudreaux's hands. One lay on his thigh. The other rested casually atop a cane, his fingers relaxed and dangling. There was a gold ring on the smallest finger, and a long scar ran across the back of his hand from side to side, just above the knuckles.

His hands are like Patrick's. Strong, capable, formed with beauty and violence. The hands of a gentleman—a dangerous one.

The longer CeCe stared at the page, the more the back of her neck tingled. More than anything else, the tingle told her what she needed to know. She was looking at a portrait of her father.

Diane watched her closely as she kept talking. "His mother was Émile Boudreaux's second wife. She was a Creek Indian. Half Creek, anyway, since her father was apparently a Scots trader. The wife's Creek family was very high-ranking, and that came with obligations. I don't imagine you know a lot about Indian affairs in those years."

CeCe pulled her eyes away from the book. "Uh, you do remember I have a graduate degree in History."

"Well, all right, then, Professor. Tell your Aunt Nicole about the Creek Wars."

CeCe sighed. "It's pretty complex, but the short version is that in 1813, when the Creek Indians got fed up with the U.S. government breaking treaties and moving settlers by the hundreds onto Creek lands, they fought back. Violently." She looked at Diane. "So, you're saying Jacques-Antoine was considered, by his Indian family, to be one of their sons."

Her aunt nodded. "One of their sons, one of their guns. When hostilities broke out, Jacques-Antoine had to go to war along with his family. His Creek family."

"What happened?"

Diane shrugged, her shoulders rising and dropping in her print cotton housedress. "We don't really know. He was captured at Horseshoe Bend, in Alabama. He got away, killing some U.S. Army soldiers when he did. Then, he disappeared. Could've died then, or later. There were Indians on both sides of that War. If he was captured by the ones on the other side, well, he might've been enslaved. Or tortured and killed."

CeCe winced. "I hope he died before that happened."

Diane stood up and dusted her dress with her hands. "Yeah, well, that's about the only thing we do know. If he was the man our sister, Gabi, ran off to Two Rivers to be with, then he was definitely dead."

FORTY-TWO

"Waste of a very expensive education, CeCe." Aunt Hélène had a frown to go along with her opinion. It was the third time in two months she'd pronounced it like Universal Truth.

CeCe didn't disagree with her aunt, but she didn't want to argue about it, either. Teaching three sections of undergrad history as an adjunct was a job leading nowhere, and nowhere was exactly what she'd programmed into her Life GPS. Until and unless she developed a taste for it again, she'd left the only history that mattered behind her, in a castle in Wales.

Despite her obvious disinterest, her aunts had a plan for moving CeCe forward. It wasn't producing results, but they kept at it, anyway.

Like, in February. "Oh, look here, CeCe!" Sophie's readers were halfway down her nose as she waved her cell phone. "There's a music festival called Stopover—"

"Drugs!" Hélène yelled from the kitchen. Contemporary music and contraband were one and the same to Hélène.

"With *dancing!*" Sophie yelled back. "Come on, CeCe, let's get tickets..."

And in May. *"CeCeeeee!"* Diane hollered from the kitchen table where she was opening the mail with Nikki peering over her shoulder. "Louise Osborne, you remember her. Her daughter Linda's getting married next month and I'm going to include you in the RSVP, okay?"

Nikki chimed in. "Reception's at Telfair Academy, sweetie. Oh my, that'll be something. Linda's fiancé is David McKay, and he's not only rich but he's got *three* good-looking brothers..."

Then, September. "I swear, CeCe. I have *got* to drop these five pounds." That was Hélène, grabbing the negligible roll of fat around her middle. None of her aunts were overweight, and they all had a mortal fear of fried foods because both parents had heart disease. "Let's get a membership at that gym downtown. They've got a two-for-one special and we can..."

When they weren't trying to socialize her out of her grief, the aunts tried to console her out of it. Nikki was especially persistent. "Think of this as a healing time, CeCe," she cooed. "When you're past it, you'll be ready to love again."

Every month of every year, no matter how they strategized it, everyone wanted her to go out and find a real live man. Everyone wanted her to forget the dead one. And everyone was wasting their time, because the dead one hadn't forgotten her.

———

She didn't want to use the red and blue bottles, but as the months turned into years and her heart refused to heal, the need to see Patrick finally overwhelmed her. She retrieved the bottles from a side pocket of the suitcase she'd brought back from Wales. With mingled excitement and dread, she sat on her bed and removed the bottles from their wrapping, the handfasting cloth. Dropping the cloth in her lap—*why did it still feel warm?*—she held up the red one, and Jana's words came back. *"That one opens the door."*

It wasn't the only thing Jana had said about the magical bottles. "When you need them," she'd told CeCe as she pushed them at her, "it won't be a laughing matter."

I'm not laughing now, Jana. She tucked the handfasting cloth under her pillow, and placed the blue bottle on her bedside table. Courage took a minute to summon, but she pried open the wax seal on the red bottle with her fingernails, uncorked it, and upended it over her mouth. She tapped it once and a drop of something sharp and citric, orange peel or lemon, surprised her tongue. "One drop," Jana had told her, so CeCe righted the vial instantly. She barely got it corked before she fell onto the bed, overcome by sleep so fast and heavy it was like she'd been chloroformed.

She dreamed.

At the end of the long twisting passage in the bowels of the Castle, she stood in front of a door. Grasping the pitted iron handle, she gave it a strong tug. The door opened on Patrick's bedchamber, lit only by the flickering light of the fire. The fire she had watched him light so many times, crouching with tinderbox and striker on the hearth.

He was in the center of the room, facing her. His clothes were the same he'd worn when they first met. Brown breeches, mustard hose, the shoes with silver buckles, the linen shirt made thin and soft by wear. Wavering in the uncertain light, he was present, but somehow insubstantial, as though the form of the man was there; the man was not. What she saw was a shade, a shadow, a pale projection.

Her feet were anchored, even as she tried to move toward him. She regarded them quizzically, as though they weren't hers. They might be someone else's feet, standing on another threshold. Another border between worlds. She dragged her eyes upward, to Patrick. Could he see her? Did he know she was there?

I'm here, my love, I'm here! Tell me you see me, want me. Say it, say it!

The vision faded. CeCe awoke in her bed, sobbing. At last, she knew what silent as the grave meant.

———

On the red bottle nights, she tried to memorize every detail of Patrick's appearance, hoping it would help her survive the drought of touch and speech. He wasn't always standing in the center of the room. Sometimes, he sat in the leather and wood armchair. A book rested on his thigh, his hand covering the pages, while he gazed into the fire. Or he stood at the wide oak table, holding the astrolabe and staring out the casement window into a gray, featureless landscape. Once, she saw him in his bed. He was naked to the waist, eyes open, one palm splayed on his chest, over his death scar.

No matter how she tried, CeCe couldn't cross the threshold into the room. Dream after dream, she tried to speak, but nothing, not a single sound, came out of her mouth. Patrick never seemed to see her. He never spoke.

Thank God Jana had given her the blue as well as the red bottle. Jana said the blue one would close the door, and so CeCe oscillated between the two. For as many nights as she could stand it, she fell into the dream. Then, on the razor edge of madness, she used the blue bottle to plunge her brain into dreamless sleep. The need to see Patrick always drove her back to the red bottle, a junkie to her drug.

The dreams weren't the worst or the best of it. She became obsessed with things undone, or never to be done again. The day she'd sewed a button on the cuff of Patrick's shirt, and his grateful kiss. The meals they might have shared, but hadn't.

The quiet conversations in the dark, before they fell asleep. Her hopeless fantasy of furnishing a room with him, a house. *Should we put the sofa here, or there?*

The child he would never hold.

She lost weight until she was thinner than she'd been before she was pregnant, no matter how much her aunts tried to feed her. She spoke in monosyllables to everyone except Aoife, her only solace. All night she clung to her dream, and all day she clung to her child. When it became obvious Aoife was turning into a life preserver on CeCe's personal Titanic, the aunts intervened. One of them would say, "Aoife, let's get you in a pretty dress. You're going to Mass with us," or, "What a pretty day it is, Fee!" Aoife struggled to pronounce her name, calling herself "Fee," and the aunts had picked it up. "Come on, sweetpea. Let's go to the park."

CeCe had stopped going to the park, and to Mass. At parks, she ran the risk of seeing loving couples, arm in arm, stealing kisses. At Mass...

She didn't go to Mass, but she always left early for her Monday and Thursday morning classes at UGA so she could spend a half hour at the Catholic Center on campus, praying the rosary for one Sean Patrick Ó Loinsigh. She had no idea if anyone in Heaven was listening or, if they were, they would help him, help her. In the moment, the prayers calmed her. By the time she got home six hours later, she was taut as piano wire again.

———

It was a piano wire afternoon, and Aoife had just turned three. The toddler was sitting on the living room floor playing with her brand-new mermaid doll, while Hélène took great-auntie photos with her phone. CeCe tried to hug her daughter, but Aoife pulled away and CeCe cracked.

"What's the matter with Fee? Why doesn't she look at me when I talk to her? Something's wrong. She's detached from me, she's—"

Her aunt tsked and kept snapping photos. "There's nothing wrong with that child. She's just in her own little world. Exactly like your mom was at that age. And just like you were when—"

CeCe shouted. "I am not like my mother! If you say that one more time, I'll scream!"

"You're already screaming, Celeste Gowdie."

"Fee's nothing like my mother! She's nothing like me! Nothing!"

Aoife stared at her open-mouthed and dropped her doll. Her face crumpled like paper and Hélène snatched her up and carried her, wailing, out of the room.

CeCe kept shouting what sounded like a curse, even to her own ears. "She's not like me! She's not! She's not!"

FORTY-THREE

But Aoife was exactly like CeCe, in the way that mattered most. A month before Aoife's fourth birthday, the drawings started. At first, it was just a block with a pointy top. Could have been a house, could have been just some shape she liked. Liked well enough to draw it and nothing else. In a few months, the shape had grown taller, with what looked like three stories, windows with cross-hatching, and fluted pilasters embedded in the façade. The pediment was pyramidal with a squiggle on the pointy top. CeCe squinted, but she couldn't guess what the squiggle was. She couldn't guess what sort of building it topped, either, until Fee explained.

"It's a theater," Fee solemnly told anyone who asked.

Aoife had never been to a theater, not even a movie one. Had her aunts taught her that word? Whatever it was, the image was amazing for an almost four-year-old, and it got more detailed and expert with every drawing. By the time she was four and a half, Aoife's theater looked almost like an architect's rendering.

As to who might be inside that theater? CeCe tried not to

think too much about him. All she could do was hope and pray he was a good, good man, who deserved her precious child.

She supposed she should be happy Fee wasn't drawing abandoned barns, or stone circles on desolate moors. Even if she was and CeCe wanted to fight it, she couldn't. She was tired, tired to death, tired all the time. She was sure she never slept, but she must have been sleeping because the dreams kept coming.

Frightened of the relentlessly silent nighttime visions, she stopped using the red bottle. It made no difference; the dreams came. There was no stopping them, and the fight had gone out of her, anyway. Despite the rosaries, she didn't think she had faith in God anymore. Improbably, illogically, immovably, she still had faith in Patrick, so she wrapped herself in that. That, and the soft strip of cloth he'd wound around both their hands. CeCe slept with it clutched in her fist.

One night, almost exactly five years after Patrick last held her in his arms, her faith was rewarded. Worn out after a long day, she fell into bed and instantly into sleep. She had a new dream. A different one.

It was Wales. Daylight there, late afternoon with a leaden mist rolling in from the west. CeCe stood on the grassy bluff above the beach, a mile from St. Rhydian's Castle. She was among the broken gravestones of the oratory, gazing out to sea.

Patrick stood next to her. She turned her head to look at him, and he met her gaze. Vivid against the vast pale green of the water and the gray, cloud-streaked sky, he was just the same as he'd been the day she last saw him. His height, his smile, his black hair disordered by the wind, his eyes the color of the tossing waves. He reached out to her, and she put her hand in his. Reunion flowed like healing water from their handclasp to her heart.

His voice banished the silent desolation of the years. The same dear voice, deep and faintly rough, speaking the only words she needed to hear.

"Come to me, my love."

CeCe woke, rested and calm. Five years ago, when the fading tore them apart, Patrick had said it wasn't her fault. She knew that, now, as she suddenly knew what to do next. Patrick's words had carried fire to her heart, lighting the way out of darkness. At last, this day, she would set out on the path to his arms.

FORTY-FOUR

It was less of a shock than she thought it might be when she told her aunts. After all, they'd been through something similar with their sister Gabrielle, Two Rivers, and the rest. But that was only a hundred miles away, in Moniac. CeCe's ghost lover was taking her across an ocean.

Right away, her aunts insisted on coming with her, and CeCe didn't go to war over it. It was their prerogative, and she wanted them there, since the idea of a final leave-taking without them was just too hard to imagine. The battle started when they told their niece they wanted to leave Aoife behind, with Cousin Andy and his wife, Ellen.

"No! Fee will go with us. With *me*. Not just to Wales but —beyond."

Her aunts' stunned silence seemed to fill and overflow the house. "But, CeCe, honey," Hélène said, "what if something happens? None of us knows how this works."

"*I* know." Did she? Or was she in denial again? "And there are people I can ask, people who will help. Even if she doesn't go where I go, she has to *see*. Not for my sake, but for hers. She'll know how I've gone, and who'll be there for her, after.

It'll help her when she's older, and she goes the way her souler mom went. The way her souler grandmother, whom she never knew, went. It's her right, don't you understand? She's a souler, and it's her *right*."

———

After the initial fussing died down, her aunts did what they did best: organize. That left CeCe's hands and heart free to spend two weeks the way she needed to spend them.

She took Aoife to the park every day. CeCe counted them off in her head. Fourteen days to be with her daughter in case her gut feelings were wrong and Fee was left behind. Fourteen days to treasure everything about her. To give her the memories CeCe wished her own mother had given her. Memories that included more than a sad, pretty face framed in brown curls, and sad, pretty eyes looking into hers. Fourteen days to explain—try to, anyway—what was going to happen. What CeCe thought and hoped would happen. She was flying by instruments, blind to everything but instinct. That, and faith in her man.

When Aoife wasn't on the swings or running circles around big oak trees in the park, she wanted to draw, so CeCe made sure colored pencils and a sketch pad accompanied them every day. Sometimes, like today, she just sat on a bench next to the daughter that she and Patrick had impossibly, perfectly, made. She stroked Aoife's black, wavy hair and memorized the silky feel of it, the baby shampoo scent of it.

CeCe looked up, into the treetops shading the bench. It was October, and the leaves were turning from green to rust. In a few weeks, there'd be more on the ground than on the branches. If everything went the way she hoped, neither she nor Aoife would be in Savannah to see them.

Her cell phone rang, and she grabbed it. The witch on the other end began bluntly, as she usually did.

"You're not really thinking of doing it, are you?"

"Jana. You got my email."

"I did, and I didn't like it." Thanks to satellites, Jana's concern came through as loud and clear as if she were sitting on the bench next to CeCe. "I asked Morgana, who knows more about soulers than the rest of us put together. She couldn't think of a single case where a child went with her souler mother."

"Single case that she *knows of*," CeCe corrected. She couldn't sit still for this conversation. Pressing the phone to her ear, she started walking, one eye on Aoife, who hardly noticed. "Is she aware of any *failed* transferences?"

Jana answered obliquely. "Morgana said to remind you that's why maidens—*maidens*, CeCe—were the ones who delivered the souls' ransom on All Hallow's Eve."

"Yes, I read that in my research. But—"

"Do you understand now why Selene kept asking if you'd bedded your leathling?"

"I do, but can we please just get back to—"

"You've made a right shambles of this, daughter."

CeCe couldn't think of a reply that sounded anything but lame, so she didn't try for one.

The silence stretched on so long she thought maybe Jana had ended the call, but finally the witch spoke again. "Selene has some antique grimoires." *Grimoires?* They were back in Magick City now. "In one of them, there's a margin note. Selene sent me the—wait, I'll show you." Jana disconnected. A few seconds later, a notification pinged. When CeCe opened the photo file, an image of a faded, discolored page filled her phone screen. The body of the page seemed to be a list, so faint it was almost illegible. Brown writing in the margin was a little bolder. She rotated the image and hit the enlarge feature. The words spoke to her across centuries.

Goody Aylewright did on this Eve of Hallowmas goe with Roberta her Dotter to the Fyre.

The phone rang. Jana began where she'd left off before sending the photo. "Selene always thought it meant they were executed for witchcraft, but there's no evidence of a trial or witch hunts in that time and place."

"Which was?"

"Every entry is dated. That one is from All Saints Day, the first of November in 1729. The grimoire belonged to Alice Berre, of Sussex."

"So, you're saying that an alternative meaning of the margin note is that Goody Aylewright and her daughter went to the All Hallow's fire. As soulers."

"It's a reach, Celeste, but yes, the souler fire. Went and did not return. At least, there's no mention in the grimoire of a return."

"Thank you, Jana."

"Celeste, wait! That grimoire note—it's very scant evidence."

CeCe ignored the comment and instead asked, "What will happen if we both don't go? I mean, if we try, but..."

There was another long pause, this one full of things CeCe didn't want to think about. Finally, Jana replied. "You're asking me to guess, daughter. Witchcraft is not guesswork."

Wasn't it? Wasn't everything guesswork? "Just posit an outcome, Jana. Based on what you know."

Jana's sigh was big, even across an ocean. "It's possible that neither of you will go. Or you might go, and the child will be left behind. Or..." An even longer pause than before, with more scary things oozing through the connection. "Since you've told me Aoife is the leathling's child, he might pull both of you to him. Notwithstanding, he knows nothing about her."

"He does. I mean, I've told him about her. Tried to, anyway."

"Keep telling him. We will work from this side." Despite Jana's doubts, the promise had a ring of determination. "And CeCe, there's one more thing."

Of course, there was. What was it this time? A secret spell? An amulet dipped in henbane tea?

"Morgana said to tell you that in all her years of studying both soulers and grimoires, she's never found a single instance of a souler making more than one...trip."

Trip. That was a delicate way to put it. Like CeCe and Aoife were going to the beach or the mountains for a week. "Go on. I need to know everything."

Jana sighed again. "I wish I could tell you everything, but all I know is what Morgana knows, or thinks she knows. She said to warn you that wherever and whenever you end up, you won't be able to come back. The souler has what you Americans call a one-way ticket."

CeCe nodded, even though she knew Jana couldn't see it. "I understand." Did she? Not really. But whether she understood or not, she and Aoife had that particular ticket in hand and were using it in two weeks.

Musing on that, she let her cellphone slide away from her ear and almost missed Jana's next remark. "What? Jana? Say that again."

"Morgana told me to tell you something else. She said the three of you—your leathling, your daughter, and you—must be bound together."

We already are. She was sure of it. Neither she nor Patrick had known at the time, but CeCe was pregnant when Patrick joined their hands in the small, cold room high in the Castle.

Jana's goodbye was as curt as her hello. "Right. Two weeks." The call ended.

CeCe walked back to the bench and Aoife smiled up at her when she sat. The building on the drawing pad had been an outline when the phone first rang. Now, Aoife was coloring it in. Her drawings got more detailed and lifelike every day.

"That's beautiful, baby." CeCe looked up to the treetops again. With one hand, she stroked her child's hair, but her mind reached for a place farther away than the other end of the call she had just taken. *Patrick, I'm here with your daughter, Aoife Gabrielle. We're coming to you, my love.*

"Fee, honey, would you like to hear a story?"

Aoife nodded. She loved stories. A born historian. CeCe had no idea if the story she was about to tell Aoife would make any sense or would stick in her child's mind. She was only four. How much did a four-year-old remember about anything? CeCe took a deep breath and let it out on important words.

"Once upon a time, in a place called Ireland, there was a boy. He lived in a house on a hill with his mother. Her name was exactly the same as yours, because you're named after her. She was very beautiful, the other Aoife, and she had a cat named Fergus..."

FORTY-FIVE

They left Savannah like a caravan about to set off across the desert, minus the camels. Instead, they had four aunts, one niece, six suitcases, five carry-ons, passports, tickets, jackets, sweaters, fruit rolls, water bottles, and a four-year-old. Somehow, they got through security and managed to board the plane to the U.K.

On the flight over, CeCe put Aoife between herself and Nikki. They both pulled up their armrests so Fee could stretch out or snuggle. CeCe was pretty sure if snuggling was on the agenda, it would be on Nikki's side of the seat. Aoife was more attached to her than any of the other aunts, almost as attached as she was to her mother. Jealousy pricked CeCe now and then, but all in all, she knew it was for the best. Just in case.

While everyone else chatted or read or dozed, Aoife drew her theater. CeCe had bought a new drawing pad for the trip, and Aoife got absorbed in her work for hours. She finally fell asleep, curled, as CeCe knew she would be, against Nikki. Love for her aunt surged in CeCe's heart. Love for all of them, of course, but especially Nikki, the one always searching for angels, when all she had to do was look in the mirror.

She took the pad from under Fee's arm and inspected what her daughter had done. It was the most intricate and perfect of her buildings yet. *Building, singular.* Only the one, over and over, like her mother, like her grandmother, Gabrielle. Their drawings had been unique, just as their leathling would be.

CeCe thought Aoife's theater looked vaguely like one she'd seen, but she couldn't place it. Certainly nothing she'd seen in Georgia. Someplace else in the South? In Europe? Farther East? As long as it wasn't Transylvania.

She flipped the sketchbook's cover over the completed drawing and closed Fee's treasured box of colored pencils, a gift from Nikki when CeCe was still fighting the inevitable and wouldn't buy her daughter any drawing tools. She was ashamed of that, now. If her own mother, and then Nikki, hadn't given her pencils when she was drawing her castle, she would have drawn on the bedroom door with one of her aunts' lipsticks, or on the sidewalk with chalk, or with toothpaste on the bathroom wall. The souler urge was too strong to be denied by any earthly prohibition. It was its own law.

Selene's voice came to her across the ocean. *"Some choose magic. Some are chosen by it. Some* are *magic. For them, there is no choice."*

CeCe turned sideways in her seat to watch Aoife sleep. So innocent, so untroubled. When the time came, what joys and horrors would her daughter's leathling bring? Would he change her, immerse her in strange realities, consume her heart with unquenchable love?

Yes, yes, and oh, yes.

FORTY-SIX

S amhain, All Hallow's Eve, October thirty-first. By something the witches called the Old Reckoning, the day had started at sundown the day before, and it was now close to noon. Everyone—her aunts, the witches including Poppy Norris—was at Basil and Bee, Rowan and Wren's farm six miles inland from the coast.

CeCe loved it at first sight. Now, she stood in front of the mossy old stone cottage, holding a mug of cider in her hand but too nervous to drink. Fee sat on the sun-warmed front steps of the cottage, cooing at No Name while the cat shifted lazily into lizard green.

A light touch on CeCe's shoulder made her turn around. It was Rowan, holding hands with Wren. Both of them smiled their shy, farm girl smiles. They wore matching tees, as they did the last time CeCe saw them together. Today's were black with orange printing. *Nos Calan Gaeaf*, the Welsh name for Halloween.

Rowan spoke first, nodding toward the cottage. "Wren's parents had it as their country place for years, but—"

"They retired to the South of France," Wren interrupted.

"So, they gave the place to Wren."

"To us," Wren corrected. She lifted Rowan's hand and pressed it briefly against her lips.

The tiny gesture brought sweet and painful memories to CeCe. Patrick, kissing her hand, her cheek. Brushing a stray hair out of her eyes. It had been so long. She pulled herself together. "You two look just the same, after—"

"Four years," Rowan finished.

"And a few months," added Wren. Smiling and waving, the two walked away, still holding hands.

Four years and a few months—nine months, to be exact. Rowan and Wren looked the same, but did she? Her palm went involuntarily to her abdomen. She'd had a baby, gained weight, lost even more, spent five years grieving, agonizing, pining for Patrick. Did it show on her face, her body? Would Patrick notice, would he still desire her?

With the uncanny way Jana had of creeping up silently, the witch was suddenly at CeCe's elbow. Jana was in witch uniform, all black from head to toe, with a large silver pentacle on a chain around her neck. She'd gone platinum with her hair again, except for a single broad streak of black in the middle.

They stood together, silent. There was no way to tell what Jana was thinking, but CeCe had a question that had bothered her since the dream in which Patrick beckoned her.

"Why so long, Jana?" She waved her mug toward the women bustling around a long outdoor table, arranging lunch, but she knew Jana would understand the larger meaning. "Why did it all take so long?"

Jana nodded slowly, considering. "It takes as long as it takes, Celeste. 'Only if the coin be whole,' that's the rhyme. You, yourself, are the tribute exchanged for a soul. You can't just plonk any old thing down on the altar."

Burnt offering. The phrase came unbidden, ringing true. The years without Patrick had burned her, body and soul, right down to her essence. She could hardly remember the person she'd been before him. Deluded by secrets, desperate for attainment, her life was driven by *nots*. Not to be like her mother, not to fail at anything, not, ever, to risk love.

Now, she was a mother, she had failed more than once, and she loved—oh, how she loved. She was all love, whole and shining with it.

It had taken five years. But if she was the coin that, when offered as ransom for Patrick's soul, might be enough...She reckoned she was twenty-four karat solid gold.

She sensed Jana watching her as understanding dawned. "How old were you," the witch asked, "when your mother went to join her leathling?"

So, one or more of her aunts had shared the now-not-so-closely-guarded family secret. Secrets, plural, including CeCe's father. Presumed father. "Five. I was five when she went."

"And had you started drawing your castle?"

"I had." CeCe waited a few seconds, then said what was really on her mind. "I understand her better, now. But I still think my mother should have taken me with her when she went."

Jana's eyes narrowed. "Perhaps. I'm sure she thought she was doing the right thing."

Am I?

"I won't ask if you're ready," Jana added.

"Ready or not, it's happening. I'm fine with everything, really. Well, almost everything." CeCe lifted her chin toward Fee. "Promise me you'll, I mean, if things don't go the way I hope, I just need to be sure Aoife will be—"

"It's all taken care of, daughter. If Aoife stays behind, then every May, one of your aunties will bring her to us for the summer. She'll stay here at Basil and Bee. It's a wonderful place for a child. You should walk around before sundown."

Sundown. It's happening at sundown. Six hours, five, four...

Jana put her arm around CeCe's shoulders. "She'll be fine, Celeste. Fine now, and fine years from now."

CeCe looked again at the little gathering of witches and aunts. Nikki was chatting with Selene. The older witch's long gray hair swung around her knees like a bell.

Jana read CeCe's mind, as she usually did. "Not all of us will be here, of course. And new ones will have joined us. But Aoife will learn what she is, and what to expect. She won't be alone when her time comes."

CeCe nodded, but fear put an edge on her next words. "If she goes with me, do you think she'll come back here when she —I mean, when her leathling…" The words died in her throat, and her eyes burned. *I won't cry, I won't cry.* The tears escaped, anyway, making slow, salty trails down her cheeks.

"I can't tell you that, Celeste. No one can. But I think, one road or another, she might." Jana squeezed CeCe's shoulder with one hand, pointing to the still-steaming mug with the other. "Bottoms up, daughter. It'll help with the fear."

———

Lunch went on for hours. CeCe was so wound up she thought she might explode. Poppy Norris tried to distract her with the backstory on what was coming next.

"There's a stone circle called Hel Solod. Nobody except us," she sidled her eyes toward the other witches, "comes here now, but most of the local grandparents know about it, and many generations before them knew. They came on All Souls' Day and left all sorts of things, cakes and puddings and fruit. Even money. All for what they called the 'messengers of the dead'."

CeCe let that sink in. A messenger of the dead. Was that what she was?

Poppy stroked CeCe's cheek. It was a featherlight touch,

but CeCe was so wired she jumped. "You needn't worry, dear," Poppy soothed. "The magic is active and strong."

Worry? CeCe had gone well past worry into full-on panic. She clung to Patrick's voice in her head. *That we never will part, not on Earth nor in Heaven...*

Poppy jostled her out of her fear-spiraling thoughts by handing her a small handkerchief. CeCe recognized it immediately. It was the square of linen and shamrocks she'd wept into after Patrick left, nearly five years before. Poppy winked. "My mother told me never to leave the house without one. For you, dearie, for luck."

CeCe was still staring at the handkerchief when the meal abruptly ended and the cleaning up began. She leaped to her feet, then realized she didn't know what to do. Apparently, others did, because Diane and Sophie came to her side.

Sophie had a brown paper-wrapped parcel in her arms, and she handed it to CeCe. "Our sister," she began, "was wearing a raggedy old shirt and blue jeans when she went to—"

"Two Rivers," Diane finished. "And I'm sure that was just fine. But we thought you—"

"You and Fee," Sophie broke in.

"Should have something nice for, well, you know. Him."

CeCe figured the witches had explained the Knight of Pentacles to her aunts. They obviously still had trouble saying it out loud.

Diane pointed to the stone outbuilding closest to the cottage. "Wren says you can change in the herb barn. We'll dress Aoife and bring her to you in a little while so you can—I mean, if you have to..." Her aunt trailed off.

Say goodbye? I won't have to, Diane, because my daughter is coming with me. Oh, please, God, let her come with me.

She smiled at her aunts, then took the parcel to the barn. It was a warm space, fragrant with the herbs being dried and readied for packaging. A mad impulse seized her. Why couldn't she and Fee just stay there, safe and warm in the witches' house? *Don't be ridiculous, CeCe. It's showtime.* Under a canopy of overhanging sheaves and bunches, she made the biggest costume change of her life.

Even though she hadn't done it in a while, it only took her fifteen minutes to cross three centuries, in clothing, anyway. *Twenty-first century historian, fare ye well. Woman of the seventeen hundreds, well met.*

Diane and Sophie were such good tailors. CeCe remembered every Christmas pageant and Halloween outfit they'd ever sewn for her. What they'd made for her now, though, wasn't for trick-or-treating. It was an eighteenth-century trousseau. A crisp white shift, stays, two petticoats, and a pair of white stockings knitted in delicate yarn. CeCe tied the stockings above her knees with silk ribbons. Atop the underclothing, she donned a wool, butter yellow sleeved bodice and a Delft blue skirt. She felt for a pocket in the skirt, then realized her aunts had made it authentically, so it had a separate pocket, a flat linen bag with ties, accessed through a slit in the skirt. CeCe lifted the hem and tied the pocket around her waist.

As at St. Rhydian's, she struggled to get her thick hair into a single braid and stuff it under the linen cap her aunts had made. She swung the dark blue wool cloak—Sophie and Diane had replaced the red one she'd left behind at the Castle —over her shoulders and fastened the pewter clasp at her neck.

A cloak, that's good. It might be cold where...wherever.

She tucked Poppy's handkerchief into the front of her bodice and slipped her feet into her old Colonial shoes. Lastly, she pulled the handfasting cloth from the pocket of her jeans, transferring it to the pocket under her skirt. A plain, ordinary action, but it pasted bold labels on the day. *Enormous. Final.*

Irrevocable. A silvery chime sounded in her heart. *I forgive you, Mom. I understand now, and I forgive you.*

Aoife ran into the barn. Jana stood behind her, a dark shadow in the open doorway.

"*Oooh*, Mommy!" Fee rushed to her mother's side, and CeCe smiled at the miniature version of herself. Same clothes, just tinier. "We look like princesses!" her daughter shouted, twirling. When Aoife's skirts lifted, CeCe saw one striking difference in their shared costumes; her daughter wore red, patent leather Mary Janes. She raised her eyebrows at Jana.

Jana shrugged. "Your Aunt Diane said your little diva insisted on the shoes."

Aoife threw her arms around CeCe's knees. Ocean green eyes—Patrick's—looked up at her, innocent and wise. "Are we going to Papa now?"

And there it was, done in one simple soaring second, like a bird taking wing. The moment she had dreaded, the journey she couldn't explain, came effortlessly from Aoife's lips. On a bench in a park, CeCe had told her little girl a story about an Irish cottage. A woman who had a son. The son who grew up to be a man, a warrior, a father. Aoife had made the story real, made it hers.

CeCe bent to embrace her, kissing the top of the white cap that barely restrained Aoife's mop of dark hair. "Yes, baby girl, we're going to him now. But listen to me." She crouched so her eyes were level with her daughter's. "Your great-aunts Hélène and Sophie and Diane—"

"And Nikki."

"Especially Aunt Nikki. They're not going anywhere. In case you want to stay."

"My new aunties, too?"

Her new aunties. The witches. CeCe nodded gravely. Aoife was quiet for a count of ten, thinking. Then, she fiercely gripped her mother's hand. "I want to go with you, Mommy."

Jana spoke from the door of the barn. "It's time, Celeste."

———

The whole day, the witches had kept one eye on the hour and the other on the weather. Now, at five o'clock, the sun had lowered and the air had the edge-of-frost feel that autumn brought early to Wales. Equipped with battery lanterns and flashlights, the witches led the others along the narrow path to Hel Solod. Deeper and deeper into the thicket of trees they went, until the woods suddenly opened into a modest-sized clearing.

It wasn't what CeCe had expected—something megalithic, or a mini Stonehenge, maybe. Sol Helod was just a circle of oversized rocks. Welsh bluestone, each chunk about four feet high, six stones arrayed around the intersection of two footpaths so worn by time they were nearly invisible. Within the embracing forest, the circle no longer felt the sun, but it seemed to give off a pale light of its own. A shallow pit had been dug to one side of the intersection of the paths, and a fire built in it. It was burned down now, to hot embers. A thin spiral of tangy smoke rose from the coals.

She went to the middle of the circle, Aoife with her. CeCe put her feet on the spot where the two faint paths crossed, pulling Aoife in close so her little feet were on it, too. The fire at their backs lent a comforting warmth. One of Aoife's hands clutched her mother's, and the other held her latest drawing, the one she'd made on the plane. She looked happy and wasn't even fidgeting the way her four-year-old usually did. CeCe wanted to hold her in her arms but she was afraid to, in case Aoife didn't go when her mother did. It seemed absurd, considering the danger she was putting them both in, but she didn't want to risk her child falling out of her arms and hurting herself.

Her four aunts stood with four witches, one pair before each of four stones, all facing her. Selene stood at the fifth stone, and Jana at the sixth. The witches' faces were calm, almost—exultant. Her aunts looked frightened out of their wits, and Nikki was crying into a hanky.

The witches' mouths began to move, but whatever they said—a chant, a song—was so soft CeCe couldn't hear the words. She felt them, though. The words snaked beneath her skin, stirring her blood, caressing her bones. Quiet power—a vibration, a thrum—seemed to pulse from the circle.

She reached through the slit in her skirt and pulled the linen handfasting cloth from the pocket. Wrapping it carefully in a figure eight around her wrist and Aoife's, she tucked the end between their hands. "Hold on tight, baby," she whispered. Little fingers clutched hers, hard.

Through a gap in the trees, a sudden flash of solar fire pricked CeCe's eyes. The sun fell, fast, toward the horizon. Wind sprang up—she could see the treetops moving—but it didn't brush her skin. Taking a last desperate look at her aunts' cherished faces, she prayed. *Hail Mary, full of grace, the Lord is with you...* She gripped Aoife's hand for all she was worth.

A huge, soundless shadow swallowed them both.

FORTY-SEVEN

I n one convulsive instant, Patrick woke and vaulted out of
the armchair to his feet. He stood, stock still, staring at
the cold hearth in his chamber. His whole body tensed as
if for battle.

He *never* slept. In his long exile between worlds, the only
times he'd been overtaken by sleep were when he lay with
Celeste. Warm and sated from their lovemaking, Patrick had a
dozen times slipped into a black chasm, bottomless, dreamless.

Tonight, though, he had slept. Not only slept, but
dreamed. In the dream, he visited a strange country, neither
wild nor tame, earth nor sea. An unnamed borderland
between the living and the dead.

But, no...he knew the place. It was the bluff above the
strand, the place where Trawsgoed ended and the Irish Sea
began. Celeste was there. In the dream, as now, a cry of aching
desire rose in Patrick's throat. She turned to him, her face
alight with happiness, and took the hand and words he
offered.

Come to me.

Had he truly spoken? Had she heard him?

A tremor ran through his limbs, and he looked again at his bedchamber's frigid hearth, the empty andirons. He took three steps to the fireplace and flattened his palm against the chimney breast. A second shudder coursed under his skin. Not of chill, but comprehension.

The hearth was too cold for any grate that had held a fire in living memory. No logs. No ash. No sign of the blaze that had warmed the night—or the year—before. Patrick let his sight touch every feature of the room. The walls, floor, bed, oak table with its familiar furnishings. All were lifeless and gray, like clay figures on a shelf.

He turned his gaze toward the door of his chamber. It was ajar. Beyond it was the passage he knew so well. He had walked its twisting length thousands of times, his way illuminated by candles in wall-hung lanterns.

Patrick crossed the room, halting with one hand on the edge of the door. Was he still dreaming? Beyond the thick oak slab, would he find the passage changed, like the room? Was this some final torture before he fell into the abyss? If he opened the door, would he see Hell? He committed himself to God and his fate, and wrenched open the door.

He saw—nothing. A white and formless murk spread in all directions, subtly wavering, like fog. He stared into the mass, his muscles tightening. Keyed to any threat, he listened.

At first, he heard only his own blood, pounding in his veins. Then, from somewhere deep in the murk, birdsong. And floating toward him, sweet and high, a child's voice. An Irish child? French? English?

American. A second voice, also American. A voice that, for years, he had heard only in longing memory. *Celeste.* Patrick plunged into the void, shouting her name.

———

CeCe was still praying when the sunlight struck her face. It was so intense that her forearm reflexively flew up to shield her eyes. Next to her, Aoife wriggled her wrist out of the hand-fasting cloth and chirruped. "Mommy! Are there swings, Mommy?"

CeCe uncovered her eyes. "Swings?" Ahead and around her, a landscape of trees, bushes, flowers, grass, gravel paths—the tamed greenery of a park. A breeze, cool but not cold, made her shiver. "I—I don't think..."

Two women strolled across the lawn a few yards away. The sleeves of their gowns ended in *engageantes*, full ruffles of lace, and their skirts swayed with panniers. They wore cloaks, like her and Aoife, but theirs were short and scarlet, with ruffled hoods.

Her historian brain dropped into gear. She and Aoife were in a French park, in the 1700s. In fashion-mad Paris? The Jardins des Tuileries?

"*Celeste!*" Her name, shouted in the rough, deep voice she had been desperate to hear for so long.

"Patrick!" She searched for the source. There! Dragging Aoife up the path, CeCe screamed, "*Patrick! Patrick!*"

He was running toward her. Great, bounding strides, his long legs eating ground as he dodged trees and leaped over hedges. CeCe thought wildly that she'd never seen Patrick run. She scooped up Aoife, who squealed and dropped her drawing, and raced to meet him. The path was uneven, Aoife bounced in her arms, and CeCe's cloak flapped and billowed against her legs. She thought, even more wildly, that the first sight Patrick might have of his wife and child would be the two of them tripping and sprawling, face down, in a Parisian park.

They collided, Aoife shrieking and laughing as Patrick lifted her into the crook of one arm. With the other, he grasped CeCe around the waist and pulled her tight against him.

Too stunned to do more than cling, she flung her arms around his neck, pressing her cheek against his chest. Scent, sight, sensation—they filled and overwhelmed her, a flood driving away all speech and thought. Traces of aromatic tobacco on Patrick's jacket. Lavender, starch, and maleness rising from his shirt. The thud of his heart, the texture of wool, the rustle of linen, the heat from his body, his mouth...

She turned her face upward and Patrick bent to meet her lips. They kissed so deeply and so long that CeCe lost every sense of standing on the earth. Dimly, she heard Aoife's giggle and the sounds of birds in the park. Swifts and pigeons and finches. No ravens.

Finally, her daughter's squirming made her and Patrick pull apart. They stared, wordless with joy, into each other's eyes.

Thousands. That was how many times CeCe had seen their reunion in her mind. Never once had she seen Patrick weeping, as he was now. Freely, unashamedly, tears coursing down the strong planes of his face. *I never saw him run, and I never saw him cry.* Now, in the space of a minute, she had witnessed both. Aoife leaned into her father, wiping his cheek with her small hand. "*Ne pleure pas, Papa.*" Don't cry.

Patrick kissed Aoife's fingers, then spoke to CeCe, his voice thick and breaking. "She—she speaks French."

"A little." CeCe's own voice quavered. "My aunts are—" Her aunts. Her aunts who weren't born yet. Whose third-great-grandmothers weren't born yet. She cleared her throat. "Say something else in French, Aoife."

Aoife's face wrinkled in thought while Patrick touched the sable curls escaping her cap. "You gave her my mother's name."

CeCe could only nod.

Aoife yelped triumphantly. "*Merde dans un bas de soie!*"

"Fee!"

Patrick threw back his head and laughed, the full, free roar that CeCe had so missed, year after year. "I see she learned the essentials first. Shite in a silk stocking!"

CeCe shook her head. "Aoife Gabrielle Gowdie, where on earth did you learn that?"

"From Aunt Sophie." Smiling coyly, Fee rested her head on Patrick's shoulder. "She says it to her computer. A lot."

With a chuckle, Patrick shifted Aoife's weight, supporting her bottom with his powerful forearm. Aoife's legs dangled, and CeCe patted one small foot in the bright red shoe that peeped out from under her skirt. *Fee's legs are getting long. She'll have her father's height to go with his eyes and hair. And from her mother, she'll have...*

CeCe glanced over her shoulder, looking for Fee's drawing. It was gone, borne away on the wind like Jana's words. "*What you are comes in the blood.*"

"*Céleste.*" Patrick's voice made a silk offering of her name, putting all the French in it. He smiled down at her, holding out his free elbow. She hooked her arm through it so he could draw her close, and they started up the path, both of them more than a little unsteady, happiness rushing in their blood like champagne. As Aoife had done, CeCe rested her head against the warm, solid strength of the man beside her. *I'm here. He's here. We're here.*

A man pushing a handcart came from behind and clattered around them, apologizing. "*Je vous demande pardon, monsieur, madame.*"

Excuse me, sir, madam. It was broad daylight, and the man saw them. Saw *Patrick*. CeCe's dreams arrived in a flurry of images. Patrick at day's end, his hair catching highlights from the sunset. Patrick waking in bed, sunshine pouring through a window onto his magnificent body. Patrick at breakfast with her, on a bright balcony.

A balcony attached to a house. Or a flat or an apartment or even a garret. CeCe didn't care which, as long as they were in it together.

She raised her head to look into his beloved face, his beloved eyes. "Where to now, *Papa*?"

Patrick pulled both his girls close. "Home, *mo chroi*. Home."

EPILOGUE

Thirteen years later. The house on Bull Street, Savannah,
Georgia

Now that she saw them sitting opposite her, all in a row on the long sofa, Fee remembered her great-aunts. A bit. She wasn't sure how much was memory and how much was her mother describing them so many times. And they were older, of course, older than either she or Mom remembered them being. Grand-Tante Diane was talking to one of her sisters.

"You're the schoolmarm, Nikki. If she wants to get into college, you'll have to fudge some test scores. I mean, we can't really say she took the SAT in Paris in 1774."

Fee tried to be helpful. "If the examiners ask, I am profi-cient in Latin and Greek. *Et Italien. Papa, il a insisté—*"

"It's very laudable that your father taught you all those languages," Nikki broke in. "Especially since you're only seventeen. But I think we're still going to have to falsify some records."

"*Mais, Grand-Tante Nicole, c'est bien possible que*—"

"English, honey. You'd best get used to it."

"Sorry." Her parents spoke English, of course, and sometimes Papa, if he was irritated, spoke Irish. But after thirteen years in Paris, Fee thought and dreamed and spoke in French. Especially when she was nervous. Perched on a chair while the four aunts questioned her—that certainly unnerved her. Compared to them, even the witches in Wales were not so *formidables*. The witches, the stone ring in the woods on La Toussaint, the flying machine across the ocean, the many women, including now herself, wearing breeches of which Papa would not approve...it all paled in comparison to *les grandes dames* questioning her from the sofa.

Not that Mom hadn't tried to warn her. She had called them *samurai aunties*, which Fee hadn't understood. Until now.

Great-Aunt Hélène, the physician, spoke next, but not about schooling. "Are you an only child, Aoife? *Une fille unique?*"

"*Mais non, Grand-Tante* —I mean, no, I have three brothers. Michael, Conor, and Liam. Conor and Liam are twins. They are now five years of age."

Nikki cried happily. "Three! Our CeCe has three sons!"

"Had." Grand-Tante Hélène's voice was bleak, reminding her sisters, and Fee, of the truth of time. "I'm sorry, sweetheart," she said softly. "They're all gone, now."

Fee's eyes filled, and she looked down at her feet. The new, bright-colored sandals did nothing to distract her from the facts. Mom and Papa had explained everything, but the final farewell was not made easier by knowing how it worked.

A silent minute ticked by. "No sisters?" Hélène asked.

Fee shook her head. "I am—I was the only girl."

Diane threw up her hands. "Well, that's a blessing."

Hélène, who sat next to Diane, elbowed her in the ribs. "Don't get ahead of yourself, Dee. CeCe was forty-two when Aoife left Paris. Momma had Sophie when she was forty-four."

Hélène's sharp eyes settled on her grand-niece again. "Aoife, *chérie*, you're absolutely sure you want to go to UNC Chapel Hill?"

Fee nodded vigorously. "Yes, Great-Aunt. I must—I feel I am called to *Caroline du Nord*." Her great-aunt said English only, but Fee didn't know how to pronounce the state's name any way but in French. *Cahr-o-leen dyu Nord.*

"You feel *called* there."

"Yes, Great-Aunt. Most strongly."

Sophie, the very stylish *grand-tante* in a marine blue suit, sighed heavily. "Here we go again."

Acknowledgments

My sincere gratitude goes to the people and places in Wales that helped me turn an idea into a novel. I'm also grateful to Cormac Buzz Ó Briain, my advisor on the Irish language passages in this book. Anything correctly written was his doing; any mistakes are my own.

There is no overestimating the support I've received from Leslie Truex: agent, editor, mentor, advocate, and friend. My editor and all the hardworking staff at Harbor Lane Books also deserve and receive my thanks and respect.

ABOUT THE AUTHOR

Annie R McEwen has lived in six countries and under every roof from a canvas tent to a Georgian Era manor house. A career historian, she's driven herself to work in everything from a donkey cart to a vintage Peugeot. For her, it feels perfectly natural to create stories of desperate love and powerful secrets in faraway times and places.

www.anniermcewen.com
https://facebook.com/Quillist/
https://www.instagram.com/anniermcewen/
https://www.bookbub.com/profile/annie-r-mcewen

About the Publisher

Harbor Lane Books, LLC is a US-based independent, digital publisher of commercial fiction, non-fiction, and poetry.

Connect with Harbor Lane Books on their website www.harborlanebooks.com and TikTok, Instagram, Facebook, Twitter, and Pinterest @harborlanebooks.